ROCK THE BOAT

Laura McWilliams Howard

ISBN# 9781695633049

Cover design by: April Burril
Edited by: Kelley Heckart

Printed in the United States of America

CHAPTER 1

Freshman Year
1976-1977

Almost!
Within my reach!
I could have touched!
I might have chanced that way!
Soft sauntered through the village,
Sauntered as soft away!
So unsuspected violets
Within the fields lie low,
Too late for striving fingers
That passed an hour ago.
- Emily Dickinson

Beth poked through the hallway of Colonel Roberts High School toward physical science class, one step behind a cute boy heading up the stairs. They were both caught in the throng of students. She hurried along hoping to spend a few precious moments talking with her friend Lynne before the next class began. Beth carried her books in her left hand and held on to the metal railing with her right. No teachers monitored this area of the high school, and the traffic jam of braces, glasses, books, and pimples traveled in an "X" pattern between the wings on the first and second floors. She always dreaded this part of the day. After lunch, it was back to the grind of high school crap!

Science was a serious drag, and Beth was barely passing. She begrudgingly memorized the element chart. Her teacher, Mrs. Brick, wore a large, natural Afro. She was pleasant, entertaining, and spoke with a distinct Georgia accent. She would say "bromide—BR" but the "R" came out as "ARahh." Beth's spot-on impersonation of Mrs. Brick always made her classmates roar with laughter.

Full of pizza burgers, pears, and a chocolate shake she bought from the Ala Carte line in the cafeteria, Beth trudged up the steps.

The boy in front of her stopped abruptly and Beth almost ran into him. She heard a voice yell loudly, "Hey, Danny! You going to the game tonight?"

The cute boy standing just above her on the stairs responded to the question with an equally offensive volume. "Yeah, man. You need a ride?"

The two guys maintained a casual but loud conversation amidst the crowd, and Beth rolled her eyes impatiently as she was forced to a full stop. Cigarette and pot smoke wafted off the hair and clothes of the two potheads waiting behind her. Clearly, they'd spent their lunch hour in the woods directly behind the school grounds.

The boy in front of her turned to face his friend. The two boys yelled back and forth to one another. Beth rolled her eyes again, this time sighing loudly and muttering "unbelievable" under her breath.

Beth waited for the two boys to move on. She figured they were seniors because they behaved so rudely. Seniors always seemed to think they were more important than everyone else. The pothead behind her plowed into her back with his stack of books and spiral wires poking out around a pencil.

"Hey man, what the...?" He groaned as he pushed past her left side, eyes opening halfway. The flow of traffic followed him.

Beth was hit from behind and lunged forward. She managed to maintain a two-inch distance from the guy in the light blue sweater. He turned to look at her. She lifted her head and glared at him.

She widened her eyes in disbelief as he turned away and continued chatting. After a few seconds, he looked down at her again. He smiled and tilted his head upward as if to say, "Hey." She waited for a spot in which she could merge into the ongoing traffic. Groans of protest could be heard behind them. He acted as if he just noticed he was holding up the line of students trying to get to class.

"Oh, excuse me," the cute but rude boy said in an exaggerated, sarcastic tone.

Beth ignored him and squeezed into the flow of traffic. He moved backwards towards the double door, grabbed the door, and held it open for her. He continued to stare, and she made eye contact with him.

"Hello," he said. "You have beautiful brown eyes. What class are you going to?"

"Physical Science," Beth answered. Suddenly, she was no longer irritated but a little unnerved at being spoken to by a senior. People often complimented her brown eyes with long lashes, and she usually took it in stride. Now, though, she was flustered.

"I'll walk you," he stated.

The two turned the corner in silence and were at the classroom door within seconds.

"What's your name?" He lifted one eyebrow.

"Beth."

"I'm Danny. Do you have a last name, Beth?"

"O'Brien."

"Well, Beth O'Brien, I'll be seeing you around," he said backing down the hallway. Danny smiled at her before turning the corner.

Beth stood outside her science class and stared at the empty hallway.

Lynne approached the classroom door and stopped next to Beth. "I saw you talking to Danny. You know him?"

She turned to her friend. "Not really. What's his last name?"

Lynne smiled. "Mitchell."

Beth processed the name quickly and realized she'd heard it before.

The two girls walked in the classroom as Mrs. Brick motioned to them that class was ready to begin.

"You don't know Danny?" Lynne whispered as they took their seats.

"I know *of* him, but I just met him now, in the hallway."

"He's a friend of mine. Looks like he would like to get to know you." Lynne lifted her eyebrows up and down several times.

Beth smiled, pleased.

Mrs. Brick droned on about pith balls and lab safety. Beth's mind wandered. This was her first year at Colonel Roberts High School, but she had attended elementary school and junior high in Colonel Roberts School District and she knew a lot of people here. She had heard of Danny Mitchell. Beth had seen him once when she was in fifth grade. She had been playing dolls with her friend Susan in Susan's backyard. Danny had ridden by on his new ten-speed bike.

She had noticed the cool bike first. The levers on the handlebars let the rider choose the pedal speed. Her attention had shifted to the boy riding the bike. He was cute. At the time, Beth didn't know who he was.

"Who's that?" Beth had asked her friend.

"Oh, that's Danny Mitchell," Susan had said as she adjusted the blanket over her baby doll's face.

Beth had watched him ride his bike for a few moments, impressed.

He passed in the opposite direction and showed off by making figure eights in the street with his cool ten-speed. The girls moved closer to the road. He passed back and forth several times.

On his fourth ride-by, he had smiled at her and said,

"Hello." He even rode with no hands clearly trying to impress Beth with his skills.

"Hi," the girls had said then grinned at each other. He eventually rode down the street and out of sight.

"Danny's the kid who hurt his back in a horrible car accident awhile back. His family thought he might die. He even rode around in a wheelchair for a while," Susan had told Beth.

Beth vaguely remembered hearing about the accident from her parents at the dinner table one night. The town they lived in was small and news traveled quickly.

She recalled standing on her tiptoes and stretching her neck over the bushes to see if he was still in sight. At the time, she'd thought he was a lot older and probably attended junior high school.

"Be careful who you choose for lab partners tomorrow..." Mrs. Brick's voice pulled Beth back to the here and now. "Read the rest of chapter eight for homework. See you all tomorrow."

The class period bell rang, and Beth joined the throng of students hustling toward the exit. She caught up with Lynne who waited for her by the door. They walked to their next classes together.

"So, Danny was talking to you, huh?' Lynne smiled, her pretty features framed by light brown hair brightened. She softly bumped her shoulder into Beth's.

"I guess so." She grinned.

"Would you go out with him?"

"He's a senior. He won't ask me out." Beth let out a sigh and drew her brows together.

"By the look on his face, I don't think it mattered." Lynne's brown eyes twinkled with mischief, and she let out one of her famous infectious giggles.

Beth reached her class door and said firmly, "See you later."

"Bye!" Lynne sang as she walked toward the opposite

classroom and waved her fingers in the air.

Beth smiled. She was lucky to have Lynne Angellini for a friend. They had been friends since elementary school. Lynne was captain of the junior varsity cheerleading squad and she exuded warmth and love. She always worried about getting in trouble and had thus been dubbed "goody two shoes." Beth and her friends had given her that nickname mostly to tease her, though. Lynne was a worrier, but it never seemed to stop her from having fun and taking chances.

Beth entered her English class and took her seat next to Susan Pallace, another longtime friend of hers. Beth thought about asking Susan if she remembered the two of them seeing Danny Mitchell on his ten-speed when they were younger but decided against it. Not that she didn't trust her loyal friend, but cousins Donna Jones and Yvonne Wright sat behind them, and Susan was already chatting with them, her green eyes sparkling playfully and her short dark hair bobbing as she talked. The older kids knew Susan well because she had an older sister, Janet, who also attended CR. Among Beth's friends, Susan was the only one with a steady boyfriend. She was dating Tyler Jenkins who was a year older. A thought that made Beth slightly envious of her friend.

Beth listened in on the conversation about boys between Susan, Donna, and Yvonne until the teacher called the class to order.

The four had great fun talking and telling jokes in class, but they never socialized outside of school. Donna was a beautiful long-legged cheerleader who smiled all the time. Everyone at Colonel Roberts High liked her because she was genuine and kind. Some of the black kids in school gave her a hard time because she had a lot of white friends. Yvonne was in the same situation, but her friends did not seem to be as tough on her. Mostly because she was not a cheerleader.

The four always talked incessantly in class and drove their well-liked English teacher out of her mind. "Please, girls," she would say, "...girls, please!" Once, they pushed her past her toleration point and Mrs. Castle finally said, "You four are so rude! I'm going to start calling you the Gruesome Foursome!"

The girls did manage to be more respectful. However, now they were known as the "Gruesome Foursome."

After class ended, Susan had to hurry to her next class. Beth hoped to see Danny again but didn't. She daydreamed about him during the rest of her classes, but she was disappointed that she didn't see him. As she walked home from her bus stop, she began to feel foolish. It was self-talk time.

One chance meeting does not mean he will ask me out on a date! Try not to think about it. Don't think about it. Stop thinking about it! Why is it that the thing you are trying not to think about is the only thing you can? Cripes!

She arrived home and did her homework but still could not stop thinking about Danny.

CHAPTER 2

"Dinner's ready!" Beth's mother yelled up the stairs.

She came to the kitchen, sat, and smiled as her mother dished out stuffed pork chops. Her mother always served her father first, and he piled lima beans and applesauce onto his plate. Beth hated eating dinner without her older sister who had married and moved away. It felt strange to sit at the table without her.

"How was your day?" was the standard opening line from her father.

"It was good, yours?" she'd always respond.

Occasionally, when he was having a good day, he would return with an outrageous comment like "I've been as happy as a bullfrog with a watertight behind," making everyone chuckle. Most of the time, he didn't talk at all. Beth and her mother talked a lot, but her Dad worked long hours at his music shop and was not home much. He left every day before Beth even made it downstairs for breakfast, and he often did not get home until after six o'clock at night. Mr. O'Brien had a strong work ethic and did whatever was necessary to please his customers. He often drove out of his way to pick up an instrument for someone who was unable to bring it to the shop. More than once, he spent a long evening repairing a piece at someone's home because they needed it for a performance the next day. People appreciated his loyalty and commitment. When he did manage to get home, he watched Walter Cronkite with such intent that an earthquake could not pull him away.

"Anything new going on at school?" her mother chimed in as she sat down with her plate.

"Not really."

All three bowed their heads to say grace. "God is great. God is good, let us thank him for our food. By his hands we all are fed, Give us, Lord, our daily bread."

They began to eat. Beth's mother and father conversed about people they knew. Beth was not interested and let her mind wander.

Since she had been in a rut lately, Beth wanted to spend more time with her friends and enjoy herself more. She had been out on a couple dates since she began high school but nothing serious. One guy had a great car, but he was a pothead and a terrible kisser. The other was adorable to look at but acted a little too geeky. He was a good kisser, though. She had not been on a date since the school dance before Homecoming. Also, her grades weren't so great on her first report card. *Things definitely need to change.*

"You're awfully quiet Beth...everything alright?" her mother asked, looking at her intently.

"I was just thinking about school and getting myself together a bit." Beth sighed and took a bite of the pork chop, looking down at her plate.

"Anything I can do to help?"

"No, Mom, but thanks anyway." Beth glanced up at her and forced a grin.

Her mother gave her a reassuring smile.

Beth reflected on her junior high school experience. It had not been a good one. She had been disliked by a group of girls known as "The Nasties." They had threatened her and called her names. No reason for it. They just didn't like her.

There were four of them, and they were a rough bunch. They dressed like boys and wore dirty clothes. Each girl looked like she needed a good shampooing, and each tried to appear hard as nails, daring anyone to say anything to them. They smoked cigarettes in the back of the bus and got in fistfights with other girls and with each other. Beth grimaced and shuddered at the thought of them. They were loud, obnoxious bullies. They rode her bus and got on halfway through her ride. They all lived in the apartment complex outside of her housing development. By the middle of eighth grade, their nastiness had reached its peak.

They smacked her in the back of the head as they walked off the bus, called her "a fucking snob," and made fun of her long dark hair. "She thinks she's so hot and she's not at all. She's so ugly." They made nasty comments over and over, day after day, saying them loud enough for everyone on the bus to hear. The other riders ignored it and pretended not to notice. If anyone tried to come to her defense, then they became the new target and were bullied unmercifully right along with her. She hated to admit it, but she was afraid of them.

The bus driver stopped Beth one day as she got off the bus saying the other girls were jealous of her and not to take any of their comments to heart. Beth appreciated the bus driver's advice but would have appreciated it more if she had put a stop to it. Beth worried about the threats the Nasties made. They hated her, and the venom spewed at her increased with each passing day. Ignoring them became impossible. One Friday, the girls threatened to kick her ass after school. The threat was a real one, and Beth knew she had to do something about it. Her friends and sympathizers approached her throughout the day to warn her of the girls' plans. She prepared to call her mother at the end of the school day to come pick her up, but during fifth period, she realized there was someone who might be able to help her.

Oscar was sixteen years old and still in the eighth grade. He was as big as some of the teachers in the school and hung out in the shop room by himself most of the time. He was cute but had long hair and smoked cigarettes behind the school next to an old, abandoned church. The teachers knew it, but he had permission from his parents. He was a genuine god to the "Nasties," and they constantly tried to get his attention. They thought being tough was something he wanted in a girl. Beth knew Oscar liked her. He was always sweet to her and blushed whenever she spoke to him. She hated taking advantage of the fact that he had a crush on her, but she couldn't see any other way to protect herself.

Beth approached Oscar after science class. He looked at her shyly but warily as she said, "Hello."

"How are you, Oscar?" She smiled.

He nodded, blushed, and looked around again.

Beth could tell he was nervous because he would not look her in the eye. She decided to get to the point quickly, told him what happened, and that she needed his help.

Oscar looked pleased with himself as he walked her to her bus that day, skipping his afternoon smoke. The Nasties stood in the parking lot at the corner of the school waiting for Beth, and they watched with gaping mouths as Oscar walked her to the bus. He stayed at her side, darting his eyes from side to side as if she were President Ford, and he were the only secret service agent on duty. After she was securely deposited on the bus, Oscar went over to the "Nasties" and shouted at each of them in turn. If they "touched one fucking hair on her head" he would "personally kick their fucking asses from here to fucking Florida and then fucking back again." The girls nodded and backed down, but when he walked away out of earshot, they shrugged and grunted as if they were not afraid of him, determined to save face.

The "Nasties" totally ignored her on the bus that afternoon. The ride home was finally pleasant for the bus driver and the passengers. Oscar continued to keep tabs on her in school and walked with her to the bus for several days to drive home his point. He clearly had a crush on Beth, and although she felt grateful to him, he was not the kind of boy she wanted hanging around. He was bad news in many ways despite his kindness to her. Oscar's friends began to talk to Beth in the hallways, making her friends uncomfortable. The two social classes did not mix well. Beth didn't know how to handle it because Oscar was kind and protective of her. She felt safe with him. They were starting to become friends.

He began calling her on the phone. Oscar had a terrible home life, and Beth felt badly for him. Thankfully, he never tried to kiss her or even hold her hand. He knew he would lose her friendship if he did.

Beth refused to stop speaking to him just because her friends turned up their noses. She finished eighth grade and made two new friends who accepted her friendship with Oscar. Her new friends had many problems of their own. Beth tried desperately to help them. One girl used a pencil eraser to rub burn marks on her skin. It looked horrible, and the marks sometimes became infected. Beth told the girl's mother about it, but she didn't do anything to help her daughter. The other girl smoked pot all the time. Beth discovered that her parents did, too, and she stopped going over to visit their family altogether. Oscar dropped out and decided not to attend high school. Only one of the "Nasties" attended the high school, and she was placed in remedial classes. Beth never saw her again.

Beth came back to earth when she realized her mother was talking to her. She knew her mother hoped things were improving for her daughter. Beth excused herself from the table, went to her bedroom and shut the door. A KISS poster hung on her wall along with other rock icons that reminded her of junior high. Seventies style mushroom stickers and peace signs decorated her mirror. If she wanted to change, Beth needed to start with her dated bedroom. So, she took these items, as well as the macramé plant holders and wall hangings down from her wall, and then picked the stickers off her mirror. She also decided to go through her album collection, but she could not throw out her favorite Deep Purple, Nazareth, or Steppenwolf albums. As soon as possible, she planned to go to the school store and buy some Colonel Roberts High School posters and pennants. Her room and her life would be transformed within a week. Beth felt better just knowing she had some goals. She would get better grades and spend time with her friends.

After retrieving a large trash bag from the kitchen, she bagged up and threw out all the hippie crap in her room. She went to the chest in the guest room and pulled out a beautiful pastel-colored patchwork quilt. Her old bedspread was early 70's gold and looked cool with her "die hard rock fan" room, but that was all about to change. She moved her furniture around last.

Her mother opened the door. "Beth? What's going on?" After glancing around the room, she looked at Beth, her brow furrowed.

"I've changed some things. I took down all the old rock posters and put up some new CR stuff."

Her mother widened her eyes and grinned. "It looks fantastic! Where's all your other stuff?"

"In the trash bag." Beth motioned to the overstuffed trash bag.

Her mother had a pleased smile as she left the room, shutting the door behind her. Beth could almost hear her mother skipping happily down the hallway. Envisioning her reaction, Beth chuckled.

Everything was about to change. Danny had noticed her! Suddenly she felt confident in making the changes she knew she must. Her friends would help her with make-up and clothes. Things were looking up.

CHAPTER 3

The next day at school, kids shouted at each other across crowded cafeteria tables and the noise level made it impossible to hear. Beth found Lynne at her usual lunch table. Girls were squeezed in at every angle. Most of them were cheerleaders. The Junior Varsity basketball team had a game after school, and the cheerleaders at Colonel Roberts High School wore their uniforms to school on game days. She waved to Lynne, and her friend motioned for her to join the table.

Beth squeezed in next to Lynne and grinned at her old friend. Lynne smiled back, her eyes sparkling. There were twelve girls squeezed into eight seats at the lunch table. They turned their trays sideways so they could all fit on the tabletop. Half of the girls were cheerleaders and the rest were called "jockettes." Both cliques were popular.

Varsity cheerleaders graced the cafeteria, too, but they didn't sit with the Junior Varsity girls. These girls had already grown into their bodies and knew how to wear blue or green eye shadow and lip gloss without looking like they belonged on the centerfold of *OooLaLa!* magazine. The JV boys desperately wanted to get their attention, but these girls wouldn't give them the time of day. The boys watched them longingly from the only lengthy table in the cafeteria, located in the back near the row of windows. Every day, it seemed, someone reenacted the infamous *Blazing-Saddles*-campfire-bean-eating scene at their table. The girls groaned from across the room, and the boys laughed until milk spewed from their noses. If the girls paid them any notice, this escalated the guys' attention-seeking behavior. They never understood why the girls said "no" when any of them needed a date for the Homecoming or Prom.

The girls' table stood in the front half of the cafeteria closer to the jukebox. They had to talk loudly to be heard over the blaring music. Elton John's "Crocodile Rock" played on the jukebox as the girls chatted.

"Hey, what did you think of algebra today?" Jackie Basile asked Beth, tossing her long curly blonde hair that cascaded down her back like Stevie Nicks' over her shoulder.

She scrunched her face at Melissa Walters who was in the same algebra class, and the girls began talking about their weirdo algebra teacher.

Jackie's hazel eyes brightened at a cute boy who ogled her as he passed by. She thrust her chest out, showing off her nice boobs in her tight shirt.

Beth rolled her eyes. The boys were always checking Jackie out.

Melissa pushed out her chest in her snug junior varsity cheerleader top, mimicking Jackie, tossing her long auburn hair over her shoulder. She tilted her head, her bangs outlining her beautiful face and playful blue-green eyes.

Beth was glad to see Melissa having fun. Since she lived with her alcoholic mother, Melissa often had to take care of her irresponsible mom and had been doing so from an early age. Sympathy for her friend panged Beth's chest. Melissa often talked about being anxious for high school to end so she could leave this small town.

They were giggling when Susan came up to the table and squeezed in next to Beth, greeting her with a wide smile. Beth was feeling more comfortable in her own skin, more so than she had in months. She had great friends and now some interesting daydreams about Danny.

Along with Lynne and Susan, Jackie and Melissa were becoming Beth's best friends. The five girls were becoming inseparable as they navigated their freshman year. This was the beginning of a special bond that would carry the girls through high school and beyond. They would be there to help each other survive life's blows and celebrate life's joys.

All five were beautiful and popular but each had unique personality traits. Jackie was a leader and boundary pusher, Susan was loyal and generous, Lynne had a strong sense of right and wrong, Melissa was independent and adult beyond her years, and Beth was sensitive and caring, earning her the nickname "Mother Mary."

After lunch, Beth and Lynne left the cafeteria together and walked through the dreaded "stairwell from hell" to the science wing.

Beth looked for Danny Mitchell, but there was no sign of him. As she and Lynne turned the corner, Beth saw him standing outside their classroom door. Was he waiting for her?

"Oh my God! What should I do?" Beth whispered to her friend.

Lynne pushed into her shoulder and said, "Go talk to him!"

Danny leaned back into the lockers and watched her approach the classroom. He crossed his arms in front of his chest and planted one foot up behind him to rest on the metal lockers. He was taller than Beth by about four or five inches and his curly dark hair framed his handsome face. Were his eyes blue or green? Beth could not tell. He flashed his perfect white smile at her.

"Hi," he said, as she approached the entrance to the class-room.

"Hi."

"Beth, right?" he asked, as Lynne butted in between them and walked into the classroom.

"Hey, Bam Bam," she said with a sly grin as she sashayed past.

Danny replied in a big brotherly kind of way, "Hey Pebbles." But his eyes never left Beth. They stared at one another for a few moments, and then he said, "So, this is pretty awkward."

Beth smiled and looked down at her earth shoes. She

wished she wore something more sophisticated today, like her clogs.

"Are you going to the basketball game tonight?" he asked.

Beth had not been going to basketball games, but she was excited to start now. Lynne would be cheering, and she could go watch without feeling too stupid about being alone.

"Yes, actually I planned to go. Are you?" She lifted her shoulders into a shrug and arched one eyebrow.

"Absolutely, so maybe I'll see you there."

"Yeah, maybe so," Beth responded.

"Well, I'd better get going. I don't need a detention for being late to geometry." Danny added, "Maybe I'll see you later." He smiled at her and did the backwards walk again.

Beth stared after him. At that moment, she was certain he was the most gorgeous person she had ever seen. His eyes were most definitely green.

Mrs. Brick came into the hallway. "Come on in here, Beth. We need to get started on our lab."

Lynne and Beth teamed up as lab partners and were wise enough to include Beth's friend Kenny Nixon in their group. He would earn them an "A."

Lynne whispered, "Well? What did Danny say?"

"He asked if I was going to the basketball game tonight. I think I'm going to call my mom after school and ask to stay for the game."

"That's great. You can watch me cheer! Tell your mom that my mom can give you a ride home. She won't mind."

"Okay, thanks!"

The rest of the day dragged on, and Beth worried about what Danny thought of her. She questioned how she looked from her hair down to her clothes. Her haircut was a Dorothy Hamill-style bob. Cute, but it didn't seem to look quite as good as Dorothy's did in the slow motion shot of her gliding on the ice. Still, it would have to do. There just wasn't a whole lot you could do with short hair.

Beth wore an off-white pair of painter pants and a sweater with calico pink, off-white, and shades of green. The sweater matched her pants perfectly. It had a hood on the back and while her earth shoes still bothered her, she could not do anything about that now. Beth was so glad she'd ditched the puka shell necklace and big hoop earrings she had been wearing recently and replaced them with the thin gold chain and small birthstone studs, which were birthday gifts from her grandfather. *Much more mature looking.*

At the end of the school day, Beth raced to the payphone in the front lobby of the high school and called her mother at work. Her mother gave her permission to stay after school and ride home with Lynne, and she sounded pleased about it. Beth went to her locker slowly instead of her usual frantic after-school routine. She got her things together and headed towards the gym for the basketball game.

Beth walked into the gymnasium and widened her eyes at the number of people in attendance and the deafening noise. Everyone prepared for the game with excitement. The players were warming up on the court, and the cheerleaders were stretching. Parents and friends poured in and found seats on the wooden bleachers. A few teachers and photographers were there as well. This high school thing was becoming fun! Beth quickly found a seat on the front bleacher so she could watch Lynne and Melissa. The girls began to cheer.

I bet I could do that, Beth thought. *But I don't know about the short-pleated skirt and bloomers. I definitely wouldn't like that!*

After a while, the horn sounded, and the cheerleaders took a break.

Lynne came over to Beth. "I'm so glad you came!"

"Thanks, me too. You and Melissa are doing great!"

The two talked for a minute, and Lynne introduced Beth to a few sophomore girls. Beth knew some of them from elementary school and had never met the others.

The game resumed its second quarter. Jackie came in and sat next to Beth. Jackie's long curly blonde hair amazed Beth. She wished she could have hair like that. The two smiled, cheered, and clapped as the home team worked its way to victory. Beth was having fun but was a little disappointed that Danny had failed to show.

Beth and Jackie cheered and applauded for Lynne, Melissa, Donna, and the other girls on the squad. After the last horn signaled the end of the game, the crowd clapped for the home team. Lynne gathered her coat and purse, and then she approached Beth. Melissa waved goodbye and left with one of the other cheerleaders. Jackie's mom waved to her daughter from the entranceway. Jackie returned her wave and said goodbye to Beth and Lynne.

The two girls went to the school's front lobby to sit on the bench and wait for their ride. It seemed strange to Beth to be in the school when it was dark outside. The door to the lobby opened, and a rush of frigid winter air whipped inside. Both girls looked in the direction of the door, and in walked Danny. He wore a knee-length tan camel hair coat, blue denim Levi's, white Tretorn sneakers, and a blue and white-striped buttoned-down shirt. His brown curly hair was windblown, but that only added to the effect he was having on Beth. Her stomach flipped with nervousness.

"My God, the hawk is flying out there tonight! Jesus!" he said to the girls.

Beth thought, *What's this all about? We're just about ready to leave, and he shows up now?*

Danny said, "Well, Pebbles, you ready to go?"

"I sure am." Lynne smiled, glancing at Beth.

Beth was not smiling. She was in the middle of a major melt down. What was Lynne thinking? She told her mother she would get a ride with Lynne's mom. She'd get in serious trouble over this. In a twenty-four-hour period, the reinvention of Beth O'Brien had come and gone. High school career —over!

"Let's go, then," Danny said.

Beth stood completely still while he and Lynne headed for the door. Lynne stopped and looked back at Beth. She walked back towards her friend.

"What's the matter?" she asked softly, moving close to her so Danny couldn't hear.

He continued towards the door, unaware they stopped.

"Well, um, where are we going?" Beth asked in a low voice.

"To the basketball game," Lynne whispered, obviously concerned. "You did call your mom, right?" she asked, drawing her brows together.

"Uh huh, but isn't that what I just went to?" Beth whispered.

Lynne laughed. "That was the JV game, ding a ling! The Varsity game is at Smythfield High School across town."

Uncomfortable heat crept over Beth's cheeks. She felt like an idiot. Obviously, everybody else had known what they were talking about except her. Danny had indeed shown up. He and Lynne were in cahoots on this one.

"Danny, go on out to the car and keep it warm. I need to make a phone call," Lynne called to him adding, "Beth, will you stay with me?"

"Sure," Beth mumbled. Lynne must have noticed she was upset.

"Hurry up, geez!" Danny groaned dramatically as he walked out the door.

"Oh my God, Lynne! I didn't know you were talking about the game at Smythfield. I need to call home. My mom is working late. She'll get mad if I call her at work again. I'll have to ask my dad. He will never let me go on such short notice." Beth's muscles tensed.

"Call anyway and sound *calm*," Lynne directed.

Luckily, Beth had a dime for the payphone.

Her father answered. "Um, Hi Dad," she said hesitantly.

What's wrong?" he asked.

Lynne mouthed the words "stay calm," and Beth did her best to sound as casual as possible. "I stayed after to watch the JV basketball game. I called Mom, and she knows I'm with Lynne Angellini. We were wondering if it would be alright if we went to the varsity game tonight?"

"It's okay with me. Is the game here in Camden?"

"It's actually at Smythfield."

There was a long pause.

Death...this was the death of Beth O'Brien. Right now, at this very moment.

"How are you going to get there?"

Shit, shit, shit! Beth's mind raced, and she thought of saying, "Well, there is this senior boy named Danny Mitchell who is going to drive us there." She quickly thought better of that.

"Lynne's older brother is going to drive us, and her mom will bring me home," she said, wincing at the lie.

"Okay, that sounds alright. Have a good time."

Relieved, Beth closed her eyes and leaned into the phone for support.

"Well? Well?" Lynne's eyes were wide and her voice impatient.

"I can go! I can go!" Beth screamed.

They squealed and took off out the lobby door into the very cold, very windy, and very icy weather. The hawk was *definitely* out.

CHAPTER 4

Danny held open the door to the back seat of the tan station wagon. The two girls jumped in quickly to escape the frigid wind. Beth sat behind the driver's seat next to Lynne, and Danny walked around and got in on the other side. There were groans from inside the car as precious heat was lost.

Nervous tension wound through Beth. She was not in the habit of lying to her parents and she had a tremendous fear of getting in trouble. She continued to shiver even in the warmth of the car. The driver was a senior guy she barely knew. He was on the football team, and his father was a big-wig politico in their small town.

Lynne leaned over and whispered, "Relax, everything will be fine!"

Beth smiled, but she really wanted to throw up.

Lynne introduced Beth to everyone in the car. Another senior boy was in the front passenger seat. Beth had never seen him before. The guys chatted and joked with one another, but Beth couldn't keep up with their banter. The senior in the front seat turned around and handed a wine bottle to Danny. He turned the bottle up and took a few deep swallows. He then passed the bottle to Lynne. Her eyes were wide as she looked at Beth. She pretended to take a small sip, and then passed it to Beth.

Oh my God, Oh my God, Beth thought.

Without hesitation, she placed the bottle to her lips and tilted it upward. She also pretended to take a dainty sip but kept her lips closed tightly. Her parents would kill her if she came home smelling like wine. Lynne mirrored Beth's slack, sick expression. Neither was in the habit of driving with boys, especially boys who were drinking. They were both terrified of getting caught.

A boy in the back of the station wagon hollered, "Hey, don't forget about me back here! Come on..."

Beth turned and offered the bottle to Rob, a book smart, rich, handsome Jewish boy. He was not athletic but managed to maintain his coolness by playing on the school golf and tennis teams. It didn't hurt that his dad was a doctor in town either. If you went to C.R. and your family had money, you were part of the "in" crowd. Beth smiled at Rob as he took the bottle from her hand. He gave her a goofy smile, and his eyes were glassy through his glasses. Obviously, some of them had already been drinking.

What a dweeb, Beth thought as they continued to pass the Boones Farm around.

Beth and Lynne tried to appear comfortable and self-assured. They were good actors. Everyone laughed, talked, and teased one another, and Beth took it all in. From time to time, she laughed out loud at the sheer stupidity of the jokes. The boys showed off for her and Lynne, and that was funny enough.

Beth started to relax slightly. The guy driving seemed to be passing on the wine, and she was relieved. Suddenly, Lynne pulled herself forward to the front seat.

What is she doing? Beth wondered.

Danny jumped over in the seat next to Beth where Lynne had been, while Lynne climbed over his lap to sit next to the window. Beth felt uncomfortable again.

The others in the car continued carrying on performing Steve Martin's imitation of the French language, singing "Swing Town" by the Steve Miller Band as they danced in their seats. Eventually, Danny did not talk, sing, or dance. He stared at Beth, and she stared back at him.

Danny's dark brown hair curled loosely about his ears and neck. His eyes were a lighter shade of green than she remembered, and she was unnerved by the intensity of which they watched hers. His nose was perfectly straight.

People would pay a lot of money for that nose, Beth thought.

Finally, she focused on his mouth and chin. He grinned slightly, and his lips were full and ruggedly formed. His chin was strong, and he held it proudly. She swallowed hard as Danny swept his stare over her features. They sat looking at each other for the last moments of the ride.

The car entered the Smythfield school parking lot, and Danny placed his arm across the seat behind Beth in an apparent attempt to steady them from jostling with the movements of the car.

They reached their destination. Now what?

Everyone climbed out of the car, and Beth followed the group to the doors of the school and into the foyer to the Smythfield/C.R. basketball game. An even larger crowd of people waited for them to arrive. Beth recognized their faces and some of their names. Amidst the greetings and high fives, the group traveled towards the visitors' side bleachers in the gym. Lynne, Beth, and another cheerleader from the JV squad walked up the bleachers and took their seats. The boys followed them with Danny leading the way. He moved up the bleachers and took them two at a time. He sat next to Beth on her right and smiled down at her.

He had the most beautiful teeth she had ever seen.

Danny leaned down close to her and whispered, "Don't look at me like that. It could be extremely dangerous."

Heat rose in her neck and cheeks. She lowered her gaze, looked away and tried to compose herself. She turned her attention to Lynne, and they chatted a few moments.

Before long, she glanced up at Danny again. He was talking to his friend Mike Crowley who was seated a few bleachers down from them. Mike was a state champion wrestler, a senior, and Lynne had a terrible crush on him. Lynne had told Beth that Mike liked her too, but he didn't want to go out with a freshman. Lynne was hurt by that. It didn't help that Mike flirted with her shamelessly. Mike was cute and blond, and Beth could envision them as a couple.

He would just have to be persuaded.

The minute she turned her attention back to Danny, he pivoted towards her and held her gaze. They both smiled and chuckled.

Danny shook his head at her. "Oh no, I'm really in for it now."

Beth didn't understand half of the comments he made to her, but she was pretty sure he wasn't making fun of her.

The game proceeded, and the group yelled and cheered for their team. Beth was having a wonderful time. She talked with Lynne and her friend but not a single moment passed when she was not aware of Danny sitting next to her. He was so close she could feel the heat from his arm as it softly brushed against hers. His left thigh pressed against her right one, and the sensation from the touch lingered. When the cool air of space met her leg, she found a way to keep the warm contact between their two denim legs. A warm flush bloomed on her face as she realized she was making the effort to keep them close.

Danny talked to her from time to time. He appeared more awkward and flustered than he had at school.

After the third period bull horn sounded, Mike yelled to him, "Hey, Mitchell! Why don't you just put your arm around her?"

The others joined in the fun by making arm gestures, smiling, and winking as they turned to look at the two smitten teenagers. Danny did not appreciate the jokes and his body became rigid as he shook his head with irritation.

"I really don't need seven or eight coaches here," he yelled. He looked down at Beth and smiled as if to reassure her. He leaned in and whispered, "They are such jerks. Don't pay any attention to them. Please!"

Beth smiled and nodded. She knew his irritation had nothing to do with her.

Once the game came close to ending, Lynne told Beth she needed to call her mother about their ride home. The boys had offered them a ride, but Lynne wasn't sure it would be okay.

Beth put on her coat and walked with her to the pay-phone outside. Surprisingly, Lynne's mother gave her permission for them to ride home with the boys. Beth dared not even call her mom. She knew she would not be allowed but she was willing to take the chance to spend more time with Danny. If her parents noticed, she would say Lynne's brother was driving. That might get her in trouble but not grounded. She shivered in the icy air. Back inside, Beth returned to her seat next to Danny. He helped her take her coat off. C.R. made a killing on the score board and had sent in the less experienced team players. Danny was ready to go and so was Beth. He held her hand and told her they needed to find someplace quiet. She wanted to be alone with him. His friends had gotten on her last nerve.

At the final buzzer, the crowd stood up and moved toward the exit. Cheerleaders grabbed their coats and purses. The two teams retired to the locker rooms, and the parents and friends of the players headed out into bitter cold air.

Their chauffeur rushed to unlock the car and hopped in the driver's seat shivering exaggeratedly. He reached around, unlocked the doors, and turned the heater vents on full blast. Everyone took their former positions in the car, and soon the station wagon was stuck in a traffic jam at the school's exit. Conversation and laughter flowed among the group. The driver offered to take Beth home first and then Lynne. She gave him directions, and they arrived at her house much too soon. Beth felt sad that the night was over. Danny got out of the car and stood with her in the freezing cold.

"I hope you had fun with us. I know my friends can be assholes, but they are really good guys."

"I know." Beth shuffled her feet, the cold air prickling her skin.

"Could I have your phone number?" Danny questioned

through his chattering teeth.

"Sure."

"Can I have it now?" He quickly added, "I'll remember it."

Beth called off the numbers, and the impatient teenagers groaned from inside the station wagon.

Danny said, "I'll call you when I get home." Quickly, without warning, he bent down and kissed her on the cheek.

She smiled and put her head down in embarrassment. Then, she ran towards the front door.

It was 10:00 p.m. Her mother was watching television in their family room when she came in, but her father had already gone to bed.

"Did you have a good time?"

"I did! Oh, Mom, it was so fun! I made some new friends, too. You'll like them very much."

"Who brought you home?"

"Lynne's brother." She hated it, but she had to keep up the lie if only for tonight. "I'm going up to bed now, Goodnight."

"Goodnight, Beth."

She climbed the steps to her room and opened the door, pleased with the redecorating she had done earlier. The room looked cool.

I love this quilt on my bed, I love the way I moved the furniture around, I love my stereo, I love that candle, I love this stuffed animal, I love everything in the whole world at this very moment!

She sat on the side of her bed. After replaying the whole night in her mind, she stood to undress and quickly wiggled into her nightgown. She turned the thermostat up on the electric blanket and started toward the bathroom to wash her face. The ring of the telephone stopped her in her tracks.

"Oh my God. Oh my God!" It was Danny, she knew it! She couldn't believe he went home and called her like he said he would. Most seniors stayed out late, and she was already in her pajamas at 10:15. Quickly throwing herself across the bed, she reached for the phone before it woke up her father.

"Hello?" she said quietly, hoping the ring hadn't gotten her parents' attention.

"Hey, Little One, how are you? What are you doing? How have you been, and most importantly, do you want to do it again?" He chuckled in a hushed voice.

Could it be he was sneaking to talk on the phone, too? Beth doubted it.

"I'm not doing much. Getting ready for bed."

"Getting ready for bed? Already?" he chuckled.

She felt like a child, and she could tell he smiled on the other end. He was making fun of her. She didn't care.

"So, what are you doing?" She changed the subject.

"Thinking about you in your jammies and wishing I were there with you right now. Wishing there hadn't been a carload of people in the car when I said goodbye to you tonight."

"Me too," Beth said boldly.

This was her first attempt ever at being provocative and well, quite frankly, she knew she had a better chance of pulling it off over the phone than in person.

The two continued to talk until after midnight. Danny played her songs over the phone, and she listened intently. She asked him to hold on while she took bathroom breaks. There were a few times when he did the same thing.

Finally, after getting to know one another over the safety of the phone, Danny said, "I'd better let you go, Little One, or you won't be able to stay awake in school tomorrow. Meet me in the Center before homeroom, okay?"

"Okay. Goodnight, Danny," Beth said quietly.

Danny let out a deep sigh then said in a low whisper, "Goodnight Beth."

Each waited for the other to hang up first. Beth said, "Goodnight" again and softly put the phone back on the receiver.

She rose and tiptoed to the bathroom. She grinned at herself in the mirror and ran the water to wash her face. The soap bubbled on her face as she splashed water on it to rinse and pretend to be in a Noxzema commercial. She patted her face dry, looked in the mirror and giggled to herself. Things were looking up for her.

Beth crawled into her bed and drew the covers up tight around her neck. She grabbed a second pillow and pulled it down next to her, putting her arm over it as she had seen so many lovers do in movies and on soap operas. Pretending she and Danny were sleeping together in total bliss, she nestled into the pillow.

She silently thanked the heavens above for her life. *Thank you, God, for everything! What an incredible invention you made with planet Earth and human beings. Amen. Oh, and please help me to stop being so giggly and stupid. I really need to get a grip.*

For the first time in a long while, Beth was excited about going to school in the morning.

The next morning, Beth sat next to a window on the bus. She felt a bit like a baby having to take the bus and hoped she might find someone who would drive her to school.

Lynne waited for her at her locker. They smiled at one another.

"He definitely likes you," Lynne said, bouncing up and down.

"I know!" Beth couldn't control her wide grin.

"I saw him kiss you at the car."

"He called me after he got home."

"He did?" Lynne sounded so excited. She reached out and hugged her friend.

"We talked forever, and I really like him, Lynne. It's kind of scary and nerve racking."

"I know but that's what makes it all so fun! Maybe Mike Crowley will ask me out and we could double date," Lynne added, her eyes wistful.

Beth smiled. *Who knows? Maybe that would work out.*

"Let's go down to the Center," Lynne said.

Excitement rippled through Beth. The "Center" was located just outside the cafeteria doors and accessible from all areas of the school with entrances at both sides. The popular kids hung out there before homeroom to socialize. It was the entire reason for going to school early.

They entered the Center, and a sea of letter jackets, button-down prep shirts, dockside shoes, and expensive perfumes and colognes engulfed them. Steve Hoffman, a high school God with a reputation to go along with it, flirted a little with Beth. He was *the* football star of the class of '77. His feathered, black hair hung down the back of his neck. He wore a letterman's jacket that was impeccably clean. Everyone knew Steve and that he drove a black Firebird with a gold bird emblazoned on the front hood. You could tell when he was approaching Burger Chef from a mile away. Beth was surprised he spoke to her.

Steve leaned his head in to speak to her as if it were a private conversation. He asked her name, if she had a boyfriend, what grade she was in, and finally, "Would you like to go out on Saturday? We could go see a movie and then hit Pippy's for pizza. Are you interested?"

Beth's head reeled. If she had not met Danny, she would have been saying "yes" without hesitation. And where was he anyway?

"Um, well...I don't think I can this Saturday. I have something to do with my family."

"Well, let's make it Friday then," Steve stated as if the date were already a done deal.

"I can't Friday either. I'm sorry." She looked up into Steve's piercing blue eyes and felt a bit faint. He was a big guy. His muscles were evident under the heavy fabric of the letterman's jacket.

"Are you kidding?" He looked at her as if he could not believe she said "no" to a date with him.

"I'm really sorry," Beth said.

Steve continued to stare at her with a furrowed brow.

She uneasily glanced around for Lynne, or Danny, or anybody that could get her away from this guy.

"Hey Beth." That guy with the familiar voice from the late-night phone call came up behind her.

She let out a relieved breath.

Danny placed his hands on Beth's shoulders in a possessive manner. "Hey Steve."

Steve narrowed his eyes and gave him a curt nod.

"How are you?" Danny asked Beth as he guided her by the elbow away from Steve and the packed crowd standing in the Center.

"I'm good. How are you?" The tension in her body relaxed a little.

"I'm a little tired. I was on the phone all night talking to the most wonderful person. I feel like I've known her forever."

Beth enjoyed him flirting with her. She smiled to herself. *You have known me my whole life.* Maybe someday she would tell him about seeing him on his bike, in 5th grade.

Danny held her hand and walked her to homeroom, and they made it just as the bell rang. They stood outside her homeroom and stared at one another. Steve walked by and headed into the classroom down the hall. He looked back at her and then at Danny. He shook his head and chuckled as if Beth were crazy for choosing Danny over him. What a pompous ass.

At the last possible moment, Danny said, "Goodbye" and squeezed her hand before he bolted down the hall. Turning one last time, he shouted, "Meet me in the Center before Science."

"Okay," Beth called back louder than she intended.

She looked around to see if she had drawn any attention and then slipped into her homeroom class. Her teacher shut the door behind her and smiled at Beth. The rest of the morning flew by.

Everyone wanted to talk to her that day, it seemed. She

had been invited to a party that coming weekend, and several boys stopped her in the hallway to say, "Hey." They were Danny's friends who had been at the basketball game the night before.

At lunch, she chatted with the girls at her table. This was the day she found out the popular girls' deepest, darkest secrets, which girl was secretly in love with which boy, etc. Girls often told other girls the details of their crushes. If she said it out loud, the boy became totally off limits to all females that stood within earshot of the table. They followed the "Girl Code."

Luckily, the girls preferred different boys. The boys were all friends, too. This certainly made socializing easier. Since Beth had been seen holding hands with Danny Mitchell in the Center earlier that day, the girls now viewed her as a "means to an end." Beth realized this immediately as each girl relayed her own tale in detail.

She listened politely, nodded, and responded with "Yes, it sounds like he does like you. I'm sure it will happen."

After saying goodbye to her friends, Beth stood to leave the cafeteria a couple minutes early to meet Danny in the Center. She walked to the trashcan to dump her lunch tray, and the custodian accepted it from her.

"Thank you, little lady," he said happily.

Beth smiled at him. *Geez, even the janitor is being nice to me.*

She left the cafeteria and entered the Center. Danny was there waiting for her and waved to get her attention.

"You're here early." She smiled.

"I got a pass from the nurse." He held up the pink paper.

Danny tucked the note into his front pants pocket, and the two walked to class together. He held her hand again, which sent a warm tingle through her. She was aware of girls watching her with envious gazes, and pride swelled her chest.

When they reached her science class, he leaned on the

locker with his right arm and enclosed Beth between him and the wall.

"Do you want to go to the wrestling match with me tomorrow night?" he asked.

"Sure," she said, trying to sound casual as she looked up at him.

Their gazes locked with such intensity that she couldn't look away or speak and sensed he couldn't either.

"I'd love to kiss you right now," Danny said in a low voice.

Beth lowered her eyes to the waxed tile floor, suddenly feeling light-headed. She smiled and glanced back up at him. He focused on her face. It was as if she could feel his gaze touch her cheeks, her lips, her neck.

"Please stop staring at me like that," Beth whispered, looking away.

Danny grinned. "Okay, but I can't wait until that match tomorrow. I'll pick you up at 6 o'clock, okay?"

"Okay."

"Later," he said in a dreamy tone.

"Bye." Her voice was low and breathy.

Danny walked slowly backward down the hallway, smiling at her as he went.

"Miss O' Bahrien? Arah you going to join us for class today?" Mrs. Brick broke into her reverie.

"Oh! Yes! Sorry..." Beth darted into the classroom.

Mrs. Brick grinned as Beth passed in front of her.

"Collect yourself Miss O' Bahrien."

Beth's cheeks warmed, and Mrs. Brick laughed.

Lynne waved and patted the seat at the desk next to her. Beth had been so enamored by Danny, she hadn't noticed Lynne in the hallway before class.

Beth could hardly wait for school to end. Finally, the last bell rang, and she rushed home and scrambled to find the perfect outfit to wear to a wrestling match. She used a blow dryer to plump up her hair and swiped on lip gloss and mascara. After pinching her cheeks until they were pink, she checked herself in the mirror one last time. She scrunched her brow. Not perfect but the best she could do. She wore a cream-colored turtleneck, straight-leg Levi jeans, and a pair of leather clogs. Over her turtleneck, she wore a thigh-length cardigan. One final purse check… Good, she had three pieces of Trident spearmint flavor left. She might need them tonight. Beth felt certain Danny would kiss her. She hoped he would be a good kisser and prayed he would think the same of her.

Oh my God! What if he doesn't show up?

If she sat in her room any longer, she would go out of her mind. She went down the stairs and sat with her parents in the family room while she waited for him to pick her up.

"You look nice," her mother said.

"Where are you going?" her father asked, looking up from his paper.

"Beth has a date tonight," her mother answered.

"A date? With whom?"

"His name is Danny."

Silence.

"Is that all you're going to say? I'd like to know a last name and a bit more about him like where he lives, and how old he is." Her father compressed his lips.

Beth had already been through all this with her mother, and she knew her mother had told her father already. She wished she had never sat down with them.

"His name is Danny Mitchell," she said quickly.

"Mitchell is it?" Her dad stared at her.

"Yes," she responded, shifting uncomfortably

"Danny?" her dad asked, continuing to hold her gaze.

"Yes, she said as she shrugged with irritation.

"Not Daniel?" her dad asked while the corners of his mouth twitched.

"No." She rolled her eyes.

"Not Dan?"

"It's Danny!" Beth narrowed her gaze.

Her father chuckled. She rolled her eyes again and sent her mother a pleading look. Her mother chuckled, too.

"Traitor!" Beth could not help but smile. "He's really very nice."

"He'd better be. What grade is he in?" her father inquired.

"He's a senior." Ugh! Beth winced and waited for her father's reaction.

Her father glanced at her mother. "A senior? What on earth is a senior doing going out with a freshman?"

"He likes her!" her mother interjected.

Beth felt like crying. *What is a senior doing with a freshman?* she thought. He should be dating older girls, girls who know how to kiss, girls who stay out past 11:00, girls who can wear eye shadow and blush. *I am a child. What is he doing with me?!*

The doorbell startled her, and her stomach fluttered. She jumped up off the couch as if a pin had been stuck in her rear end.

Her mother placed her hand on Beth's shoulder. "Relax," she instructed her daughter and followed Beth towards the front door and away from her father.

"You certainly are nervous tonight, Beth. You have never acted this way before. You really like this boy, don't you?"

Beth lowered her head and said, "Yes, I do."

"Well, let him in. Let us meet 'Danny Wonderful.'"

Beth noticed the lit oil lamp on the vestibule table. She smiled and thought about how much she loved her mother. Her father remained in the family room as Beth opened the front door.

Danny looked like a deer caught in the high beams. Beth felt better now. Even he was nervous! She told him to come in and made the introduction to her mother.

Her mother smiled. "Hello, Danny, it's nice to meet you."

"You too, thanks," he said with a shy grin.

Beth walked toward the family room, pulling Danny by his arm. Her mother followed behind them.

"Dad?" Beth walked up behind him in his chair. Her father turned around as if he were surprised someone stood there.

"Oh, hello." He casually put his newspaper down.

Beth introduced them to one another. Danny shook hands with her father. It was a whirlwind of politeness and chitchat as Beth guided him back towards the door. Danny picked up her coat from the stairwell banister. She turned her back, and he helped her into the coat. The two of them maneuvered coats and gloves. Beth caught her mother watching them with a broad grin, and she smiled at her mom.

The two walked out, and her mother quietly closed the door behind them.

Danny opened the door on the passenger's side of his car, and Beth slid in. The interior of the silver mustang was black leather and smelled of musk.

He quickly crossed the front of the car, hopped in the driver's side, and put the key into the ignition without a word. Beth felt a little uncomfortable at his silence. He turned the ignition, and the heater vents blew hot air at them. Danny fumbled as he quickly flipped down the vent. He took a deep breath and blew it out hard. Putting the stick shift in reverse, he stopped, turned towards Beth, and put his right arm over the seat behind her.

"Thank God *that* is over!" he said, referring to meeting her parents. He smiled, and the two shared amused laughter.

"Were you that nervous?" Beth inquired with a giggle.

"Good Lord, I almost crapped my pants!" Danny lifted his eyebrows.

They laughed again, and Beth did not feel quite so young after all.

The ride to the high school was a quick one full of chatter and laughter. After Danny parked the car, he turned to Beth and told her she looked beautiful. She blushed, smiling at his compliment. The temperature outside was only five degrees, and the wind blew fiercely. The windchill had to be below zero. Danny pulled her close to him and held on tightly as they walked to the school entrance. He smelled wonderful. She was willing to stay in the cold forever if he held her like this.

"You smell good. Is that Sweet Honesty?" he asked her.

"No, it's Grass Oil."

Danny turned her around and bent down toward her neck to sweetly take in the scent of her perfume. They stood outside the high school doorway with people surrounding them on all sides. Beth's face heated at the thought of being seen by grown-ups.

A sense of euphoria washed over her as Danny held her and placed his face close to hers. It was almost more than she could bear. Her skin became gooseflesh, and she turned her face towards his cheek. Beth leaned into the smoothness of his freshly shaved cheek and kissed him softly. She intended to do it quickly, but neither of them moved. She kept her lips pressed to his cheek for several seconds before pulling back slightly without a sound. Danny did not move to break the moment. Neither did Beth. He turned his head to look at her, and she held his gaze.

"We'd better go in." He grinned at her.

Danny and Beth walked in holding hands, and immediately their friends surrounded them.

They took their seats in the middle of the bleachers. Danny held her hand throughout the entire match. The only time they broke their clasp was when they both yelled and cheered for their school's wrestlers along with the rest of the large crowd. Danny's friend Mike Crowley won his match. His friends were happy.

Just before the last wrestling match, Danny said, "Let's get out of here."

She sensed he wanted some time alone with her before they headed to Burger Chef.

After sports events, students at Colonel Roberts High

always packed the local hangout. They ran together towards the car, and he held the door for her. He closed the door softly and stood there at the window long enough to attract her attention. Beth turned her head up toward the window to see Danny standing in the light from the streetlamp. He stood in the frigid cold wind staring at her, smiling. A soft cloud of breath came from his nose and mouth as he shivered, pulled his coat together and crossed the front of the Mustang. He entered the car with a thump. Beth's teeth chattered uncontrollably as Danny struggled to get the car started and the heater turned on at the same time.

"It's going to take a minute for it to warm up," he said with his upper body shaking.

"O-k-k-kay," Beth stammered. Her jaw shivered with cold.

She gazed straight ahead. He reached over to take hold of her gloved hands and began to rub his over them in a warming motion. Beth looked at him and smiled.

"Come here," he gently commanded.

Beth slid over as close to the edge of the bucket seat as she could get without sitting on the parking brake.

"Keep coming." He tugged her closer.

"I can't. The brake is in the way," she protested.

"You're not going to break the brake." He reached both arms around her back and lifted her up. He deposited her onto the offensively uncomfortable parking brake.

"Ouch" she said, teeth still chattering.

"Funny, I always liked this car until this very moment." Danny laughed as he held her in his arms and rubbed her hands with his.

He reached down just under the front of his seat. Without warning, his seat flew backward with a thud. Beth tumbled to the side and back onto him. Danny shifted her body and positioned her more comfortably in his lap. She was seated with her back to the driver's side door and turned her head sharply to look in his face.

His body shook with laughter, and she decided not to play the indignant schoolgirl by getting angry at his man-handling. Instead, she laughed along with him. The car warmed up, and the windows fogged from their body heat. Beth immediately became aware that her full weight was on Danny. She struggled to get up. His arms were still locked around her waist, and he pulled her to him even more tightly.

"Don't get up," he said in a low voice.

Beth's palms started to sweat. She tried to lighten the weight by pressing her back into the side door, but then she became tense and uncomfortable. After a few moments, she finally let her body relax.

I am not going to act like a child, Beth thought with determination. She looked into Danny's eyes. They sparkled, and he looked down toward her mouth.

"Umm, I don't want to hurt you," she said.

"You're not." He still stared into her eyes and held on to her tightly.

"Well, it's starting to get a little warmer in here now." Beth searched for something to talk about. She removed her gloves.

"Yes, it is" was his only reply.

Danny removed his hand from around her back, and she relaxed. He removed his gloves with his teeth and reached up to touch her hair. As he ran his fingers through the hair on the back of her head and neck, Beth shut her eyes, and her mind raced wildly. *Oh my God! Do not be a baby, Beth, do not be a baby*.

In a bold and determined move, she reached her right arm over his head to rest it around the top of his shoulders. She touched the softness of his skin around his ear and neck. Danny closed his eyes. Beth was pleased and smiled to herself. He opened his eyes, and they widened. Danny broke the silence.

"Look, I know you're a freshman and I don't want to

do anything that will frighten you or make you uncomfortable."

Beth tensed with anger. How dare he treat her like a child right now? Danny held on to her as she tried to pull away.

"Wait a minute, wait a minute," he said.

Beth stopped struggling but the moment was ruined. The back of her throat tightened. Why was he with her if he thought she was a baby? Was she so awkward that he didn't want to kiss her?

"Beth," he whispered, "just relax."

She turned to look at him, unable to hide the hurt in her eyes.

"There is nothing in the world that I would rather do than kiss you right now. I just don't want to be an ass and make you uncomfortable. We'll take things as slow as you need to take them. I'm never going to pressure you. Okay?"

His soothing words helped Beth relax, and she softened her gaze. He was trying to be a decent guy.

She looked at him boldly. "Do you think I've never been kissed before? I have, you know. I don't think there is anything wrong with kissing, do you?"

Danny stared at her for a long moment then placed his lips on hers. He pulled her into him so purposefully that Beth didn't have time to take a breath. He pressed his mouth to hers firmly at first, and then lightened the pressure.

Danny drew away. She opened her eyes halfway to look at his face. Her lips were pursed, and she was waiting to be kissed again. He didn't kiss her again but regarded her with regret in his eyes. Danny's face was so close she could feel his breath mix with hers. He smelled like cinnamon.

Beth decided not to wait for him and leaned into him this time. She kissed him and slanted her head to the left. Danny pressed his mouth against hers and pulled her body toward him. He opened his mouth a bit and she followed his lead. Their timing was perfect. He moved his tongue forward, and she met it with hers. The two blended into a kiss that eliminated the rest of the world. She loved the way he tasted, the way he smelled, the way he felt. She put her hand on the side of his face and continued the kiss.

He broke away and took off his coat. Beth leaned forward into him as if she were not done. Danny didn't smile but watched her intently as he helped her remove the sleeves of her coat. Beth felt sleepy, dreamy, strange. She followed Danny's lead and wriggled out of her coat. They banged elbows and knees as they tried to untangle from the heavy winter clothing.

Beep! Beep!

Beth and Danny froze.

Beep! Beep! The sound of a car horn next to them invaded their mini paradise.

"Hey man, what the hell is going on in there?" Mike Crowley guffawed. His hair was still wet from the shower after his wrestling match.

He was driving a group of his friends in his green Duster.

Beth and Danny straightened themselves up quickly.

Danny rolled down the window. When the other boys saw Beth, they gave catcalls and yelled "woo-hoo!"

"Hey Beth," he said pleasantly, then looked at Danny. "Are you guys going to Burger Chef?"

"Not at this exact moment," Danny said in an irritated tone.

"Yeah, well, maybe you'd better," Mike responded in a serious tone. He gave his friend a "be careful" kind of look.

Beth understood the cryptic comment and the look. *Be careful Danny, she is too young.* Why did these idiots have to intrude?

"We'll see you guys there," Mike yelled as he drove off.

Danny rolled the window up and sat perfectly still. He stared out of the fogged front window. Then he picked Beth up and put her back in the passenger's seat.

Beth thought, *What? He's not going to pay any attention to Mike, is he?* She pouted her lips.

He pulled his seat up to the steering wheel and handed Beth her coat. The special moment between them was over.

Danny looked at her and said, "We really ought to go. I don't want your parents to get mad if you're late."

"Aren't we going to Burger Chef?" Beth asked.

"We'll go for a little bit."

Beth tried to turn on the radio, but it didn't work. She glanced at him.

"Broken," he replied.

Beth leaned back in the seat and sulked as they pulled away from the parking lot. Who didn't have a radio in their car? That wasn't acceptable. She began to hum "Hey Jude."

Danny drove in silence.

"I can't believe you don't have a radio in here!" She crossed her arms over her chest. The magic was gone.

Cheerleaders, wrestlers, and a whole host of other teenagers packed Burger Chef. Beth and Danny strolled in, and a small roar greeted them. Beth excused herself to go to the restroom while Danny went to find them a place to sit.

When she came out, she caught sight of him waving her over to a table of their friends. Lynne sat on Mike's lap and grinned at Beth.

Hmm, good for Lynne, Beth thought with a smile. As she walked toward the table, she cut though the massive lines of students ordering fries and Cokes.

"Beth O'Brien." Steve leaned in a little too closely to her.

"Hi." She tried to maneuver her way around him.

He moved into her path and blocked her from getting through.

"I didn't know you were Mitchell's girlfriend. Why didn't you tell me that the other day?"

"I'm not his girlfriend, but we have started dating," Beth responded, trying to get past him on the other side.

He moved again and blocked her attempts to walk by him.

"Why?" he said with a sneer.

Beth glared at him.

Steve raised his eyebrows. "Why him? He didn't even play football."

This jerk was serious. He really didn't understand.

Steve was beginning to make Beth nervous. Danny could not play contact sports because of the back and leg injuries he received in the car accident. In their first phone conversation, he had admitted he was self-conscious about not being able to participate in football, wrestling, or basketball. He ran cross-country and played on the tennis team. He also liked to water ski, but his favorite sport was surfing.

She looked across the room at Danny, but he was deep in a conversation with his buddies at the table. If Danny saw Steve hassling her, he would get upset. Steve was confrontational, and Beth feared they might get into a fight. She certainly did not want to have Danny fight with anyone over her. It would kill her if he were seriously hurt.

"Leave me alone." Beth pushed Steve out of the way and hoped he would not make a bigger scene.

As she walked by, he said, "I don't know what he wants with a freshman anyway. I'm sure you don't put out, and I'll lay twenty that you don't even know how to give a blowjob."

His no-neck friends laughed.

Beth ignored the rude comment and continued walking toward Danny. Her legs shook, and she felt like screaming.

"Hey." Danny patted his right thigh for her to sit down, and Beth plopped on his lap and removed he coat. He asked her quietly, "You're shaking. Are you alright?"

Beth wanted to tell him about Steve but didn't dare. "I'm fine," she said and consciously made the decision to ignore Steve and his bulldog buddies on the opposite side of the room. She did look over once, but he was occupied with two girls who looked at him adoringly. She was glad he didn't focus any more attention on her.

Twenty minutes passed quickly.

Danny said, "We need to get going. I don't want you to be

late."

Beth reached for her coat, but he took it from her and helped her with it. She loved that. He hugged her from behind and kissed her on the cheek in front of everyone.

Lynne smiled at Beth and winked. She still sat in Mike's lap.

Mike looked at Danny again and said seriously, "Be careful, man."

Danny focused on his friend and replied in an equally serious tone, "Shut up, Mike."

Beth wanted to shout, "Yeah Mike, shut up!"

Lynne turned to give Mike a questioning look, and he shifted and gently pushed her out of his lap.

"Get up, rug rat. You need to get home," Mike said.

Beth could see the hurt in Lynne's eyes.

Mike shook his head sheepishly as if he knew he hurt her feelings, and then said more gently, "Come on, I'll give you a ride."

Beth wondered why Mike was so complicated. Was he going to be a friend or a foe? How come it was all right for him to have a freshman in his lap but not Danny?

The night air was unbearably cold. Danny joked and laughed with her while the car warmed during the short ride back to her house. He made her smile and she teased him playfully. It was strange how well they got along.

The Mustang pulled into her driveway. Her mother had left the front light on. Danny reached for the car door handle.

Beth said, "Wait a minute. I'm home on time. They won't care if we sit here and talk for a few minutes."

Danny raised his eyebrows and eased back into his seat.

He pulled her close again over the parking brake. "I love the way you smell. I have never smelled that perfume before. I really like it."

Beth felt a flutter in her stomach as he brought his face close to her neck. She moved her hand up to his face and guided his mouth to hers. Their kiss was intense and fierce.

He took her breath away. She pulled away from his mouth and kissed his closed eyelids, his cheeks, his nose, his chin, and then she traveled down to his neck and back up to his ear. Danny groaned. His breathing became heavy as she used her mouth to gently tug on his ear. She felt him shudder. He placed both hands on her shoulders, sat her upright and pushed her away.

Beth gaped at him. In the past, the guys she dated were like Kung Fu with their hands everywhere. Danny acted like he enjoyed kissing her, and he acted as if he liked her a lot. But he kept pushing her away.

"You need to go in now," he said with a ragged breath.

"I don't want to." She leaned back toward him.

He held her shoulders more tightly now and forced her away.

"Beth you've got to go in, or I'm going to have a real problem." He smiled at her tightly.

Beth did not get it, but she surely wasn't going to sit here and beg someone to kiss her.

"Okay, I'll see you," she said as she opened the door and exited the car much too quickly.

Danny scrambled out his side of the car, but she was already at the front door. He stood there looking at her with narrowed eyes.

"I'll call you when I get home," he shouted.

Beth walked into the shadow of the front door while Danny got back in the car.

True to his word, he called when he got home. Beth had already changed into her nightgown, crawled into bed, and was listening to a Linda Ronstadt album on her turntable. She grabbed the phone quickly so her parents wouldn't hear the ring and tell her it was too late to be on the phone.

Danny must have been in bed, too, because he whispered when he said, "I need to tell you something and it's important."

Beth was sure he would say he didn't want to see her anymore. Hold on, here it comes. She braced herself.

"I'm crazy about you. I think you can tell that. You and I both know there are some problems with us being together, though. I mean, it's my senior year and there are going to be times when I want to go out later than 11:00."

Yep. Here it was! She began to feel a pain deep in her throat. The only time she ever got that pain was when she was about to sob, and she was trying hard not to.

"I'm just asking you to trust me. I care about you, and I don't want to be with anyone else, but I do want to hang out with Mike and the guys a little. They are starting to give me a hard time because they can tell how I feel. So sometimes when I take you home, I might go back out, but I swear I will not be with another girl. You're the only girl I want to be with."

Then there was silence.

"Beth?"

"Yes?" Beth could hardly breathe.

"Beth?" he repeated. "Is that okay?"

Beth finally took a breath and said, "Of course, absolutely, I completely understand. I'm sorry that I can't stay out later, but I really can't help that."

"I know. It does suck but like you said there's nothing that can be done about it." He paused and then moved to another subject.

"You make it very hard for me to behave myself with the way you kiss me and look at me with those eyes."

Beth was instantly assured and felt warm and cozy again. Her throat pain disappeared.

"Why did you run from the car earlier?" he asked.

She was upset that he kept dismissing her advances. But that sounded too juvenile to say out loud.

"It was really cold outside, and I didn't want you to have to get out of the car to walk me to the door," she said in a feeble voice.

"It's good I didn't walk you to the door. I don't think I

could have walked anyway if you know what I mean."

Beth didn't know what he meant. He was great at confusing her. She decided she needed to quit pretending to understand things he said when she did not.

"What *are* you talking about?" Beth asked.

He laughed, and her temper flared. "Well, I'm sorry I'm so stupid, but I really don't get it."

He laughed again and had to excuse himself from the phone. She felt like hanging up on him, but if she did, he would call back. At this hour, her parents would be unhappy with the phone ringing.

"Beth...?" he asked as he returned to the phone.

"What?" she snapped.

"I stopped kissing you in the car because I was getting... well, you know, excited."

A rush of embarrassment came over her. Oh my God! He couldn't walk to the door because he was hard? She remained silent on the phone but inside her head was bursting. She squeezed her eyes tightly shut, and she muffled a strangled sound. Finally, she pulled the covers up over her mouth in humiliation.

"Do you understand now?" Danny asked.

"Yeah, I get it," Beth said.

She was sure he could hear the embarrassment in her voice. Embarrassed or not, Beth was elated that she had that effect on him.

The two quickly established a routine of talking on the phone until the wee hours of the morning. They got to know each other very well in a short amount of time through the late-night marathon conversations. Danny and Beth became an item at school and were seen at all extra-curricular events. Beth's teachers teased her about him because he always walked her to her classes. Her parents and family joked about Danny with her, too. She was happy. Danny seemed happy, too.

CHAPTER 5

Several weeks of dating bliss passed in a blur. Beth and Danny were getting along well and became awfully close. When they weren't out together, they spent their time talking and laughing on the telephone. They spoke over the phone in whispers for hours after their dates. Danny never once dropped her off to go back out with his friends as he had indicated. It would be close to one or one thirty in the morning before they would begin to doze off. Sometimes, Danny would hang up after Beth had fallen asleep. She would hold the phone close to her ear and curl under the bed covers. He would whisper, "Good night" and replace the receiver on his end of the line. The conversations became more personal and tender, as they grew increasingly comfortable with one another.

When they were on a date or at school, they held hands and looked adoringly at each other. They laughed a lot, and their friends rolled their eyes at their inside jokes. Beth enjoyed the necking Danny allowed them to do. He had taken on the role of "Make-Out Police," and he made Beth stop whenever things went too far.

It was Valentine's Day, and Beth could hardly contain her excitement. She and Danny planned to attend a wrestling match and then head to a party afterwards.

After school that day, Beth's mother asked, "Are you going out with Danny tonight?"

"Yep, we're going to the wrestling match and then his friend Billy Englehart is having a party. Mom, could I please stay out later tonight since its Valentine's Day?" Beth pleaded, giving an Oscar winning performance of a pathetic, sad, love-stricken teenager.

"Oh alright, but be home by 12:30. No later, understand?"

Beth nodded.

Her mother asked, "Do you have a present for Danny?"

She didn't hear the question right away. She was still rejoicing over the curfew. Twelve thirty? Yahoo! Even the seniors she knew had to be home by then. She wasn't going to miss anything tonight...alright!

Then the question finally registered. Beth's mouth dropped open, and she locked gazes with her mother.

"A gift?" Cripes! Beth widened her eyes, and she was on the threshold of flipping out.

Her mother interrupted the panic attack. "Don't worry. I think I might be able to help you out. Come with me."

Beth followed her mother upstairs to her parents' bedroom. Her mother opened her bureau drawer and pulled out a small square box.

She handed it to Beth and said, "I think this would be an appropriate gift."

Beth accepted the box and opened it. It was a beautiful pewter keychain. She smiled at her mother then hugged her hard.

"It's something I had for your father but..."

"Oh, thank you, Mom!" Beth danced about the room holding the keychain in the air. She swung it in happy little circles. Not for one minute did Beth honestly think this was ever meant for her father. She loved her mother.

"Here's some wrapping paper," her mother added.

"Thank you so much!" Beth accepted it.

"You're welcome, but you will have to buy your own card for this boy. Do you need a ride to the drugstore?"

Beth nodded. "I do."

She carried the items to her bedroom, and then joined her mom downstairs. They climbed into the car and drove to the drugstore.

At the store, it took Beth forever to find the right card. It couldn't be anything too sappy because Danny hadn't said he loved her or even asked her to wear his class ring yet. After choosing a humorous card with a large ape on the cover, she and her mother returned home. Beth wrapped the gift in her room.

"Oh my God! Mom?" Beth screamed.

In an instant, her mother was in the doorway, her eyes wide. "What? What's the matter?"

In a barely audible tone, Beth whispered, "What if he doesn't give me anything?"

Her mother smiled and relaxed. "Well, that's the great thing about a small gift and a big purse." She turned around and opened the hallway closet.

She pulled out a nice leather pouch purse and dangled it at her daughter by the long strap. It had plenty of room in it.

"Keep the gift out of sight in your purse. If he gives you a card, you give him the card. If he gives you a gift, you pull out the gift. If he doesn't give you anything, then by gosh, you're so sorry, you didn't shop for him either," she said smiling.

Beth jumped off her bed and bounced toward her. She reached for the purse and said sincerely, "Thank you, Mom, you're the best."

The phone rang off the hook for Beth while she tried to get ready for her date. Everyone would be at the wrestling match and then at Billy's party. Lynne called her three times. Jackie, Susan, and Melissa called, too. The girls added to her stress with questions like, "Do you think he'll give you a gift?"

Danny would be there in less than fifteen minutes and the phone rang again. Beth groaned out loud at the constant interruptions.

Beth's mother appeared in her doorway. "It was Melissa. I told her you couldn't talk right now. You look beautiful."

"Thank you for everything." Beth put her earrings in.

She turned around and hugged her mom. Her mother held her hands. Beth felt something being pressed into her palm, and she looked down at a small makeup bag. Beth smiled and opened it. She saw a tube of blush and a small four-shade pack of blue eye shadow, a lip gloss stick that was berry flavored and a small bottle of Love's Baby Soft perfume.

"I'll help you if you'd like," her mother said.

Beth started to cry but stopped herself. She didn't want to ruin her mascara. Composing herself, she looked in the mirror. The beautiful reflection looking back was her own.

It was already dark outside, and the dimmer switch by the door was turned to low. The lighting was perfect.

"I want you to have a good time tonight, but you must be home by twelve thirty, so don't be late," her mother said.

"I won't. I promise," Beth assured her.

The phone rang again, and it was Danny. He said he would be there in five minutes.

Beth decided not to enter the family room where her father was watching *The Undersea World of Jacques Cousteau*. She was an emotional wreck tonight, and her dad's teasing was the last thing she needed. Her mother sat with her in the kitchen, and they talked quietly.

The doorbell rang. Beth jumped out of her seat, and her mother stood and put her hands up to stop her daughter from darting toward the front door.

"You wait here. I'll let him in and bring him to you."

"Okay," Beth said as she bit her berry-flavored bottom lip. Yum!

Danny walked into the house and began talking a blue streak to her mother. "I love your house Mrs. O'Brien. The wallpaper in here is nice. I like the oil lamp, too. Is this butter churn new? I really like it."

Her mother responded to all his questions and comments as she guided him into the kitchen. Danny stared at Beth, his mouth slightly parted.

"Hey," he finally said weakly. "You look very nice."

Beth's cheeks grew warm and she smiled. "Thank you."

He picked up her coat from the back of the kitchen chair. "Are you ready?" he asked.

"Yes."

Her father came out to the kitchen to recheck their plans and to see them off. Thankfully, he didn't say anything to embarrass her.

Danny helped her with her coat, and they said goodbye.

The night air was cold but still. Beth wore blue jeans and brown socks that matched the leather on her new pair of clogs. Her V-neck brown and tan angora sweater hung low past her waist. It was incredibly soft and one of her favorites. She didn't wear the Baby Soft perfume because Danny liked the smell of Grass Oil. More importantly, she didn't wear it because of the name. Life was rough enough around his senior friends without wearing a perfume with the name "Baby" in it.

They got into the car, and Danny complimented her over and over. He had showered, shaved, and he smelled wonderful. She pulled his arm toward her, leaned into the side of his face, and kissed his cheek. He always seemed surprised by that gesture.

Beth quickly scanned the car and did not see a gift. She experienced a small wave of disappointment. Her friends thought he would buy her something. She was hoping for a stuffed animal at least. Oh well. He had never asked her to officially be his girlfriend despite the fact they had been dating only each other and talking on the phone every night.

Time for self-talk. *Get over it, Beth, it's just another day. Pretend it's not Valentine's Day and under no circumstances do you let him see the gift in your purse.*

He held her hand during the drive to the high school.

"Guess what," Beth said, breaking the silence. She hated that he didn't have a radio.

"What?" He checked the rearview mirror and merged onto the highway.

"I get to stay out until twelve thirty," Beth said quietly.

It took Danny a minute to register what she said. His eyes widened, and he smiled at her. "So, we have extra time, huh?"

They locked gazes, and she giggled. They would have over six hours together.

"That's cool. How did you pull that off?" he asked.

"Mom's being really cool today," Beth said, careful not to mention Valentine's Day.

Danny smiled and glanced at his watch. He squeezed her hand, but he didn't say anything about it being Valentine's Day, though. Beth tried not to be disappointed.

They arrived, parked the car, and climbed out into the cold air.

He wrapped his arm around her as they walked in the building. Their friends were already seated in the bleachers, and the match was just beginning. Danny took a seat and guided Beth by the hand to the bleacher in front of him. She leaned back, fitting perfectly between his knees. His thighs were pressed around her sides and her arms were wrapped under his calves and knees. Danny lowered his arms down in front of her and clasped his clasped just above her chest. He kept his chin close to her head and played with her hair throughout the first few matches. His breath on her neck raised goose bumps on her skin. There were people all around so the touching and closeness could not get out of hand. Danny lightly rubbed the tops of her arms and her back. Beth ran her hands up and down his calves. She leaned back into him and felt his obvious reaction to the sensual, private touching they were doing in a very public place.

He placed his coat over his lap. The movement caused Beth to look up at him. He bent down and kissed her deeply. Emotion overwhelmed her, and she sensed the same from him.

He leaned into her ear and whispered, "Let's go."

She wanted to be alone with him, so it didn't take her long to collect herself and follow him down the bleachers.

They were slightly drunk with emotion, weaving towards the car. They held on to one another for support as they tried to kiss and walk at the same time. Danny opened her door and reached down to pull the lever that moved the front bucket seat forward. Beth willingly climbed into the back seat. He came around the other side and slid in next to her.

The car was parked in a darker section of the parking lot, and they quickly resumed where they'd left off in the gymnasium. The windows fogged because of the cold weather and the heat rising between them.

In between passionate kisses, Danny said, "I won't do anything to hurt you."

"I know."

Danny moved his lips away from her mouth and slid them to her ear. He helped her take off her coat. Beth attempted to help him with his coat, but it was already off. His lips caused a trail of gooseflesh down her neck. Danny picked her up underneath her arms and put her on his lap, so she faced him. While exploring her mouth with his, he put one hand up the front of her sweater and felt the silky seamless bra Beth wore. He had never done anything like this with her before. She was surprised he was going a step further. His hand remained in that area for a moment or two as if he waited for her to protest. She did not.

Soon, both his hands were hidden in between the brown angora and white satin. He groaned quietly. Beth had never been touched by a boy on her bare skin, but she was ready to let Danny do whatever he wanted tonight. She reached down to unbutton the front of his shirt. He moaned again as he kissed her. She smiled slightly and touched his bare chest. It felt like Christmas morning. Danny brought his hands down and rubbed his palms on the tops of her thighs.

"I won't do anything to hurt you," he assured her again.

Beth made eye contact with him and nodded slightly. She leaned into his lips, and their kisses were slow, deep, and filled with passion. Danny slid his hand over the denim fabric up to her waist and then down her backside. She moved forward, and he drew her closer. He breathed heavily and sighed. The feel of his hand between her legs made Beth sit straight up.

Danny froze at her startled movement. Beth looked at him with wide eyes. He held her gaze and shifted his hand slightly, pushing his luck a bit further. Beth closed her eyes, overcome with the sensation, and then dared to open them. Danny focused on her face, his eyes brimming with affection. Pleasant warmth spread through her chest. He removed his hand and leaned forward to get more comfortable. In doing so, he jostled Beth, and she hit her head on the interior light of the car.

"Ouch!" she said.

"Oh God, I'm sorry." He touched the top of her head and rubbed away the offensive pain.

She giggled, and so did he. They fell silent, embraced, and remained still.

"Look, we can't do this anymore," he said.

"Why?" Beth asked. She hoped for more of the same.

"It's just not a good idea." He sounded agitated.

"Yeah, but it feels so good to be with you, kissing you." She tried to recapture the moment by placing her hands back on his chest.

"You have no idea what you're talking about." Danny groaned as if he were in pain.

Beth continued to touch him and moved in closer.

"Stop it, Beth!" Danny grabbed her hands and stared at her.

Beth pulled back as if she had been stung. She shifted her body off to the side, and Danny quickly stepped out of the car and slammed the door.

She flinched. *Now what did I do?* She had never seen him angry before and now she had to pee. Shit!

Danny stomped to the other side of the car and yelled into the night sky, "Damn it!" He jerked her side of the door open, and Beth slowly exited the vehicle. She didn't understand his anger, and she feared he would abandon her in the parking lot. Her eyes welled up with tears, and she looked up at him. Danny's expression softened.

"Don't cry," he said and embraced her. "It's just...I don't want to hurt you, and we have to be careful. It would be a disaster if we got carried away. It would be worse than a disaster if you got pregnant. There are other things we could do but...you are a lot younger than me. I care about you a lot, but I don't want us to do anything we'll be sorry for."

Pregnant? Geez, she wasn't going to let him do *that*! What kind of a girl did he think she was anyway? Why can't we just kiss? What's wrong with that? It certainly feels wonderful. Why isn't that enough?

Beth challenged him. "You act like you're afraid to kiss me."

"I am," he said softly into the top of her head and held her tight. "You make it very hard for me to stop."

No way was she ready to have sex. She figured Danny knew everything about it because he wasn't satisfied to just "make out." She was angry with him for that. She was angry with herself, too. She was angry that she was such a baby and knew nothing about sex. Danny's kisses and caresses had felt wonderful. Now they terrified her.

"We've got plenty of time, Little One," he said, trying to comfort her.

"Don't call me that."

Danny hugged her and convinced her to return to the wrestling match. While she fixed her hair and makeup in the rearview mirror, he faked impatience and sighed deeply, shivering, and chattering his teeth. She giggled at his drama, and he chuckled back. Both relaxed a bit.

They returned to the gym where they watched and cheered the team on to victory. The tension between them relaxed in the comfort of the gym. After the match, they gave Lynne, Billy, and Jackie a ride to Burger Chef. Beth complained about the broken radio, and she encouraged the others to fuss at Danny, too. She hoped it would prompt him to get the damn thing fixed. They sang "Black Water" by the Doobie Brothers and did animal noise impersonations. Amused laughter filled the car, and Beth laughed so hard her belly hurt.

Once they were inside Burger Chef, Beth and Danny had a private moment at the table while the others headed for the restrooms.

Danny said, "You know the Prom really isn't all that far away. Things seem to be going rather good with us, and I think we should probably start thinking about going together. I know you girls need time to find a dress and all the extras."

Beth gaped at him. Her insides exploded with pleasure. He just asked her to his Prom! The rest of their friends arrived and took their seats, and the moment for her to answer was lost. Beth assumed Danny knew her answer was "yes."

He reached for her hand and held it under the table.

Beth brimmed with happiness. Even Mike Crowley tried to be cordial to Beth.

"You know he really cares about you," Mike said to her when Danny left to purchase their shakes.

"I care about him, too," Beth replied softly, hoping Mike was finally accepting her as Danny's girlfriend.

"Well, don't get him in trouble." Beth didn't know what he meant, but Mike's tone was serious.

Billy interrupted Mike to ask for a ride home. The rest of the gang soon left, and Danny and Beth remained in a virtually empty restaurant.

"Should we go?" Beth finally asked.

Danny only nodded as he sucked down his vanilla shake. They rose and headed toward the door and squeezed their trash into the overfilled trashcan near the exit. Beth got in the Mustang first. Danny took his position behind the wheel and turned on the ignition.

"By the way, Happy Valentine's Day," he blurted.

Beth looked at him, blinked, smiled, and then could not suppress a yawn.

"I'm so sorry. Thank you. Happy Valentine's Day." She assumed someone had reminded him.

Danny started to back out of the parking space, and then he quickly pulled back in.

He reached into his pocket and showed Beth a small blue velvet box. "This is for you. Happy Valentine's Day."

Beth stared wide-eyed at the box, touched by his gesture. She hoped it was a necklace instead of a pair of earrings.

He offered the box to her. She took it from his hand and gently opened the lid. Inside was a delicate, gold diamond ring. Beth was overwhelmed by its beauty and unable to speak. He took it out, placed it on her finger, and kissed her. Time seemed to stop for her. Was this really happening?

"I never bought a class ring, and I wanted you to have something nice. If I had a class ring, I would be giving that to you now."

Beth squealed with delight and held her hand out to admire the ring. This was much better than a necklace.

Danny beamed at her reaction. "So, you'll wear it?"

She laughed and bounced up and down, nodding emphatically. After squeezing her arms around his neck, she kissed him squarely on the mouth. Their teeth clicked from the contact, and they both laughed.

"Alright, alright." Danny composed himself.

Prompted by renewed confidence, Beth lifted her chin and locked gazes with him. "By the way, I'd love to go to the Prom with you. I already have a dress picked out. My older sister worked at Hannigan's Department Store. My mom and I shop there a lot. There's one on display that is my favorite! It's a pale pink halter with a darker pink and white sash across the waist. It's so beautiful."

Danny raised both eyebrows and smiled. "I'm sure it is. I will rent a white tux, so we'll match. We'll be the best-looking couple there." He leaned over and kissed her again.

The lights went out inside Burger Chef, and he said, "We'd better get to Billy's."

Beth glanced out at the empty parking lot.

"Oh! Wait!" She reached in her purse and retrieved his gift. "Happy Valentine's Day."

Danny slanted his head. "I wasn't going to get this if I didn't give you something, right?"

"Right! I might be young, but I'm no idiot!" She smiled, and he laughed.

Beth loved to watch him when he laughed. His eyes turned a brighter shade of green, and his smile was intoxicating.

Danny grinned like a little boy on Christmas morning as he opened the card and key chain.

He kissed her and drew back. "Thank you." Then they headed to Billy's.

There were about fifty cars parked on Billy's street. Jackie was there with Melissa and Lynne. Susan came with her boyfriend, Tyler. The girls ogled the ring, and Beth beamed with pride.

Danny informed her that Lynne had gone with him to pick it out. She had known for days but kept his secret. Beth hugged Lynne. She couldn't believe her friend had made her wonder if he would give her a gift or not. Lynne told Beth that she would have told her about the ring, but Danny wanted to surprise her and pressured her to keep his secret.

Danny's friends soon took him away from Beth's side. Standing at the keg, he caught Beth's eye and winked at her several times. Beth frowned, slightly annoyed at his friends for keeping him from her, but she was having fun hanging with her friends, so it didn't bother her that much.

A drunk Mike flirted with Lynne from across the room. It bothered Beth that he was so hot and cold with Lynne, and Beth worried her friend was in for a heartbreak. She was glad that Lynne seemed happy, but doubt nagged at her. She worried her friend would get hurt. Beth accepted a can of Budweiser beer from one of her friends and pretended to drink it.

Danny came over and took the beer from her. "You'd better not. I don't want you to get in trouble."

Beth shooed him back to his friends. She enjoyed hanging out with the girls.

Beth stifled a yawn. It was 12:00. She and Danny usually talked on the phone much later than this, but the romantic scene in the car earlier had taken its toll. Now she was sleepy. Danny fake-yawned at her from across the room, and she smiled at the teasing. Unfortunately, the yawn was not lost on Mike. He worked his way across the room and stood near Lynne.

His words slurred as he leaned forward across Lynne and said to Beth, "Oh, is it past your bedtime?"

Beth bristled and wanted to slap him. Mike made a few more rude bedtime comments.

Danny came over. "Let's go." He handed Beth her coat.

"Oh, you'd better get the little girl home in time for bed," Mike slurred his words, laughed, and snorted.

Lynne curled her lips in disdain and narrowed her eyes at Mike.

"Fuck you, man," Danny shouted, and the two boys exchanged a barrage of curses and insults as Danny led Beth out to his car.

Beth and Danny were both silent for most of the ride to her house until Danny broke the silence.

"Do I get bonus points if I get you home early?" he asked, as if trying to conjure up a more pleasant mood.

"Probably," she replied and smiled slightly.

She should be feeling on top of the world tonight, but Danny was unhappy. They turned onto her street, and Danny pulled over and stopped the car. There were no other cars around, and he kissed her passionately.

He drew back. "I'm not going to let them get to me.

Okay?"

Beth nodded and pursed her lips. She hated when he kissed her like that and then started talking immediately.

He turned to look out the front window and took his foot off the brake. Beth leaned over and kissed him on the cheek. Danny pivoted and crushed his mouth to hers. He managed to drive the car and kiss her all the way down her street without crashing.

Danny drew away to pull into her driveway.

Beth lifted one eyebrow. "Very talented. You can drive and kiss at the same time." She looked down at the ring, and her stomach fluttered. Would her parents be upset over the diamond ring?

Her mom would be cool, but her dad may not like it.

"Danny, will you keep this until tomorrow? I'd like to tell my folks about it first before I start wearing it."

Danny raised his eyebrows and licked his lips. "Uh, okay. Do you think they're going to be mad?"

"No, but I think it's best if I tell them about it first."

"Alright, whatever you think is best."

She placed the ring in his hand. They kissed a long good-bye.

Beth recalled his pained expression. "Bring my ring to school tomorrow. I want to wear it as soon as possible." She gave him a dazzling smile.

He grinned and winked at her, apparently reassured. "Hey, since it's so late, I won't call you. Is that okay?"

"Sure." She was ready to fall asleep anyway.

They shared another quick kiss, and Beth went into the house.

Beth's mother waited up for her. "Well, did you give him the gift?"

"Yep."

"Did he like it?"

"I think so," she said smiling.

Her mom tilted her head and arched an eyebrow. "Did he

give you something?"

"Yes."

"Beth, what was it?" She smiled at her daughter.

"Oh Mom, he gave me a beautiful ring!"

Her mother focused her attention on Beth's finger. "Where is it?"

"Well, that's the thing..." Beth began nervously.

"Oh Beth, you didn't break up with him on Valentine's Day..."

"No, no! I asked him to keep it until tomorrow. It's a mini diamond, Mom. It's beautiful."

"Oh my!" Her mother paused and then added, "What does that mean?"

"He bought the diamond ring because he doesn't have a class ring to give me."

"Well, you'll have to tell your father tomorrow." Worry lines creased her mom's brow.

"I'm wearing the ring in school tomorrow, so I eventually I have to tell him." Beth sighed. "Do you think he will be mad?"

"Why don't I break the news to your father."

Beth hugged her mom. "Thank you."

"You're welcome. Now, get to bed. It's late." Her mother rubbed her shoulder and shooed her toward the stairs.

Beth went to bed and hugged her pillow tightly until she fell sound asleep.

In the morning, Beth's father came in to wake her up. He pulled the chair from her desk over to the bed.

"I need to talk to you," he stated in a firm voice.

She sat up and rubbed her eyes.

"I need to talk to you about this boy. Your mom says he gave you a diamond ring last night for Valentine's Day."

"It is a *mini* diamond, Dad."

"I don't care if it's the goddamned Rock of Gibraltar, you are too young to be accepting a diamond ring from a boy, especially this boy who is getting ready to graduate from high school. How old is he anyway? It doesn't matter. You are only fourteen years old! Do you understand?"

She assumed the question was rhetorical, so she didn't answer.

"Just exactly how close are you two anyway?"

Beth threw herself back onto her pillow and groaned. "Dad, it's a mini diamond, it's ridiculously small! He didn't own a class ring, so he gave me that instead. It would be the same as giving me his class ring." Beth attempted to get all the correct information out to him immediately before he got more upset. As she had feared, this was not going well.

Her dad's face twisted into a scowl. "Well, you're too young to be dating this boy anyway, and your mother should never have allowed it. I don't want you to see him anymore."

His words shook Beth's world to the very core.

She sat upright in the bed. "What? You're kidding, right?"

"No, I'm not kidding, and your mother and I agree on this so don't think she'll go along with it either. You tell that boy today that you aren't allowed to see him anymore." He rose from the chair and exited her room.

Beth could tell by the hardness in his voice that this was the end of the discussion. Where in the hell was her mother? *She is such a traitor! I will never forgive her for this.*

I can't see Danny anymore. Beth's stomach lurched. She was so stunned she couldn't even cry. Fists clenched, she got up, stomped to the bathroom, and jumped into the shower.

Beth couldn't remember ever being this angry in her entire life. She was beyond angry. *My mom better not try to talk to me this morning!* Beth fumed and scrubbed her hair and body so hard that her skin turned pink.

After she dressed, she went down into the kitchen. Her mother was washing breakfast dishes in the sink. Thankfully, her dad had already left for work. Maybe her dad was just being overprotective, and this would blow over. Her mother had always been on her side and seemed to be pulling for her and Danny. Maybe she should try and talk to her mom.

Beth ran up to her mother. "Oh Mom, what am I going to do? Dad is being so unreasonable!"

Her mother paused from washing the dishes and glanced at her. "I don't want to discuss this. I was wrong. That boy should not be buying a diamond ring for a fourteen-year old girl."

At her mother's firm tone, Beth stopped cold and began to cry.

"Can you just let him come over today and we'll show you the ring? It's tiny. We will do whatever you and Dad want. Just please don't do this! Please?"

Her mother went back to washing the dishes.

"Go wash your face, Beth, and get ready for school. I'll drive you."

Beth was a zombie on the ride to school. When she arrived at the front entrance of C.R., she reached for the door handle.

"Beth, I would advise you not to bring that boy to the house today, and don't let your dad and I catch you with him or wearing that ring." Her mother compressed her mouth into a stern line.

Beth's mind screamed out *Jesus Christ! You bitch!* She slammed the car door shut and stormed off into the front of the school building.

CHAPTER 6

Beth avoided the Center that morning, but Danny waited for her at her homeroom class.

"Hey, how are you?" He gave her a nervous smile.

Her heart was breaking. She decided not to obey her parents.

"Did you tell your folks? Everything's cool?" he asked

"Yeah, all is well. May I please wear the ring?" Beth grinned and held out her finger.

He retrieved the ring from his pants pocket, slipped it on, and kissed her quickly on the lips.

"I have to go. I'm going to be late!" He smiled and ran down the hall.

Beth stared after him, a lump forming in the back of her throat. It was large and painful. She was getting ready to sob, and there was nothing she could do about it. The final morning bell rang. She stood outside the classroom unable to go in. Her homeroom teacher, Mrs. Hart, could see Beth from her desk and watched her closely. The rest of the hallway was now empty. Mrs. Hart got up and approached her in the hall.

"Is everything alright, Beth?" she asked, concern wrinkling her brow.

Beth began to sob soundlessly. Her body racked with the force of it.

Mrs. Hart wrapped her arms around her. "There now, nothing could be all this bad. I've seen the way Danny looks at you. He will come around. Do you want me to send you to the nurse?"

Beth nodded. Mrs. Hart thought Danny had broken up with her. She decided not to correct her.

"Would you like me to send Susan with you?" Beth nodded again.

Her teacher wrote a pass to the nurse's office for the girls and wrote a later time on the slip. This gave the two of them time alone. They just needed to find a place to hide and not get caught.

Susan met Beth in the hallway. The two went to one of the empty school stairwells. Beth tearfully relayed to Susan what happened with her parents.

"They won't even look at it. They think we are having sex. They think it's a pre-engagement ring or something!" After a few minutes, she stopped crying and composed herself. Beth made the bold decision to wear the ring in school. She would have to meet Danny for dates instead of having him pick her up. How would she ever explain that to him? Making the decision to lie to her parents left Beth feeling upset but she was angry enough to see this through. Her parents were not going to ruin this for her.

Susan patted Beth's shoulder. "Your parents will come around. I know they will."

Beth nodded, but she wasn't so sure.

After a brief stop at the nurse's office, they returned to class.

All her friends and acquaintances approached her to look at the ring that day. Even her teachers got into the act and asked to see it. Beth avoided Danny as much as possible for fear she would break down and cry in front of him.

He caught up with her at the end of the day. "Beth! Let me give you a ride home."

"No!" Beth snapped.

The busses were filling up. If she stayed there to talk to him, she would miss hers. She didn't know what to do.

With concern etched on his brow, Danny took hold of her hand and asked what was wrong. Beth insisted she needed to catch the bus, but Danny finally demanded she answer his question. Beth relented and walked with him to his locker, missing her bus ride home.

She told him the whole story.

He shook his head and smacked the wall with his hand. Danny's reaction to her parents' decision was understandable. She knew he was hurt because they didn't give him a chance and would not listen to reason about the diamond. Why would they assume he would take advantage of her just because he was a senior and she was a freshman? He was probably embarrassed as well as hurt and angry.

After he calmed down, he said, "Let me take you home. We'll show them the ring, and we can talk to them together."

Beth was angry enough with her parents to defy them face-to-face.

"Okay."

The two left the building, got in the Mustang, and headed toward her house.

As he turned onto her street, Danny slowed the car and stopped. "Maybe we ought to give them some time to cool off a bit."

Beth agreed, relieved. She wasn't ready for another confrontation.

They pulled in the driveway. There was no kiss goodbye. Beth handed Danny the ring without a word.

She got out of the car, turned back to him, and said, "Bring it to school tomorrow, okay?"

He winked at her and nodded.

She smiled and walked inside. No one was home. Thank God!

Beth went upstairs and stayed in her room all night. Neither of her parents called her for dinner, and she was fine with that.

The next day at school it seemed everyone knew about Beth's parents, Danny, and the ring. The girls wanted to talk to her about it at lunch. Lynne could not believe Beth's parents had jumped to all the wrong conclusions. Beth was exhausted from crying, and Danny had not called the night before. The situation weighed on him, too, because he was grouchy and tense. They walked together from the Center to his locker holding hands. He smiled at her and handed her the ring. She leaned her face up to him, and he kissed her. A teacher saw the exchange and told them to let go of one another. Public displays of affection in Colonel Roberts High were not allowed. It felt like the whole world was against them.

"Christ!" Danny said loudly. "I am not a child!"

"Be careful, young man," the teacher told him.

Beth and Danny approached his locker as one of Steve's goons walked by. Danny slammed the locker door shut out of frustration.

"Hey, what's the matter with you, man? Your girlfriend too tight for you? Ha! Ha! Ha!" He bent over and walked dramatically to the end of the hallway, stomping his feet and holding his sides.

"Very funny. You're a riot, man," Danny said in a resolute tone.

Her eyes widened, and her chest swelled with air as her temper rose. Who would say such a disgusting thing like that to someone right in front of their girlfriend?

Steve was standing nearby. He and his cronies broke into malicious laughter.

She took a deep breath, refusing to give him the satisfaction of seeing her upset.

Beth said, "Danny, let's just ignore them."

"It's not that easy, Beth." He turned and strode away from her.

She followed him but said nothing.

That day and the next several days at school, Danny pulled away from her. His attitude toward her was changing, and this annoyed Beth, but she didn't know what to do. Danny rarely made eye contact with her, and he ignored her around his buddies. She couldn't understand how he could be so different, acting like the old, attentive Danny, when they were alone. That Saturday, Mike Crowley was having a huge party, so she and Danny planned to meet each other there. She hoped he wouldn't act like a jerk.

Saturday night arrived, and Susan's older sister Janet drove the five girls to the party. People were packed inside the garage, and the stereo blared out into the street. Everyone congregated by the turntable and the food. A senior boy did his best imitation of James Brown as the loud music played. Beth, Lynne, and Susan squeezed their way up to get a better look. He put on quite a show. The kids gathered around him, sang along, and encouraged him.

Beth saw Danny and approached him.

"How are you?" she shouted over the music.

At first, he ignored her and was swaying a bit from side to side. Beth correctly guessed he had been drinking. She rubbed his arm to get his attention. He leaned down to hear what she had to say. She smiled at him, and he hugged and kissed her. They stood together and watched "James Brown." When the show was over, the place went nuts. "James Brown" waved his hand, bowed, and then pretended to pass out. The crowd roared.

"That's pretty cool," Danny said and lumbered away in a bit of a stupor.

She narrowed her eyes at him. The music picked up again with the piano intro to "Thank You for Being a Friend." Everyone threw their arms around each other, and the crowd sang the song in unison, laughing and rocking back and forth to the beat. Several girls were crying, overcome with love for their friends. Beth joined in with Lynne, Susan, Jackie, and Melissa.

Beth drank Coke and pretended it had Bacardi in it. Danny proceeded to get stinking, stupid drunk. Beth was concerned, but he stayed away from her. Several times she went over to him, but he walked away with an annoyed look on his face. Her feelings were hurt, but she kept her distance. Beth went into the house to use the restroom. Once inside, she began to cry.

There was a knock at the door. "Beth, can we come in?" It was Lynne.

Beth opened the door and saw her four friends. The girls squeezed in one by one, shut the door, and locked it.

Beth sat on the closed toilet lid, trying to make room for all of them in the small space. She started to cry again.

Lynne grabbed the tissue box and handed Beth a handful.

Susan patted her hair. "It'll be alright. He's just drunk."

Jackie rubbed Beth's back. The girls eventually convinced her his callous behavior was because he was drunk.

Beth wiped her eyes and blew her nose with the tissues. She managed to pull herself together. The girls stayed in the bathroom and before long, they were laughing and giggling, waiting for Beth's eyes to de-puff so she could exit the restroom looking dynamite.

They returned to the party. The music lulled, and a couple continued to slow dance to music playing in their drunken heads.

Billy made a grand arm gesture towards the girls and hollered, "Well, there are the rug rats! Isn't it past your bedtime, girls?"

Mike laughed and pretended to check the time on his watch. He made a snorting sound and bent over so far, he staggered to stay standing.

Beth and her friends exchanged mortified glances as all eyes focused on them.

Lynne dropped her gaze to the floor.

Beth looked up at Danny and mentally tried to convey *Stop him from doing this.*

His eyes were glazed over from the Budweiser and the gold stuff in the large bottle Mike held in his hand.

Danny held up his cup to Beth and said defiantly, "I really think you should go home now before your mommy and daddy come looking for you."

Mike roared with laughter.

The other guests at the party groaned at his lack of sensitivity.

Beth gaped at him.

Billy sobered up a bit and said, "Aw, come on, man."

Suddenly, Steve appeared in front of Beth and blocked her view of the disappointing scene Danny had created with his friends.

"I told you he was an asshole. Let me drive you home."

Beth wanted to accept his invitation to show Danny he wasn't the only senior who was interested in her. She wanted to hurt him just as badly as he had her. She reached for Steve's arm, but a junior cheerleader Beth barely knew intervened.

"Come on, Beth. I'll drive you." She pulled Beth's arm and guided her out the door.

Beth glanced back, and her four friends urged her to leave with the girl.

Danny staggered behind them mumbling, "Go on and go, just run away."

Anger rose to the surface, and Beth turned and glared at Danny.

"What the fuck?" Steve said to his friends as he looked back and forth at Beth and then his friends. The no-necks shrugged and went back to the keg.

"Come on. They aren't worth it," the girl said, and she guided Beth out and to her car.

The cheerleader gave her a continuous stream of advice on the way home. "He's a senior. They all act like jerks this time of year. It's called 'senioritis.' Forget him. He will be gone next year, and you'll find somebody new. You'll be better off if you split now rather than later."

Beth directed the girl to her home, wishing she would just be quiet.

Finally, they arrived at her house. She thanked the girl and got out of the car. Beth was relieved to reach her front door. Shortly after she got inside, the phone rang. Beth ran to her room to answer it. Maybe Danny was calling to apologize for being an ass.

Jackie was on the other end asking, "Are you alright?"

"Not really." Disappointment washed over her. Danny hadn't called the house since her parents forbade her to date him.

Her father came to her bedroom door in his pajamas.

"Who's on the phone?" he asked sternly.

"It's Jackie Basile."

"Well, it's too late to be on the phone."

"I have to go," Beth said. "Call me tomorrow."

Her father shut the door, and Beth stuck her tongue out at the closed door.

~

Beth spent Saturday night at Jackie's and Sunday at Susan's. Being with her friends helped her laugh and stay sane. She was bound and determined not to be home unless she absolutely had to. It had been weeks since "the ring incident," and she still could not bring herself to talk to her mother or father at any length. Plus, she hadn't heard from Danny the rest of the weekend. She sensed their relationship was fizzling, but she hoped if they could go the Prom in five weeks everything would be okay. The Prom was the most romantic date, and Beth decided she would "go all the way" with Danny if he wanted to. She really didn't want to do it in a car the first time, but she would if that's what it took to keep him interested in her. She'd prove to him she was not a "little girl."

On Monday morning, Danny sat in a chair on the outer edge of the Center. Beth approached him hesitantly and smiled gently. She hoped he was in the mood to be kind.

He smiled back at her and reached for her hand. "I'm so sorry about Friday night. I was really drunk and stupid."

"Yes, I know." She sat next to him.

Danny handed her the ring, and she put it on her finger, just like she had done every day for the last few weeks. He watched her put it on her finger and smiled.

His friends joined them to shoot the breeze. They avoided eye contact with Beth. At least it appeared they were ashamed of themselves for the way they had treated her.

Beth got up to go talk to her friends. The girls had bonded over the weekend, angry at the same boys they had been crazy about before "Humiliation Friday." Before she got far, Danny grabbed her hand and squeezed it, silently asking her to stay close. He gently tugged at her. She paused, and as he continued to pull her back toward him, she offered minimum resistance. He continued talking to his friends as he guided her back to him and maneuvered her onto his lap.

Mike shook his finger at them. "Be careful. No PDA's allowed."

Beth shot him a heated look. She couldn't believe his nerve.

Mike's expression softened. "Beth, I was just kidding. I will even be your lookout if you two want to kiss goodbye. I'm sorry about how I acted before. If you two are happy, then I'm happy." He gestured by placing his hands over his heart.

Beth wasn't sure she trusted what he said, but she was pleased he'd said it in front of the rest of the group. The other guys nodded and apologized for the way they'd behaved on Friday.

"I'm not the only one you guys need to apologize to." Beth turned her head towards her heartbroken friends. She pressed the envelope further by adding, "You guys think you are so mature, but you all have a lot of growing up to do."

The guys remained silent as if pondering her comment. At least they weren't mocking her.

The warning bell rang, and everyone turned to go to homeroom.

By lunchtime apologies had been made, and the girls forgave the boys. Things were back to normal. The girls shared the details of the apologies at the lunch table while the jukebox screamed out "Jackie Blue," and "Hello, It's Me."

"Carwash" played four times in a row. The students loudly groaned each time it replayed. "Carwash" was the only song on the jukebox that the black kids liked, and they protested the song selection by playing that one song over and over. No one at Beth's lunch table really understood why a bigger effort wasn't made. It would have been easy to have culturally inclusive songs.

After lunch, Danny waited for Beth at her science class. "Do you think your parents have cooled off yet? I'd like to take you to the movies this weekend."

Beth wanted to cry. He was not accepting the situation at all.

"Maybe I could meet you there?"

"Damn it, Beth, I don't want to have to sneak around to see you. I can't stand that! What do they think I am?" He pushed his hand against the locker as he spoke in a forceful whisper. "There's no way they are going to let you go with me to the Prom."

Beth touched his arm. She had a plan. "I don't think they'll change their minds, but it isn't because of you. They don't even know you. It's because you're a senior. We could still go to the Prom, though. I could pretend to spend the night at Lynne's, and you could pick me up there. I will find a way to sneak the dress and shoes to Lynne's house."

"Absolutely not," Danny declared and marched away without looking back.

I hate my parents! Beth thought fiercely.

Danny was in a bad mood the rest of the day. He didn't call her that night either. Beth was used to it by now but remained hopeful that he would at least try. She missed talking to him at night. She missed talking to him during the day. She just missed him...terribly.

The next day in the Center Danny was cold and distant. He looked past her and over her head and wouldn't make eye contact with her. He was angry, and she knew why. She felt terrible. It was the last marking period of his senior year, and he should be happy. Instead he was grouchy and miserable.

He remained that way for several more days. Their friends noticed Danny's behavior and started giving Beth concerned looks. He would break up with her soon. She could feel it. Why would a senior who is eighteen want to be dating a fourteen-year old girl whose parents wouldn't let her see him? He was giving up on their relationship, and she didn't blame him. Beth went into survival mode. She did her best to ignore the pathetic glances she received from others when Danny walked her to class and abandoned her after a half-hearted "See you." They didn't kiss at all anymore, and he didn't talk to her much anymore either.

That Thursday after school, Beth sat with Danny in the Center. She was talking with Lynne and Jackie as he goofed around with his buddies.

She'd made her decision and didn't want to wait. "Danny, I need to talk to you."

Mike raised his eyebrows. "Uh-oh!"

Danny peered at her through narrowed eyes. "Now?"

"Yes, please," she said softly, and her voice cracked. *I can do this.*

They walked into the stairwell where they had some privacy, and Beth handed Danny the ring. "Things don't seem to be working out very well. I want you to take the ring back and keep it. I won't be wearing it anymore."

Danny stared at her intently. "I don't even know what to say. I've been thinking you might break up with me, and I don't blame you. I guess I even wanted you to. I have been so angry. I wish you were older and that your parents were cool with us dating."

Beth stared at him for a long time and began to feel that pain in her throat again. She wanted him to say something like "Don't do this, stay with me. We'll work it out, everything will be okay." But he said nothing more, not one word.

He looked down at the floor. Fighting back tears, she turned and walked away before he could see how upset she was. She got a ride home from school with Susan's sister Janet. Beth didn't mention what happened, and somehow, she managed not to cry the entire ride home.

Beth got home, fixed a glass of iced tea, and walked over to visit her grandmother. She was so lucky her grandmother lived next door. When she was a little girl, her grandparents' home had been a comfort to her. Her grandmother made cakes and pies from scratch, and Beth would help her chop, grate, or grind the necessary ingredients. She was sure her grandmother knew the entire story about Danny from her parents' point of view, but she needed to tell her side to someone, preferably someone who would feel sorry for her. Beth needed kindness, so she knocked on the door. Her grandmother welcomed her in with hugs and kisses and steered her to the kitchen table.

Beth poured her heart out, telling her grandmother all the details of the story and how she felt. She complained about her parents and then mentioned they had implied that she and Danny were involved sexually. Beth looked sideways at her grandmother's face to see her reaction.

Her grandmother remained calm and unaffected. "I believe you when you say you and Danny haven't made love, but I want you to think about something. I can tell how much you love this boy. I'm guessing you would do anything for him. I mean, you broke up with him for his sake not yours. You were willing to break your own heart, so you can't tell me it wouldn't have been a matter of months or weeks before you would have been willing to give your virginity to him, too."

Beth smiled through her tears at hearing her grandmother talk about sex. It was funny to hear her say the word "virginity" out loud. She also smiled at her grandmother's perceptiveness. She had planned to have sex with Danny on Prom night.

Her grandmother handed her some tissues. "You know I'm right. That's why you are smiling, and that is exactly what your parents know, too. Honey, your parents were your age once. They also know you are too young, and you are not ready for the responsibilities of an intimate relationship."

Beth stiffened, clutched a tissue in her hand, and rolled her eyes.

"I know you're angry, but it is the downside of being a young teenager. It will pass. We all had to go through it."

God, she understood everything.

"Your parents want what's best for you and if things are really meant to be for you and Danny, it will work out. You'll see."

"How can it possibly work out when he'll be graduating and going off to college?" Beth began to cry again. "He'll be dating college girls and won't want to come home and hang out with some stupid high school girl."

Her grandmother sighed and put her arm around her. "You know, stranger things have happened when two people want to be together."

"Well, it doesn't matter now. He thinks I hate him," Beth said with a slight whine.

"Oh pooh, he knows you don't hate him any more than he hates you."

Beth blew her nose, tossed the tissue in a nearby trashcan, and hugged her grandmother, grateful for the warmth and understanding she received. "I love you Mom Mom."

"I love you, too. Now, go home and talk to your parents. From what I understand that has been one unhappy household for the last few weeks. They only did what they thought was best. So, forgive them and make up." She picked up the dishtowel hanging over the sink and started drying the dishes in the rack.

Beth grabbed a windmill cookie from the cow-shaped cookie jar on top of the kitchen cabinet.

"Go on now." Her grandmother shooed her out the door, playfully flicking the dishtowel at her.

Beth smiled and headed home feeling a bit better. Although she would miss Danny a lot, at least she no longer had to lie to her parents, and that part felt particularly good.

CHAPTER 7

The next two weeks passed quickly for Beth at Colonel Roberts High. Danny and Beth didn't speak to one another, and every time she saw him, he showed off with his friends. He wouldn't even acknowledge she was in the room. Because she had dated Danny for a while, guys were coming out of the woodwork to ask her out. Beth refused them all. Even Danny's friend Billy tried to get her to ride in his car with him at a party one Friday night.

Beth looked at him through narrowed eyes. "Have you lost your mind?"

"Yes." Billy leaned in to kiss her.

Beth backed away. She was not nor had she ever been attracted to Billy.

One Friday night, Beth was leaving a party, and Danny showed up. He had to walk past her to get in the house. First, he tried to ignore her as he passed, but he finally made eye contact with her.

"Hi," he said grudgingly and stopped in front of her.

"Hello." She glanced down at her feet.

"Are you leaving?" he asked.

"Yeah. I'll see you later," she said quietly.

"Later."

He rubbed the back of his neck and gave her an anguished look. Beth wanted to cry, but she simply walked away determined that nobody else would see her cry over Danny Mitchell.

She piled into the station wagon with Janet, Susan, and the rest of her friends to head home. The girls talked excitedly about the party. Beth sat next to the radio speaker in the back of the car. She focused on the music. "We used to laugh, we used to cry, we used to bow our heads then wonder why..."

"Great! Radio torture!" Beth said as America continued singing "I Need You."

The girls laughed and belted out the song in screaming voices.

Beth could not help but smile at their antics. She looked out the back window and watched the streetlights pass as the song played. "You know I need you... Just knowing you were thinking of me. Then it came that I was put to blame..." She could have written this song for Christ's sake. She quickly wiped the tears from her eyes while her friends screamed out the chorus.

"Please God, get me home quick," Beth prayed silently.

Jackie flipped her long curls behind her back and put her arm around Beth. She tugged on her attempting to snap her out of her sadness. Beth reluctantly sang along with her friends on the last chorus. When the car reached her house, she got out, said her quick goodbyes, rushed inside, and went up to her room and put on the America album. The next hour was self-imposed, emotional "album torture."

In school on Monday, everyone was buzzing as announcements were made over the PA about the upcoming Prom. "The theme of this year's Prom will be "Stairway to Heaven." Tickets should be purchased from the junior class sponsors, Mr. Keller, or Mrs. Bilderback. Please make your purchases in their classrooms prior to homeroom. Tickets are on sale beginning today. They are $25.00 per couple..."

Beth's heart sank. She wondered if Danny would take someone else. The prom was two weeks away and she still hoped that he would come to her and agree to the plan she had proposed.

The days passed slowly. Danny did not speak to her at all. By Friday she had lost all hope of going to the Prom. The week before the big night, Melissa Walters had a party. Her mother was on a drunken binge in Atlantic City with her latest beau and had left her daughter home alone. Again.

Beth took extra time to get ready for the party and wore a new pink gauze blouse and platform sandals. She had been growing out the layers of her hair and had recently been to the salon to get a trim. Her makeup was perfect, and her nails were painted. She left the house with a satisfied smile.

Jackie's mother drove the girls to the party. They entered Melissa's house, and it appeared as if some kids had come right after school. Several junior boys were already trashed. Melissa had some guys bring in and set up a keg of Budweiser. Mike and Danny's friends were there, but the two of them were nowhere to be seen. Where was he anyway? It was very strange.

Steve walked up to Beth with a drunk girl draped about him. "Well, if it isn't Miss O'Brien."

"Hello, Steve," Beth said curtly.

"Who's this?" the girl slurred as she turned her drunken rag doll head toward him.

"This is Beth. She *used to be* Danny Mitchell's girlfriend."

"Aww, what happened?" the girl said with sincere drunken compassion.

Beth sent Steve a cold stare. He responded with a snide smile.

The drunken dishrag continued in her own private conversation. "That sucks when people break up…"

Steve swept his gaze over Beth. "I tried to tell you he was an asshole."

"Oh? Maybe it takes one to…never mind." Beth sighed and shook her head. She was too tired to trade barbs with him.

"Damn, Beth, I'm wounded. I'm only an asshole when I'm trying to be." He leaned in and whispered into her ear, "I promise I wouldn't be an asshole if you went out with me. I'd be the perfect gentleman, and I would certainly be able to take care of you better than *Danny Boy*."

She scowled at him.

Steve stuck out his tongue and flicked it back and forth at her. Miss Dishrag was unaware of her escort's perverted advances. She was still talking to herself about breakups.

Beth's stomach turned, and she walked away looking for friendly faces. Steve was laughing behind her, and she quickly moved away from him. Where was Danny?

From behind, someone poked their knee into the back of her right leg and caused her to lose her balance and dip down. She whipped her head around ready to snarl at the offender, but Billy's mischievous face stopped her.

"Very funny, Billy." Beth grinned.

He came around to face her and said he needed to talk to her. Billy looked so serious that Beth was sure something terrible had happened. They went into the laundry room for privacy, and Billy shut the door.

"I wanted to apologize for coming on to you the other night."

"Don't worry about it, Billy, there was no harm done."

Beth wasn't upset with him. She liked Billy. He was always nice to her, but she did not want to date him.

"So, we're okay then, right?" he asked.

"Right. We're fine," Beth said, relieved that was all he wanted to discuss. She reached up to give him a friendly hug and then turned to leave the laundry room.

"Um, wait Beth..." She faced Billy, and he shifted his feet, his cheeks flushed.

Beth's stomach tightened. "What is it?" She expected to hear news that Danny had been injured in an accident.

"Danny asked Kathy Bishop to the Prom," Billy blurted out.

The laundry room spun, and Beth's adrenalin kicked in. She opened the door that led outside to the backyard and stepped into the evening air.

Billy was right behind her. He grasped her arm and gently turned her toward him. She knew Billy felt terrible about being the one to tell her, but she was glad he did despite the pain it caused.

"Aw, he's an idiot, Beth. None of us know what he's doing. But we did know he was really hung up on you. We all knew that."

"He's mad at me, Billy. He's mad at me over things I can't help," Beth said.

As she began to cry, Billy wrapped his arms around her.

This is the worst. What a head rush Danny would get when he learned she cried over him. She composed herself and pulled away.

"That's why I haven't seen him lately. He's probably avoiding me."

"I guess so," he said. "I thought you should know."

"Thank you for telling me," Beth said quietly.

Billy handed her a handkerchief.

Beth looked at the cloth, arched one eyebrow and smiled. "Do you really use this thing?"

"Yes." He offered her a goofy, warm smile.

"Lord, Billy, my dad uses these. They're gross!" Still, she stuck it up to her nose and blew into it.

"Well, it's definitely gross now." He chuckled, and she laughed again.

"Want to walk for a while?" he asked her.

"Sure."

They left the party, and she was glad to be away from the crowd. "Is Danny bringing her here tonight?" Beth asked, and her shoulders slumped.

"No way. She's just a nookie date."

"What?" She clutched the handkerchief.

"There's only one reason why he's taking her to the Prom."

Beth's heart sank. "Well, he's an idiot then because I would've done anything for him Prom night."

Billy put his head down. "Don't say that, Beth."

"Well, I would have." The tears flowed again as she envisioned Danny kissing and being intimate with Kathy Bishop.

"That's probably why he knew he couldn't go with you," Billy said.

"That is crap!" Beth swiped at her stupid tears with the handkerchief.

"Beth, Danny is eighteen! He could go to jail for...you know, being with you." Concern knitted Billy's brow. He shrugged and waited for her response.

Beth pursed her lips. She had heard the word "jailbait" before and knew it had something to do with young girls. Now, she understood.

"Danny and me never should have happened." Beth looked up at the night sky.

"That's what we all tried to tell him. I really don't think he could help it," Billy added.

"Yeah, me either and now look at me. What a mess." Beth held the handkerchief out for further demonstration.

Billy smiled. "You're not a mess."

"And you're sweet. I'll never forget you, Billy." She moved beside him and wrapped her arm around his waist.

He put his arm around her shoulders. They walked silently for a while until they made a circle around the block. The party was in full bloom, and the house was rocking. Loud music spilled outside.

"Boom, Boom, clap! Boom, Boom clap! Boom, Boom clap!" The crowd inside started a raucous sing-along of Queen's "We Will Rock You."

"Shall we?" Billy asked.

"Onward ho!" Beth replied.

Billy opened the door, and the music shot out into the street.

Beth followed him into the sea of teenagers, stuffing the handkerchief in her pants pocket.

"Where have you been?" Lynne asked. "I have to talk to you."

"If it's about Danny, I don't want to hear it," Beth said.

Lynne looked at her friend with genuine concern.

"You've been crying."

"Yeah. I already know about Danny and Kathy." Beth glanced around the party, trying to act uninterested in what or who Danny Mitchell was doing. She boldly walked over to the keg and took a plastic cup.

Having never worked a keg before, she wasn't quite sure how to do it. She stood and stared at the contraption.

"Here, let me help you with that," said a male voice to her right.

Beth turned. The speaker had light brown hair, blue eyes, and a beautiful smile.

She smiled. "Okay, I've never done this before." For once, she was honest about her inexperience.

"Never done what before, poured a beer or drank one?"

"Either!" She laughed.

"Here, put the cup at an angle like this." He placed his hand over hers on the cup.

Beth did not object.

"Then you take the handle here and squeeze it like this." Again, his hand wrapped around hers as he demonstrated. The beer trickled slowly and then dripped into the cup.

Beth widened her eyes at him.

He laughed. "And when *that* happens, you need to pump this…" The cute stranger pumped the handle, and the beer flowed more quickly into the cup.

"Ah, I see." Beth said. "Thank you very much."

"May I offer you a bit more advice?"

"Sure."

"Well," the boy continued. "If you've never drank alcohol before, you need to pace yourself. Only drink about one beer per hour and you will stay sober for the evening. If you don't want to stay sober and you want a little buzz, drink one each half hour for about three cups and then pace out to one every hour."

Beth appreciated this information. She never tried to drink alcohol, too fearful she might get drunk and lose control. A spark of hope ignited inside her. She liked this helpful, cute guy.

"You're Beth O'Brien, right?"

Oh God.

"Yes, I am. Who are you?"

"I'm Charlie Cahall. Very nice to meet you." With a kind smile, he extended his hand.

Beth shook his hand and smiled back.

"What grade are you in?" Beth asked him.

"I'm a senior."

Beth's back stiffened. "I've never met you before, have I?"

"No, but Danny Mitchell and I have been good friends since we were kids. We live next door to each other."

"Oh? Why haven't I met you then?" Beth asked a little bluntly.

"Well, I had a serious relationship going this year and I wasn't out socializing much."

"Where is she?" Beth scanned the room for a girl she did not know.

"She's not here. She broke up with me a couple weeks ago."

Beth took a big gulp of the beer and shuddered at the bitter taste.

Charlie laughed at the scrunchy face she made.

"Remember what I said and take slow sips." Charlie nodded toward the cup of beer in her hand. "So, anyway, now I'm back out on the social scene."

"Lucky you..." Beth said dryly and burped.

"I'm beginning to think so." He grinned.

The two stood side by side near the keg. They didn't talk but neither moved away.

Beth admired Charlie's jacket and noticed he lettered in football. Colonel Roberts High had gained quite a reputation in athletics the past few years. They were football State Champions the year before last and Division Champions this year. They missed the State Championship by 3 points—a field goal scored in overtime.

"So, are you interested in football?"

She shrugged. "Uh, I don't know."

Charlie looked amused so Beth threw caution to the wind and suggested they go outside.

"Sure." He arched one brow and followed her through the laundry room and out the back door.

The night air was chilly but warm compared to the winter weather they had been experiencing.

They sat at a picnic table across from one another and talked. He seemed kind and spoke with a gentle manner. The beer went to her head a little, and he teased her about it.

Beth laughed at herself. Charlie went inside to refill their cups and returned. She decided that Charlie's girlfriend was a total idiot for dumping him. He had quickly become one of her favorite people. He shared the details of his failed relationship with her, and she talked about the failed Danny saga.

"I'm not sure what he wanted from me," Beth said, referring to Danny.

"I'm sure he really liked you. He's a good guy."

Beth looked at him sideways and glared at him through tapered eyes.

His amused laughter echoed in the night.

"I miss him," she said, surprising herself with the honesty of her comment.

"I know what you mean," Charlie replied.

She hiccupped, and her eyes widened.

Charlie's widened, too, and he laughed.

She giggled. A lot. Before long, they were laughing hysterically. When their laughter died down, she hiccupped again and said, "So much for my first beer!"

Charlie smiled as Beth took a deep breath.

They grew silent. The noise from the party was muffled. Charlie reached across the table and placed his hands over hers folded on the table.

"You'll be alright. Everything will be fine. By this time next year, you won't even remember Danny's name. There will be so many guys who will want to date you. You'll see. It's his loss."

Beth wanted to hug him. Many people had told her she would be okay, but Charlie was the first one she believed.

"What the hell is going on out here?" yelled a drunken Mike Crowley from across the yard.

He staggered up the driveway and stumbled across the yard toward the picnic table. Danny followed behind him. Billy ran to catch up with them and appeared out of breath.

"Oh my gosh!" Mike continued to shout. "It's Charlie and Beth! Glad to see you back on the social scene, man." He reached out and shook hands with Charlie.

Charlie stood to greet his old friends.

Danny nodded. "Sorry to hear about your breakup."

"Yeah, well…life's a bitch. What can I say?"

Beth stood to go back inside. She did not want to be near Danny.

As she walked away, Mike said, "Well, it looks like Beth hasn't wasted any time trying to land a new boyfriend."

Beth halted. That was it. She lit up like a firecracker. Before Billy, Charlie, or Danny could say anything to put Mike in his place, Beth clenched her hands into fists, and her body shook with a rage she could not restrain.

In a flash, she was inches from Mike's face. She pointed her finger at him. "Mike, I've had just about as much of you as I can stand. No wonder you're always alone except for your *friends.* You are obnoxious and mean. You could have had a beautiful relationship with Lynne, but you couldn't even pull that off. Clue in. She is too good for you. As a matter of fact, anyone is too good for you! Don't speak to me again, Mike Crowley. Ever!"

Charlie furrowed his brow and swiveled his head from Beth to Mike and back again.

She turned to stomp away but pivoted back again. "Don't

even look in my direction because I could care less what you have to say about me, my age, my looks, my dates, my anything. Do you get that?" she yelled.

Mike stood there, dumbstruck while Beth waited for a response. There was none.

No one moved. Danny looked at her with a small smile that Beth interpreted as pride. Tension thickened the air.

Billy smirked at Danny and turned to their friend. "Well, there you have it, Mike. I'm thinking she doesn't like you very much. Kind of makes you wonder why?" He reached over and gave Beth a high-five.

Beth took a deep breath, picked up her cup that she'd left on the table, drank the rest of the beer in her cup, and then threw the empty container at Mike's feet. He stood with his mouth hanging open, and his friends laughed at him.

She turned around and marched back into the house.

Danny, Billy, Mike, and Charlie walked in the back door. Out of the corner of her eye, Beth watched as Danny searched the room. Was he looking for her? Charlie searched the room, too. She guessed Charlie was taken off guard. She sighed and decided she had to leave. She found the junior girl who gave her a ride last time and offered her money for gas if she would take her home.

Beth returned to school the following Monday after a sad weekend of missing Danny and feeling jealous of Kathy. This week would be hell for anyone who did not have a date to the Prom or who was going with one person and secretly wanted to go with someone else. Beth could barely get through morning announcements. Each day was going to be a countdown to the major event of the year, Prom Night: "Stairway to Hell in a Hand Basket." That would be the night Beth O'Brien would officially lose her mind and be carted off to a sanitarium by her parents. She imagined Danny touching and making love to Kathy Bishop, telling her he loved her and then giving her the ring that he had bought for Beth.

A student walked into her homeroom and handed her teacher a note.

"Miss O'Brien, you are wanted in the nurse's office," Mrs. Hart said, glancing over at her.

Beth looked at Susan, and she shrugged. Perhaps she should tell the school nurse she was considering throwing herself off a bridge. As she got up from her desk, she envisioned her parents sobbing at her graveside, and Danny standing near the casket saying, "What a baby!" He would torment her even at her own funeral.

She entered the hallway, which was empty except for a tall figure coming towards her from the opposite end. The sun shone brightly outside, and the window at the end of the hall shadowed the figure. Beth trudged on through the sea of gray metal lockers and black knobs. Soon they were close enough to see one another and speak. Beth's mouth dropped open. It was Kathy Bishop, Danny's Prom date! *Oh God, why have you forsaken me?* Beth thought dramatically, and a knot tightened in her stomach.

"Hello," Kathy said with a snotty 'I'm better than you are' tone.

"Hey," Beth responded in a 'say one more word to me and I'll punch your fucking face in' tone.

Once they walked past each other, Beth rolled her eyes and made a face. She was quite sure Kathy did the same.

Beth continued on to the nurse's office. The school nurse, Mrs. Schumacher, was adorable. Everyone at C.R. loved her. Beth had known her since she was five years old and always called her Aunt Mary. Beth's sister was married to her nephew. Aunt Mary favored the athletes at the school and went above and beyond in her care for them. Beth turned and walked into the nurse's office. Aunt Mary looked up from her desk over her reading glasses.

"Hello, my sweetheart. How are you doing?" She

rounded her desk to take Beth into a big hug.

"I'm fine." Beth breathed out and hugged her back. "How are you?"

"Oh, I'm just fine," she said.

"There was a note for me to come see you."

"Oh that...well, uh yes, I did send a note. However, there is someone else who needed to see you. I believe he's in room number 1." Aunt Mary removed her glasses and smiled at her.

Beth leaned forward and whispered, "Is it Danny?"

Aunt Mary shook her head. "No sweetheart." She patted her on the shoulder as Beth frowned. "Go on in. You'll find a nice boy waiting in there for you."

There were three rooms with cots in the nurse's office so students could lay down to rest if they felt sick. Room Number 1 was the first on the left. It took a moment for Beth's eyes to adjust from the fluorescent lights in the main office. A figure sat on the first cot. Beth walked over, and her eyes adjusted to the darkened room.

"Charlie!" she said happily.

"Hey girlie, what are you doing?" She could hear the smile in his voice.

"Well, I guess I'm getting out of homeroom now. Did you want to talk to me?" she asked.

"Yeah, I did."

Beth nodded. She could see him clearly now and moved to sit down next to him on the cot.

"I've been trying to see you all week. I guess our schedules must be totally different. You haven't been down to the Center?" he asked.

"No. I'm avoiding it this week."

"Why?"

"Because I'm losing my mind!" Beth said a little too loudly.

Aunt Mary popped her head in the doorway. "Everything alright in here?"

"Yep, we're fine." Beth said.

"You're not losing your mind," Charlie replied tenderly.

"I am." She grinned.

"You are not." He put his arm around her. "I need to ask you something and I'm a little uncomfortable for a few reasons."

"Okay, go ahead." Beth was a little concerned given his serious tone.

"I'd like to know how you really feel about Danny."

Beth sat quietly for a moment. Danny must have asked him to pump her about this. She took a moment to really think about it.

She replied sincerely, "I like him a lot, more than anyone else I've ever known. He is not the guy he pretends to be around everyone else. You know? The way he was when we were alone, when he was relaxed and laughing or when we were having a real conversation, was real. He wasn't trying to be Mr. Big Shot. He is so different when no one else is around. Do you think he misses being like that? Do you think he's like that with everyone he dates?"

Charlie hung his head and looked at the floor. "You don't give yourself enough credit. No, I don't think he's like that with everyone. So, do you love him?"

She nodded, and Charlie smiled

"Well, that's what I thought you'd say. So, that's what I needed to know. I'd like us to be good friends, Beth. I can't seem to see you in school, so I'm not sure how we will run into each other. I will be graduating soon, but I won't be far away. The University is only an hour's drive. I can write to you if that's alright." Affection glimmered in his blue eyes.

Beth suddenly realized why he asked her about Danny. It wasn't because Danny wanted him to. He wanted to ask her out, but he couldn't now. Damn! Any girl would be lucky to have him. How come she couldn't feel the way she wanted? It was Danny's fault, of course. Lately, everything was Danny's fault.

"Sure. I'd like to be your friend. We can hang out on weekends and I'll write to you. Definitely! I'll tell you where all the parties are, and you can come home on weekends."

Charlie's smile lit up his handsome face. His arm was still around her, and she turned to hug him.

"Thank you," she said softly. Hopefully, he knew she was flattered.

"Yeah, Yeah," he said. "You'd better get back to home-room now."

She stood as the first period bell rang. He smacked her on the butt.

"Hey!" She rubbed her tush and groaned.

"Charlie, are you going to the Prom?" she asked.

He rubbed the back of his neck. "Yeah, Jill and I are going together, but only because it was planned before we broke up. I don't think either of us is really into it."

"Well, have a good time. I'll see you later." She left him sitting in the dark.

Beth hoped Jill would change her mind about Charlie. She wanted him to be happy.

Aunt Mary gave her a hall pass and another hug, and Beth returned to class.

CHAPTER 8

On Friday morning, Beth woke to the beeping of the alarm clock radio. It was the day before the Prom, and she dubbed it "Living Hell Day." She rolled over and pressed the snooze button. The beeping stopped, but the radio played lightly. She closed her eyes and hoped to shield herself from the world for an extra ten minutes, but Gladys Knight began to rip her heart out. "It's sad to think we're not gonna make it, and it's gotten to the point where we just can't fake it, ooh, for some ungodly reason, we just can't let it die, I guess neither one of us wants to be the first to say goodbye."

Beth moaned and pushed the pillow over her head, but she could still hear the song. She jerked herself up and slammed her index finger down on the tuning button. "Darlin' if you want me to be closer to you, get closer to me, Darlin' if you want me to be closer to you, get closer to me, darling if you want me to love only me..."

Slam! Her finger hit the next button. "I feel the warmth of her hand in mine, I hear laughter in the rain walking hand in hand with the one I love..."

Slam! She pressed the last button, and Peaches and Herb assaulted her with a final insult. "I was a fool to ever leave your side, me minus you is such a lonely ride, the breakup we had has made me lonesome and sad, I realize I love you cause I want you back hey, hey. I spent the evening with the radio, regret the moment that I let you go... Reunited and it feels so good..."

Damn it! *What is it with the stupid radio this morning?* Beth kicked the covers off with a jerk and stomped her way into the bathroom.

She showered and prepared for school, glad she saved a

new outfit to wear today. Beth hoped it would lift her spirits on a day her spirits needed lifting. She put on a pastel pink, cotton, two-piece spring sweater with tiny pink pearl buttons down the front, black Bobbi Brooks slacks, and black slide-on leather shoes. The clothes fit her well, and she felt good.

Beth stared at her reflection in the bathroom mirror and applied her makeup. She had blown her hair dry and was amazed it turned out perfect. Today, she decided to get to school early. For the first time this week, she was going to the Center. Hopefully, Danny would be there to see her at her finest. She would not talk to him, though. She wouldn't even look at him. Instead, she'd talk to Charlie and laugh and smile and do her best to annoy the crap out of Danny. If Charlie didn't show up, she could hang with the girls.

Beth hitched a ride to school with the girl who lived down the street, and they arrived early. They parked in the side lot, and Danny's Mustang pulled in not far from them.

Beth waited for Danny to get out of his car. Kathy got out of the passenger's side, and Beth's heart sank.

"Don't forget to lock the door," instructed her neighbor.

"Right," Beth replied as she exited the car.

She pressed down the metal lock, slammed the door shut and headed inside without a glance at Danny and his stupid girlfriend.

Beth's hands were shaking as she fumbled with the black knob on her locker. Self-talk time. *Don't cry, don't cry, do not cry!*

Watching Kathy getting out of her spot in his car caused her to be unreasonably jealous. Her locker not opening added to her frustration. It was very touchy. "Damn it!" Beth shouted as she slammed her hand into the metal. She took a deep breath and started over. *You turn it...to...just... the exact...spot...at...just...the...right...speed.* There! The door popped opened.

Lynne, Jackie, Susan, and Melissa stopped at her locker to

talk.

"Come on down to the Center. It will be alright. Danny hasn't been hanging out there anyway," Lynne said.

Beth decided to skip the Center this morning after all.

"Oh, it's not that. I'm not really in the mood for all the noise today," Beth lied.

Her four friends looked at each other knowingly. Susan and Melissa changed the subject, and soon the girls were laughing, telling jokes, and sharing secrets.

Steve Hoffman and one of his Neanderthal sidekicks came by. "Hello girls," they said in unison.

Beth shrank back on her locker as if trying to make herself invisible. It did not work. Steve pushed his way past the others to get to her.

"Are you headed to the Prom tomorrow, Beth?"

"Nope, are you?"

"Most definitely. I wouldn't have minded taking you. I still will. All you have to do is say yes." He kissed the air towards her.

Gross. Beth rolled her eyes.

"You'll be sorry. I'll be gone from here soon and you will have missed your chance."

"I don't know how I'll ever survive." She pursed her lips into a slight sneer.

He glared at her, and his buddy said, "C'mon, man. Who needs that hassle?"

Steve continued to glare at her as he turned to walk away.

"Rotten little bitch..." he said under his breath.

The girls rolled their eyes at him, and then discussed going to the high school on Saturday night to watch the Promenade of Couples on the auditorium stage before the dance. Beth listened to the conversation but remained quiet.

Lynne leaned closely to Beth. "Do you want to come over tomorrow and spend the night with me?"

Beth could always count on Lynne to look out for her.

"I'm afraid I won't be very good company," Beth said honestly.

"Oh, come on, we'll have a couple of highballs and listen to Richard Pryor. Come on, it will be better than sitting home crying. I will get my mom to pick you up after she gets off from work. She's done on Saturday around noon."

"Okay." Beth nodded.

Lynne did her cheerleader bounce and squealed her pleasure. She hugged Beth.

"We'll have so much fun!" Lynne said as the first period warning bell rang.

The girls headed towards their homerooms. Beth smiled at Lynne, but seriously doubted she would have fun at all this weekend.

Homeroom went quickly and the announcements about "Stairway to Hell Night" were minimal. The next announcement went through Beth like a spear to her gut. "Seniors, please see your advisor to order your caps and gowns for the graduation ceremony. Seniors' last school day will be May 28. Underclassmen will remain in school until June 12."

Beth walked to her first period class without stopping to talk to anyone. Danny wasn't waiting for her. Oh, that's right…they weren't dating anymore. She would be left behind. He wasn't waiting for her outside her English class, either. The period dragged on as they finished an oral read aloud of *Romeo and Juliet*. Next week, her class was going to the theater to see the film, so at least that was something to look forward to. She loved the story but had finished reading it long ago. The pace of the classroom was slow, and she was bored stiff.

At lunch, someone loaded the jukebox with dimes pushing M-32 at least twenty times. After the ninth playing of Neil Sedaka's "Breaking Up Is Hard To Do," the students in the cafeteria yelled their protests. The assistant principal went over and stared at the jukebox. He scratched his head and waved his hands at the students, indicating they needed to relax. He fumbled around for a couple of minutes and tried to figure out how to stop it. The song began a tenth time, and the groans got louder. Finally, he pulled the jukebox away from the wall and yanked the plug from the electrical socket. He was thanked with an explosion of applause, howls, and whistles. He dramatically took a bow, and everyone laughed.

After lunch, Beth and Lynne walked together to science class. Danny was in the stairwell and had fallen in line about seven steps behind Beth. As she went through the door, she glanced back. He looked intently at her, offered her an awkward smile and slight wave. Beth ignored him and continued toward class.

Was she imagining things, or did Danny appear like he wanted to say something to her? She was sure she noticed a regretful glint in his intense stare. She sighed heavily. It didn't matter anyway. He would be gone soon. She managed to make it through the rest of the day without seeing Danny and went home, trying to forget about him.

Beth spent Friday night talking on the phone to her friends. She gave herself a manicure and stacked Jackson Brown, Billy Joel, and Eric Clapton albums on the stereo. Her stereo was decent, but if she stacked more than three albums, they wouldn't drop properly. They would all fall at once.

Finally, she turned on the small black and white television in her room and watched a rerun episode of *I Love Lucy*. She turned off the television, read a book of poetry by Emily Dickinson and went to bed. Beth cried herself to sleep thinking about Danny and Kathy in his car. Was Kathy doing all the things he never let her do?

She awoke the next day and forced herself not to think about Danny. Saturday morning went by quickly as Beth dusted and vacuumed the house and ironed the laundry. Mrs. Angellini picked Beth up after she got off from work Saturday afternoon. Lynne exited the car and bounded up the front steps to retrieve Beth. Her excitement was infectious. Beth laughed at her friend's goofy behavior.

They reached Lynne's house, and the girls lay on the bed in Lynne's basement room, checking out photo albums and keepsakes. Beth pointed at a picture of them on a third-grade field trip, and they burst out laughing. Then they went for a long walk in the neighborhood, and Lynne told Beth that Melissa had taken Jackie to the free clinic to get birth control pills. Beth didn't believe it at first. Lynne swore it was true and told her not to tell anyone. She said Jackie had spent the night with her the previous weekend and showed her the pill packet and told her about the appointment. Jackie had confided in Lynne and told her she was tired of freaking out about late period scares. Beth could not believe Jackie hadn't told her about this, but Beth had been preoccupied with Danny. Melissa's mother wouldn't care if her daughter were on the pill, but if Jackie's mother and father found out, they would be upset. Jackie probably didn't care, though.

After returning home from their walk, the girls returned to Lynne's room and talked about what school might be like next year with the seniors gone. Beth avoided the topic of Danny, and she began feeling better.

Lynne's father called them up for dinner. Beth glanced at the clock on Lynne's dresser. It was six thirty already. All the Prom goers had already picked up their dates, had their pictures taken, and were probably at their tables at The Dinner Bell Inn or The Gold Key Restaurant. Danny and Kathy would not be at The Hudson House, the popular restaurant Danny's parents owned. Beth had been there several times with her family. It had an authentic old Delaware style with genuine antiques and historical artifacts, plus beautiful lake views. Danny had nixed the idea of going there when the two of them discussed going to the Prom. He didn't want his older sister or parents staring at them all night.

At the dinner table, Lynne's parents included Beth in

their conversations and showed genuine interest in her. They always were kind and gracious. Beth could see where Lynne got it from.

When they bowed their heads to say grace, Beth closed her eyes. She immediately pictured Kathy sitting in the black leather chair at the Dinner Bell wearing some fancy flawless dress and Danny next to her in his white tux. There was that pain in her throat again. She was afraid to raise her head for fear Lynne and her family would notice the tears in her eyes. Damn it. *Why did I allow Danny into my thoughts?*

Lynne reached under the table and patted Beth on the leg. Mrs. Angellini told everyone about her day. This gave Beth time to get her emotions under control, and it worked. She was able to blink back her tears.

Lynne's mother smiled at her, concern gleaming in her eyes.

Lynne must have told her mother about the Prom and Danny. The woman was being truly kind. Beth's own parents didn't know how she felt tonight. For weeks now, she hadn't been allowed to bring up Danny's name in front of them. They still didn't want to hear about him. If she showed any sadness, her parents quickly dismissed it. They probably thought if they didn't talk about him, she might get over him faster. Her parents weren't very sympathetic to her plight.

"Beth, would you like a piece of carrot cake?" Mr. Angellini asked.

He had prepared the entire meal, and she was fascinated by their arrangement. Mrs. Angellini worked, and he stayed home to take care of the house. Mr. Angellini retired from the Air Force several years ago, and he was an excellent cook.

"Oh, no thank you. Dinner was delicious, though," Beth said.

"Well, I think I'll slice you a little piece anyway. We are all having some and it'll seem strange having you sit there with nothing. How about a cup of coffee?"

Beth had never been offered coffee before. She perked up and smiled.

"Yes, I'd like that please." She felt a bit more grown up.

She grinned at Lynne, and her friend smiled back. Mrs. Angellini continued to tell funny stories about her day at work and her life while Mr. Angellini served the coffee and cake. The cake was delicious and to her surprise, Beth liked the coffee, too.

Soon, they were done eating. Beth had never dined at a table that long in her life. It felt calm, relaxed, and she was thoroughly entertained. Lynne was right. This was better than staying at home tormenting herself with love songs and poetry.

Beth offered to help clear the table and wash the dishes, but Mr. Angellini refused her offer.

Lynne and Beth retired to her room. They talked about movie stars, teachers, and Danny for about an hour and a half. Lynne wondered aloud with a wistful look in her brown eyes who Mike took to the Prom, but Beth didn't know either. Her friend figured Mike's date might be a senior from Dullard High School, which was C.R.'s archrival.

For the most part, Lynne seemed to have gotten over her crush on Mike. Beth envied her for that. Lynne tried to reassure Beth that Danny really did love her, but the situation was just impossible. That didn't make her feel much better.

When she was sure her parents were asleep, Lynne smiled secretively, excused herself, and went to the kitchen. She returned with two smuggled highball cocktails. Lynne pulled out three different Richard Pryor albums, and the girls got drunk on one highball each and laughed uncontrollably at Richard Pryor. Then Lynne taught Beth cheers. At eleven thirty, they went upstairs to watch *Saturday Night Live.* Joe Cocker was the musical guest, and John Belushi did an impersonation of him as he performed. The girls roared with laughter. Surprisingly, they didn't wake Lynne's parents.

Between the physical exercise, the highball, Richard Pryor, and *Saturday Night Live*, Lynne managed to pull off the impossible. She saved Beth from her darkest night ever. They crept back down to Lynne's room and got ready for bed.

Soon, an exhausted Lynne was sleeping like a baby. Beth checked the clock. The Prom and the After-Prom dances were over. Danny and Kathy were probably headed to the beach. Beth's parents would never have allowed her to stay out that late and they certainly wouldn't have allowed her to go to the beach afterwards.

The trip was customary, and Beth envisioned "Miss Long and Tall" looking like a goddess in the sun and Danny applying lotion to her back. A huge tidal wave washed over the beach and sucked them both up into it as they screamed at the top of their lungs. HA! Beth's dreams were fitful, but she did manage to sleep.

The next day, Beth's mom picked her up. She barricaded herself in her room Sunday and dreaded going to school on Monday. The phone rang Sunday evening, but Beth did not rush to answer. She didn't feel like talking to anyone.

"Beth, telephone!" her mother called up the stairs.

"Okay." She turned down the stereo and picked up the phone in her room.

"Hey girlie." It was Charlie.

"Hey!" Beth smiled for the first time that day. "How are you? How was the Prom?" She hoped it had worked out for him and his ex-girlfriend.

"It sucked," Charlie told her.

"Really? I'm sorry."

"Yep, the whole thing was a disaster for *everybody* if you know what I mean," he said.

"Charlie, you're lying to me."

"I swear I'm not," he added. "None of the guys had fun at all."

Charlie was going to be a close friend if he acted as a spy for her.

"*None* of your friends? Not one?"

"No. It sucked."

Beth grinned and then prayed to God to forgive her for being happy Danny had a miserable time. "Well, I'm really sorry about that," Beth said, trying to sound like she meant it.

Charlie laughed, "No, you're not."

Beth chuckled, too. "Well, I wanted you to have a good time," she added with sincerity.

"Thanks, but it didn't happen."

They continued to chat for a half hour. Mike and his date got kicked out of the Prom for drinking. Danny skipped the After-Prom, and no one saw him at the beach until later the next morning. Kathy wasn't with him. Billy and his date got into an argument, and he took her home mid-way through the evening.

Charlie had to get off the phone to go eat dinner. Beth hung up and went downstairs for a Diet Pepsi.

Her mother was in the kitchen stuffing envelopes for her boss, something she did once a month when the bills were mailed.

"Who was on the phone?" she asked.

Beth opened the fridge and grabbed her drink. "A friend of mine, Charlie Cahall."

"Did he call to ask you on a date?"

"No, he's just a friend." She retrieved the bottle opener from the kitchen drawer and popped open the cap.

Her mother pouted her bottom lip and said, "You know, you really do need to start dating again. What grade is Charlie in?"

"He's a senior," Beth said nonchalantly as she dropped the bottle opener back into the drawer and threw the lid in the trash.

Her mother sat stunned as Beth walked out of the kitchen. She couldn't help the smug smile that twisted her mouth. This night didn't turn out too badly after all. While she drank her Diet Pepsi, she prepared her clothes for school the next day, and then she went to bed.

CHAPTER 9

Beth no longer saw Danny and Kathy hanging out together, and he started turning up in the Center again each morning. Little by little, Beth was able to be in his presence without feeling like she wanted to cry. He and Beth were polite and spoke a little, but he was so full of senioritis she could hardly stand him. The boys were giddy about being "free" soon, and everyone else was green with envy. Charlie came down to the Center every day, too. Beth had fun with him.

Charlie brought a spool of fishing string one day and asked Billy to hold one end. He began unraveling it as he walked through the crowd. No one knew what they were up to until someone tried to leave the area. "What the hell?" Beth heard people say as they lifted their arms to try to figure out how to detangle.

Unintentionally, Charlie had gotten Beth and Steve tangled together in the same pocket.

Steve got way too close to Beth and said, "Let me see you wiggle out of this one."

Beth rolled her eyes.

Everyone laughed, squealed, and tried to get free.

Steve grabbed Beth's arm and squeezed his fingers into the flesh of her upper arm. "What is your problem, you little bitch?" he said through clenched teeth.

"Let go, Steve, you're hurting me." She flinched and tried to pull away.

He seized her other arm and held her up against his chest. Then he wrapped one arm around her waist and the other behind her neck.

He yanked her close to him, whispering in a vicious tone, "You think you're too good for me? Is that it? Let me tell you something. I wouldn't fuck you if you were the last girl on the face of the earth."

Beth's stomach lurched, and panic had her heart racing.

He brought his mouth close to her ear and whispered, "Don't ever let me catch you out alone. Do you understand?"

Beth nodded, and he placed his teeth around the bottom of her earlobe and started to bite down.

The crowd continued to laugh as they tried to detangle the fishing string.

She called out, "No!" startling him into releasing her.

He sneered at her and laughed because he managed to leave a red mark on her ear.

Danny walked over to help remove the fishing line from Beth.

Steve backed away, and Beth trembled as Danny lifted the string. She quickly ducked underneath it.

"What's wrong?" Danny asked.

"Nothing I gotta go." Rattled by Steve's behavior, Beth turned and ran toward her homeroom class.

She was jumpy the rest of the day. She told the girls at the lunch table what Steve had said and done, and the stories began pouring out about him. Apparently, he had forced himself on more than one girl in the school. The girls he abused were wrecked over it, and one girl had even quit school because of it. His victims hadn't admitted what he'd done to anyone because they felt guilty. They had agreed to go out with him and had been drinking alcohol. They didn't want their parents to find out.

"I don't understand why so many girls throw themselves at him," Susan said.

"I guess they assume that because he's a big football star and good looking he is nice," Lynne added.

Jackie added, "Well, my mother always says, 'Handsome is as handsome does.' That doesn't make Steve Hoffman very handsome does it?"

By the end of the day, the stories about him were flying

all over school, a result of the girls' chatter at lunch. The boyfriends and brothers of the girls Steve had assaulted were finding out the truth about him.

Beth watched from an open second-floor window in an empty hallway as a group of guys met up with Steve in the parking lot after school for a little "chat." He held up his hands and said, "Now look, guys, I never meant any harm. Please don't hurt me."

"Get in your car, Steve, and don't come back," a former teammate said. "I don't care where you go but do not come back to this school ever again."

"Okay, okay." Steve jumped into his car and peeled out of the parking lot.

A town police officer was parked on the opposite side of the street and running radar. The lights and siren came on immediately, and the police officer turned to flag him down. Everyone in the school parking lot laughed out loud, and then grew silent as they walked away from the group to return to their girlfriends, sisters, and friends.

Steve's reputation is ruined now Beth thought with satisfaction.

"Beth?" She whirled around, relieved to see Danny and not one of Steve's goons.

"Oh Danny, hi." Beth put a hand on her chest and said, "You startled me."

"What's going on?" he asked. "I heard Charlie say the guys were meeting up with Steve Hoffman in the parking lot after school. I asked him to tell me why, and he said I needed to talk to you. I've been looking for you everywhere. What's up? Did he do something to you?"

Beth's bottom lip started to shake as she looked around to make sure they were alone.

She shook her head. "No. Well, sort of. He has been pressuring me to go out with him for a long time. He got nastier and meaner as time went by. This morning, when you saw us together, he threatened me." Beth removed the pink sweater jacket she had on to show Danny the bruises where Steve's fingers had dug into her flesh.

"Oh my God. Why didn't you tell me this?"

"I was afraid." Beth lowered her head.

"Why on earth were you afraid to tell me? Tell me now, Beth."

She shrugged.

"I thought you'd fight him, and I was afraid he'd hurt you," Beth said weakly.

"Jesus, Beth!" Danny curled his hands into fists at his sides. "Jesus! Do you know how that makes me feel??"

"I didn't want you to be hurt," she whispered now with her head down.

"Do you have any idea how embarrassing it is that my girlfriend thinks I could get my ass kicked by a moron?" he continued shouting at her.

"Stop yelling at me, Danny."

"I'm not yelling at you!" He looked around to see if anyone was listening to them.

They stood in silence, him running his hand through his hair staring at her in disbelief, and her staring at the floor. Each stood perfectly still for several moments.

"We just can't seem to work things out, can we?" he said softly. "We are either all over each other or angry and fighting. There is no in-between, is there?"

"You hurt me worse than Steve Hoffman ever could. I thought I would die when you took Kathy to the Prom."

Danny took a deep breath and let out a heavy, frustrated sigh.

"Beth, you broke up with me, don't forget that." His tone was short.

"Oh, you know damn well you were being obnoxious to me so I *would* break up with you. It was all just too difficult, and you couldn't handle it." She turned back toward the window away from him so he couldn't see the tears in her eyes.

Danny walked closer to her, leaned forward, and wrapped his arms around her.

Beth let him hold her.

"I'm so sorry. What a mess. I didn't want to break up with you or take Kathy to the Prom. I have no idea why I've been acting the way I have. He kissed her sweetly and then again more passionately.

They stood in the empty school hallway kissing for a long time. Beth felt him reacting to her, and the pleasant warmth in her stomach meant he was having the same effect on her. Was Danny her true and lasting love?

"I want to be with you, Danny," she said to him quietly. Beth was convinced if she had sex with him, he would want her as a girlfriend and never leave her.

"You are with me." He kissed her neck.

"No. I mean, *be* with you." She reached inside his coat and ran her hands down his backside and then towards the front of his Levi's.

She felt him through the heavy denim, and Danny let out a deep breath. His tongue continued to tease the inside of her mouth, and it was becoming agonizingly wonderful. She didn't want to stop, and he didn't seem to either, but they couldn't go any further in the high school hallway.

Once again, Danny was the one who heard the voice of reason in his head. "Beth, Beth, Beth. What am I going to do about you?" he moaned as he held her tightly to him.

"Don't leave me. I don't want you to go away," she whispered.

"I have to, you know that. You knew that all along. I'll come back, though. I promise."

"It's all passing by so fast. I'm not ready to be here without you." She looked down at her feet.

He grasped her hand and walked her to the stairwell. They sat down on the steps. Danny cupped her face and gently forced her to look at him.

"Beth, I take full responsibility for this mess. I should

have never let this get out of hand. I'm so sorry. I wish I could take away all the bad feelings you have. If I were smart, I would try to make you hate me. I don't want you to hate me. I love seeing you look at me fondly like that. I'm just a selfish person."

He let go of her, hung his head, and then turned towards her again. "This year has gone by too fast, and it doesn't seem fair. I want you to know I'll always care about what happens to you."

"This is it, isn't it?" she choked out in a whisper, a tear sliding down her cheek.

He nodded. "Please try to be happy for me, Beth. I'm going off to college, and it's exciting. I can't stand to see you near tears every time I look at you."

Beth sniffed and said, "Okay, no more tears. I promise."

"You won't even remember me this time next year. You'll probably have a boyfriend and you'll be in love," he said, his voice cracking.

"Yeah, probably," Beth replied in a shaky tone.

"Next week is my last week here. Are you going to come to graduation?" Danny asked.

"I don't know."

"I'd like you to be there."

"Okay. I'll think about it." Beth stood. It was time to go. They had said all there was to say for the moment.

"Good luck, Danny."

"Thanks, Beth." He remained on the step as she walked away.

She needed to find a ride home. Luckily, Jackie was still in the Center. She had been to a tennis team meeting in the cafeteria.

"Can I get a ride home with you?" Beth asked her friend.

"Sure, my mom is picking me up any minute. We can drive you home. Are you alright? Did you hear what the guys did to Steve Hoffman? He deserved that."

Beth nodded. She was too tired to think about anything

else today.

While Jackie talked on and on about everything from boys to graduation, Beth remained largely silent as they climbed into the car.

Jackie's mom dropped Beth off in front of her house. Still in shock from what had happened with Steve followed by her disappointing encounter with Danny, she went straight to her room.

Beth called Lynne later that night and told her about the conversation she and Danny had in the stairway. Lynne just kept saying, "Christ, Beth...Christ, Beth."

"Have you seen Mike lately?" Beth asked her.

"No, I've given up on that. He's been acting too bizarre lately. I'm not sure I'd want to go out with him anyway. When he gets drunk, he flirts with me something awful but has never kissed me or asked me out. I think he is out of my system. I don't even think about him much anymore."

"Are you going to the graduation ceremony?" Beth asked.

"I wouldn't miss it. Let's go together okay?"

"Okay," Beth agreed.

~

The last days for the seniors flew by, and the students added an extra unofficial day off on "Senior Skip Day." Beth went to the Center, and it was practically empty. The same girls were there, but the boys weren't. It was both sad and boring for Beth. Someone had started up the jukebox. Boston belted out, "More than a Feeling." The warning bell rang, and the underclassmen went to their homerooms.

Beth trudged to class, her shoulders slumped as she maneuvered through the mostly empty halls. Danny was officially gone. An ache spread throughout her chest. This was going to be tough on her.

The year finished with final exams. Beth received her report card, and her grades had improved by leaps and bounds since the beginning of the year. She was proud of that. Her parents were happy, too. They were even happier that the upcoming graduation ceremony was almost over, and Danny would finally be gone.

On graduation night, Mrs. Angellini drove Beth and Lynne to the ceremony. They sat with the other Center girls and watched the seniors graduate. A festive mood filled the air, and the well-organized ceremony was impressive. When Danny's name was called, Beth yelled and clapped with the rest of the group. After all the announcements and speeches were over and the hat toss done, the guests filtered out on to the football field looking for their loved ones.

Beth walked toward Danny. He smiled at her, and they hugged.

Tears came to her eyes, and he said impatiently, "I'm going to be back. I haven't died."

Beth composed herself and left so he could take pictures with his family.

Mike and Billy stood nearby with their families, too. Mike caught sight of Beth and ran up to her, picked her up by the waist and swung her around shouting, "Woo hoo! We're done, baby!"

Beth struggled to get out of his grasp and back on solid ground.

Danny glanced over and laughed at the scene.

Beth smacked Mike's shoulder. "Put me down, you idiot!"

He swung her around a few more times and placed her down very softly on the ground.

Beth looked at him with wide eyes. "What the hell is wrong with you?" She adjusted her blouse and skirt.

Mike leaned forward and whispered in her ear, "I always liked you, Beth. I was jealous. I deserved everything you said to me a few weeks ago." He leaned back, holding his cap on his head, and he smiled at her, winking devilishly. Then he ran off to join his friends.

Beth waved to Billy who smiled at her as he posed for pictures. Her girlfriends were busy congratulating their friends. Danny posed for a picture, and he no longer watched her. Charlie ran to her, and Beth threw her arms around him.

"I'm so jealous you are out of high school now!"

He hugged her and said, "I'm going to be working at the beach this summer. I'll let you know for sure where I'll be. You come see me down there, okay?"

"Okay," she smiled at him.

The beach was a forty-minute ride from her home, and she had spent many summer days there with her friends. It was a family resort town and parents were comfortable dropping their kids off to hang out.

"You have to promise." He smiled sweetly at her.

"I promise!"

His parents called him over to take pictures with his grandparents. Beth looked around. Her friends talked with their relatives and other friends. She went out to the parking lot to find Mrs. Angellini's car.

Beth walked by Danny's silver Mustang. She gazed across the parking lot to the streetlamp where his car had been parked the first night they'd kissed. After she glanced around to see if anyone was watching, she strode over to his car. She peered inside the passenger's side window one last time and smiled. The memory of the night they were interrupted by Mike and the rest of the guys made her smile. She pressed the inside of her hand to her lips, kissed it and then closed her eyes and pressed her hand to the window. The pain in the back of her throat started again, and she swallowed hard. She would always love Danny.

Throngs of people spilled into the parking lot. Beth walked to the other side of the lot toward Mrs. Angellini's car. Lynne ran up from behind and asked if she were okay. Beth nodded and smiled sincerely. In the car, Lynne told Beth they could go to Danny's graduation party.

Beth raised one eyebrow. "Danny's having a party?"

She was hurt, but not surprised he hadn't told her. He was happy and excited about his future, and Beth was depressed and ready to cry all the time. No wonder he didn't want her around.

"Didn't he say anything to you about it?"

"No," Beth replied.

"That's strange." Lynne narrowed her gaze. "You know he wants you there. You want to go?"

"I don't think so." Beth frowned.

Mrs. Angellini smiled at Beth in the rearview mirror, and Beth forced a smile. She raised her head and looked out the side window as Lynne's mom chauffeured her home.

As of today, I am no longer a freshman. No longer a "Baby" or "Little one" or "Rugrat." She sat up straight and compressed her lips. Maybe Danny was right. Perhaps it was best that he was going away. But why did it hurt so much?

CHAPTER 10

Sophomore Year
1977-1978

Heart, we will forget him!
You and I tonight!
You may forget the warmth he gave,
I will forget the light.

When you have done, pray tell me,
That I my thoughts may dim;
Haste! Lest while you're lagging,
I may remember him!
-Emily Dickinson

Beth's summer flew by. She was in better shape than she'd ever been, and her tan was dark. Her mother had arranged for her to do volunteer work because Beth was too young to be employed. She worked from early in the morning until late in the evening at a day camp program sponsored by the YMCA. The Camp Director was a teacher from the high school. Beth enjoyed getting to know her on a personal level. She would be teaching her Biology class this year. Although, she enjoyed the children and the swimming activities at the lake, she felt miserable inside. Beth worked hard and was so exhausted by the end of each day she had only gone to the beach twice. She had run into Danny a couple of times and had barely seen her girlfriends.

By the end of the summer, the air was hot, humid, and buggy, and she could not possibly tolerate one more Popsicle arts and crafts activity. Beth was certain her mother's motive for having her volunteer was to make sure she didn't spend time with Danny.

Beth learned that Danny, Charlie, and Mike were working and sharing a house at the beach all summer. Without a driver's license, Beth would not have been able to see him regularly anyway. Her mother had driven her, Susan, Lynne, Melissa, and Jackie to the beach twice that summer. None of them knew where the boys lived or where they worked.

The first time Beth had run into Danny was in July at a sweet sixteen birthday party for a mutual friend.

Danny looked tan and gorgeous. He saw her immediately as she entered the door and walked quickly towards her to say hello. His swift interception kept any other guys from reaching her first. He hugged her tightly. She could tell he was a little buzzed. It seemed the only time he showed any feelings for her was when they were in front of other people or when he had been drinking too much Genesee Cream Ale. She didn't care to think about it, though. It thrilled her to see him and feel his embrace. Maybe absence had made his heart grow fonder of her.

They ended up outside on the front porch but didn't talk at great length. He said it was a blast working at the beach, and she told him about the kids at the camp. Soon they stared into one another's eyes and before long, they sat on the curb under the streetlight. They held hands and hugged and kissed. Danny had gotten a ride to the party, so they had nowhere to go for privacy. The situation frustrated them both and Beth pulled away.

Beth looked at him regretfully.

"Maybe we should go back." Danny appeared reluctant.

They held hands and returned to the party. For the rest of the night, they sat together and flirted with each other. Beth went home feeling sure he would call the next day. She waited patiently and kept busy. She read a book and wrote poetry. But he didn't call.

Finally, she decided it wouldn't be so terrible if she called him just this once. Her mother told her time and again that it was in-

116

appropriate for a girl to call a boy. All her friends were doing it, and it didn't seem to be that big of a deal. Still, her mother said...

It took her exactly one hour and fifty-two minutes to work up enough nerve to call him. After picking up the phone and dialing half the phone number several times then hanging up, she finally managed to follow through. The phone rang only once. His mother answered.

Beth said, "Hello, this is Beth. Is Danny there?"

"Hello, Beth. How are you?" his mother said in a sweet tone.

Beth was caught off guard by the question and stuttered a reply.

"I'm fine thank you. May I please speak to Danny?"

His mother apologized and explained that he wasn't home. He had returned to the beach that morning.

The words slammed into her. "Oh, I'm sorry to have bothered you. Thank you."

Beth was disappointed and hurt. She wouldn't be calling him again anytime soon.

Their second, and final, meeting was at Baskin Robbins near the end of August. He had finished his seasonal job at the beach. With Labor Day around the corner, the beach season was winding down. Danny was heading to Salisbury State College. He was leaving Monday morning and was excited over his new path in life. Beth smiled like a trooper and told him to have fun at college. That was the extent of their conversation.

Beth sighed and returned to the present. She tried to be happy for Danny, but she was miserable for herself. She believed she would wither away and die from a broken heart. He never said, "I'm sorry I didn't call you," only "I can't wait to get to the dorms. Well, I'll see you."

Later that day, Beth decided to update her freshman style bedroom. It was a new year after all, and she was a sophomore now.

She moved her dresser down one wall and made room for a chair in the corner. Her mother gave her permission to use a cushioned rocking chair from the spare bedroom. She set up a small table and put her black and white TV on it. Now she could sit in the chair and watch it or talk on the phone. It felt like her own dorm room. She removed the *Sergeant Pepper's Lonely-Hearts Club Band* movie poster and with it, her secret crush on Peter Frampton. Then she threw away the old candles and put the pastel quilt back in the closet. She searched through the trunk and found a dark green bedspread that matched the upholstery on the chair. Her white curtains remained but she took down the C.R. pennants, scarves, and pom-poms and arranged them neatly in her closet.

Beth went to the basement and scrounged around for anything that would match her décor. Her mother allowed her to put different colored glass bottles on her shelves. She placed her stereo on top of the dresser, and Beth asked permission to move several of her mother's plants into the space. A spider plant hung in front of one window, and she placed the smaller vines and ferns strategically around the room. She found a stack of hardback books she wanted to read in her father's book collection and placed them in neat stacks on her shelves. When she finished, the room was truly transformed. Her mother loved it. She began reading *Jaws* that very night. She heard the book was quite a bit different than the movie.

On the first day of school, Beth got a ride with a friend from her neighborhood. Lockers had not been assigned yet, so the Center was buzzing with people. Beth gaped at everyone. She had assumed it would be empty and boring. Her friends rushed through the entrance in small groups, hugging one another and ready to start another year. They were thankful they weren't freshmen anymore. It was strange not to see Danny, Mike, Billy, or Charlie.

It sank in like a heavy stone in her gut that Danny was gone. Yet she was still alive, still breathing. Lynne, Melissa, Jackie, and Susan were scoping out the boys and trying to figure out who was part of the "in-crowd." Beth joined in, but she honestly had a difficult time finding even one person she thought was cute. *This is just pathetic.*

Her homeroom teacher passed out the class schedules. English was first period. That was cool. She would prefer to take English all day and never sit in another math class. Beth enjoyed writing and thought she might join the school newspaper or the poetry club. This year, she decided to take some business courses and felt a little nervous about Typing and Accounting classes. Fourth period was Biology, then lunch, Spanish, and a study hall to end her day. As she worked her way through the hallway to first period, Beth smiled at the freshmen who were trying to figure out how to use their lockers.

When she entered her English class, she was thrilled to see Susan and Melissa. She quickly took a seat behind Susan, and they all slapped each other high fives. The teacher entered and introduced herself, and Beth immediately liked her.

Beth decided she better take the time this year to get to know some of the kids in her own class a little better. She would be stuck in high school for three more years, and she would need some good friends.

At the end of the day, one of the cheerleaders offered to drive Beth home every day since they lived near each other. Hurray! No more pathetic bus rides. She was happy she could hang out in the Center after school a little longer.

The first two weeks passed quickly, and everyone staked out their spots in the Center and the cafeteria. Beth reestablished several friendships with her classmates during lunch, especially with a boy named Kenny Nixon. They had known each other since the fifth grade, and he'd helped her and Lynne pass Mrs. Brick's Physical Science last year. He was kind and easy to talk to, so they quickly became close and shared many secrets at the lunch table and in homeroom.

Kenny was the first boy Beth was able to confide in and trust completely. He was much taller than she was and wore glasses, braces, and his hair was way too short. The two sat next to each other at lunch every day. He was left-handed, and she was right-handed. They would bump elbows constantly and soon it became a huge joke. "Elbow fighting" was always good for a laugh when either one of them needed a little cheering up. Kenny watched out for her, and she often loaned him lunch money. He teased her a lot and got mad at her about her interest in "older guys." He told her she should start accepting invitations for dates, while she told him to break up with the newest nutcase with whom he was involved. They made each other laugh, and she enjoyed his company.

This year's lunch table was different from last year's, though. The boys and girls were no longer divided. They all sat together and all of them were tenth graders. It was packed. Beth, Susan, Melissa, Jackie, Kenny, and several other boys they had known since elementary school were there. Lynne was the only one of the girls who had to eat lunch at a different time during the day. She was upset about it, and the girls felt badly for her and missed her at the table.

The jukebox had new tunes, which pleased everyone. Beth found herself having fun with her classmates and slowly putting Danny out of her mind. She was convinced going to parties would be a lot more exciting this year. There would be no one there to agonize over, and every time she thought about it, she felt light and free.

CHAPTER 11

Beth's friend Melissa hosted the second party of the year. Her mom went on a trip to Atlantic City with her new boyfriend, and she left Melissa home alone. Parties at Melissa's were always great fun. Beth carried a half full cup of warm beer, for looks only. She stood in a circle with the girls. They were cracking jokes and dancing as stupidly as possible. Jackie sported a couple new hickeys on her neck and flipped her blonde curls so they would be noticeable. Susan fussed at her about it. Jackie rolled her eyes at Susan's disapproval and laughed.

"Who gave you those love bites?" Melissa asked.

Jackie would not divulge the information and sniffed with annoyance when they pressed her. "You guys don't need to know everything."

The girls stared at one another with raised eyebrows as Jackie left to go talk to a boy in eleventh grade.

Lynne shook her head and wondered out loud, "What if her mom sees those? I would be in so much trouble."

Susan and Beth nodded in agreement, but Melissa just laughed.

Beth relaxed as the night progressed, and everyone laughed and joked. She enjoyed the party because she wasn't waiting for Danny to walk through the door at any moment. She didn't have to worry about how she looked or if he would show up with a date.

There were a lot of guys there, and her friends were in a tizzy of excitement. Beth soon noticed a tall, very handsome guy staring at her. She looked at him several times, and each time he was watching her. His attention made her smile, but she looked down to avert her eyes from his.

Eventually, Jackie told Beth that a guy named Brian Knight had asked who she was. Beth was flattered. The guy looked like a catalog model. Several other giggling girls approached her and gave Beth more details. He graduated in 1976, he worked for the local A & P grocery store as a meat department manager, and he didn't have a girlfriend. Beth would never be permitted to date him but decided she would have fun flirting with him anyway. They continued to play eye tag with one another, and he finally approached her grinning broadly. The girls around Beth dispersed quickly.

He seemed to grow taller as he walked toward her. "How are you?" he asked.

His teeth were perfect. He had the broadest shoulders of any guy she'd ever known. His eyes were dark and twinkled as he flirted with her. Lord, he even had a five o'clock shadow. He must need to shave every day. Brian didn't ask her how old she was, and he certainly didn't treat her like a baby. He made a couple of racy jokes that were quite witty. Beth liked that he spoke to her as if she were mature. He was chatty. She liked that, too. They were getting along quite well. He asked for her phone number, and Beth gave it to him. She was sure he would never call her, but if he did, well, she would keep his real age a secret from her parents. God knows she had learned that lesson.

~

Brian called on Wednesday and asked her to a movie on Friday. Beth said yes. She was thrilled when her parents gave their permission, but she felt guilty about lying to them concerning his age. She told them he was seventeen. He called her Thursday night, and they talked on the phone for over an hour. On Friday afternoon, he called just to let her know what time he would be there to pick her up.

When he came to the door, Beth introduced him to her parents. They were polite and kind to him. Beth was glad they had not asked her what grade he was in. She really hated to lie.

Beth and Brian went to the Capitol Theater to see *A Bridge Too Far*. It was an exceptionally long war movie, and Beth was bored out of her mind. Brian enjoyed it but must have noticed Beth was a little less enthusiastic. He whispered conversations with her during the film. She smiled, thankful he was talkative and interesting. Luckily, there were no other moviegoers around them to worry about. Beth studied him as he watched the screen. His earlobes peeked under his dark brown curly hair. She figured he had nice ears. His well-defined muscles strained under his light brown sweater, and she decided he was incredibly handsome.

He turned and smiled at her. Beth smiled back and wondered why she wasn't embarrassed at getting caught looking at him so intently.

Later at Burger Chef, Beth noticed his gorgeous dark brown eyes They were so dark they were almost black. He reminded her of the lead character in the romance novel she was reading. Truth be known, he was more handsome than Danny. So, what was it about Brian that didn't do it for her? Oh, that's right. He wasn't Danny. Her quest for true and lasting love might always end at Danny.

Beth and Brian went out on several dates. She felt comfortable around him, but he tried too hard to please her. This made her nervous and a little edgy. Brian went out of his way to wait on her and tried to predict her every need, but all it did was annoy her. He was nice, though. She found herself talking to him about everything. He laughed at the same things she did, and they realized they sometimes knew what the other one was thinking. Sometimes, even insignificant things would send them into gales of laughter. She really liked him as a friend.

She and Brian went to the Homecoming football game together on Friday and then to the dance on Saturday night.

They double dated with Melissa and her new boyfriend, Eric. Eric made the dinner reservations, and they went out to eat at The Hudson House, the restaurant owned by Danny's parents.

The restaurant was full of high school students dressed in long gowns and suits. Brian was a perfect date. He didn't seem bothered to be seen with a girl younger than him.

Danny's sister welcomed and seated them. Even though Beth had never met her, she and Danny looked a lot alike. She was helpful and kind to everyone that came inside. Beth admired their view from the window at their table. The setting sun hovered over the lake, and pink and yellow hues exploded in the sky.

Melissa's date was a year older than Brian, and the two guys got along well even though it was clear they had different interests. Brian was into playing and talking about sports while Eric liked to talk about cars and rock music. When the meal was finished, they headed to the dance at the high school.

Brian liked to dance, and they were on the floor often. *I'm an idiot. I should be falling for this guy like a rock.*

Her friends were there with their dates, and everyone got along well. The girls loved Brian and thought he was perfect for Beth. Melissa referred to him as Mr. Universe. Beth wasn't so sure about her feelings for him, though. She was constantly comparing him to Danny.

The band began to play "Some Kind of Wonderful," and the dance floor was soon crowded with teenagers. Brian and Beth laughed as they did the Bump. Afterwards, the band followed with "I Want to Kiss You All Over." No one moved from the floor, and you could almost hear a collective sound of excitement as the boys grabbed their girls and held them close. That song got everyone's hormones stirred up.

Brian pulled her to his chest. He wrapped his large arms around her and rested them on the small of her back, clasping his fingers together. Beth placed her hands on his biceps.

The guy was built, she had to give him that. Her breasts pressed against him, and he moved in rhythm with the music. Her dress swayed gently at her feet. At that moment it hit her, and she realized she and Danny had never danced. Brian tugged her closer. *That can't be right. Danny and I must have danced somewhere. No. I don't think we ever did. Well, I just can't get over that! I could've sworn we had danced somewhere. Geez, it's hot in here!* Her mind raced, and the heat of the room became unbearable.

Beth raised her head to see if she could get a breeze on her face. Brian kissed her, slipping his tongue into her mouth before she could stop him, and her heart skipped a beat. This was different than the kisses he had given her after their other dates. She wasn't expecting it, and he had never French kissed her before. Shock spread through Beth as he continued to caress her tongue with his. Oh my God! Oh my God! *Hmmmmmm, this isn't too bad. Wait! What am I doing?* Beth ended their kiss.

She looked into Brian's eyes. He was a goner. *Oh shit.* He pulled her close. She could almost hear him purring, and she wanted the song to be over now. The rest of the evening Beth ducked Brian's advances and made excuses to go to the restroom often.

After the dance and the drive home, Brian pulled his car into her driveway and turned off the lights and ignition.

Does he think I'm going to invite him in? She wasn't planning on it.

He spoke to her softly, "Beth, I think I freaked you out when I kissed you."

"Oh no, not at all," she said, lying with bravado.

"Well, we were having a good time until then. After that, your mind ended up somewhere else, like you didn't want to be there with me." He had his head turned towards her and tried to make eye contact.

Beth sat with her face toward her lap. She let out a deep sigh, and her lips bounced together making an unpleasant noise. If he had been Danny, they would have laughed hysterically at the noise, and the tension would go away. Brian stared at her and waited for a response. Finally, she broke their silence.

"I'm sorry. It's not you, it's me..."

Brian took a deep breath, and she braced herself for his anger. He only stared straight ahead as she looked at him.

"I'm sorry," she repeated, her palms sweating.

"Me too," he said.

After a moment, Beth reached for the door handle.

Brian stopped her by speaking again. "Listen, I really like you. I think you're a great person, and I understand where you're coming from. I'd like us to stay friends. Is that okay?" He smiled at her.

"Absolutely!" Beth was relieved he was being so cool about it. "Thanks for everything, Brian. I really did have fun."

He held out his hand, and Beth thought he was going to shake hands with her. Instead, he took her hand in his and pressed it against his lips.

"Thank you for going out with me." He was so polite and so sweet.

She should be smacked for dumping him.

He got out of the car and walked her to the door. Beth continued up the steps, and Brian stayed on the sidewalk. She opened the door, turned, and waved to him. He smiled at her, waved back, and walked back toward the car.

CHAPTER 12

If I can stop one heart from breaking,
I shall not live in vain,
If I can ease one life the aching,
Or cool one pain,
Or help one fainting robin
Unto his nest again,
I shall not live in vain.
Emily Dickinson

The first marking period ended in a flash. The football team worked its way to the division championship. Beth and the girls rode with Susan's longtime boyfriend, Tyler Jenkins, to the game. The sky was overcast, and it was twenty-five degrees out. The spectators were bundled in blankets, earmuffs, scarves, and heavy coats. Some people drank hot chocolate and coffee from Thermos jugs. Beth and Jackie stood near the fence that outlined the football field. Beth watched the crowd in the stands, shivering and wishing she had thought to bring a blanket. Susan was with Tyler somewhere in the crowd. The girls did their best to stay warm, moving around and standing close to each other. Lynne and Melissa were cheering, and the crowd was tense.

"Hey Girlie."

Beth jumped at the deep male voice and turned. She threw her arms around Charlie, and the two began chattering a blue streak. He asked her about the classes she was taking, which teachers she had, and if she was dating anyone. Likewise, she wanted to know every detail of his college life. Charlie confided to her that he wasn't happy at college and had made plans to quit. He had promised his parents he would finish out the semester, though.

"They think I'll change my mind," he said, sullen and unhappy.

Charlie asked her why he hadn't seen her at the beach this past summer. Beth told him about her volunteer job at the day camp, and he was suitably impressed.

"I think my mother was just trying to keep me incredibly busy and out of trouble," she grumbled.

"Your mother is a smart woman."

Beth stuck her tongue out at him, and they both smiled.

The two headed to the bleachers to find a seat.

"Your nose is red." He tapped it with his gloved hand.

"It's freezing! My toes are frozen solid, and they are hurting." She winced.

They headed toward the bleachers and found a small opening they could squeeze into. As they watched the game, they talked. The air seemed to get colder, and soon a light snow began to fall. She noticed how Charlie watched her lips as if he might be thinking of kissing her, and she decided to ignore it. They were only friends. At halftime, they bought hot chocolate and stomped their feet to keep warm. Kenny walked by and gave her a warning look. *Be careful of those older guys*, she could hear him thinking. Beth shot him a smug smile. She was safe with Charlie.

Beth and Charlie lost their seats in the bleachers when the second half began, so they returned to the fence to watch the rest of the game. Her girlfriends stopped to chat and say "hello." Charlie enjoyed the attention, and Beth was happy. Brian was there, too, and they chatted while Charlie spoke to the others in the surrounding group.

When they were left alone again, Charlie asked, "Have you seen Danny?"

The familiar knot pulled inside her stomach again.

"Not since August." Beth looked out towards the field and pretended to be more interested in the game than she was.

"Has he written to you?"

"Nope," she said softly and glanced at the scoreboard.

She hoped to prevent the tears threatening to form in her eyes. Charlie must have noticed her expression change from happy to sad because he winced.

"Damn, Beth, I shouldn't have brought it up. I'll write to you. Here, give me your goddamned address." He took off his glove and reached in his back pocket under his coat, making dramatic movements to make her laugh.

Beth giggled at him, and he chuckled.

He handed Beth a small yellow piece of scrap paper he had taken from his wallet. She took a pen from her purse and scribbled her address down for him and smiled as she handed it to him. He was just the best.

The day was a type of homecoming day for the football stars of the past two graduating classes. They were the teams that had brought glory to C.R. and coming back to visit gave them a sense of pride. Beth and her friends saw many of the former players standing together by the fence so they could see the action. After the defeat of C.R., Beth said goodbye to Charlie.

"What's going on next weekend?" he asked before she walked away.

She shrugged. "Not a whole lot. There's a dance at the Fire Hall."

"Really?"

"You want to come?" Beth lit up, hoping he would say yes.

"I will most likely be there," he said, nodding.

"I have to go…they're waiting for me." She glanced at her friends waving for her to hurry.

"I'll write you!" he called.

Beth didn't believe him but was thankful he cared enough about her to try and make her feel better.

On Wednesday Beth received a letter from Charlie. She jumped up and down in the kitchen with excitement when her mother handed it to her. She was thoroughly touched that he made the effort and was true to his word. Her mother questioned why he was writing her.

Beth replied with frustration, "We're just friends, Mom."

In the letter, Charlie complained about life on campus and said he would see her this weekend.

Friday night arrived quickly, and Beth grew excited about the dance. The local volunteer fire company hosted dances every other month, and the high school kids crowded in with hidden fifths of pre-made screwdrivers. Older boys brought in beer iced down in coolers. They would be paid well for their purchasing power, and that way, everyone stayed happy. No one ever seemed to watch for underage drinking. Beth and her friends arranged for a ride to and from the dance. Jackie's mother drove them in her station wagon and dropped them off at the entrance.

CHAPTER 13

Beth, Lynne, Jackie, Melissa, and Susan entered the dark, smoky dance hall after paying a dollar cover charge at the door. The band began to play "Free Bird," and some couples slow-danced. A group of friends from their lunch table waved them over to some empty seats on the far side of the room. The girls barely settled in when they were asked one by one to dance. The five of them danced through the entire first set. Beth started to sweat from the stifling air, and her friends complained about the heat. Thankfully, someone opened the side doors to let some cooler air in. The band took a break, and the Stones played on the stereo system through the speakers. The young crowd continued to drink heavily.

Beth scanned the hall for Charlie. He should have been there by now. Lynne ran breathlessly up to her.

"He's here! He's here!" She did her cheerleader bounce, up and down, and she grabbed Beth's shoulders, causing her to rock back and forth.

"Who's here?" Beth asked, anxious to see who it was that had Lynne so excited.

Lynne hadn't had a crush for quite a while, not since Mike.

"Who?" she asked again as Lynne grinned at her.

"Danny Mitchell!" she squealed.

Beth felt a pit in her stomach.

What was Danny doing here? she thought frantically.

"Is Charlie with him?" Beth hoped the two had not ridden together.

"No, I didn't see Charlie. I think he's alone." Lynne was still smiling.

Beth turned around as Danny entered the room. He smiled at everyone, shaking hands, looking like he thought he was important. Mike was behind him.

"Oh Lord," Beth said with a groan.

"Charlie!" Beth heard Lynne say, and she began bouncing again. "Beth was just looking for you!"

Beth turned to see Charlie entering from the opposite doorway. A sense of dread washed over her. If she were a nice person at all, she would focus her attention on Charlie, dance with him and have him sit next to her. If she were rotten, vile, and disgusting, she would let herself fall victim to Danny again and dance with him and let him take her out to the car, get her all worked up and then dismiss her again. It was a real dilemma.

"Hi Charlie," Beth said with a nervous smile as he approached.

"Hey. Is the band on a break already?"

Beth nodded.

"You having fun?" he asked.

"Not at this particular moment," Beth replied truthfully.

Danny approached her from behind. She knew it. She could *feel* him. The disappointed look on Charlie's face confirmed it. He forced a gallant smile in true Charlie style.

Beth's heart broke for him a little. She focused on Charlie's face as he held out his hand. Danny reached around Beth to shake it. He and Danny greeted one another cordially while Mike went to buy a couple of beers from a guy with a cooler.

"Hi Beth," Danny said, as if it were an afterthought.

He thinks he is so hot. She was jumpy and edgy, and she was getting on her own nerves.

"Hello," Beth said shortly.

Danny glanced at Charlie with a "what's up with her" expression.

Charlie shrugged and rubbed the back of his neck.

The band re-assembled on stage. Danny started to lean in

toward Beth but before he could say anything, Beth abruptly turned to Charlie and said, "You want to dance?" She felt Danny tense next to her, and Charlie widened then narrowed his eyes.

"Uh...sure."

She turned and walked away from Danny. Charlie followed behind her.

Beth glanced over at Danny who took a deep drink from the beer Mike had handed him. By his angry expression and tense body language, he was pissed off. What did he think she would do? Sit around and pine for him? Well, of course that's exactly what she was doing, but she didn't want him to know that. Danny turned and asked Jackie Basile to dance, and she accepted. Danny guided Jackie towards Charlie and Beth on the dance floor. Was he trying to make her jealous?

The song was finished, and Beth could feel him looking at her. She refused to look at him. Beth cautiously peered around Charlie's shoulder at Danny and Jackie Basile, fury building inside. *If he thinks I am going to fall all over him tonight, he is sorely mistaken.* She had been irritated with him before, but now, after he asked Jackie to dance, she was plain angry.

During the next several songs, Beth danced with Charlie and refused to leave the dance floor. After downing beers and shots of Lord Calvert supplied by Mike, Danny was becoming livid, his voice rising above the music.

Beth rolled her eyes and focused on her dance partner.

A half hour later the band took another break, and Beth went outside to cool off in more ways than one. Jackie and Susan followed her out, and then Lynne approached.

"What is going on?" Lynne asked. "Danny looks so pissed!"

Jackie flipped her long curls over one shoulder. "He asked if you and Charlie came here together tonight. He thought you were on a date."

"Oh," Beth replied with a casual shrug, but her tone was

sarcastic. "Did he ask that when you were dancing with him?"

Jackie's eyes opened wide. "That wasn't anything. Hey! You were dancing with Charlie!"

Beth glanced away and refused to look at her or speak to her.

"I'm going back in," Jackie said, thrusting her scowling face in front of Beth, and then she turned and stomped away.

Suddenly, Beth's mood was worse, and she had put Jackie in a bad mood, too.

Lynne and Susan stayed with Beth, and Lynne put her hand on Beth's shoulder. "You haven't seen Danny for so long. He probably came here tonight to see you. Why don't you talk to him?"

After ten minutes, the persuasion worked. She returned to the dance hall. The band was still on their break, and the crowd moaned its displeasure. The guys in the band had been drinking shots of something and weren't in a hurry to return to work.

Beth scanned the room for Danny. He was not with Charlie or Mike. She continued searching for him, and her chest tightened. He stood close to Jackie, and Jackie was leaning into him. She groped his chest and flipped her long blonde curls. Jackie was drunk. Danny had a half pint of Lord Calvert in his left hand and a beer in the other. He stared at Beth and then laughed dramatically at something Jackie said.

Fuming, Beth marched over to Charlie. He smiled when she approached. She knew Danny watched her from across the room. She forced her sweetest smile at Charlie and stood next to him. Beth imagined Danny and Jackie talking about how bitchy she was tonight, and it made her want to cry.

"Hey Beth," Mike greeted her.

"Hi Mike, how's college?" she asked politely, glad to have a distraction.

"Sucks," he said.

Beth couldn't believe everyone was so unhappy at college. Danny certainly wasn't coming home on a regular basis. It was probably going very well for him. Charlie excused himself to talk to some high school friends he had not seen in a while.

Dubbing himself "Shot Man," Mike ran up to Jackie and Danny and offered them two shots of amber alcohol. Danny lifted his bottle of Lord Calvert and indicated he didn't need a shot. Jackie accepted one and tossed it down. Danny put his bottle of Lord Calvert up to his lips and drank deeply. He lowered the bottle and made eye contact with Beth. His expression was strained and unkind. Unnerved, Beth left the dance hall to go to the restroom.

"What's wrong with you? You have missed him so much! What are you mad about?" she muttered to herself. *You're mad because he left you back in high school and he didn't even care. That is ridiculous, Beth. Stop being such a brat. You might as well just go out there and talk to him. You haven't seen him for so long. It would be nice if you two could finally dance together."* She made up her mind. Her mood lightened as she returned to the room.

The band was back on stage, and the crowd applauded. The music began. It was a slow ballad by Boz Scaggs, and the lead singer was doing a great job. "Outside the rain began, and it may never end, so cry no more…"

Beth searched for Danny, hoping he would see her, and they would dance, touch, and kiss. He wasn't there. She went to the table where the girls had staked out their spot for the night and sat down.

Brian came over and sat next to Beth. He tried to make small talk, but she was distracted and ignored him. He said his goodbyes, smiled at her politely, and walked back to talk with Charlie and the other guys.

Susan was dancing with her boyfriend, Tyler. Lynne danced with Mike, and she made eye contact with Beth. She shot her friend a quick smile to let her know she was okay and continued looking around for Danny.

The song was half over, and they were going to miss it all if he didn't show up soon. If he'd gone to the restroom, he would have been back by now. She got up to see if he left out the side door. No one was out there. She wanted to apologize to Jackie, too, after being so miserable to her. Beth went back inside. The song was winding down. Now she couldn't find Jackie. Where in the world had everybody gone?

The couples on the dance floor kissed as the song came to an end. Beth became increasingly frustrated. It dawned on her that everyone wasn't missing, just Danny and Jackie. The blood drained from her face. Beth checked again and couldn't find either of them. She remembered Jackie's face when she'd snapped at her earlier. Pain swelled in her throat, and she hurried outside again, hoping she had just missed one of them. Beth feared the worst. Jackie was on the pill and frequently sported hickeys on her neck, so those two details didn't calm Beth's suspicions.

She stood in the darkness and scanned the parking lot. There was no one there. She didn't see Danny's car, but he could have gotten a ride with Mike. Only she didn't see Mike's green Duster either. Where could they have gone? Why did she let him make her so miserable?

Charlie exited the hall and appeared by her side. "Are you alright?"

"Did you see Danny leave?" she asked in a panicky voice, not ready to hear the answer.

Charlie nodded and lowered his head.

"Did he leave with Jackie?"

Charlie nodded only once then looked up into her eyes.

Beth turned away from him and wandered the parking lot. A painful lump lodged in her throat.

Charlie grasped her hand and led her back to the Fire Hall.

"I need to go home." Tears welled in her eyes.

"Okay. Let me drive you. Don't move. Wait here while I get our coats and your purse. I'll tell your friends I'm taking you home. Don't go outside." He let go of her hand and left to get their belongings.

She was grateful that Charlie offered to take her home, but she grew suspicious. Why was he so insistent that she wait for him inside the door?

Brian approached her and asked if she was alright.

She shook her head. "I don't feel so great. Charlie's taking me home."

Brian waited with Beth until Charlie returned. She crossed her arms around her chest as she leaned against the wall just inside the building. Hurt and confusion draped over her shoulders. Charlie returned quickly, handed Beth her purse, and helped her with her coat. They said goodbye to Brian, and Charlie drove her home.

CHAPTER 14

Who?
My friend must be a bird,
Because it flies!
Mortal my friend must be,
Because it dies!
Barbs has it, like a bee,
Ah, curious friend,
Thou puzzlest me!
Emily Dickinson

For the next two days, Beth tried to find out what happened between Jackie and Danny. She realized Charlie and Brian had been keeping something from her, and she suspected Danny and Jackie were having sex in the parking lot. No one could or would tell her what happened.

Finally, she asked each of her friends one by one, point blank, "Do you think Jackie slept with him?" They avoided eye contact and their responses confirmed her worst fears. "I'm not sure," "I really don't know," "It would be hard to say," were the replies. Not one person said, "No way, Jackie wouldn't do that."

Convinced they had been together, Beth was numb. Now one of Beth's former best friends was her enemy. She wanted to wring Jackie Basile's slutty neck.

On Monday, Beth confronted Jackie at school.

Beth planted her feet apart and wouldn't let Jackie pass. "Did you have sex with Danny?"

Jackie gaped at her. "Danny was upset that you were with Charlie, and he just needed somebody to talk to. Why would you waste a perfectly good opportunity to be with him after all this time of pining for him?" she asked in a louder than necessary voice. "I felt sorry for him."

"Oh really? Just how *sorry* did you feel, Jackie? Sorry enough to comfort him in the back seat of his car?" Beth yelled.

Jackie's face turned red and her eyes slanted, "You were nasty to me when all I did was dance with him so perhaps it's your jealousy talking!"

"Whatever, Jackie. Don't talk to me ever again!" She stomped away.

Intuition told Beth that Jackie had slept with Danny, but she couldn't prove it. She was totally heartbroken to lose a best friend and Danny all at the same time. She couldn't help but reflect on her friendship with Jackie, and she wondered if it was worth it to lose Jackie because of Danny. He couldn't seem to make up his mind about Beth. One minute he was nice to her, and then he ignored her. Beth was so confused.

Plus, Jackie had had a few heartbreaks of her own. Her father had been distant, angry, and mean to her mother. Jackie's mother was constantly turning herself inside out to please him, but it never worked. He found fault with everything she did. When Jackie turned eleven, her father began to find fault with her, too. Jackie had had many conversations about this with her friends. Before she got braces, her dad called her Bucktooth Beaver and thought it was funny. After she got them, he called her Tinsel Teeth. She hid from him in the bedroom most of the time. When he did see her, he would tell her she was going to get fat if she kept eating so much and told her that her hair looked like a rat's nest. When she began to come out of her preteen awkwardness and develop into a beautiful young lady, he ignored her completely. Beth was aware that Jackie's parents had huge arguments. The elderly couple next door once called the police while Jackie and her brother hid in her room. Jackie told Beth that was the night she found out her father had a girlfriend. Eventually her parents had divorced, but Beth knew

Jackie had many scars. Beth didn't know what to do. She hated to lose her friend, but she wasn't ready to forgive her.

CHAPTER 15

Beth still felt strongly that Jackie and Danny had sex in his car, and she wanted nothing to do with her. She didn't need confirmation. She could feel it. Unable to have contact with Jackie, she decided to pull herself out of the social scene.

She felt betrayed by Melissa, Lynne, and Susan as they continued to talk to Jackie and make plans with her. The only person she really talked to was Charlie. They wrote letters every week, but even Charlie hadn't been coming home the past couple of weekends. When he did, he went hunting with his brother. Beth felt lower than she ever had. Even Charlie didn't want to hang out with her. After three weeks of self-imposed isolation, she dragged herself out of her foul mood and decided she needed to forge ahead.

The newest topic of conversation at the lunch table was sex—who put out and who didn't. That was all everyone seemed to talk about. Privately, the girls shared intimate information about their boyfriends and dates. Apparently, it hurt like hell the first time, and you could make an anonymous appointment at the free clinic to get birth control pills at no charge. If you did manage to get pregnant, you could go to the clinic and get an abortion for about $275, and they wouldn't even tell your parents. There were rumors and stories about several girls in school, but the stories were hard to believe.

Beth once heard the entire Junior Varsity football team got a case of crabs from one girl in the eleventh grade. No one would talk to the girl anymore. To be seen with her was social suicide. The boys, however, came through the incident unscathed and unaffected. The girl did not fare so well. She transferred to the only private school in town.

There was another rumor about a senior girl who almost died after having an abortion at the clinic. She never returned to the high school, and everyone assumed it was because she was too ashamed. Beth wasn't so sure the girl didn't just move out of town and felt terrible for the reputation she had. She wasn't even around to defend herself.

The boys seemed to be the winners in the sex world. They didn't suffer any consequences from their actions. A few of them wore the number of times they had contracted gonorrhea like a medal. The more girls they screwed the better. The boys refused all responsibility regarding unwanted pregnancies, because birth control pills were so easy to get and use. They were packaged in small containers, making them easier to hide from nosy parents. Most of the boys flatly refused to wear a condom. If you wanted to get and keep a boyfriend, then you took care of birth control yourself.

Whenever anyone got a cold sore on their lips, it was a disaster. Students were convinced they had syphilis and would go insane, or even die thanks to the gruesome movie they'd seen in health class. Other rumors floated around about a short list of girls who used abortion as a means of birth control, having five and even six during their years in school. Most understood the rumors were exaggerated and probably untrue, but they still held an element of intrigue. Beth wasn't ready to have sex, even though she desperately wanted to be. She was too self-conscious to let anyone see her naked, and she would rather die than risk being seen at the clinic or worse, found out by her parents.

All that aside, who would she sleep with anyway? She wasn't interested in anyone, and she would never speak to Danny Mitchell again, let alone sleep with him.

Winter vacation was coming up soon, and Beth was excited to have the time off from school. Charlie would be coming home and would call her. Perhaps she should just let him take her out. Maybe she should let Charlie take her virginity. He was certainly nice to her, and he was cute. Wouldn't that be the best "get even" scheme of all time?

At the lunch table that day, the girls made plans for sleepovers and movies they wanted to see over vacation. Until now, Beth and Jackie had been able to avoid each other by talking to the people around them and sitting on opposite sides of the lunch table. Today, it was impossible.

Jackie looked at Beth nervously and asked, "Beth, do you want to go see *Kramer Vs. Kramer* with us on Saturday?"

Astonished, Beth stared at her and blinked hard. She would not be able to ignore her without looking foolish. No one else at the table except Susan and Melissa knew why Beth and Jackie hadn't been speaking. Beth had a choice to make... Would she forgive Jackie and allow the girls' friendships to remain intact?

Her two friends were aware that Jackie had set the dynamite underneath their friendship by her ill-fated actions with Danny. However, Beth was the one who could diffuse it and save the group. Melissa and Susan turned towards Beth with anxious expressions. They held their breath and waited for Beth's response.

She glanced down at the table. "I guess. Sure."

The girls were ecstatic and began to talk at the same time. After several moments, Jackie smiled gratefully at Beth, but Beth looked away.

Later that day, Melissa rode her bike over to Beth's house. It was an older style red boy's bike with newspaper baskets on the back. She could carry groceries and overnight bags in it easily. Everyone in town knew it was Melissa when they saw the bike from a distance. The bike and her auburn hair were hard to miss.

They went upstairs to Beth's room, plopped on the bed, and talked about the conversation at the lunch table.

Melissa said, "You know, Jackie has never said anything to me about Danny. I really don't know if anything happened or not."

Beth handed her a diet soda she had taken from the refrigerator on their way up to her room.

"*I* know," Beth stated bluntly, looking her friend in the eyes. "You know," she choked out, not letting the subject drop.

Melissa belched softly after taking a large gulp from the bottle.

"I'm so hurt."

"I know you are," Melissa said quietly.

Beth remained calm. "I feel betrayed and angry. I don't know which one of them to be angrier with. Danny has been nothing but a pain in here." She pointed to her heart as she began to cry.

"I know," Melissa said as she moved next to Beth to comfort her.

"I think I really need to make an effort to let go of these feelings for him, forever."

"I think that's a good idea." Melissa patted her shoulder. "Why don't you come out with us on Friday? We're going to a party. Billy Englehart's cousin is having it. Tell your mom you're spending the night at my house so we can stay out late."

Friday arrived, and Beth's mother dropped her off and told her she wanted her home by twelve. Beth tried to convince her to let her stay at Melissa's house with Jackie and Lynne, but her mom gave her a firm no.

Beth sighed but didn't argue with her. "Bye, mom," she said as she got out of the car.

Her mom's response wasn't a huge surprise.   She'd overheard her parents talking a few nights ago in the family room as she eavesdropped from the stairs. Susan's mother had told Beth's mom about Melissa's home life earlier that day in the grocery store, and her mother shared the information with her father. Melissa's mother was an alcoholic and was known as a bit of a floozy in town. She permitted the teenagers to drink and smoke cigarettes at her house and often left Melissa unsupervised for long periods of time. Since her parents' divorce several years ago, her father had virtually disappeared, and Melissa had taken on the role of caregiver. In junior high school, she would go out on her bike and search for her mother at the local bars. Beth had often cried at the thought of her friend searching in the dark for her mother.

Both her parents had expressed concern for Melissa's well-being and briefly talked about inviting her to live with them. They liked Melissa a lot. She was always kind, respectful, helpful, and incredibly mature for her age. Thankfully, her parents agreed not to make Beth stay away from Melissa, but they decided to monitor their daughter's visits to her house.

The following afternoon, Beth's mom talked with Beth about the situation at Melissa's. Beth assured her that Mrs. Walters had never done anything inappropriate while she was there, and her mother was relieved.

Of course, Beth had lied to protect their friendship.

The sad truth was that Mrs. Walters was a classic drunk. It didn't help that she worked as a bar waitress at the local club called The Back Door. The woman was tanked every night when she came home from work. Melissa always tried to be in bed sleeping so she wouldn't have to face her mom. Mrs. Walters regularly smoked pot in her bedroom, too. She was also a beautiful woman, and there was a different guy in and out of the house weekly. Melissa tried to ignore her mother's behavior as much as possible by keeping her bedroom door locked and shut. No way could Beth tell her mother that.

Melissa had the same pretty facial features as her mom, though her coloring differed. But unlike her mom, she was a good girl and did her best to keep her head above water. She did the laundry, cleaned the house, and she used the money her grandparents sent her each week to grocery shop. She made iced tea and kept the Kool Aid pitcher full. Her and her mom ate a lot of baloney and cheese sandwiches, macaroni and cheese, and hot dogs or tuna fish. Beth adored her friend and wasn't going to give up the friendship, no matter what.

CHAPTER 16

Beth walked into the house. Her friends greeted her, but Jackie hung back as if hesitant. Beth scoped out the alcohol choices just to focus on something other than Jackie. There were a couple of bottles of wine, and two boys managed to purchase beer for the small party of about twenty people. Beth wasn't in the mood for drinking, so she just held on to a beer so she wouldn't look like a party pooper. A card game started, and the boys played penny ante poker while the others stood around the kitchen and talked.

Jackie flirted heavily with Billy's cousin Mick. It started to get on Beth's nerves as she watched her friend flip her blonde curls around her shoulders. Guys loved Jackie's hair. Beth kept picturing her with Danny. Maybe Danny liked her hair, too...

Beth stepped out into the back yard. Her mind had tortured her enough over Danny and Jackie, and tears threatened to fall. Everyone else seemed to be having a great time, and she didn't want to bring anyone down. She still could barely stand being around Jackie. A slight chill raised goose bumps, but it was unseasonably warm for this time of year.

She strolled over to the fence by the pool, leaned on it and looked up into the night sky. A full moon illuminated the yard. She left the fence and went to sit on a swing that hung from the tree. It had a flat wood seat and wooden ropes holding it in place. She rocked slowly back and forth without letting her feet leave the ground. A shiver crept over her shoulders, and the weird sensation that someone was watching her had her glancing around the yard, but she didn't see anyone.

One of Mick's friends came walking around the back of

the house toward her.

"Hi," he said.

"Hello," Beth replied.

"What's a good-looking girl like you doing out here all alone?"

Beth smiled at him in the moonlight. He had no idea how much she needed to hear a compliment. She glanced down at her feet, relishing the flattery.

"Well," he continued, "do you mind if I stay here with you for a minute?"

"I don't mind." She wasn't lying.

"I don't think I've ever met you before. My name is Rocky Mulinero."

"Beth O'Brien. Did you say your name was Rocky? Like Rocky Balboa?" Beth looked up at him, her eyebrows raised.

He nodded. "Yep. Yo, Adrian!" he imitated the star and the famous scene from the movie.

Beth chuckled at his poor rendition.

Rocky continued to talk to her despite her relative silence. He spoke slowly, deliberately and said the nicest things. Rocky acted surprised when she told him she didn't have a boyfriend. He asked her about school, her family, and what she liked to do. Before long, the two were seated side by side on the back steps. Beth was happy to be with someone who wanted to know her better, and she warmed up to him. She reciprocated in kind and learned a lot about him in the process.

Beth was surprised to hear he'd been at the junior high with her. She didn't remember him. He told her his short hair had been long hair then. Beth still didn't remember but pretended she did to avoid hurting his feelings.

They sat outside for quite some time. Beth shivered slightly from the coolness of the late-night air. Rocky took off his letterman's jacket and thoughtfully wrapped it around her shoulders. It was too dark to see what sport he'd lettered in.

Rocky was only a year older than her. She liked that, too. He had short dark hair and intense brown eyes. His gaze unnerved her slightly. He was ridiculously cute and had a beautiful smile. Rocky complimented her freely and then asked her if he could drive her home. Beth agreed.

They went back inside. The kitchen was a mess, and the house was empty. Jackie's purse sat on the counter, but she was nowhere to be seen. The stereo had stopped running, and it was nearly 12:30 a.m. Her mother had told her to be home by twelve.

"Shit! I'm late!" Beth said to him in a rushed whisper.

"I'll hurry. It'll be alright. You haven't even been drinking."

They walked to his car at a brisk pace. Beth's mouth fell open at the beautiful 1972 black Thunderbird. It had chrome metal wheels with white wall tires, and the inside was as immaculate as the outside. Wow! Much nicer than Danny's car.

Oops! Self-talk time. *Don't compare, don't compare, don't compare.*

Rocky glanced at her every so often as he drove her home. By his intense, calm demeanor, he seemed much older than sixteen.

"Is this your parents' car?" Beth asked.

"No, it's mine. Do you like it?"

"Yes, it's really nice." Beth was still wearing his jacket when they reached her house.

"I'll walk you to the door," he stated.

Beth thought it would be okay. *Why shouldn't it be? Screw Danny and his superior "I'm older than you" attitude." Not to mention his mean "let me screw all your friends" attitude!*

"I'd like that." Beth fluttered her eyelashes at him.

His smile lit up his face, and his eyes flashed in an appealing way.

Rocky walked her slowly to the door. He took hold of her hand, held it tightly and looked deeply into her eyes.

"I really enjoyed meeting you tonight. Would it be alright if I called you this week?"

Beth giggled self-consciously and nodded.

He started to walk away, and she called to him, "Oh my gosh! Danny! You forgot your coat."

He returned to her with a furrowed brow.

As he took the coat from her hands he asked, "Who's Danny?"

"What?" Beth narrowed her eyes.

"You just called me Danny."

Beth's face grew hot.

"I am so sorry! Rocky-Rocky-Rocky. I know that, really I do," she stammered.

"I like the way you say my name," he said.

His smooth smile made her all tingly.

Rocky walked away and left her staring after him. He waved goodbye as he opened the car door with his free hand. She waved back, turned, and quietly entered the house. Thankfully, her parents were already in bed.

Excited about Rocky, she could hardly sleep.

The next day, Beth and Jackie rode with her mother to Lynne's house. They didn't talk during the ride, partly because Beth was still upset with her, and partly because she didn't want to say anything incriminating in front of her mother. Melissa and Susan were already there when they arrived. Despite Beth's feelings about Jackie, the girls were spending more and more time together as a group. They gossiped about the party, and they teased Beth about meeting Rocky. It was the first time they had seen Beth smile about a boy in a long time. They knew Rocky Mulinero. He was a bigwig on the soccer team, and they all thought he was cute. This pleased Beth, but she still couldn't stop comparing him to Danny.

Beth asked Jackie what happened between her and Mick Englehart. She acted innocent and claimed she didn't know what Beth was talking about. Since her friend was acting defensive, Beth let it drop and didn't mention seeing her purse on the counter at the party after everyone else had gone.

After spending the day with her friends, Beth got home around dinnertime and helped her mother set the table. Her grandmother was coming for dinner. Beth placed ice cubes in the glasses and filled them with tea when the phone rang. The front door opened at the same time. Her grandmother came in as Beth reached behind her to pick up the receiver. "Hello?"

"Hello, may I speak to Beth please?" Heat spread over Beth's face, and her stomach flipped.

"This is Beth," she managed to say calmly. She walked out of the kitchen into the laundry room for some privacy, pulling the phone cord with her.

"Hey, it's Rocky. If you aren't busy tonight, do you want to go to the movies?"

"Hold on. Let me ask my mom."

Beth's mother approved, and the two made final arrangements for the date. Her grandmother and mother smiled at one another as they watched Beth grow flustered while speaking on the phone.

Beth smiled and chatted during dinner. Her parents and grandmother appeared happy to see her excited about going on the date, and her dad teased her. Beth answered questions about Rocky and how they met. Her grandmother wanted to know more details than Beth could tell her, but she smiled at her grandmother's interest. Beth asked to be excused from the table at six thirty so she could be ready by seven o'clock.

Rocky arrived five minutes early. This scored him a few bonus points with her mother and grandmother. Her mother liked him immediately and was thrilled to discover he was a junior in high school. Rocky was a gentleman from the moment he shook hands with her father to when he smiled kindly at her grandmother and said, "Hello." He helped Beth with her coat and opened the car door for her. Beth slid into the impressive, clean car. Every detail shined and it smelled good, too. Rocky got in and flashed a gorgeous, white smile at Beth.

They drove to the movie theater at the Blue Hen Mall to see *The Spy Who Loved Me*. Rocky bought a large tub of buttered popcorn for $1.25 and two small cokes for 35 cents without asking Beth what she wanted. She felt conflicted about his self-assuredness. On one hand, it thrilled her that he took charge. On the other hand, it seemed narcissistic and annoyed her.

Rocky followed her halfway down the darkened theater aisle to the seats she chose. Beth looked at him for approval of the location. He smiled and nodded. Rocky sat in the aisle seat, and Beth sat next to him. The cinema showed previews of upcoming attractions as the two got comfortable. Soon the film began.

After they ate half the tub of popcorn and set the bucket and their drinks on the floor under their seats, Rocky held her hand for a long while. He used his thumb to trace a feather light outline over her thumb and wrist. The touch and movement were quite soothing. Beth placed her right hand on his elbow, and Rocky smiled.

Before long, he moved his hand onto her left knee. Quickly, Beth placed her right hand over his to keep it in place. Rocky chuckled.

The second half of the movie was a dance of hand placements and avoidance between them. Beth became exhausted as she ran interference with Rocky's roving hands. He eventually gave up trying to cop a feel and returned to holding her hand. Beth was comfortable but still sat in "high alert" mode.

Once the movie ended, Rocky held her hand as they walked to the car. He slipped into the driver's seat, pushed the cushioned armrest up and patted the seat next to him. She smiled and moved closer to him. The impressive car added to his appeal. She was ashamed to admit it, but she liked people seeing her in it. At red lights people looked over at them, checked out the car and then checked out the people inside.

They went to Pippy's Pizza. Rocky sat across from her in the booth. This time he asked her what she wanted and then handled the ordering. The conversation was easy and light. Beth found herself enjoying his attention and his sense of humor.

From that night, the two dated one another exclusively. Beth liked Rocky a lot. He was nice and truly kind to her. He complimented her all the time, and he was an excellent kisser. The two spent more and more time together as the weeks passed by. They were together at all the parties. He took her out to the movies, to Pippy's, and to Burger Chef. They hung out with her friends. He was close with Tyler Jenkins, Susan's boyfriend. Rocky fit comfortably in her life, and it felt good.

Beth continued to correspond with Charlie. She told him about Rocky because people had begun to refer to them as a couple. She wanted him to hear about it from her first.

As she feared, he soon stopped writing to her. Brian knew Rocky a little. They had worked together at the local gas station in town when he was a senior in high school. At a party one night, Beth talked with him about Rocky. Brian seemed to approve of the match, and she was glad.

Rocky constantly told her how much he liked her and gave her notes every day in school. With each week that went by, he wanted to get closer. He'd visit her house, and he introduced her to everyone in his family.

The only problem was Rocky pressed the sex issue with Beth and had a hard time taking no for an answer. He was relentless as Beth refused him time and again. He became more and more frustrated and then began to get angry. It took eight weeks for Rocky to break up with her because of it. Beth was surprised, but she wasn't heart broken. It seemed Beth's friends and parents were more upset about it than she was. She didn't like the fact that he dumped her, but she wasn't crying about it either. This breakup wasn't as devastating as her split with Danny. She couldn't believe she hadn't seen Danny Mitchell since November.

The next weekend was the Valentine's Day Dance at school. Beth went to the dance with Donald Jackson, a friend of hers from English class. Donald was sweet, kind, and very hung up on Jackie. He asked her all kinds of questions about Jackie during their date, which annoyed Beth. The next day Lynne called Beth on the phone to tell her Jackie was jealous because Beth had gone out with Donald. Truth be told, Beth felt slightly vindicated.

CHAPTER 17

Beth focused her attention on her friendships and the kids in her own class. Her group of friends took turns hosting sleepovers each weekend. She had finally convinced her parents she was safe at Melissa's house. Rocky wrote her notes from time to time. He always seemed to know when she was down and vulnerable. He developed a predictable pattern. He would date a sleazy girl for a week or two. When he tired of what she had to offer, he'd try to get back together with Beth. She managed to dodge those bullets as they came at her.

There was talk of a huge "Sweet Sixteen" party Friday night at Donna Harris' house. Everyone was welcome, and Beth and Lynne made plans to go. Susan and Tyler were going later after he got off from work. Jackie had a date with a senior she met at the mall. Melissa wasn't going at all. She and Eric had plans to go to his friend's house. Beth's older sister was home for a visit and volunteered to drive the girls to the party. She almost didn't let them stay when she saw how many kids there were outside the house.

It was the first interracial party Beth had been invited to, and the house was in a predominately black neighborhood. Beth knew it was important to Donna to have all her friends there. It was difficult for her to choose between her friends because of the color of their skin. She confided in Beth that she hoped the party would ease the racial tension at the high school.

The tension between the black kids and white kids had lessened a bit over the past few years at Colonel Roberts High School, but they all had a long way to go. Everyone wanted equal treatment and harmony, but it seemed neither group knew how to get there. Few were willing to leave their comfort zones and branch out. Donna was one of the few exceptions to that and Beth admired her for it.

Over a hundred kids jammed into the house. Anyone who had graduated in the past two years or who still attended high school was there. It was cold outside, but there wasn't enough room inside for everyone, so some kids were outside bundled up in coats and huddled in groups. Pockets of kids stood together with friends of their own race, but there was no tension, and the atmosphere was friendly.

Inside the packed house, Donna introduced Beth and Lynne to her mother as she took their coats and put them in her bedroom. Her mother was beautiful, and Beth saw where Donna inherited her good looks.

Beth and Lynne pushed their way through the crowd on the basement steps and reached the beer keg. A few candles lit up the smoky, dark basement, though it was still difficult to see. *The Long Run* album by the Eagles played on the stereo. Kids sang along loudly. "The moon shinin' bright, so turn out the light and we'll get it right. There's gonna be a heartache tonight, I know." The crowd and the noise overwhelmed Beth. She wanted to get her beer and go upstairs.

A familiar voice spoke into her ear. "Hi Beth. She jumped and turned to see Danny's face inches from hers. He looked into her eyes. The tops of her legs went weak. Heat rose in her cheeks.

"Hey Danny," she stammered out the words.

Beth couldn't fake the overwhelming emotions rushing through her. She wanted to punch him in the face and throw her arms around him all at the same time. Her adrenalin kicked in, and her legs began to shake.

"You're wearing your hair longer," he said.

"Uh-huh."

He swept his gaze over her. "I like it."

Lynne watched the exchange and excused herself from their company.

Danny placed his hand on the ceiling beam above Beth's head and leaned in close to her.

"Can you and I get out of here?" he asked softly.

She nodded and silently hated herself for not having any willpower whatsoever. He put his hand at the small of her back in a protective, possessive manner, and then guided her outside.

The night air had grown colder with the increase in wind, and they raced to his car. Danny didn't turn the ignition on, and the two sat quietly for a long moment. She didn't know what to say or do and it appeared he didn't either.

Danny finally broke the silence and asked her about her year in school. Beth replied without much detail. She didn't like being reminded that she was so much younger than him. He asked her if she were dating anyone. She told him about Rocky Mulinero, but before she could tell him they were no longer dating, Danny let off a streak of reasons why Rocky was an "asshole" and she shouldn't "waste her time on him."

Speaking of assholes, Beth didn't bring up the dance at the Fire Hall. Instead of accusing him of sleeping with Jackie, she stayed on her side of the car and held her hands in her lap.

"I've missed you, Beth," he finally whispered with his head down.

She sat perfectly still and stared out the front window, willing her pain to go away. Remembering how she felt when Charlie confirmed that Danny and Jackie had left the Fire Hall together, Beth's eyes filled with tears.

Danny turned his head to look at her. He covered her hand with his.

"Beth, I am so sorry for everything. Things got so screwed up. It's all my fault."

She lowered her eyes, and tears dripped into her lap. One fell on his wrist. She removed her hand and brushed the tear away and then quickly wiped her face. Danny continued to watch her and monitor her emotions.

"Things will get better for us. I know they will," he said.

Beth studied him, her brow furrowed. She had been wanting to hear those words from him. He was the one she waited for. Her true and lasting love. She smiled at him.

"Can I kiss you?" he asked.

Beth looked into his eyes and nodded silently as he moved toward her.

Danny slowly pressed his lips to hers. He used his mouth to brush hers lightly from side to side at first, and then he traced her lips with his tongue. His kiss set her blood on fire. Danny's breath was a mixture of beer and cinnamon.

Pleasant tingles rippled along her body, and she wanted to throw herself onto him and hold him tightly. Beth dared not break the spell. She opened her eyes slightly and sat completely still with her hands in her lap. If she encouraged him and he rejected her again after he had been with Jackie, she would die from anger and humiliation. He continued to use his tongue to trace lines up and down her neck and back to her mouth. He had yet to put his tongue to hers. Passion swept over his features, and she was sure he loved her as she did him.

Danny cupped her face and turned her head slightly to the right. He kissed and pulled away from her mouth several times as if trying to draw a response from her. She finally leaned in for him to complete the kiss. As she did, she reached up behind him, and she tugged him close to her. Danny let out a groan.

He opened his eyes halfway, and the two stared at each other with overwhelming emotion.

"I'm sorry. I'm sorry about everything," he declared again.

She touched his face. "Danny?" *What do you want from me? How long are you going to do this to me? Will you always want me?*

He seemed to understand and pulled her tightly to him. The two shared a very deep and passionate kiss. Beth began to feel a need she did not understand. She wanted him to touch her. She wouldn't stop him. She wanted him to love her. She was ready.

As she continued to return his kiss, she moved her hand down his arm and to his left thigh. She glided her hand up his jeans and sucked in a sharp breath. His obvious passion pressed against her, and Danny quickly took hold of her wrist.

"Beth," he breathed out her name and tried to get her attention.

"Hmmm?" She leaned back and looked at him through sleepy eyes. Her lips tingled from his kisses.

Danny stared at her, as if searching for something in her eyes. What was he trying to see? What was he trying to figure out? He drew back from her. She did not expect his rejection again.

Before she had a chance to react, he tugged her close to him again and held on to her tightly. She rested her head on his chest, and they sat in the silence of his car for a long while. The faint sound of Chaka Khan played inside at the party. She could feel Danny's breathing pattern. His chest swelled, and then he exhaled, his breath moving her hair slightly on the top of her head. She paced her own breath with his. His heart beat in time with hers. He played with her hair in a soothing manner. Beth wished they were in a bed together so they could simply fall asleep.

Danny broke the silence. "I'm quitting college."

"What?" Beth sat up to look at his face. "Why?"

He scrubbed his hand through his hair. "It's just not working out. I'm going to come back here and work for my folks at the restaurant. I don't want to, but I need to. I'm going to take courses here at the community college."

Beth tried extremely hard not to squeal and jump for joy. Alright! This will work out after all. He is coming home. They were destined to be with one another. She was going to marry him one day.

He ran his fingers down her face, looking at her strangely. "I'd like to call you tomorrow. I'd like to take you out. Do you think your parents will let you date me now?"

Beth went from pure joy to total despair in one millisecond. Her parents believed he wanted to take advantage of her. They were unreasonable where he was concerned. Ever since the mini-diamond incident, they worried Beth and Danny were too serious and she was too young for him. She was fifteen, but she wasn't a child. Still, her parents believed they were protecting her.

"I don't know, Danny, but I don't care. I want to be with you."

He smiled and hugged her tightly.

"I still have the ring. I'll never get rid of it. Who knows, maybe one day you will wear it again." He lifted an eyebrow. "Let me drive you home?"

Beth agreed. Her parents were probably in bed and wouldn't be watching to see who dropped her off.

They reached her house, and Beth told him good night. After a brief kiss, she climbed out of the car and practically skipped up to the door.

Her mother waited for her inside. "Was that Danny Mitchell's car?"

Dammit, I was wrong. "Yes," she said honestly.

"Beth, your father and I have told you time and again. He's too old for you, and you are much too serious about him for your age. We will not permit it."

Beth turned her head up in defiance and held her mother's gaze. The two stood with a silent struggle hanging in the air.

Her mother caved first. "Well, I won't tell your father about this now, but you have to promise me you won't pursue this any further."

"I can't promise."

Without waiting for her mom's response, Beth climbed the stairs to her bedroom.

She lay awake late into the night practicing what she would say to her parents to convince them to let her see Danny.

Eventually, she drafted and memorized the most perfect, persuasive speech ever to be performed by a fifteen-year old girl. It wasn't until she was convinced it would work that she allowed herself to drift off to sleep.

Beth slept in late the next day. The ringing phone woke her, but someone else in the house answered it. She went down to the kitchen, rubbing sleep from her eyes. Her mom sat at the kitchen table, flipping through a magazine.

"Who called?" Beth asked.

"Wrong number, honey. Want something to eat?"

"Sure." Beth plopped into a chair, hope swelling in her chest. She couldn't wait to hear from Danny.

He didn't call that day or the next...

CHAPTER 18

Beth felt ill all week in school. She was pale and had dark circles under her eyes. She had never known such hurt and despair. Her friends knew why she was distraught and looked at her sympathetically. She had waited all weekend to hear from Danny. Luckily, she had not approached her parents with her well-rehearsed speech. She would have looked like a class "A" fool if she had. It was obvious to her now. Danny was playing with her heart again.

She didn't sleep at night and slept most of her free days away. Her mom sent her worried stares but remained quiet. She had to know Beth was distraught over Danny since she knew he had brought her home on Friday night. Her mother never brought up the conversation they'd had. Her dad would never relent and let her see Danny anyway. Besides, Danny had made his choice, so it didn't matter what her parents did or didn't allow.

As Beth and her parents finished dinner on Wednesday, Beth's father said, "Beth, I've found you a job."

"What?" Beth and her mother responded together.

"You'll be working at Hannigan's downtown. You need to report on Saturday at two o'clock. You will work until five. You can come across the street to the shop, and I'll drive you home."

Beth sat stunned and gaped at him. Hannigan's was a department store with a reputation for high-quality clothes. Beth's older sister had worked there when she was in high school, and now it looked like Beth would, too. Her father owned the music store across the street from Hannigan's.

After a stretch of uncomfortable silence, her mother finally said, "How can Mrs. Hannigan hire Beth? She's not even sixteen yet."

Whew! Her mother would get her out of this. Why couldn't they just leave her alone? Didn't they think she could handle anything on her own? They were so interfering and so frustrating! Beth's heart raced as she waited for her father's response.

"It's all been taken care of. You will drive her there before two," he said to his wife.

Her mother got up and started clearing the dishes from the table. Frowning, Beth got up as well. It would do no good to argue with her dad.

Her father left the table and headed to the family room to watch the news. Beth and her mother were silent as her mother washed, and Beth dried the dishes.

After a considerable amount of time, her mother said, "Aren't you happy to be starting your first job? It will be exciting for you."

Beth felt like she was being sent to prison. She wasn't happy or excited. She shrugged and said nothing in response to her mother's comment.

The week ended without much fanfare. There were no major parties or events planned. The girls scheduled a sleepover at Lynne's house on Saturday night. At least that was something to look forward to. Beth dreaded going to work on Saturday and felt ill. At 1:30 p.m., her mother called to her. It was time to go to work. Beth trudged down the stairs and headed silently to the car. The ride to the store was unnerving. Beth's mother told her not to be nervous. She told her to smile often and relax. Beth was relieved to finally exit the vehicle.

She entered the store from the front entrance and found herself in the elegant men's clothing department. There were suits of every size and color, silk ties, and handkerchief boxed sets. There was a rack of men's socks and belts and a beautiful sweater selection. The men's department smelled wonderful like leather and spice, and the man working in that department approached her.

"May I help you?" he asked.

"I'm here to see Mrs. Hannigan about a job."

He looked her over. "Is she expecting you?"

"Yes, yes she is. I'm Beth O'Brien, thank you," she said.

He was dressed immaculately in a gray pinstriped three-piece suit. The white dress shirt contrasted smoothly with his brown skin. His pale pink tie had silver stripes slanted across it. He looked quite a bit older than Beth, probably thirty-five or forty. His cologne smelled strong and manly, and his shoes were shined to perfection. He wore a short Afro and a thinly trimmed mustache.

Mrs. Hannigan came out of a doorway to the side of the department.

She smiled broadly as she approached Beth. "Beth! It's so nice to see you. I was so excited when your father told me you were old enough to work with us. We loved your sister, and we're looking forward to having you with us for a long time."

Beth returned the woman's warm smile and felt instantly at ease.

Mrs. Hannigan gave Beth a tour of the store. Further inside, past the men's department, was the ladies' department. The clothes were exquisite, and the displays were attractive. Two girls close to Beth's age were working that day. Mrs. Hannigan introduced them to Beth. They were friendly and beautiful. Next, they traveled back to the men's department where she was introduced as a new employee to the man who helped her when she had first arrived.

Mrs. Hannigan gestured toward him and said, "Andrew has been with us for twelve years now."

Beth smiled as he shook her hand warmly, nodding softly.

The two then walked through an opening and down several steps to the casual wear department. Everyone in town bought their jeans and corduroy pants there. Beth looked around the store with new eyes as Mrs. Hannigan guided her around. She noticed the light fixtures, the carpet color, and the condition of the telephone on the wall behind the counter. Wooden bins covered the back wall. Each bin contained a stack of Levi jeans. The bins were marked with a printed white label revealing the size of its contents. Surrounding the store were waist-high shelves holding every color of corduroy slacks imaginable. The colors added sparkle to the place, and Beth touched the pants as she stood near the shelf. Kelly green, aqua blue, teal blue, and a pastel yellow shade dazzled her eyes. Well-placed clothing racks holding men's casual pullovers and button-down shirts commanded the center of the store.

The cash register stood next to two glass display cases. One held belt buckles with rock group names such as Hot Tuna, Zappa, the Stones, and the Eagles. Beth smiled to herself. *Who in the world would wear those?* The next display case carried nice leather wallets and key chains. She thought of Danny and remembered how nervous she was when she gave him the key chain last year on Valentine's Day.

Mrs. Hannigan clapped her hands together. "So! That's all I'm going to show you. I'll introduce you to my daughter, Nancy. She can fill you in on everything else you need to do and help you fill out your paperwork."

"Thank you so much," Beth said.

She realized her neck felt tense, and she let out a breath to relax. At that moment, Nancy came out of a small hallway located in the back of the casual wear department. Like a hippie, she didn't wear any make up or a bra. She had on a pair of faded overalls and a shirt with a peach tube top underneath. Her hair was a short, wild tangle of red curls. She looked nothing like what Beth expected the conservative Mrs. Hannigan's daughter to look like. Beth was no longer uncomfortable.

Nancy's warmth and friendliness were contagious. Beth finished her tour of the stockroom. The room was packed with boxes and stacks of jeans, corduroys, rabbit fur jackets and coats, suits, dresses, skirts, prom gowns, and more. The layaways were hung on two long racks, and Nancy showed her how to read the number I.D. on the bag. The two walked up a flight of stairs, chatting comfortably.

Nancy helped Beth fill out her paperwork in the office upstairs. "Remember, if anyone comes in here and asks how old you are, you need to tell them you're sixteen. Got it?"

Beth smiled warmly at her. "Got it."

After the paperwork was completed Nancy said, "Each person who works here is assigned to a particular department. We try to have several girls working here from the different high schools in the area. We want your friends to come in and visit. Then they will buy stuff. See? We could use another girl or two from C.R. Let me know if any of your friends are interested."

Beth nodded.

"You will be working in the Casual Department," Nancy said.

Beth was thrilled. The girls assigned there had been friendly to her earlier that day and displayed a good sense of humor.

"Oh, and by the way, we do three fashion shows a year. All the employees are expected to model. We just had our summer show last week. The next one will be for the fall line."

Beth's mind raced at the thought of modeling in a fashion show. She had modeled clothing from their now-defunct children's department when her sister had worked here. The ladies at the country club had always smiled at her and patted her on the head as she'd walked by their tables and down the runway. Doing fashion shows now was altogether different, and it made her stomach queasy just thinking about it.

The rest of the afternoon Beth shadowed a girl named Debbie. She showed Beth everything in the store from the brands of clothes they sold to the hottest styles. By the end of the day, Beth chose over twenty different outfits she just had to have.

"Did Nancy tell you about the employee discount?" Debbie asked.

Beth shook her head.

"We get thirty percent off. No other store in the area gives that much. Usually it's twenty, at most twenty-five with no discount for sale items. Here you get your discount on sale items, too. They like you to wear the clothes from this store when you're on the floor." Debbie was excited about that, and Beth caught her enthusiasm.

The last hour of the day flew by, and Beth was genuinely excited and happy about this new job her father had arranged for her. At five, she punched out on the time clock in the employee break area with Andrew's help and headed over to her father's music store.

During the ride home, Beth and her father talked more than they had in months. He offered her advice on how to handle irate customers and what to do if your boss ever got mad at you for a mistake you made. Beth listened and learned.

"I have to call on Monday to find out my work schedule for next week," Beth told him.

"Well, call right after school and don't wait. Bosses like it when their employees are enthusiastic."

Later that night, Beth went to Lynne's for the sleepover. She told her friends the details about her new job. The girls were excited for her and couldn't wait to come in and visit her. She told them Hannigan's was looking for more help, and the girls squealed with the prospect of working together at the store. They spent the next hour discussing how much fun they would have.

The prospect of working with her friends became less likely as the week wore on. Susan's parents said her grades were more important than working right now. Jackie's mother said she was too young. Lynne's parents said she would be allowed but only if she gave up cheerleading. Of course, Lynne did not want to give up cheering. Melissa only shook her head no. There was no need to explain. She needed to be home to take care of her mother.

Beth felt disappointed but hoped maybe when they got older, they would be able to do something together.

CHAPTER 19

Over the next few weeks, Beth became more comfortable at work, and her friends visited her often. She saw them more now that she worked at Hannigan's. Brian Knight came in at least once a week to chat with her. The two of them became good friends. The girls Beth worked with thought Brian was gorgeous. They went nuts whenever he visited. Brian was more than pleased with their attention and Beth laughed at him. Charlie Cahall came in whenever he was home from college. Even Billy visited a few times on long weekends when he was home. Her friends bought clothes just as Nancy said they would, and everyone was happy. However, one person never came into the store to see her—Danny Mitchell.

Rocky came in often, too. Debbie and the other girls she worked with at Hannigan's teased her about him all the time. He always complimented Beth on her clothes and told her how pretty she was in front of her co-workers. Beth enjoyed the attention and began to soften towards him. She needed someone to validate her since Danny's latest assault on her self-esteem.

Rocky asked her to come and watch his soccer match on Friday night. Beth considered it. He acted differently this time, and he promised if she went out with him again, he wouldn't pressure her about s-e-x anymore. Still, she hoped she would see Danny, find out what was wrong and be able to fix it.

Beth believed now that she was working, it might be easier for them to maintain a relationship. It would be easier to lie to her parents. She could tell them she was going to work. Also, he could come see her at the store. She refused to call him because maybe he had simply changed his mind. It may have nothing to do with being in high school or her parents' disapproval. She hoped she would run into him in town somewhere, and she couldn't believe she hadn't seen him at the gas station, or Pippy's, or at any of the usual spots. It was as if he completely dropped out of sight. Perhaps he'd changed his mind about quitting college after all. She wished she knew, but she refused to put her life on hold for him.

Beth did indeed go to the soccer game to watch Rocky play. She and her friends made a night of it, and Lynne was thrilled to have them come watch her cheer. Not many people attended the soccer matches, and sometimes it could be disheartening for the players, cheerleaders, and coaches.

The field lights were on, and it was chilly. Beth and her friends sat in the bleachers at mid-field. The stands were virtually empty except for the parents and family members of the players. Rocky's team was winning more games than ever before, and they were attracting local attention. If they kept up their winning streak, they would go to the State Championship. The team ran out on the field. Rocky looked up at Beth and waved. She waved back. Her friends smiled at her and teased her about how much he liked her.

Beth had never been a soccer fan and was surprised when she got caught up in the action of the game. C.R. won 5-2, and Rocky was elated. The team remained undefeated now at 7-0. She met him at the fence after the game. His face was flushed, and he looked so handsome. She agreed to meet him at Burger Chef later after he showered and changed. Susan's boyfriend, Tyler, had bought an old station wagon, so he drove them all to Burger Chef.

Beth saved a seat for Rocky. He arrived and took her aside away from the others. Again, Rocky asked her to go out with him. Beth considered it. She had a lot of fun with him, but she didn't love him and didn't think he was her true and lasting love. She asked him to please be her friend. He was disappointed and angry at the rejection but tried hard not to show it. She knew how he felt. The two agreed to be friends, though. Rocky continued to visit her at work, and she was always happy to see him. He made her laugh at his stupid jokes, and she continued to attend his games and cheer the team on to state championship victory.

There was a huge party the night of the championship game, and the boys on the team got miserably drunk. Rocky wasn't fit to be around, so Beth went home early. He continued to date other girls, while Beth went on several dates with guys she'd met through her friends at work.

Prom season arrived. Beth turned down an invitation to attend the dance from a boy she barely knew. She hoped Rocky would ask her to go. They would have fun if they went together. Susan was hoping he would, too, so they could double with Susan and Tyler. Instead, Rocky asked a girl with a slight reputation for being easy, and she accepted. Beth and Susan were both disappointed. Susan would be the only one of her friends to attend this year's Prom.

On Prom night, Beth's mother took her, Lynne, Jackie, and Melissa to the mall. They saw a movie, *Heaven Can Wait*, and swooned over Warren Beatty. They ended up at the ice cream shop eating bubble gum ice cream cones and having a contest to see who could blow the biggest bubble.

Her mother picked them up at nine. The girls exited the mall from the rear entrance. Cars parked there as customers came to attend the nine o'clock show. The rest of the mall was closed now. Beth's mother dropped Jackie off first, then Lynne. Melissa spent the night at Beth's house.

Melissa told Beth everything about her boyfriend, Eric. He rented a house near hers with a few other guys, and he worked at a car dealership as an auto mechanic. Melissa thought he was the cutest boy she had ever dated. Beth was excited for her friend but warned her of the perils of dating older guys. None of them really knew Eric. He had graduated from C.R. in 1975 so that made him somewhat okay. Then, they talked about Susan and Tyler. Melissa said she knew they weren't having sex yet, but they were doing other stuff. Beth wasn't sure what she meant, and Melissa explained she was referring to touching like masturbation. Beth wondered if Rocky would be satisfied doing that. She didn't think so. He was clear about what he wanted. Besides, it all sounded embarrassing anyway.

After Beth's disdainful reaction, Melissa explained that other kids were doing even more serious stuff like oral sex. She strictly denied that she and Eric were doing *that*. Melissa and Beth agreed anything like that should only be done after you really knew each other well and had already been intimate through intercourse.

CHAPTER 20

The last day of school finally arrived.

Beth was pleased with her report card, but she was more grateful that the school year was over. She was thrilled about working longer hours at the store. This summer she wouldn't be volunteering, she would be making money.

All the girls except for Susan had been taking driver's education classes. Susan would not turn sixteen until November of next year and couldn't take the class until next year's first marking period. The girls felt sorry for her, and Susan was mad as hell about having to wait longer than the others. Lynne already had her license, but her parents wouldn't let her drive with any friends in the car. She was a little skittish behind the wheel anyway. Beth was next in line to receive her license, then Melissa, Jackie, and Susan.

The best thing about being fifteen was turning sixteen. Your parents drove you to the Department of Motor Vehicles and you got your license. Then your parents let you drive home, and you took the car out that night with strict guidelines, of course.

Saturday was her birthday—the day she would get her license. That morning Beth's mother drove her to the Department of Motor Vehicles. They were only open until noon. She walked out with her license and a huge smile on her face. She skipped and jumped during the walk back to the car, then danced around her mother who laughed at her daughter's excitement. Beth begged her mother to let her drive home. She had gotten a 100 in Driver's Ed class and was given the highest marks on the road experience section, so her mother agreed. She was a good driver, and her mother commented on it during the ride home.

Beth asked permission to use the car that night. Her mother said it would be fine. So, Beth called the girls, and they made plans to go out with Beth driving. At 5:00, Beth picked them up one by one and headed to Burger Chef. She had gotten paid that day, and she had enough money to treat them. The girls sat at a table and looked around at the deserted restaurant.

Several kids came through and stopped at their table to talk. "You guys going to any parties tonight?" they asked.

"Probably," said Susan. She wanted to get definite plans going so she could call Tyler and tell him where they could meet.

Beth and her friends didn't know which party they wanted to attend. They received invitations to three, but none of them were people the girls were close to.

Jackie said in a singsongy voice, "Look what I got..." She held something in her hand and waved it around as the others leaned in to see what it was. It was a license.

"How did you get that? You haven't had your birthday yet." Melissa's brows knitted together.

"It's a fake ID. It says I'm twenty!" Jackie grinned and raised her eyebrows up and down several times.

The girls squealed in delight. Each examined it for authenticity.

"This doesn't even look like you!" Susan said while holding it.

Jackie snatched the license back. "It'll do fine. Let's try it out! I have money."

Beth and her friends rushed to toss their trash away and scurried to the car. It was still light outside, and none of them wanted to go to the liquor store in the daylight. Beth didn't want to go at all, not in her parents' car anyway. Lynne looked like she would pass out. Jackie was persuasive, though, so they all agreed to go.

They rode around for a while. The car traveled down the highway with the windows open and the music blaring.

They sang and bounced to the beat of the music.

"Let's ride by Tyler's house," Susan yelled to Beth.

If his car were home, she would make Beth stop so she could let him know what they were doing.

The girls laughed and began a trip around their hometown that took about an hour. They drove past Tyler's house, but he wasn't home. Next, they drove past Mike Crowley's house for Lynne. Then they drove past Danny's home. His car was parked in the driveway, and her four friends screamed at Beth.

"You guys are so stupid!" She laughed.

They were caught up in the celebration of freedom that turning sixteen brought.

Dairy Queen was their next destination, and they and got ice cream cones before heading to the mall. They shopped for a while and tried to pass the time.

"It's dark out now. Let's go," Jackie said with a wicked grin.

They ran out to the car, and Jackie directed them to Chester Black's Bar located in the next town over. According to information Jackie had received, if you went to Chester Black's, you could go in, walk to the end of the bar, tell the bartender what you wanted, and he would sell it to you as long as you had an ID. It didn't matter if it was real or not.

It took them a half hour to work up enough nerve just to pull the car into the parking lot. The bar sign read "Everyone comes back to Chester Black's."

Jackie instructed Beth to park to the far left of the entrance door so the guy working inside wouldn't see a carload of "dipshits" waiting for her. The girls moaned at her.

Beth finally parked the car but kept the engine running. Jackie fixed her makeup and hair in the rearview mirror. She hiked up her boobs and unbuttoned the top buttons on her blouse.

The girls watched her quietly. They looked at one another with raised eyebrows. Susan giggled nervously while

Lynne bit her lip and fingernails.

Melissa appeared unfazed. She laughed at Jackie and said, "Hurry up. This is going to be fun!"

Susan worried out loud, "What if they call the police and we get arrested?"

Lynne added, "Or what if someone sees the car and tells Beth's parents?"

Susan whispered, "We're going to get in so much trouble."

Beth turned white and felt slightly nauseated.

Jackie and Melissa said, "Shut up, Susan!" in unison.

"Okay, I'm ready. You're come with me." Jackie pulled Beth's hand.

Beth almost fainted. "Me?"

Outside the running car, Beth drew back. "Take Melissa. I don't want to go!"

Jackie ignored her and dragged her along with her. "Melissa needs to stay with Lynne and Susan, so they don't have heart attacks."

Beth pulled back and halted. "I can't..."

Jackie turned and snapped at her. "I can't do this by myself!"

She flipped her long curls and strutted into the bar without looking back. Beth reluctantly followed behind as her heart pounded wildly in her throat.

A huge fog of cigarette smoke filled the bar, and the only light came from the beer signs that hung on the walls. About ten old men sat at the bar. Jackie walked the length of the bar with Beth as her shadow. They reached the end, and a handsome young guy smiled at them.

"Can I help you?" the guy asked.

The old men made lewd comments and laughed.

Jackie flipped her massive mane of curls and looked the bartender in the eye. "I'd like two pints of Sloe Gin Fizz, premixed please."

He smiled with amusement and looked at Jackie's face

and then her chest.

Beth felt like she might hyperventilate. She started to perspire. They were going to get caught and get in major trouble.

The guy seated on the bar stool to her right stared at her. She could feel his eyes on her but didn't dare glance in his direction. She tapped her foot nervously.

Eventually, she looked at him out of the corner of her eye. *Damn, he is watching me!* He nodded at her. He was extremely handsome and seemed out of place in the hillbilly bar. Beth's eyes flashed back to the bartender without responding to his nod.

"You got an ID?" the bartender asked Jackie.

She handed him the fake license.

He looked at it for what seemed an eternity, handed it back to Jackie, and then went to the back room to get the liquor. After a short stretch, he returned.

"This'll do?" he asked.

Jackie focused on the label as if pretending to be a connoisseur of Sloe Gin Fizz mix. Beth's stomach took a painful dive, and she wanted to die.

"Yes, that'll be fine."

The bartender chuckled, and the customers laughed at the show.

"Don't give those girls a hard time, Al, your Uncle Chet wouldn't approve. He always takes care of the ladies."

Al Black smiled at the old man at the end of the bar. He made eye contact with the handsome guy seated at the bar next to Beth as if he needed permission to sell to them. The guy nodded, so Al shoved the liquor bottles in a bag and accepted the money from Jackie. She held onto his hand just a bit longer than necessary.

Beth rolled her eyes as she watched her friend flirt with the goddamned bartender. When the transaction was finished, Beth walked back down the length of the bar to the exit. The customers shouted goodbyes to them along with other suggestive remarks. Beth wanted to crawl under a table.

They exited the bar, and Melissa called out excitedly, "There they are! There they are!"

Jackie sauntered toward the car with a brown paper bag in her hand, swaying it back and forth as if she just won it at the State Fair. Beth followed behind her, her heart beating fast.

Jackie hopped in the passenger's seat with a smug grin. The girls jumped up and down silently as Beth got in and put the car in reverse. She headed out of the parking lot a little too fast.

Jackie and Melissa screamed and laughed as they pulled quickly way. Beth, Lynne, and Susan relaxed and started to get color back in their cheeks, and they joined in the laughter.

Jackie told the story of what happened in the bar three times. Each time, she added new details.

Beth drove the car down a back road and headed out of town.

"Where are we going?" Melissa asked Beth.

"Jackson Farm."

The girls hollered again. "Alright!" Susan yelled.

CHAPTER 21

Susan's grandparents once owned Jackson Farm, but they sold it when they got too old to farm. Beth and Susan used to play there when they were small children. Neither had been there in over six years. Beth pulled the car onto a narrow dirt road that led back to a little pond hidden within a thick patch of woods. A dilapidated old boat sat up on the embankment wall. Beth stopped the car about twenty-five feet back. She put the car in park. The girls fell silent as they stared out into the darkness. They listened to the silence around them. Bullfrogs and spring peepers called out to one another from the pond. Once Beth was satisfied there were no *Deliverance* men about to run out of the woods, she turned off the ignition and flipped the switch backwards to keep the radio on.

"It looks the same except for that *Gilligan's Island* boat," Beth said to Susan.

She agreed but added, "It's creepy being here in the dark."

"This will help!" Jackie pulled a pint bottle out of the brown bag she had set on the car floor.

"You go first," Susan said to Jackie.

Jackie took the bottle and cracked the paper seal open. She turned the bottle up to her mouth and took a large drink.

The girls watched her with serious expressions. She passed it to Susan and then to Melissa, Beth and finally, Lynne. The pattern repeated several times while the girls sang along to the radio, "Why do you build me up, buttercup baby just to let me down? I need you more than anyone darlin', you know that I have from the start. So, build me up buttercup, don't break my heart!" Soon the bottle was near empty.

Beth felt warm but was afraid to open the car window. "You guys? Make sure your doors are locked," she directed.

It made her nervous to be out in the middle of nowhere in the dark.

Each girl near a door checked and pushed the lock buttons down. They started telling jokes and cracking themselves up. The bottle was now officially empty.

Melissa asked, "Is that all you got?"

Jackie reached down into the bag and pulled out another pint. "Do you think this will be enough?"

The girls squealed with delight. Beth's buzz felt rather good, and they were all in the mood to feel better. Lynne belched loudly. The others sat startled for a moment then burst into gales of laughter.

"Oh my, scuse me!" she slurred and giggled.

The girls laughed hysterically for a good five minutes. It was so funny to see Miss Goody Two-Shoes become uninhibited.

The second bottle worked its way to empty in much the same fashion. The energy in the car had relaxed considerably. Melissa, Susan, and Lynne propped their feet up on the back of the front seat and lounged effortlessly. Beth and Jackie turned their backs to the doors and had their stocking feet on the dash. The volume of the radio was low, and Susan told them that Tyler planned to join the Air Force next year.

Melissa listened to Susan talk about Tyler as long as she could stand it and then she said, "Hey, let's play Truth or Dare! We haven't played in a while."

Everyone perked up and started to laugh.

Susan shook her head. "Oh no! I'm not playing that...you guys will ask too many personal questions!"

Beth held up her hands. "If we all don't play, then none of us play. It's not fair. I don't know what you're so worried about. You tell us everything anyway!"

The girls laughed at Susan, and she rolled her eyes. After a bit of groaning, she gave in. "Oh, alright! But be nice."

The game started, and everyone let Susan go first. The girls rarely chose "Dare." They didn't mind sharing all the details of their life with one another. They adhered to only one rule—all questions had to be yes or no questions.

Susan asked, "Lynne, Truth or Dare?"

Lynne groaned and kept her eyes closed during the exchange.

"Truth."

"Are you still hot and heavy for Mike Crowley?" Lynne winced and began a fake whine. "Yes and no. I swear, I have a hard time making up my mind!"

The rest of the girls exchanged knowing smiles.

Then Lynne asked Melissa if she and her new boyfriend Eric had sex yet. Everyone jumped to attention.

Melissa hesitated a moment, then said, "Yes. It just happened recently."

The girls went nuts. She then shared the details, details, and more details. She told them all about her mother taking her to the clinic at the beginning of the school year to get birth control pills. Her mother was cool with Eric sleeping over, too. She said it seemed to help them get along better when Eric was there. Her mother was always on her best behavior. Beth was a little envious of the freedom Melissa had to be with the man she loved. Her parents were so uncool.

When Melissa took her turn, she asked Susan if she had done it with Tyler, and she confessed that she had. Beth and Lynne were the only ones left in the group who had not lost their virginity. It was embarrassing. Jackie suggested they all get off the sex topic. Beth wondered if she was uncomfortable about the direction in which their questions might lead.

They resumed their relaxed positions and spoke in hushed tones. When it was Susan's turn, she asked Beth if she had ever gotten high. Beth said no and was pleased it was now her turn. The alcohol buzz had worn off, and it left her relaxed but moody. She turned her head towards Jackie.

Her eyes opened in slits as she said in a serious tone, "Jackie. Truth or dare?"

Jackie stared at Beth wide-eyed.

Everyone turned to stare at Jackie.

"I don't want to play anymore," Jackie said quickly.

Melissa chimed in nervously, "Yeah, let's quit. This isn't fun anymore."

Beth got angry at their feeble attempts to stop the question she wanted to ask more than anything in the world—had Jackie done it with Danny?

Beth sat up and said with determination, "That's not fair! It's my turn and I am taking it!"

No one objected. Maybe they feared upsetting her more. It grew quiet inside as if they waited for the bomb to drop.

She repeated her question, "Jackie, Truth or Dare?"

Jackie held her chin in the air, looked Beth straight in the eye and said, "Dare."

Beth scowled at Jackie. Nobody ever said dare.

The rest of the girls seemed relieved while Beth fumed silently.

She leaned forward. "Okay, Jackie. I dare you to walk over to that boat and climb in. You will have to sit there for sixty seconds. You will count out the seconds so we can all hear you."

The girls all sucked in a deep breath.

Jackie gaped at her. "You want me to go out there in the dark?"

"Yep," Beth said coldly.

"In the boat?" Jackie's voice shook.

Beth crossed her arms over her chest. "Yep."

"And sit with who knows what is crawling around in that nasty old boat?"

"Yep," was all Beth would say.

"Fine." Jackie pulled the lock on the door up, pushed the door open in a huff, and slammed it shut.

Lynne looked at Beth imploringly.

"Come on, Beth."

"Shut up, Lynne," she snapped back as she rolled down the window.

The boat was tied to a stake and floating in the water at the edge of the pond. Jackie stomped over to it. She hesitated as she stood on solid ground and bent over to peer inside.

"Will you turn the headlights on?" she yelled back at Beth.

Beth yelled back, "Nope."

Jackie muttered under her breath. She stepped in the boat and sat down.

"One! Two! Three!" she spoke loudly and continued to count.

The girls in the car stared at the scene. Jackie's voice started to break up as she counted, and they winced when she began to cry with fear. Beth began to feel awful as she watched Jackie fall apart. The others were right. This wasn't fun. Beth turned the headlights on, and they lit up the boat and the surrounding woods. She jerked the lock up on her door, pushed it open and stepped out.

"Fourteen, fifteen, sixteen." Jackie's voice was loud but shaking as she hugged herself, rocking back and forth.

"Okay, Jackie, that's enough," Beth hollered.

"Oh no, Beth, it's not!" she screamed back at her.

Beth walked over towards the boat.

"Don't be stupid. Get out and get back in the car."

Jackie made eye contact with her and continued counting loudly, "Seventeen, eighteen, nineteen."

"Get out of the God damned boat, Jackie!" Beth clenched her hands into fists at her sides.

Jackie looked up at her, and Beth noticed tears and snot running down her face.

She said softly, "Come on, Jackie. Really, that's enough."

Jackie stopped counting and in a low voice said, "It will never really be enough will it, Beth?"

Beth stared at her friend with compressed lips.

Jackie stepped out of the boat and slipped, falling into the pond with a splash. She started screaming, and Beth's heart skipped a beat. She had no idea how deep the pond was. Composing herself, she moved towards Jackie's voice. Lynne, Melissa, and Susan clambered out of the car and ran towards them.

Oh my God! Oh my God! Beth was at the edge of the pond, frantically searching for her friend. She couldn't see a thing in the dark.

"Jackie! Jackie!" she screamed in terror.

Beth waded into the water and scanned the pond for Jackie. All the girls were yelling. It was hard for Beth to follow the sound of Jackie's voice.

Please God. Please God... She strained to find Jackie in the black water. Then she heard a splash and saw a ripple near the boat. Beth dove in and swam towards it. Breathing hard, she grabbed for the flailing Jackie who was making it difficult for Beth to get close enough to grab her. After several attempts, she was able to grab Jackie's hair and pull her up out of the water. Jackie gasped for air and cried as Beth hauled her back to shore. Soaking wet, they fell into each other's arms, sobbing and apologizing over and over.

"It's okay," Beth said as she hugged her. And it really was.

They hugged each other as if they would never let go while their friends watched. Beth and Jackie shook off as much water as they could as the other girls helped them back to the car. Luckily for them, it wasn't winter.

They all sat silently in the car for several minutes.

Finally, Susan said, "Hey, do you guys think there's a bathroom out here?"

They all burst out laughing.

"I really, really have to pee," she added.

Beth said, "I think we ought to go. What time is it anyway?"

Lynne answered, "Eleven thirty."

Still shivering, Beth backed the car out, her heart still

beating faster than normal. She had almost lost one of her best friends because of a stupid boy. Never again would she put one of her friends above a guy.

CHAPTER 22

After Beth, Melissa and Jackie acquired their driver's licenses. The five girls spent a lot of time that summer at the beach and at Jackson Farm. They'd gotten familiar with the surroundings and the secluded woods and had come to love the boat. Beth missed out on several trips because she worked longer hours. She even worked the huge sidewalk sale the downtown merchants decided to have. It was excessively hot that day, but she was able to get some sun in her hot pink sundress. Brian came and bought a few shirts from her. Her commission sales for the day were her highest ever, mostly thanks to Brian, and it earned her a day off from work with pay.

On Sunday night, Beth asked her mother if she could use the car to go to the beach on Monday. She had not asked to take the car on a long drive before, and she was afraid her mother would say "no" because it was a forty-minute ride. Her friends had been going down on the weekends, but maybe one of them would be able to go Monday. Beth was surprised but pleased when her mother said she could use the car.

She called all her friends, but only Melissa was able to go.

Beth left her house at eight thirty that morning. She wore a fluorescent orange bikini with a halter style top. It had spaghetti straps that tied behind her neck. Her suit had a paisley style print of bright green, white, and blue, and it was outrageously bright. Over that, she wore a pair of cut-off Levi jean shorts and a white T-shirt with a huge yellow smiley face on the front.

She picked up Melissa, and they were quickly on their way. They reached the beach and found a great parking space. Melissa remembered to bring dimes for the meter machine. Each dime gave them a half hour. They filled the meter, and the two girls grabbed their towels, bags, blanket, and radio, and they headed toward the boardwalk. They chose a spot near the public restrooms and lifeguard station on the boardwalk then walked down the steps onto the sand.

The ocean water was calm and serene. Sea salt and caramel popcorn scented the air. There weren't many people on the beach yet.

Beth laid out an old patchwork quilt and tossed her bag onto one corner. Melissa did the same on her side. They placed the radio on another corner and laid their towels on the fourth corner of the quilt. All corners were now secure from the ocean breezes and helped keep sand off the blanket.

Beth pulled off her flip-flops and headed across the cool sand towards the water. They had chosen a spot close to the water but far enough away so the incoming tide wouldn't soak or wash away their things. The seagulls screamed noisily to one another, and Beth looked far out on the ocean water past the breaking waves. A group of porpoises dived in the water as they traveled south along the coastline. Beth called to Melissa and pointed towards them. Melissa smiled, and the two of them watched the porpoises swim out of view.

She gathered her dark hair back in a high ponytail. Melissa piled hers on top of her head with a large brown barrette. The sunlight made the red in her hair stand out. They took off their T-shirts and shorts and applied tanning oil. The smell of the cocoa butter added to the beach scents of briny ocean and clean air.

Finally, they lay down on the blanket. Melissa fooled with the knob on the radio until she got a station that came in clearly. It played "Silly Love Songs" by Paul McCartney and Wings. Melissa looked at Beth to see if the station suited her. She nodded her approval. Using their beach towels as pillows, they sunbathed and talked with their eyes closed against the brightness.

Melissa shared details of her relationship with Eric. "Eric had a rough home life. I know it sounds weird, but I'm sort of glad. I don't feel embarrassed about my mother around him because he gets it. You know?"

"Uh-huh," Beth said.

Melissa continued, "I'm a little concerned that he smokes too much pot, but he's so good to me in so many ways. He takes me to the grocery store, and he helps me clean the house. He spends the night at our house most nights and my mother doesn't even care. That sounds weird, right?"

Beth opened her eyes and shaded them with her hand. "Not really."

Melissa looked at Beth apologetically. "Your parents would be appalled if they knew my mother."

Beth wasn't sure how to respond. She felt bad for Melissa and understood Eric was a buffer between Melissa and her mom. Beth could hardly blame her. She just smiled at her and said, "My parents are too over the top in the other direction. In some ways, I envy you your freedom to do as you please."

Melissa gave Beth a grateful smile. "He tells me he loves me and makes me feel beautiful. He stays at my house and I make him coffee and fried egg sandwiches for breakfast. It's nice to have somebody there who cares about me."

Beth listened intently and wished it were she and Danny instead of Melissa and Eric. She envisioned herself and Danny in their bathrobes at the breakfast table, sipping coffee and eating toast with black raspberry jam. Beth had never wished to have a mother like Melissa's, but it did seem to have some benefits. How cool was it to have your parent's permission to have a guy sleep over and help you get the pill? It was totally outlandish and unrealistic. The woman had to be a lunatic. Soon Melissa wore herself out talking about Eric. Around ten thirty, the heat became unbearable.

"We need to go in the water," Melissa said. "Come on."

Beth hesitated. "I don't think so. What if there's a shark?"

She had sworn off swimming in the ocean after the girls had gone to see *Jaws* last year. The book had scared her more than the movie.

Melissa perched her hands on her hips. "Don't think about it, Beth. It was just a movie. I don't ever remember anybody being attacked by a great white shark in Delaware."

She ran into the water and dove through a wave. Beth walked slowly to the edge and watched her friend, a bit jealous of her fearlessness.

Beth slowly eased her way into the cool ocean up to her waist. The waves were low and the water calm. She grew braver with each step she took. Melissa encouraged her to go farther and farther until she eventually ended up out beyond the breaking point of the waves. She and Melissa bounced in the surf and swam for a while enjoying the coolness of the water.

The beach crowd had grown considerably. By the time the girls were ready to get out, they had traveled with the tide about fifty yards south of their blanket. They emerged from the water dripping and squeezing the water out of their hair, yakking up a storm.

Beth laughed out loud at something Melissa said about peeing in the ocean when someone grabbed her from behind by her middle and swung her up on a pair of sturdy male shoulders. She saw the back of his head and a pair of red O.P. swim trunks. Was it *Charlie?* The guy swung her around, and another guy hugged Melissa and laughed.

Beth tried to maintain the position of her bathing suit top and bottoms and yelled, "Stop it! Put me down!"

When she finally stopped spinning, she landed on the sand with a thump. She checked her top and adjusted the back of her suit bottoms. She heard laughing and she looked up. Oh my God, it *was* Charlie!

"You!" she said excitedly as she jumped up onto him

again.

This time, she slapped him on the arm as she hugged him tightly. He laughed and struggled to maintain his balance.

"Hi Beth." She turned and saw Mike standing next to Melissa.

"Hey Mike," she responded politely but a little less enthusiastically.

Mike hugged her awkwardly, and Charlie greeted Melissa. The girls invited them to share their blanket, so the guys left to gather their things.

Mike brought a paddleball game, and they played partners until the heat overcame them. They swam in the ocean for another hour after that. Eventually, all four were breathing hard and exhausted. They returned to the blanket. Charlie laid next to Beth on his stomach at the edge of the blanket. He used his towel as a pillow. Melissa was on Beth's other side with her head next to the radio. Mike lay on a towel at their feet. Beth propped herself up on her elbows to look around.

Mike was sound asleep, his mouth relaxed and his breathing regular. For the first time since Beth had known Mike, she finally understood what Lynne saw in him. He had been relaxed and friendly all day. Melissa was also asleep. The music on the radio was barely audible as Paul Simon smoothly sang out "Fifty Ways to Leave Your Lover."

Beth turned her head to the right and looked down at Charlie. His arms were fanned out up by his head. How many freckles did he have on his back and shoulders? She contemplated counting them, but it was too big an undertaking. His face was turned towards her, eyes closed. He was relaxed, but she couldn't tell if he was asleep or not. She turned and looked towards the water. An advertisement plane flew down the coast pulling a flag with the words "A Half-Bushel of Crabs for Twenty-two Dollars and Nickel Beer Night at the Rusty Rudder Restaurant."

She tilted her face up to the sun and closed her eyes

tightly.

"Where's that mind of yours right now?" Charlie asked in a low tone.

Beth opened her eyes and smiled at him.

"I wasn't even thinking. I'm relaxed, but I'm not tired." Beth almost whispered the reply.

Mike began to snore softly, and they chuckled.

Beth lay back down on the blanket. She squinted as she covered her eyes with her hand to protect them from the sun and turned to look at Charlie. He was such a good friend, and she loved him so much. She was feeling proud that she hadn't asked him about Danny all day.

"Your freckles are showing," he teased.

Beth smiled and scrunched up her nose. "Your butt crack is showing."

Charlie reached back to quickly adjust his trunks, and Beth laughed. He joined in with his deep male laughter. Beth complained of being thirsty and hungry. Charlie agreed, and they decided to go for something to eat.

"We might as well leave them here." He pointed to the two sleeping figures on the sand.

Beth pulled on her T-shirt and grabbed her wallet and flip-flops. They tiptoed across the hot sand to the steps and headed back up to the boardwalk. Beth threw on her shoes at the top of the steps, and they headed to George's Fries and Funnel Cakes.

As they walked, Charlie asked Beth if she were dating anyone. She shook her head. Then he asked if she had seen Danny lately.

"I haven't seen him at all."

Charlie's eyes widened.

"You'd think I would at least run into him at the store or see his car on the road. A few months ago, he said he was leaving the University and heading home to work at his dad's restaurant. I haven't heard anything at all. Maybe he changed his mind," she replied and looked down at her feet. "I really don't know what's wrong with him."

Charlie gazed towards the water. "I didn't mean to bring you down. Can I do anything to make it better?"

Beth took hold of his arm. "Yes. You can say you'll pay for the fries." Flashing him a playful grin, she thought what a nice guy he was.

"I'll do better than that. I'll even spring for the drinks." He puffed his chest out with drama.

Beth began singing, "Hey big spender..." while bumping her hip into him.

"Knock it off." He grinned as they approached George's Stand to place their orders.

Charlie was true to his word and would not let Beth pay for her or Melissa's share of the food. Beth carried two large cardboard trays of fries—one with vinegar, the other plain. There were four large Cokes and about one hundred ketchup packets. She stopped frequently to pick up fallen ketchup packets. Charlie carried the drinks and chuckled at her lack of grace. "You'd make a terrible waitress." The sand seemed to be even hotter as they jumped up and down saying, "Ouch, ouch, ouch!" the entire way back to the blanket.

Charlie called Mike and Melissa to attention with the announcement that food had arrived. Melissa appeared grateful, but Mike grumbled as he forced himself awake. The four sat on the quilt and talked while they ate. A few seagulls had spied the food and were flying over them hoping for a handout. Mike fed them and talked to them gently. Beth was happy to see the best side of Mike. She tossed a fry in the direction of the gulls near him. Mike looked back at her and smiled appreciatively. He had gotten a little sunburned, and his blue eyes shone brightly as his face crinkled up in pleasure. That was the moment she would describe to Lynne when she told her about today. Lynne would want to know every detail, and Beth tried her best to see and remember everything good about Mike.

After eating, everyone reapplied suntan lotion and

played another game of paddleball. The heat of the mid-afternoon sun beat onto their skin. Mike headed to the equipment rental shed and rented two rafts. The four went into the water. Beth felt a little nervous about going in the water again when Mike and Charlie sang the musical score to the movie *Jaws*—"da dum, da dum."

"Ignore them." Melissa rolled her eyes.

Beth had enough and removed herself from the water. It started to get late, and they needed to head for home anyway. The guys walked them to Beth's car. Charlie and Beth hugged goodbye, and the girls were soon headed back up the highway toward home.

Melissa said, "Eric would have a fit if he knew the four of us hung out today."

"So, don't tell him."

Melissa looked out the window on the passenger's side of the car.

"He really is a great guy, you know." She sounded defensive of her boyfriend.

CHAPTER 23

The rest of the summer flew by and Beth worked most of it. However, she had managed to spend a bit more time at the beach the last few weeks.

Hannigan's planned the annual Back to School Fashion Show, and Beth and her coworkers scurried to get ready. Each girl had to model three outfits. On the day of the show, all the girls were jammed into one small room to change their clothes with the hairdresser trying to fix everyone's hair. White folding chairs lined the store's walls along the women's and men's departments. A long white carpet wheeled down the length of the store. The girls were instructed to walk the length of the carpet, pivot at the end and return. Then, they would exit the runway into the dressing area to get ready for their next cue. In the rehearsals, they barely had enough time to change clothes let alone worry about hair and makeup.

The day of the show arrived, and the store was packed. As Mrs. Hannigan prepared to start, Beth was a nervous wreck. She considered herself lucky that all her friends had shown up to support her. Her mother and sister were also there. The music started, and Mrs. Hannigan began the show. Debbie walked out of the curtains first, then another girl, then...

"Go!" Nancy called to Beth, and she stepped out of the dressing room onto the white carpet.

She walked in time to "Stayin' Alive" just like they had practiced for weeks.

Mrs. Hannigan read off an index card and gave all the information about the outfit she had chosen—everything but the price. The retail cost was astronomical. Beth smiled down at her friends and family seated in the audience, and they waved to her as she passed by. Beth's stomach fluttered with nervousness and excitement. She loved the clothes and felt good in them. As she strutted and focused on not tripping, she spotted quite a few of her regular customers in the audience. Kids from her lunch table at school were also there, along with Brian and Charlie. Her former camp director came to watch with her homeroom teacher, Mrs. Hart. She kept her chin up and tried not to be distracted.

Beth reached the end of the carpet where she would pivot and turn to head back to the dressing area. She caught sight of a familiar figure and almost stumbled, her eyes widening.

Danny stood near the store's entrance in his restaurant uniform, probably on his break from work. He looked at her without smiling. Beth was overcome with nerves. She hadn't seen him in five months! The adrenaline started pumping and her pulse quickened. She made the pivot and returned to the dressing area without tripping. In a rush, she was helped off with her clothes and dressed in a new outfit. The hairdresser came over and fussed with her hair. She checked her makeup and teeth in the mirror.

"Go...Go...GO!" Nancy yelled to her.

Beth was out on the runway again. Donna Summer's "Hot Stuff" played loudly. She passed her friends and flashed them a smile. As she approached the end of the carpet, she made eye contact with Danny. He winked at her. She lowered her eyes self-consciously and blushed.

Beth walked on air to the tune of "Funkytown." It was her third and final walk down the runway. Dammit. Danny no longer stood by the door. But her father did. Her gaze darted back and forth across the packed seats on each side of the runway and the crowd that stood at the entrance.

Danny was gone. Her stomach knotted, and a pain rose in her throat.

After the show, the store held a reception, and the girls had to wear the last outfit they had modeled. It wasn't easy wearing a mid-length wool, pleated plaid skirt, matching burgundy sweater, and leather cowboy boots in the middle of August. Beth felt like she would die from the heat even with the air conditioning on.

Her mother, father, and sister ate refreshments.

Her sister noticed her somber mood and asked, "Are you okay?"

Beth smiled and replied, "It's just really hot in here!"

Ann Marie searched her eyes but let it drop.

After her family was finished eating, they left the store.

Melissa, Jackie, Susan, and Lynne stayed longer to talk and shop. Beth told them about seeing Danny.

"Who does he think he is anyway?" Susan asked.

Melissa said he needed to get a life.

Beth was surprised by their responses. She was accustomed to her friends being excited for her whenever something good happened with Danny. She wasn't used to hearing negative comments about him.

She became sullen, but Lynne explained, "We all love you, Beth. We get upset over the way he hurts you. It hurts us to see you unhappy."

Beth hung her head, and the other girls waited for her response. Finally, she looked up, hugged them, and told them they were the best friends in the world. She meant every word.

Brian and Charlie came over and spoke to her and the girls for a hot minute, and then they hit the food table hard. Beth smiled to herself. She was sure they had come mostly for the free food.

She was glad when the show ended, and she was able to get out of her winter clothes.

~

The fashion show kicked off the official "back to school" shopping rush, so Beth worked long hours over the next two weeks. She found time at work to shop for herself, and some of her new clothes hung in her bedroom closet with the tags still on. The rest hung in a bag with the rest of the store layaways. She was exhausted from helping people with their requests, and her fingers were turning blue from handling so many pair of jeans.

Beth had accumulated quite a client list since she started working in March. The store paid the girls a small commission on the total dollar of sales they made. More and more people came in and asked for her. Several customers even came in from Mexico. They spent over two thousand dollars on clothes twice a year, and they took the jeans back across the border and sold them at a huge profit. Since Beth had two years of high school Spanish under her belt now, they always came to her for help. Her hard word had paid off. She scored a pay raise to $2.78 an hour. Pride in herself helped her deal with the pain of not having Danny in her life.

The Saturday before school began, customers packed the store. Mrs. Hannigan scheduled all the employees to work that day. The salesgirls ran around helping as many customers as they could at one time. Their constant trips back and forth to the stockroom began to wear the carpet away. Customers became frustrated because the store had sold out of the sizes they needed.

Brian stopped in to see her, but she was too busy to talk to him. Rocky had been in earlier to buy some new clothes. She was able to wait on him, but they couldn't talk long.

The store had been crazy busy for the past two weeks. Beth's head pounded, her feet hurt, and she was hungry. Nancy told her to take a break. Beth had the urge to hug her. Nancy never covered for anyone for any reason, and Beth certainly appreciated the gesture.

Beth went back to the break room and bought a Tab from the soda machine for 35 cents and a pack of peanut butter crackers for a quarter. She removed her slide-on heels and propped her feet up on another chair at the mini table. A coworker from the women's department came in at the same time. She immediately kicked her shoes off and groaned. The two shared the misery of being worked to death and in pain.

The fifteen-minute break was the shortest Beth had ever known. She had three more hours to go. Thank the Lord in heaven, she was off tomorrow and the day after. She stood up and put her shoes on, wincing at the pain. The other girl groaned out loud at Beth's tortured expression. She walked to the door, took a deep breath, and headed back to the floor. The place continued to be insanely busy for a couple of hours. Finally, a lull came. It was close to dinnertime, and people didn't usually shop at that time of day.

The salesgirls took advantage of being alone on the floor. Shoes were removed and placed strategically under a clothes rack. In case someone came in, they could be quickly slipped on. Beth only had one more hour on duty. Everyone was getting punchy and falling into fits of laughter for no good reason. Even Andrew from the men's department joined in their silliness.

Two young girls entered the shop. Debbie looked at Beth and rolled her eyes toward the customers. Beth got the message, squeezed her swollen feet back into the Candies and approached the girls.

"Hi, is there something special you are looking for?" she asked.

"Oh yes. I really need to buy some jeans," the short blonde said dramatically.

Beth got the size information she needed and guided the girls back to the bin area. Only one girl spoke, but the two exchanged looks and smiles often. Beth thought they were weird, but she was too tired to really be interested in what their deal was.

"I will need to try these on. My boyfriend is very particular. He loves looking at me in Levi's. I'll need to see if they are perfect."

Beth agreed she should try them on.

Both customers entered the dressing room. She and Debbie exchanged knowing looks. Debbie stuck her nose in the air and pranced around in an exaggerated hip sway walk. Beth giggled, and they chatted quietly while the customers were in the dressing room. Finally, the girls exited, and the short blonde walked towards Beth.

"These will be perfect. I may need to have them altered a bit. Does your seamstress here do that?"

"Yes, we will be happy to alter for you. There's no charge for the hem," Beth said helpfully. She looked at her watch. Only twenty-five minutes to go.

"I think I will need them altered about a quarter of an inch, don't you think?" she asked her friend while she looked at herself in the full-length mirror on the wall.

Her friend giggled under the palm of her hand.

What the hell is going on here? Beth wondered.

The girl continued to talk about her boyfriend...a lot. He liked her jeans to be a little tight and not too long. He loved her in pastel blue. The girls didn't seem to be in any hurry to be done shopping, and the night shift salesgirls started to come on to the floor.

"Is there anything else I can help you with?" Beth forced a smile at her customers.

"Well, I'd like to find some corduroys, but the fit has to be the same as these jeans. My boyfriend won't be happy if they aren't perfect."

By now, it was past the end of Beth's shift. Debbie was still there waiting. Beth was more than ready to leave work and sick of hearing this lunatic talk about her obsessive boyfriend who was concerned with how her ass looked in a pair of jeans.

"Well, might I suggest you come back with your boyfriend and let him help you decide?" Perfect solution. Hurray!

"I suppose I could do that. You know, you look awfully

familiar. Do you go to St. Mary's High School?"

"No, I go to C.R." Beth was going to cry if these girls didn't leave soon.

It was already twenty minutes after her shift. Her feet were swollen, and she could barely fit them into her shoes after removing them earlier.

"C.R.? Really? My boyfriend is from C.R. Maybe you know him. His name is Danny Mitchell."

Her friend tried to control her laughter and turned to walk away from the scene.

Beth's mind began to race. Danny's *girlfriend*? This is Danny's *girlfriend*? Then it hit her. This girl was trying to get to her. She came in the store to taunt her! Beth composed herself.

"Oh yeah, I knew Danny pretty well last year," Beth replied and struggled to maintain her decorum.

"Really? He and I met about two months ago, and we fell in love immediately. I just love the way he kisses. He's so good at it."

Beth smiled blankly at her as the girl's friend cracked up with laughter.

"Well, I put a leather coat on layaway for him for Valentine's Day. I love the smell of leather, and I think Danny would like to get that. Don't you?" the girl continued her merciless assault.

Beth nodded. *She's talking about Valentine's Day in August! What's up with this girl?* She couldn't believe Danny dated this piece of work.

"I want to make Valentine's Day special for him. I have a feeling Danny will be very romantic on Valentine's Day."

This stupid girl just wouldn't quit.

Beth stared blankly at her, and her anger rose to a boiling point.

"Come on, Dena, we need to go," her friend finally spoke. She darted a wary glance at Beth.

Debbie and the other night shift girls had walked over

near them after hearing the conversation. They stood close to Beth in a protective manner.

Dena's friend appeared nervous about making a scene.

Beth fumed, and she was sure her eyes flashed with anger. Who the hell did this chick think she was? Why was she being so nasty to her? She didn't even know her, for Christ's sake.

Self-talk time. *Don't do it, Beth. She isn't worth it...Don't do it, Beth...Beth! Don't...*

Harnessing her fury, Beth smiled fake-sweetly at Dena. "You're absolutely right. Danny does love to celebrate Valentine's Day. Last year he gave me a diamond ring. It was sweet and *extremely* romantic."

There! Trump card, checkmate, I win! Beth thought as Dena's eyes widened and her mouth dropped open. Beth sneered back at her, blinking her long lashes in pretend innocence.

Debbie and the other night shift girls smiled.

"Ouch," Anne said as she shook her right hand as if it had been burned.

Dena looked at her friend and said, "Let's get out of here."

The girls hurried back to the dressing room. Dena quickly removed the jeans and changed back into her clothes. The two walked out with Dena in the lead.

The other girl ran to catch up and put her arm around her. "Are you alright, Dena?"

"Bitch!" Dena yelled as she stomped up the steps into the men's department and towards the exit.

Heat spread over Beth's face, and she turned to face her coworkers. Debbie walked over to her and held out her palm. Beth slapped it soundly.

"Way to go, Beth! What was that anyway?" Debbie's brow wrinkled.

Beth had no idea, and the four stood and marveled over the audacity of the girl.

"Well, I suppose she'll run to Danny and tell him I was

bragging about getting a diamond. I'll look like the idiot." Beth nibbled her bottom lip.

Debbie put her arm around Beth. "Honey, that little thing won't say a word to him about this. I can promise you that. Even if she does, and he doesn't see through her little act, then he doesn't deserve you."

Beth smiled and said goodbye to the other girls as she and Debbie limped on their blistered feet to the break room to clock out.

CHAPTER 24

Beth went over to Jackie's house the next day. The other three girls were already there. They decided to hang out in Jackie's room and be lazy. Her room was on the second floor of her parents' home. It was a split-level house, and her mother had her room set up like a teenager's dream. Her bed and dresser were on one side. A window faced the front street directly over the roof of the porch. That was Jackie's emergency exit when she needed to sneak out. On the other side of the room was a lounge set made from huge pillows and a small wicker couch and chair. A huge stereo sat on a shelf on the opposite wall.

Beth parked herself on the floor, removed her shoes, and propped her bare feet up on the chair next to Lynne.

"Ew! Look at your feet, Beth!" Lynne said a little too loudly.

Her feet were terribly blistered and still swollen from the week she had just been through at work.

The girls expressed different levels of "Ew," and Susan told her to put her feet down.

Beth lowered her swollen feet, her eyes tearing as they throbbed with pain.

Jackie went to the bathroom located off the side of the lounge area and returned with a small hand towel soaked in water and rung dry.

She wrapped it around Beth's feet and said, "Put this on them for a while. I think the damp, cold towel will help."

Beth sat back against the bed and sighed. She opened one eye and looked at the girls. "Do I look as bad as I feel?" she asked with a chuckle.

They laughed at Beth as she sat with a cold, wet towel

wrapped around her feet.

It felt like heaven, and she thanked Jackie every ten seconds or so.

The girls decided they would head out to "The Boat" on Jackson's Farm the next day for a picnic. Jackie would drive her mother's station wagon. It was their last official day of summer before their junior year began.

They spent the rest of the day hanging out in Jackie's bedroom, discussing their expectations for the next school year.

The cold, damp towel worked wonders on Beth's swollen feet, and she continued the treatment when she got home.

The following morning, Jackie picked up Beth around ten thirty. They stopped at a sub shop across from the high school and picked up sandwiches, sodas, and a large bag of chips. Jackie stopped at Chester Black's Bar and bought a fifth of Bacardi. Jackie had developed a crush on the handsome bartender. Lynne and Susan worked up the nerve to go inside with her. Melissa and Beth waited in the car. Soon, they were driving toward The Boat.

In the daylight, it wasn't a scary place. The girls arranged logs in a circle in front of the dilapidated sky-blue rowboat. Beth spread the patchwork quilt she had used at the beach on the grassy area near the logs. They slathered on sunscreen and wore bathing suit tops to get a tan. They wore shorts in case someone came and chased them off the property. Melissa brought her battery-operated radio, and the dial was turned to a rock station from Philadelphia. They enjoyed the privacy of the surrounding woods, and they drank too much too soon. Lynne began to cry and tell them how much she loved them. She hugged them, and the other girls laughed at her drunkenness.

The radio station played, "Another Little Piece of My Heart" by Janis Joplin, and a drunken Jackie did an outrageously funny impersonation. The girls screamed and rolled with laughter which made her act even more dramatically.

Beth performed as Cher singing "Half-Breed." Susan did a dance routine she had made up in fifth grade to "Respect." Lynne could not have been more convincing as Gladys Knight as she sang along with "Midnight Train to Georgia." Melissa refused to be a part of the show. She said her contribution would be as a supporter, laughing and giving standing ovations.

They ate their lunches and finished off the Bacardi, and then they played Truth or Dare. Jackie talked about her parents' separation, and the mood turned serious.

She picked at the grass as she spoke. "My dad has a whole other family that I didn't know about. My mom knew about the affair but only just found out they had a child together. She kicked him out. They screamed at each other, and he refused to go until my mom pulled a knife out of the kitchen drawer and threatened him."

The girls stared at her wide-eyed as Jackie continued, "It was so scary! My dad held his hands up and left without taking his clothes or anything else. My little brother and I watched as my mom fell to the floor sobbing."

Beth and Lynne had tears rolling down their faces, and Susan reached out and touched Jackie's arm to comfort her. Melissa looked pained, knowing full well what family problems were like. Jackie didn't shed a tear. However, she appeared heartbroken as she shared the sad details. But then her features twisted into defiance, she straightened her back, and said, "I'm glad the son of a bitch is finally gone. Mom should have kicked him out a long time ago." The girls stared at her for several seconds.

Melissa wiped her eyes and let out a sigh. "My mother was in rehab for thirty days last month."

"I didn't know you were home alone. You should've come and stayed with us," Beth said.

"Eric was there with me," she said as if it weren't a big deal.

The rest of the girls glanced at one another, and Beth

thought it was strange for her to be virtually living with her boyfriend. She was a sophomore in high school, for heaven's sake.

"Is your mother okay with that?" Beth gently asked.

"I don't give a damn what my mother thinks. She's still working as a waitress at The Back Door disco club, so I doubt she will stay sober, but for the past two weeks things have been weird. My mother cries and apologizes to me all the time. She told me she didn't think it was a good idea for Eric to be living at our house, and then implied he wasn't good for me." Melissa paused and ripped up some grass, enclosing it in her fist. "How dare she pass judgement on Eric? I told her he is the *only* one who has been there for me. My mother relented and allowed him to stay." She scattered the grass on the ground.

No one said anything for a while, and Beth didn't know what to say to her friend.

"How are you and Eric doing?" Lynne broke the awkward silence.

"Great. I love him so much," Melissa said, and her friends smiled.

Susan chimed in, "I know how you both feel. The circumstances are different but similar. My parents divorced and my dad left town four years ago, and we haven't seen him since. It hurts that he doesn't care about me or my sister. Mom is remarried, and my stepdad is ok I guess, but he has three kids and they live with us, too. My sister and I had to move to the basement so they could have the bedrooms upstairs." She began to cry.

Obviously, she missed her dad and her old life. The girls became teary-eyed again, feeling compassion for their friend.

"Thank God you have Tyler," Jackie said, sounding a bit envious.

"He's really wonderful. My mom likes him too and that helps.

Beth felt a pang of envy.

Lynne remained quiet as the others spoke.

Beth thought about her family. She had been angry with her parents over Danny for so long she had lost touch with what was important. She loved them, and they loved her. She also made a mental note to be more kind and helpful around the house and to go next door to visit her grandmother more often.

The day grew late, and they packed up their things and climbed back in the station wagon.

As the girls drove back to town, the mood in the car was pensive. They were sharing more and more and becoming more dependent on each other. It was comforting to Beth to have them in her life. She hugged each girl goodbye when she was dropped off at her home.

CHAPTER 25

Junior Year
1978-1979

The Return
Though I got home, how late, how late!
So I get home it will compensate,
Better will be the ecstasy,
That they have done expecting me,
When, night descending, dumb and dark,
They hear my unexpected knock.
Transporting must the moment be,
Brewed from decades of agony!
Emily Dickinson

The evening before her junior year began Beth went to her mother. "Guess what I want to do right now?"

Her mother looked up from *Chesapeake*, the James Michener novel she was currently reading. "What, honey?"

Beth stood silent, slanted her head and grinned.

"Beth, it's 6:45! It's too late to get into redecorating your bedroom. We can do it this weekend, okay?"

"Let me do it, Mom, please? I promise if you don't like it, I will change it back. I want to switch my full-size bed with the twin bed in the sewing room, though. Is that okay?"

Her mother stared at her, her lips pressed tightly together. After a few moments, she said, "Okay. I trust you will do a great job of arranging things. Do what you want, but I'm tired and don't want to hear a lot of thumping and bumping."

Beth jumped up and down and clapped as if she were Lynne.

She headed upstairs and recruited her dad to help her move the beds. Within a couple of hours, she finished transforming her room. It looked more like an efficiency apartment than a teenager's bedroom. The twin bed hugged the wall like a couch, and she added pillows of different shapes and sizes she'd found in the basement. She returned the pastel-colored quilt to her bed and moved all the plants back to the living room. Beth moved her desk under the window that faced her grandmother's house. She peeked out her bedroom window, and her grandmother was standing at her kitchen window doing dishes. Beth knocked loudly on the window and waved to get her attention. Her grandmother looked up and waved with her yellow Playtex-gloved hand.

Beth turned the stereo on and played a Bob Seger album. Her room had more open space with the bed change, and she could dance around the center. She pulled her C.R. memorabilia out of the closet and positioned it around her dresser mirror. Then she removed the black and white television and put it in the sewing room. She hardly ever watched it, and no one had a black and white TV anymore anyway. Her bare walls bothered her. She searched the sewing room and the spare bedroom. She found two framed floral prints that matched the quilt on her bed and hung them on one wall.

Beth also found a dried floral wreath in the basement that once hung on the front door. She hung it on the center of the other wall in addition to an old cork bulletin board that used to belong to her sister. She covered the shelves with older lace doilies she found in the linen closet, and she moved her candles to the shelf with one ivy plant in the center. The final touch—a table lamp she unearthed in the basement. Her father made it in wood shop when he was in high school. It was made of pine wood stained in a rich tan color. Beth couldn't believe she had never seen it there before. It was perfect, and she loved it. She put it on the nightstand next to her clock radio.

A soft knock sounded at her door around nine thirty. "Beth, it's me. Can I come in?" her mother asked.

Convinced her mom would love the changes, Beth smiled as she opened the door.

"What have you done? You look like the cat that swallowed the mouse." Her mom chuckled.

Beth moved aside, and her mother walked in and admired each wall. She wore a long dark blue velvet robe. Beth liked the feel of it and wished she had one like it.

"I love it, Beth. It looks like an adult's room," she said quietly as she walked over and touched the old lamp and childhood pictures of her and her husband.

"So, you're ready for another school year?" her mother asked.

Beth nodded, excitement thrumming through her veins.

~

The first week at school was a fun one for Beth. She had at least one class with each of her friends. That first weekend, the girls tried to make plans to head out to "The Boat," as it was now affectionately referred to, on Jackson Farm, but Beth had to work until nine. Susan had plans with Tyler to attend an AC/DC concert. Melissa had a new job at the local bowling alley and then had plans with Eric after work. He was taking her to a restaurant in Maryland for steamed crabs and shrimp. She was going to try to order wine with dinner and hoped she wouldn't get carded.

"I look eighteen, don't you think?" she asked Beth on the phone.

"Yes, of course you do," Beth said.

Lynne told Beth she would wait for her to get off work and pick her up at nine thirty. The two went to Burger Chef, and since there was no one there that they knew, they turned around and headed up the highway to the new Arthur Treacher's Fish and Chips Restaurant. People in town were excited about the new restaurant, and it was crowded. Lynne approached the counter and smiled at the boy ready to take her order.

The boy blushed and asked, "Can I help you?"

Beth poked Lynne in the back from behind to let her know she was aware the guy noticed her. He was cute and his name pin said "Joey."

After taking Lynne's order, he waited on Beth.

She asked him, "So Joey, what high school do you go to?"

"Smythfield."

He leaned over the counter in an apparent attempt to get closer to Lynne. She leaned in towards him, and Beth waited for one of them to say something else. Neither said anything, so Beth stated, "Well, we go to C.R. This is my friend Lynne Angellini. I'm Beth O'Brien."

Joey nodded, grinning shyly.

Beth sighed, deeply frustrated by the lack of language these two were displaying.

"We're juniors. What grade are you in?" Beth asked.

"I'm a junior, too. My name is Joey Griffin." He glanced over at Lynne again.

She continued to grin at him. He ducked his head in embarrassment but then looked at her again, this time right into her eyes. There was another awkward long pause as they waited for their orders. Beth grew impatient, but her eyes lit up when she read the sign on the counter.

"There's a sign that says you're accepting applications."

"Oh yeah, we're looking for some help."

Beth raised her brows and tightened her lips at Lynne, but Lynne kept staring at Joey.

"May I have an application please?"

Lynne looked sharply at Beth. "What do you need an application for?"

"Well, I don't need one, but I might have a friend who needs a job."

It finally registered, and Lynne said dramatically, "Oh! Oh, yes." Lynne focused on Joey. "Is this a good place to work? Will they work with you on schedules? I'm a cheerleader so I need to work around that."

Joey nodded as he grabbed an application off the back counter and handed it to Beth with their food order.

Beth turned to Joey. "Thanks for the food and the info."

Joey seemed to forget Beth was there. He turned to Lynne again and said, "The manager is great about working schedules around school and school activities." He smiled at her and she smiled back and said, "Thank you."

"You're welcome," he said.

Lynne waved goodbye, and he waved back. The girls took their fried fish and chips and Cokes and left. It didn't take long for Beth to convince Lynne to fill out the application. They ate at The Boat, and Beth helped Lynne with the form. She started working there exactly one week later.

School went well for Beth. Her classes were interesting, and her grades were the best she'd ever earned. She was thrilled she didn't have to take any more Math classes. Instead, she signed up for a creative writing class with Mrs. Castle. Beth loved writing and did a lot of it on her own. She particularly like writing short stories and poetry. Her former ninth grade teacher had really encouraged her, and she looked forward to having her again.

Beth couldn't wait for lunch. The student council had updated the music in the cafeteria jukebox to include Tom Petty and the Heartbreakers, Foreigner, The Commodores, REO Speed Wagon, Rick James, and a dance mix from the movie "Grease." The cafeteria manager added a salad bar to the lunch choices. Beth, Melissa, and Jackie hit the salad bar line every day and then got chocolate shakes from the ala cart line. It was mostly the same lunch crowd from sophomore year, but this year Susan and Lynne had lunch at a different time. Beth still sat next to Kenny Nixon. It was familiar and comfortable. Even the topics of conversation were the same. The girls were sick of hearing the boys speculate on who was a virgin and who wasn't.

Rocky sat at a table across from Beth's. He made "puppy dog" eyes at her all the time and had started coming around to visit her at work more frequently. Beth was flattered but still not interested. So, when he asked her out, she again refused.

He's a nice guy. What's wrong with me?

CHAPTER 26

Beth went to work on the following Friday night, and her coworkers told her some guy named Danny had called for her. The news stunned Beth, and she thought Debbie and Ann were playing a cruel joke. Debbie swore to God that she wasn't joking.

"I told him you'd be working tonight, and he said he would call back."

Every time the phone rang, Beth waited nervously for the intercom to pop and tell her there was a call for her. Finally, Andrew from the Men's department called over the intercom and informed her she had a call on line one. Beth walked up to the phone and pressed the button.

"Hello?" Her heart was beating wildly, but she forced herself to remain calm.

"Hi Beth, this is Danny."

"Hey Danny, how are you?" She casually masked her jitters.

"I'm good. I'd like to see you if it's okay. I want to tell you something, and it's important. Will you meet me at Pippy's tonight?"

She had plans to go to The Boat with the girls. Jackie had bought a newly released cassette tape of Bad Company, and they were going to listen to it. Beth had the quilt and soda in her trunk. The girls were counting on her to be there. They would be upset if she blew them off after one phone call from Danny.

"I can't meet you tonight, but I can on Saturday after two."

"Oh, okay. I will meet you at Pippy's at 2:15."

"See you then." She fought to keep from losing her cool.

"Bye, Beth." He ended the call, and she hung up the phone, barely able to contain her excitement.

Debbie was standing by the counter in the mostly empty store. Beth looked at her anxiously and said, "Danny wants me to meet him. He has something to tell me. I just don't know if I should go."

"Of course, you should, silly." Debbie gave her a sympathetic smile. "He probably dumped that piece of work he was dating and realized you're the one for him."

Beth grinned at her friend's positivity, but the tense sensation in her gut warned her this would not go well. She wanted to see him, but it never ended well with Danny.

Still, she couldn't stop thinking of him. She mentioned the phone call to her friends at The Boat, and they weren't that enthusiastic about her meeting him, but it didn't surprise her. They didn't understand why she continued to pine for him after the way he'd treated her. She could hardly sleep that night, and the next morning, she fussed with her hair and makeup before heading to work. The day seemed to drag on forever. Finally, she rushed to clock out.

She drove to Pippy's, and Danny waited for her at the entrance. He looked good, and that really annoyed her. Her pulse pounded on the side of her neck. He walked her to a booth and smiled at her as they sat.

"It's good to see you again." He sounded sincere.

Beth smiled and tried to look calm, but inside her heart was jumping like a cat on a hot tin roof. She had decided to wear a Gunny Sack dress because the pale lavender color complemented her skin tone. The platform sandals that laced at her ankles had killed her feet all day, but they looked good. She fretted over what Danny thought of her appearance.

She was so anxious, she blurted, "Just tell me what you want, Danny."

Beth had convinced herself Danny would tell her that "Dena aka Customer from Hell" was pregnant and the two would be married soon. She braced herself for the heartbreak.

He cleared his throat. "Remember when I told you I was quitting college and that I felt like I would die if I had to stay around here and work in the restaurant?"

Beth nodded for him to continue.

"Well, I'm moving. I'm going to California and I probably won't be back."

She waited for him to add that "Customer from Hell" would be with him. He didn't, and it seemed clear Dena was out of the picture.

Beth stared at him and calmly said, "Danny, what in the world are you going to do in California?"

He sat up quickly, excitement dancing over his features. "I'm going to work in a surf shop and give surfing lessons. I already have a job lined up. The place is listed on the new pro surf circuit nationwide. I get room and board at a beachfront hotel, and I get paid a weekly salary, too."

Beth blinked at him several times but said nothing.

Feeling the need to flee, she slid out of the booth as the waitress walked up with a tray containing water glasses and menus.

"That's great, Danny, have a great time."

Danny quickly reached out to her and took her hand. "Please sit down for a minute. I don't want you to leave yet," he said softly.

Her heart hammered in her chest. The waitress blocked her escape route and gave her a pleading look as if she felt sorry for Danny. Beth obliged the waitress and him by returning to her seat.

Danny waited for the waitress to leave before speaking.

"I wanted you to hear it from me," he said, searching Beth's face.

She glanced away and wouldn't make eye contact with him. *Damn him*, she thought. When she realized he was waiting for her to say something else, she looked into his eyes and asked, "Why?"

Danny told her how excited he was for the chance to work on the pro surf circuit and what a great opportunity it would be for him. He added that there were a lot of people with money getting into the sport, and there were some celebrities who were frequent visitors to the resort where he would be giving lessons.

She listened to him speak as the waitress brought a pitcher of Coke. He paused as the waitress took their pizza order. Once she left, he continued to talk, and Beth sat silently listening and looking at him. A million questions screamed in her brain. He finally stopped talking, an expectant gleam in his eyes.

"I understand all that, but why did you think I needed to hear all this from *you*?" she asked dismissively.

Danny narrowed his eyes. "I don't know, Beth. I wanted to see you I guess."

"Why?" She held his gaze.

"I don't know why," he said, quietly diverting his attention to the table.

Beth grew fidgety, and that urge to flee resurfaced. *If he doesn't say something...*

After a few moments, he rubbed the back of his neck and stared into her eyes. "Look Beth, you still have two years of high school to finish. When you do finish high school, you'll probably go off to college. You'll meet someone there who is much better for you than I am. You are the kind of girl that a guy would marry. I'm not ready to get married, and I don't know if I ever will be."

Beth's mind flashed to a memory. She was sitting on the kitchen counter in a Winnie the Pooh flannel nightgown with pin curls in her hair. She was about six years old, and her mother held a spoon with bitter yellow liquid in it trying to convince her that swallowing the liquid might taste bad, but it was the best thing for her. It would make her feel better.

Her father entered the kitchen and said, "Just swallow the damn stuff."

Jolted back to the present, Beth's entire body tensed. She didn't want to *marry* Danny. Well, not yet anyway. She just wanted to be with him. Why wasn't he asking her to go with him? Because she would, that's why. He was killing her. He enjoyed killing her. Well, if he thought he would get the pleasure of watching her cry over him, he was sorely mistaken.

"Say something," He slanted his head, his eyes imploring.

What was she supposed to say? A year ago, he expected her to say, "Bye Danny, have a great time in college." Now it was "Bye Danny, enjoy your life in California." This was worse. He had paid no attention to her the entire year he was home. Now he was going away for the second time and he wanted her *blessing*?

Meeting Danny had been a disaster. There was no hope for them, even from the beginning. She was miserable because she was stuck in high school, and here he was leaving again, this time for good. Before long he would be screwing Farrah Fawcett in some beach resort in a heart-shaped hot tub.

She had lost her appetite. Beth rose and brought her purse up to her shoulder.

"Bye Danny, have a great time in California."

As she began to walk away, she paused. She looked back at him, and he had his head hung low.

"Danny?" He looked up as she said, "I really do hope you enjoy yourself and find some happiness. I hope this move helps you figure out what you really want. You're always telling me how young I am, but you're the one who needs to grow up." She turned and left the restaurant.

Beth cried the entire drive home. It dawned on her she had never asked him exactly when he planned to leave. She second-guessed how she had responded to him. Maybe if she had said nice things, cried, and hugged him, he would have changed his mind. Probably not. She got home and went straight to her bedroom. Whenever there was a problem with Danny, she found she just couldn't stand being around her parents.

She got on the phone and called Lynne, Melissa, Jackie, and Susan for an "Emergency Girl Summit" at The Boat. Melissa drove Eric's car and picked everyone up. The girls knew Beth had a meeting with Danny, and she was sure they were dying to know what happened. Beth had told them not to bring any sad songs, only hard rock stuff to play. Jackie had gotten red wine this time, and the girls drank it in Dixie cups while listening to Aerosmith, AC/DC, Molly Hatchett, and Lynyrd Skynyrd.

Beth sobbed as she recreated her encounter with Danny. She got very drunk and cried a lot.

The girls were kind and sympathetic for a while, but Susan finally got frustrated with her self-pity. She put the girls in stitches by saying, "Beth, you need to get yourself together. You look like shit."

After falling over with laughter, Beth got sick from the wine. They decided to stay put until she felt better. It took Beth a full two hours to recover. She had a massive headache and moaned pathetically the entire ride home.

"We sure have had a lot of these summits lately," Melissa said as she drove. "First Susan and Tyler, then Lynne and Joey. Now Beth and Danny. Makes me nervous that Eric and I might be next."

"Well, I guess we're lucky to have each other when we need one," Beth said.

She was grateful for her friends. They shared a special bond. Their philosophy of life was pretty simple.

Survive the blows life dealt by ignoring them as much as possible when you can. And when you can't? Call your friends.

CHAPTER 27

On Monday morning, Beth still felt a little rough around the edges. Her stomach had been upset since she'd drunk too much wine on Saturday night. While driving to school with her neighbor, she told her carpooling friend about Danny meeting her at Pippy's and about the drunk fest at The Boat. Her neighbor laughed at her for still having a hangover.

Beth continued to carpool to and from school with her neighbor. Forking up a little gas money was a small price to pay for the benefit of not riding the school bus. Beth's parents wouldn't allow her to buy a car, but she was generally able to use theirs for work and to see her friends. If she'd been a boy, her father would have let her get a car, she had no doubts about that. She voiced her objections to her mother often but never once said anything to her father. Her mother was obviously unsuccessful at convincing him otherwise, so it was useless to complain.

Beth and her neighbor sat at the stop sign at the end of their street and waited for a long line of morning traffic to pass. It seemed to take forever to pull out onto the main street which headed into town. A silver Mustang headed towards them. It was Danny's car, and her stomach did the familiar flip. She used to get excited and happy about that feeling, but today it annoyed the hell out of her.

"That's Danny right there," she said calmly.

Beth pointed, and they watched as he passed directly in front of them. He stared straight ahead, possibly heading to the restaurant. Clearly, he hadn't left for California yet, and he hadn't told her when he would. Beth rolled her eyes and scrunched down in the seat. She hoped he would leave before they ran into each other again. With a slight squeal of the wheels, the two girls pulled onto the road and finally headed towards the high school.

They arrived at school and walked in opposite directions. Beth went to the Center where she ran into Rocky. He asked her if he could speak with her a minute. They found a quiet corner away from the crowd.

"Look Beth, I know things didn't go well for us the last time and I know we agreed to be friends, but I would really like to try again. The last time it was totally my fault and I know why. I promise I won't pressure you again. We'll take all the time you need."

Beth appreciated his candor and sincerity, though she'd heard this same speech a thousand times. She looked at him, this time considering his proposition.

An expectant gleam sparked in his eyes. "Will you let me take you out on Friday?"

She decided to give him a chance. Why not? Danny was out of the picture now. She smiled at Rocky and nodded.

"Is that a yes?" Rocky raised an eyebrow.

She nodded again, and he jumped for joy.

"You won't be sorry, Beth," he said excitedly.

Rocky grabbed her face with both hands and kissed her on the forehead.

Their friends let out whoops of approval, and heat crept up Beth's cheeks. Apparently, they had some eavesdroppers.

Rocky met her every day in the Center after that, and his eyes lit up when he saw her. He always asked, "How are you doing? You look beautiful." He left her sweet notes taped to her locker throughout the day.

Touched and flattered by his attentions, Beth warmed up to him now that she wasn't worried about being pressured into having sex. On Friday, he left a single rose taped to her locker with a note that read *I can't wait to see you tonight.*

She was charmed by his attentions and wondered why she still thought about Danny all the time. Rocky treated her way better than Danny had. He wasn't moody and difficult like Danny, and she appreciated the easiness of their relationship. But still...she didn't get that rush of heat when she saw him. Could he be her true and lasting love? She didn't think so. It was self-talk time. *Danny isn't good for you. Rocky is much better.* Maybe eventually she would believe it.

That night, Rocky and Beth arrived early at Susan's house to help set up for a party. Susan's mom and stepdad were away for the weekend, and her stepbrothers and stepsister were out of town visiting their aunt. Susan and her sister were home alone. Rocky and Tyler were busy setting up the keg. The four got an early start on the beer and danced around the house to Cheap Trick as they waited for the other guests to arrive.

Soon a crowd filled the house. Rocky stayed by Beth's side for about an hour. Eventually the beer and his friends around the keg called him away. It didn't matter. Beth had fun talking with the girls. Melissa came for a little while but had to leave after a half hour to meet Eric at home.

As the four girls talked and drank the draft beer from plastic cups, Rocky flirted with Beth from across the room. He would stare at her or wink, and every half hour or so, he walked up to her and complimented her, kissed, and hugged her. Her stomach fluttered at the attention, and her face heated with pleasure. Beth was warming up to Rocky. She loved the way he let everyone know exactly how he felt about her. The two never played head games with each other. Beth thought, *That's a real plus for Rocky. Danny was always messing with my mind!*

Brian Knight arrived with Charlie's older brother, Joe.

Beth approached him and asked, "How's Charlie? I haven't seen him in ages."

Joe replied, "He was working as a bartender near the university. I think he will be returning to town soon. Charlie doesn't seem happy there."

Beth looked at Joe with concern. She liked Charlie and hated to think of him being unhappy. She said, "Maybe he will feel better once he's home. Please tell him I asked about him."

Joe flashed her a smile and answered, "I will. He'll be glad to hear it. I think he's always had a crush on you." He winked at her and Beth blushed.

Brian leaned forward at that moment and kissed Beth on the cheek saying, "Hello, Gorgeous."

Beth smiled at him and they chatted for a moment. She wondered why he never had a girl with him. As handsome as he was, she thought he would have several.

Rocky walked over, and Joe said, "Hello."

First, Rocky nodded at him and then at Brian. The three spoke briefly about the performance of this year's soccer team and then Joe and Brian excused themselves to find beer.

"You certainly ran up to him quickly," Rocky said in an accusing tone.

Beth gaped at him. She had never seen Rocky jealous about anyone, even Danny, the one boy he probably should have been worried about. Rocky had a scowl on his face, and his shoulders appeared tense beneath his shirt.

She pointed toward Brian. "You mean him?"

Rocky nodded, his eyes narrowing. The house was packed, and Beth didn't want to argue with him. She tried to be serious and remorseful, but she began to giggle. It was funny to her that Rocky was jealous of Brian.

People continued to pour through the door and some bumped into them on their way to the keg. Rocky rolled his eyes at her as she laughed uncontrollably. She covered her mouth with her hand and tried to stop. Finally, she leaned in to kiss him squarely on the mouth, smiling and laughing at the same time. Rocky widened his gaze, and his body relaxed.

Apparently, she had caught him off guard. She kissed him to silence him but also to reassure him. She was flattered by his jealousy. The kiss grew more intense and became more passionate as she held her body closely against him. A cool breeze passed over them as the front door opened again. Beth could have sworn Rocky smelled just like Danny at that moment. She kept her eyes tightly closed to prolong the sensation.

Beth continued to kiss Rocky. His cheeks were smooth like Danny's, and she reached up to touch them with her fingertips. Her body instinctively reacted to the scent and feel of him. She was a little disoriented when she finally pulled back from him.

"Can you do that again?" Rocky said with a roughness in his voice.

Beth stood and stared at him, stunned by her own actions and reactions. He smiled at her, and she lowered her eyes with embarrassment. When she looked up at Rocky, she saw Danny out of the corner of her eye. When had he come in? Immediately, her stomach dropped, and she wondered if Danny had seen her kiss Rocky. She struggled to keep her emotions off her face. Luckily, Rocky was so overcome by the kiss, he didn't notice.

"I want you to hear something. Let's go." He pointed toward the door.

Beth went back to the bedroom and got her coat and purse. She was happy to get out of there. She said a quick "goodbye" to her friends, and soon she was seated in Rocky's car.

He jumped in the driver's seat and told her he made a cassette tape for her. Rocky started the car, and they drove off. He reached over, took Beth's hand in his, and pulled her close to him. She willingly moved to the exact spot where she used to sit.

The first song came on. Rocky had the volume up slightly. "A gypsy wind is blowing warm tonight. The sky is starlit, and the moon is bright. And still you're telling me you have to go, before you leave there's something you should know..."

Beth's gaze traveled from Rocky's face to the blackness

of the night sky outside his window. She closed her eyes, thought of Danny, and wondered if he'd left the party. She had to stop this. Would she waste more time thinking about Danny or would she put her whole self into this relationship with Rocky? Danny was never coming back. Why would he? He hated the restaurant, this town, and anyone in it.

She decided then and there. She was done with Danny. Beth leaned forward and kissed Rocky on the cheek. He was surprised and turned to smile at her. They drove to Burger Chef and pulled into the parking lot.

CHAPTER 28

For the next few months, Beth and Rocky were an item. Beth was deep "in like." A few people gave her warnings about him. Kenny Nixon didn't like Rocky at all and made comments about him every day at the lunch table. Beth ignored him, thinking he would get over it. Brian Knight continued to visit her at the store. He liked Rocky but told her he wasn't sure how he felt about the two of them dating again. She was surprised. Usually Brian was supportive of her.

Charlie had moved back to town, and she saw him frequently at the store, too. He never indicated one way or the other how he felt about her and Rocky. Even though everyone assumed they were, Beth and Rocky weren't officially a steady couple. Rocky hadn't given her his class ring yet.

True to his word, Rocky didn't pressure her for sex. Beth began to appreciate that enough to have it affect her decision. She was one of the last virgins in her class because she'd always felt that having sex was special, and she wanted to do it with someone she loved. She had assumed her first time would be with Danny, but now she was beginning to accept that she and Danny were over. Thankfully, having sex was no longer a major topic at lunch. Everyone assumed that everyone else had "done it" by now.

Today, the Center was loud, and the energy was palpable. Christmas vacation was beginning after today. Brian was having a party at his house on Friday night. He asked Beth to let everyone know so she spread the word in the Center and to her friends at the store. A large crowd planned to attend. Brian graduated in 1976, and his football buddies from '75 would be there along with their former teammates in the class of '77. Anyone still attending C.R. who knew him was also invited.

On Friday, Beth and Rocky headed out on the back roads. They passed Jackson Farm to Brian's rented house and pulled up in the dark. Beth counted over two hundred people. The bonfires roared on each side of the driveway. A crowd of kids cheered and danced to the loud live music coming from the garage as Rocky parked the car. They smiled at each other with anticipation. Rocky held Beth's hand as they joined the gathering. Beth had been to a party at Brian's old apartment in town but had not been out here since he moved.

A line formed at the beer keg set up in the garage next to the band. The kids hanging in the garage were a rougher crowd than Beth was used to. Some of them had been known to use drugs, and she knew several had a police record. Melissa's boyfriend, Eric, stood with his roommates and friends, but Melissa wasn't there because she had to work at the bowling alley until eleven. Eric made eye contact with Beth, smiled, and nodded a hello to her. He eyes were red and glassy, and he appeared to be stoned. She waved politely.

Rocky suggested they check out who was inside. They entered the packed house, and Beth was excited to see their friends. Lynne had brought Joey Griffin. Beth was happy to see him because he made Lynne so happy. Susan sat on Tyler's lap, and she was already a little tipsy. Jackie was with a date from Dullard High School. From inside the house, Beth could hear the loud rock music from outside. She decided to stay in the house.

Rocky and Beth chatted and laughed as they socialized with their friends and flirted with each other. He either held her hand or had his arm around her the whole time. It was early in the evening, and things geared up. Liquor bottles of all kinds jammed the counter in the kitchen in addition to another keg. Coke and 7 Up filled two coolers.

They left the kitchen, and Beth admired Brian's Christmas decorations. An artificial tree sat in front of the large glass window.

Brian saw Beth, smiled, and approached her. Pretty buzzed from the alcohol, he slurred slightly and said, "Hey, Gorgeous. I hoped you'd come tonight."

Rocky stiffened slightly at the greeting but soon relaxed when Beth reached over to take hold of his hand while speaking to Brian.

She said, "With this many people, a lot of shit could happen, Brian. How many beers have you had?"

"Okay, I get it. No need to nag me further."

Rocky and Brian chatted together as Beth excused herself to get Brian a can of soda from the kitchen.

Mike and Billy stood in the kitchen along with people Beth had not seen in ages. Billy was home from college for the holidays and seemed happy to see her. Mike was drunk but pleasant. Beth decided to be careful not to talk too long to any one guy. Rocky might get jealous.

She returned with the Coke and handed the can to Brian. He thanked her.

Rocky and Brian spied some friends and headed towards them. Beth looked around and located her girlfriends nearby. Rocky chatted with a group of guys but caught her eye and winked at her from across the room. She smiled back and resumed a conversation with her friends. It occurred to her again how easy their relationship felt compared to the constant tension she'd always felt with Danny.

The party continued with driving force for a couple of hours.

Eventually the band finished, and the activity outside wound down. Many of the kids left, and the band members sat around the fire very, very drunk, and extremely high. Several girls reclined around them at the bonfire as they passed joints to one another. Brian asked the band to pack it up and head out.

Beth became more relaxed once the group left. She wasn't used to being around people using drugs, and it made her uncomfortable.

Inside the house, about forty people remained. A little after twelve, the drunk guys in the kitchen started to play "Quarters." The girls circled around to watch, but the boys became unbearably intoxicated. Some of them went outside to vomit and attempt to recover near the fire in the back yard. Rocky approached Beth several times to talk to her, letting her know he wasn't drunk. This pleased her. She drank a little at first but stopped once she saw the people around her becoming more and more intoxicated or stoned. Beth was worried about the drugs and the sheer number of people still there. She figured it was best to keep her wits about her. A couple of fights had already occurred outside at different times throughout the evening. She worried the police would show up and then call her parents.

Despite the feeling of dread that haunted her, Beth convinced herself it would be okay now. The rowdy band members had left, and the drunk kids had been taken home. It was nice to spend time with her old friends and talk with the girls. They hadn't been getting together as often lately, and she missed them. The front door opened as someone came in from outside, and a wind gust blew snow into the house.

"It's snowing!" Jackie shouted.

Everyone walked outside and stood in the snow. Brian had put music on the stereo, but it stopped, and the snowfall caused a deafening silence. Rocky kissed Beth softly on the lips. She drew away from Rocky and saw Brian looking at them, and she smiled at him. He smiled back. Beth thought he needed a girlfriend.

More guests left and Beth, Rocky, and her friends returned inside to help clean up the house and sober up.

Brian asked Beth to put on a pot of coffee. Thinking he was joking, she laughed at him. He looked back, his brows drawn together.

"I don't know how to make coffee," she explained.

Brian shook his head in disbelief. He and Rocky chuckled.

"I'll do it," Rocky said.

Beth immediately felt young and incompetent, and she was determined to have her mother show her how to make coffee tomorrow morning. Rocky told her he wanted to leave in a half hour, and she agreed.

The group inside now numbered about fifteen. Rocky went to the kitchen to make coffee as Brian and the others bagged up the trash. Beth went down the hallway to the bathroom.

Inside, she couldn't find the light switch, and it was pitch black. She reached around in the dark until she found a chain hanging in the center of the bathroom. Beth pulled it, and the light came on. She checked her face in the mirror. Her cheeks were red from the cold wind. Snowflakes had fallen and melted, leaving water droplets on her hair. She found a towel on a rack and dried her hair off. As she began to use the toilet, she heard a commotion in the hallway near the bathroom. Oh great. There must be another fight. There were more loud bumps and thumps but no spoken words. Beth quickly finished peeing and pulled up her jeans. She stayed inside the bathroom for fear of walking into the scuffle. She kept the bathroom door locked and listened intently.

Brian's voice called out in a half whisper, half shout, "Mitchell! Mitchell!" His voice softened as he got closer to the bathroom door.

Beth was propelled into a state of shock. Danny's here? *What on earth is going on?* Her heart began to pummel inside her chest, and she stayed where she was. What would she do if he saw her? Would she be able to ignore him, or would she fall apart? And what about Rocky? What would he think? Her mind and her heart raced as she pressed her ear to the door.

Brian continued, "Hold on to him." There were more shuffles and bumps. "Let go of me, goddamn it!" Danny said loudly. The noises stopped, and she heard Danny's pathetic voice.

"I just want to see her. I just want to talk to her. That's all!" He stood just outside the bathroom door.

She placed the palm of her hand on the door, closed her eyes and leaned her forehead against it. Beth continued to eavesdrop.

"You're too drunk, and this is not the time. She's here with someone else," Brian said.

"Fuck him!" Danny groaned loudly, and the scuffling began again. She heard Charlie's voice now. He must have come with Danny. He and Billy said, "Settle down, man. Just chill out."

Brian spoke in a stern, loud voice. "If you bother her tonight, I will kick your ass. Got it?"

Beth pictured him standing with his chest out. There was no audible response. Everything grew quiet. Beth's entire body shook with panic, and she wondered where Rocky was. Had he heard any of this?

Danny assured the guys he would be alright.

"Stay calm, Danny," Brian warned. "Leave her alone. You've done enough, don't you think? Let it be."

The noises faded from the bathroom door and moved down the hallway back to the main area of the house, and then there was silence. Beth felt like she was going to throw up. She took several deep breaths to calm herself down, but she was a wreck knowing Danny was out there. She thought she would never see him again, but he must have come home for Christmas.

She glanced in the mirror and smoothed her hair down and pinched her cheeks. A bottle of scope stood on the counter, and Beth quickly swished some in her mouth, telling herself Brian wouldn't mind. She spat, licked her lips, and straightened her jeans and sweater. She worked up every ounce of nerve she had and left the restroom. She walked slowly down the long hallway towards the front living room and scanned the room from side to side. Rocky must still be in the kitchen cleaning up. She didn't see Danny either, thank God. She took a deep breath and headed towards the kitchen.

She looked straight ahead and locked eyes with Danny. He leaned back against the bookcase directly in front of her. Charlie, Mike, and Billy stood around him, but he had a direct view of Beth and stared at her intently. Beth returned the stare as she paused trying to decide what to do. Adrenaline began to pulse through her veins, and she wanted to dart out the front door. Instead, she froze and stood perfectly still. Danny pushed his body away from the bookcase and walked through his friends encircling him. He headed toward her with a purpose. Dizziness hit Beth as he moved toward her.

Billy saw where Danny was headed and called out to his friend, "Hey, Hey! Get back here!"

The remaining guests turned to see what Billy was yelling about. Brian entered the room from the kitchen, but Danny had already reached Beth. She looked up into his eyes. He stared at her for a long, silent moment and without blinking or speaking, he leaned in and kissed her deeply.

Beth felt like she was suffocating. Danny put his arms around her, bending her backwards. She remained perfectly still. For a moment, she was lost. He assaulted her senses all at once. Beth was so happy. She never thought she would ever see him again. His body next to hers sent an electrifying tingle coursing through her body. Danny's kiss tasted of beer and the leftover sweet flavor of Scope. His smell and his love overwhelmed her, and she started to respond to the kiss. The moment she did, Tyler said, "Aww, man," and she quickly collected herself. Rocky stood in the kitchen doorway, watching.

Beth pulled back from Danny, but he held on to her. She attempted to wiggle free, and Danny held tightly and refused to let go. He said things to her that made no sense. They contradicted every one of his actions toward her. "I've missed you. I need you." He was drunk out of his mind.

Brian walked up and put his hand on Danny's arm. In a soft but deadly serious voice, he said, "Let her go, man."

Danny closed his eyes, and the two stopped struggling. However, he didn't let go. Beth watched Danny's face intently. He looked sad, miserable, unhappy. She wished everyone would just go away.

Beth looked over at Brian. He stood tall, and his chest was thrust out in a "take charge" posture. She didn't want him to hit Danny. She shook her head at him. Everyone in the room was silent as they watched the exchange. Brian didn't move but glanced away from her and removed his hand from Danny's shoulder. His jaw clenched, and the muscles in it were flexing. He conveyed to her with his eyes that Danny was walking on thin ice. Danny opened his eyes and looked at her. He slowly let go. From the corner of her eye, Beth could see Rocky still standing in the doorway. His hurt expression stabbed at her chest.

Beth turned and walked silently down the hallway. Away from Danny, away from Rocky, Brian, and everyone else. Lynne, Jackie, and Susan ran after her, but she walked away from them, too, as she headed towards the back bedroom of the house. She silently picked up her coat and purse. She passed her friends in the hallway without looking at them or even saying a word. When she returned to the front room, Danny was seated, slumped over in a recliner. Brian continued to keep a close eye on him, and Charlie had a protective hold on Danny's shoulder. *God bless Charlie*, she thought. Everyone watched her, but she couldn't make eye contact with anyone except Rocky.

"Please, take me home," she begged with tears in her eyes.

Rocky's hurt expression changed to determination as he walked her out of the house to the car. Beth heard Danny come out the front door calling her name. She heard the muffled sounds of Brian and Charlie's voices calming him down, persuading him to come back inside. Rage seemed to envelop Rocky as he turned on his heel and marched swiftly back to Danny. He gave Danny one punch to the side of the face and easily knocked him down. It happened so fast that the other guys had no time to react.

Widening her eyes, Beth ran over but remained behind Rocky, too afraid to get closer.

Rocky leaned over Danny and said quietly, "If you ever touch her again, I will kill you."

Beth clamped her hand over her mouth and backed away toward the car. Danny made sounds she couldn't interpret. Was he sobbing? Oh God, Oh God, don't let him be hurt. Rocky returned to the car, helped her inside and took her home. Neither of them mentioned the incident on the way home as they each tried to come to terms with what had happened.

CHAPTER 29

Christmas week came and went. Rocky and Beth didn't attend any more parties that week, and he didn't call Beth for several days. Beth was a wreck. She knew Rocky was angry, but she wasn't sure how to fix it. She fully understood that Danny had been drunk, and his behavior didn't mean he wanted to be with her. Did he think she was stupid? How many times did he need to hurt her for her to learn? She was determined to fix this with Rocky. After a few days of feeling miserable, she worked up the nerve to call him. His mother answered the phone, and Beth politely asked to speak to him.

"Hello," he muttered.

Beth shut her eyes and said hopefully, "Rocky, can we talk? Please?"

"About what?" he asked coldly. "About my girlfriend kissing another guy right in front of me?"

"Rocky, please. That's not what happened."

"That's what it looked like to me." His frosty tone made her shudder.

Beth realized this wasn't going to be easy. Rocky tended to be jealous anyway, and she understood how he must be feeling. She'd been jealous about Danny taking Kathy to the Prom, and she hadn't even seen them kissing, for Heaven's sake!

Beth took a deep breath and asked, "Can you come over? Can we go somewhere? Can we please talk?"

Rocky was silent for several seconds, then said, "I can't imagine what you can possible say to make me feel better but, yeah, we can talk. I'll pick you up in fifteen minutes.

Beth told her mother she and Rocky were going out for a

soda and when he pulled in, Beth ran out and got in the car. Nether said anything as Rocky drove to the high school and they pulled into the empty parking lot. He left the ignition on because it was so cold, but he put the car in park and turned to look at her.

"What do you want to tell me? It better be good..."

Beth took a deep, shaky breath. "I didn't kiss him. He kissed me. I don't care about Danny, honestly I don't."

Rocky exploded in anger, his fists clenching, "What the hell, Beth? It didn't look like you stopped him to me! Am I supposed to believe what I saw with my own eyes didn't happen?"

"I was stunned. I had no idea what was happening, and I also had no idea how to handle it! I didn't want him to kiss me! He was drunk out of his mind, you know that."

"Yeah, but you weren't, were you? It took you an awfully long time to react! How the hell do you think it feels to see another guy kissing my girlfriend?" He raged and slammed his fist against the steering wheel.

Beth flinched and her eyes welled up with tears. Quietly, she said, "It must feel awful. I am so, so sorry. I wasn't equipped to handle it. I just wasn't. I handled it badly, I did, but it's not Danny I'm concerned about. It's you. Please forgive me."

A look of misery crossed his face. He was angry, yes, but Beth could see he was also very, very hurt. That made her feel awful.

"Rocky, I promise you nothing like that will ever happen again. I don't want to be with Danny. I want to be with you." She reached out and put her hand over his.

Rocky shook his head at first. She could see he was indecisive. His eyes were shiny with tears. He looked at her intensely as if he were trying to read her mind. She held his gaze and silently willed him to forgive her. After a few minutes, he shrugged as if in defeat, and pulled her to him and kissed her softly, lovingly.

"Don't ever make me feel that way again," he said.

"I won't." She leaned in and kissed him again.

After the party episode, the girls were worried that Beth would break up with Rocky and pine after Danny. She surprised them all when she didn't. At The Boat, she refused to discuss what had happened. When the party was mentioned, she narrowed her eyes at them and straightened her lips. They got the message and dropped the subject.

Rocky invited Beth to his house for dinner on Sunday. She had been to his house often but was still nervous around his family. She was afraid she would embarrass herself or Rocky and that maybe they wouldn't like her. Rocky told her she was being irrational. They loved her. Maybe, but this was the first time she would eat with them. Rocky had two older brothers. The oldest lived at home and his girlfriend lived there, too. Beth had never met the other brother because he lived farther away. Rocky picked her up and assured her everything would be fine. When Beth entered the house, it smelled wonderful.

Mrs. Mulinero cooked up a well-orchestrated storm in the kitchen—a huge Italian meal that included salad, breads, wine, and several different dishes Beth had never heard of. This was not any Ragu spaghetti or lasagna meal. It was fabulously authentic Italian. She'd even made the pasta by hand.

Rocky's father and brother sat in front of the television watching football. His father sat back in a recliner, and his brother had his girlfriend draped over him on the couch. Mr. Mulinero greeted Beth when she came in and then handed an empty Schlitz can to Rocky and said, "Hey get me another, would ya?"

Beth said hello to his brother and girlfriend. They smiled at her but didn't speak. They looked high as kites.

Beth followed Rocky into the kitchen. Mrs. Mulinero

chatted with them as she worked, asking Beth about her family, her job, and school. Rocky took a beer to his father.

Beth asked, "Is there anything I can do to help?"

Mrs. Mulinero stopped working and looked around the kitchen. She assessed the situation and asked Beth to fill the glasses with ice and water and place them in the dining room. Beth was happy to help and wanted to do more. Rocky helped his mother in the kitchen while Beth filled the glasses. Then the two of them sat at the kitchen table and stayed out of his mother's way. Eventually the meal was served at the large table. The television was visible from the dining room table, and it stayed on during the meal. Beth's father would never have allowed that.

Mrs. Mulinero had timed the meal perfectly to take place during halftime. The woman's skill amazed Beth, but no one else seemed to notice. The meal was delicious, and the atmosphere was easy as they chatted and teased one another. Mrs. Mulinero told Beth she wished she could meet her other son, but he lived and worked in Florida. She began to tear up and cry. The remaining men at the table paused and looked at one another. Beth scanned the table for reactions. His brother's girlfriend continued to eat.

Mr. Mulinero patted his wife's hand. "Alright now. He'll be home to visit soon enough."

She dabbed her eyes and collected herself.

Mr. Mulinero looked at Beth and said, "She hasn't been right since the Pope died in September."

Thinking it was a joke, Beth smiled, until she noticed his serious expression. She said, "Oh. I'm so sorry."

"I'll get over it soon enough," his wife replied. "What did your family do when they heard the news?" she asked Beth.

Beth swallowed the bite of "eggplant something" she was eating and said, "I don't really remember. It was a few months ago, right? We're not Catholic. It was terrible though. I do remember watching it on the news."

Everyone paused and stared at her. Beth looked around

the table, wondering what she had said to get this kind of re-action. She looked at Rocky.

He stared at his mother wide eyed. "Ma?"

Mrs. Mulinero continued to stare unblinking at Beth.

"Ma?" Rocky repeated, his eyebrows raised.

His brother and girlfriend shared a knowing look and re-turned to their food. Mr. Mulinero placed his napkin on the table, thanked his wife for the meal and started to stand.

"Sit still," Mrs. Mulinero ordered her husband as she held up her finger to drive home the point.

He sat again.

"You aren't Catholic?" she asked in a hard tone Beth had never heard from her before.

"No, I was raised Methodist."

Mrs. Mulinero sat and stared at Beth for several mo-ments. She stood up and ran to the kitchen in tears.

Mr. Mulinero looked severely at Rocky and pointed his butter knife at his son. "You should've known better than this."

"Ma?" Rocky called after her as he got up and went to the kitchen.

Beth froze in her seat. She had never been more uncom-fortable in her life. Thank God the potheads weren't staring at her but were instead scarfing down the last of the bread. Rocky returned to the dining room. Beth pleaded silently with him for an explanation. He nodded towards his bed-room, and Beth followed him. Boys would never have been allowed in her room at home. But girls were allowed here it seemed.

"What's going on? Is she upset because I'm not Catholic?"

"Yes. But she will get over it," he said, despite the look of uncertainty on his face.

"Let's go Rocky, please," she begged.

"No, we're not leaving. This is stupid and..."

"I want to go home now, Rocky. Beth compressed her lips and crossed her arms over her chest. She needed time to process and react. Apparently, everyone did. Rocky relented and agreed to drive her home. He apologized to her the entire way.

Beth walked in her house to find her parents finishing up their own meal in the kitchen. She stomped in the kitchen, plopped her purse on the counter, and turned around to face them.

"What's the matter?" her mother asked.

"Rocky's mother doesn't approve of us dating...she doesn't approve of me!"

Her father said, "That's ridiculous, Beth. Why on earth wouldn't she approve of you? Did something happen?"

"It's because I'm not Catholic!"

Her parents shared a knowing look, and then her father smiled at her. "Beth, she'll get over that."

"No, she won't! You should have seen the way she looked at me. It was as if I were Rosemary's Baby or something!"

"For Heaven's sake, Beth, don't be so dramatic," her mother said. "Your father's right. She'll come around."

Beth heard the front door open and a "yoo hoo!" It was her grandmother. She walked in and everyone said hello, but Beth couldn't hide her emotions.

"Is there something going on?" she asked as she sat at the table.

Before either of her parents could speak, Beth blurted, "Rocky's parents hate me because I'm not Catholic. It was awful, Mom Mom! We were at the table and she asked what we were doing when the Pope died. I'm only glad I remembered it from the news a couple months ago. I told her I wasn't Catholic, and she flipped!"

"I'm sure the woman did not 'flip,'" Beth's mother interjected calmly.

"She ran out of the room crying and wouldn't come back out of the kitchen!"

Her parents looked at each other, concern etched on their brows.

Her grandmother said, "I'm sure they won't forbid him to see you over it. What did Rocky say to you after all that?"

"Oh, Rocky wouldn't care if I were from Mars and worshiped the rings around Saturn!"

Her grandmother chuckled.

"May I make a suggestion?" her grandmother asked Beth's father.

"Go ahead," her father grunted.

"Well, it seems to me the woman is strong in her faith. To understand it, you need to learn about the religion itself."

"Mom, you're not suggesting Beth become a Catholic?" her mother asked in disbelief.

"No, not at all! I am suggesting she make an effort. There is only one Catholic church in town—St. Mary's. Perhaps you could go check it out. I'm sure the woman would be pleased to see you there."

Beth was nervous about the idea. She didn't want to convert to Catholicism, and she didn't want Mrs. Mulinero to think she did. Her father didn't think it was such a bad idea. Her mother didn't approve of the idea at all. Beth could tell by her silence. Her children were raised in the church in which she grew up, and there would be no deviation from that. The subject dropped, and the four talked of other things.

After dinner, Beth went to her room. She picked up the phone and called Lynne Angellini. She asked if she could go to Sunday mass with her and her family next weekend. Lynne was thrilled and said they would love to have her attend church with them. Mass was at eight a.m. Good Lord, the crack of dawn! Methodists wouldn't even have Sunday school that early let alone a whole service.

She prepared for bed and said prayers that night asking for grace and blessings on everyone, especially her family members and friends. She said a special prayer for Danny and promised to stop cussing so much. "Amen." She lay awake in bed thinking how awful it was to have Rocky's parents disapprove of her for reasons she couldn't help. It was uncomfortable. It seemed too much to handle, almost not worth the effort to keep dating him if this were to become a huge deal. Now she understood how Danny felt when her parents disapproved of him. It was miserable and gave her a pit in her stomach.

That next week Rocky tried to pretend everything was fine and that nothing had happened. Beth told him about her plans to go to St. Mary's on Sunday. He hugged and kissed her deeply, relieved that she was trying.

That Saturday the two went to the movies to see *Alien*. The theater was packed, and the movie caused Beth to scream out loud. Rocky laughed at her. Afterwards, they headed to Pippy's for pizza. The place was full. Susan and Tyler were there with Lynne and Joey. They squeezed two seats up to the table to make room for Beth and Rocky. It was almost ten o'clock when they left the restaurant. They got in Rocky's car, and he put the radio on. The music and holding his hand gave her the reassurance she needed. She was nervous about attending church in the morning and how his mother would react to seeing her there.

Beth looked around. "Where are we going?"

"I know a perfect place where we will be left alone, and we can listen to the music."

They traveled down a long country road in a part of town she didn't know well. It was pitch black outside. Rocky turned onto a narrow dirt road. The sign read "Nature Preserve. Absolutely No Visitors After Dark. Violators will be prosecuted for trespassing."

Beth grew concerned. She looked out the front window and couldn't see anything but a small piece of dirt road and tall weeds on each side of it.

"I don't know about this, Rocky. I don't want to get in trouble."

"It will be fine, Beth," he said gently.

He stopped the car, then turned off the engine and headlights. The cassette player was still on, and the dash lights shone a bright fluorescent green.

Rocky reached behind the front seat and pulled out a small Playmate cooler. Inside the cooler was a half pint of Beefeaters Gin, a small bottle of tonic water, and a lime cut up in wedges in a Ziplock baggy. Two beautiful cocktail glasses were chilling on the ice. Beth's eyes widened. She watched the expression on his face as he fixed each of them a drink. Rocky handed her a glass and stared into her eyes. He had a determined look in his gaze. Beth nervously took a big gulp, suddenly understanding why they were there. She had never had gin before, and it was bitter but not unpleasant.

Rocky put the tape he had made in the stereo and turned the volume up. He slowly began to kiss her. "Feel Like Making Love" started to play. Beth returned his kisses but wasn't relaxed. She gently pushed him away and took another sip of her drink.

It would almost be a relief to finally get it over with, Beth thought. The alcohol warmed her face, and her arms and legs relaxed slightly.

Rocky watched her face intently. Her heart pounding, Beth leaned in, and the kissing resumed. Much too soon, Rocky placed his hand up her sweater.

Beth took hold of his hand and pushed it away. "Wait, Rocky, wait."

He pulled away from her and tried not to get angry or frustrated with her. She could see his restraint in his face.

"I'm afraid," she tried to explain.

"I won't hurt you, Beth, and I won't get you pregnant. I brought everything we could possibly need." He pointed to the back seat.

She looked behind the seat and saw a pillow and blanket on the floor. She looked back at him. He reached forward and pulled open the glove compartment. He had a small box of condoms in there.

"You need to relax," he said.

"I know that," she said sharply and bit her bottom lip. "Fix me another drink and just give me a minute."

He did as she asked and waited for her to drink it.

"What time is it?" Beth asked.

"It's ten thirty."

She didn't have to be home until twelve thirty. Beth craned her head and looked out of all the windows in the car.

"What if someone sees us?" she asked, glancing back at him.

"There's no one out here, Beth. No one is going to see us. I swear." A tic pulsed in his jaw.

"Okay," she said in an audible whisper. "Okay, but if I say stop, you have to swear you will."

"I swear." Rocky smiled as he pulled the pillow and blanket to the front seat and moved the front seat back as far as it would go.

He kissed her neck and placed the pillow on her side door. Beth was trying to ignore the fact that he was putting the pillow down, adjusting the blanket, taking a condom out of the glove compartment, and kissing her all at the same time. She felt an urge to laugh but thought better of it. Nope, she was going to giggle. He would be so pissed!

Just focus on the music, focus on the music, Beth thought. "Born to Run" finished up. "Whoa oh, oh, oh, oh."

It worked. She didn't have the urge to laugh anymore. A new song began, "Hello it's me, I've thought about us for a long, long time. Maybe I think too much but something's wrong, there's something here that doesn't last too long. Maybe I shouldn't think of you as mine..."

Beth thought of Danny. Immediately, guilt seized her, and she focused on the fact that Rocky was kissing her. He flipped the armrest up and allowed her the room to lie down on the seat with her head on the pillow. Beth moved closer to him as they kissed. Her body shook with nerves and she wanted to cry. She was so scared, unsure if this was the right thing to do. She felt pressured but he had been patient with her. She tried desperately to relax. Despite her doubts, she was determined to see it through.

She pulled herself over to the right to make room for his leg. Her left hand pressed against the bottom seat cushion for support. Something poked into her finger from inside the cushion seam.

"Ow!" she said.

Rocky ignored her and repositioned her so he could lean up and remove her sweater. She moved with him but gingerly felt around the area where something had pricked her finger. She felt a piece of cardboard and lifted it up behind Rocky's back and head. It was a Polaroid picture. Her eyes widened in shock.

"Oh my God!" She pushed him up and away from her.

"What? What's wrong?" he asked with a furrowed brow.

Beth sat straight up staring at a photo of a rather large red-headed girl wearing a black teddy with black garters and stockings. Her breasts were exposed, and she wore large amounts of makeup. She smiled seductively at the camera. *At Rocky?*

"Who is this, Rocky?" she demanded.

He glanced at the photo, his eyes widened, and he leaned back in the driver's seat and put his head back.

"Rocky?" Beth asked louder.

He paused for a long time before he spoke. "She is nobody. I swear. She is no one you need to be concerned about."

Rocky pushed down the power button on his side window, grabbed the picture from Beth, and flung it out the window. "See? I swear. It's nothing. She put it there on purpose so you would find it. I will never see her again I promise."

Beth was stunned, and she opened her mouth wide.

"She knows about me?" She glowered at him. "Am I sitting and laying in her spot here, Rocky? Is this the place you bring her?"

He didn't say anything. Beth stared at him for a moment and then sat back and shook her head.

"I can't believe this," she said quietly.

Beth wasn't sure whether to scream or cry. Her pride was wounded.

He pinched the bridge of his nose. "I'm so sorry, Beth. I promise it's over. I want to be with you."

"Take me home, Rocky," she demanded.

Now she knew why he hadn't been pressuring her for sex. He'd been dropping her off and heading out here with "Miss Porn-Lucille Ball."

Rocky slammed the palm of his hand against the steering wheel.

"Don't get mad at me! I'm not the one riding around with nude photos of my sex partners. Were you going to ask me for one, too?" Beth yelled at the top of her lungs.

"Don't be stupid, Beth," he said quietly.

She grabbed the condom, threw it back in the glove compartment, and slammed it shut. Then she opened the glove compartment again with a jerk. She picked up the box of condoms, read the front panel, and counted the contents. Sure enough, the box wasn't even full. She held it up as further evidence. He just sat still and waited for her to finish letting him have it. Beth slammed the glove box shut, grabbed the pillow and blanket, and threw them in the back seat out of sight.

Rocky leaned down slowly and pulled the seat forward. "I don't know what else to say."

"Don't talk to me anymore."

Beth turned her body away from him and stared out the side window.

"I was going to give this to you tonight."

Beth looked at his hand holding his class ring and then at him, "Oh that would've been rich, huh?"

Rocky jammed the ring in his pants pocket, turned the ignition with a jerk, and took off swerving backwards down the dirt road. He put his car in drive and squealed his tires. Once out on the highway, the tape still played. "Will you meet me in the middle? Will you meet me in the end? Will you love me just a little? Just enough to show you care?"

Rocky slammed his finger on the eject button and pushed down the power button for her window. Cold air rushed in at her face, and her hair to flew back. Rocky tossed the tape out her window. Beth folded her arms sharply in front of her and rolled her eyes. *Jerk*, she thought viciously. She remembered hearing those exact words of warning long ago. Wasn't it from Danny? She thought about how mad Rocky got when Danny kissed her and how bad she felt. Asshole! She was NOT going to church for him or his stupid mother the next day.

CHAPTER 30

It took exactly one day for the news of Rocky and Beth's breakup to work through the social scene at C.R. Beth was glad it was quick and virtually painless like ripping off a Band-Aid. She didn't cry or call the girls for a summit. She was angry and refused to let anyone know how much he'd hurt her. Rocky had made her believe she was special and important, and it turned out she wasn't of much value to him at all. Her self-esteem hit a new low. There was nothing anyone could say or do to help her regain her former confidence and fun-loving demeanor.

Rocky left a note for her in her locker. It was three pages long and explained how sorry he was. Beth didn't believe a word of it. She ignored him completely for a month. Rocky finally gave up and began to date other girls. In the fifth and final note, Rocky accused her of acting as if she didn't care. She was glad he thought that. It served him right.

It was almost time for the Valentine's Day dance, and Beth wasn't the only one with relationship problems. Melissa had broken up with Eric, and she called a summit.

When they arrived at The Boat, Melissa explained why she called the meeting. "My mother started drinking again a few weeks ago. She calls me names and hits me when she flies into a rage...which is often now that she's drinking again. I started staying with Eric and his friends because I couldn't stand it. Mom came out to get me the other night and was so remorseful that I agreed to go home with her. Eric didn't want me to go, but she is my mother... I didn't know what to do. I spent one night at home and realized I'd made a mistake. I rode my bike out to his house the next morning and took him coffee. When I got there, he was leaning into the window of a yellow Volkswagen bug, passionately kissing some girl. He didn't even see me!" Melissa's face twisted into an anguished grimace, and Beth's heart ached for her.

The girls had some choice names for him, and they hugged Melissa as she cried.

"I can't believe I wasted so much time on him." Melissa sighed.

She drank most of the bottle of brandy they'd brought with them. Susan held Melissa's long auburn hair as she threw up into the pond, and Lynne fixed a glass of ice water for her to drink.

Jackie stood close and told her she was going to be okay. She said all the things Melissa needed to hear at that moment. "Eric is a jerk, you deserve better. You are beautiful and someone else will think so, too."

Beth had radio detail and quickly changed the station when "Bridge Over Troubled Water" came on. No sad songs. Only rock was allowed. The radio began to play "Flirtin' With Disaster."

Surprisingly, the night ended without anyone getting too drunk or injured.

The next day, Melissa came over to visit Beth. She listened as Melissa sobbed again. Beth's mother knocked softly on the door and opened it.

"Is everything alright?" she asked.

Beth said Melissa was upset but that everything was fine. Her mother nodded and left them to their privacy.

Jackie ended up at Beth's house, too, complaining about her crush on Al, the bartender at Chester Black's Bar. She had been turning herself inside out trying to get him to ask for her number, but so far, he wasn't taking the bait.

"I really wish he would ask me out," Jackie told the girls. "Do you think it's because he thinks I'm too young? I flirt with him all the time, but nothing I do seems to work."

"I don't know. Why don't you write your phone number down and hand it to him along with your real name?" Melissa asked. "You can give it to him the next time you go into the bar."

"But what if he's just not interested?" Jackie fretted. "Anyway, then he would know I have a fake ID. We'd lose our only way to buy liquor."

"Susan could get Tyler to get us beer and wine from the liquor store over the Maryland line. He's eighteen now. He'd do anything for Susan," Beth said.

Jackie took a deep breath and nodded in agreement then smiled and said, "I guess it's worth a try. Can you guys come with me?"

The girls agreed to support their friend.

The following Saturday, Susan called Beth in a panic. "I need you guys at The Boat. I'll drive."

Beth had planned to go see *Animal House* at the theater with her work friends that night but cancelled her plans. She was the last one picked up.

They headed out on the familiar back road towards Chester Black's Bar to purchase alcohol for their summit. They pulled into the parking lot, and Jackie privately showed Melissa and Beth a half index card with her name and phone number written in beautiful cursive handwriting. She had sprayed it with perfume for added effect. Melissa and Beth followed Jackie inside and smiled from ear to ear. Al the bartender was going be surprised tonight. He appeared smitten with Jackie whenever she came in.

Susan and Lynne waited in the car. The girls were completely confident walking in the bar now and no longer broke out in a sweat. The regular patrons knew them, just not by name. They would shout out "Hello Girls" and always ask them to stay and hang out with them. The girls would laugh and say, "Maybe another time, guys."

Jackie's long hair was unbound, and she wore her blouse unbuttoned to show her cleavage. Her jeans were tight and her heels high. She looked amazing. Beth felt a little guilty doing something fun when Susan was distraught and in need of a summit.

"Girls!" the men shouted as they walked in the front door.

"Hey, Hey!" Jackie said confidently.

Melissa and Beth smiled and waved to the dark figures seated at the bar. Jackie strutted her way to the back. Beth marveled at her confidence.

"Hey Al," Jackie said.

Al was wiping the counter and smiled at her. He always seemed to be amused by her.

"What'll it be tonight?" he asked.

The girls bought two six-packs of Michelob Light in bottles and a pint of premixed screwdriver cocktail. Jackie handed him the money and slipped the index card with it. Al took the money, and the three watched him. Beth sensed Jackie's nervousness.

He put the money on the register drawer, paused, and then moved the small white paper to the top of the money pile. His eyebrows rose as he read it.

He turned and looked at Jackie. "Jackie, huh?"

She smiled seductively at him.

Damn, she is good! Beth was a little envious of her confident friend.

Al nodded a few times as he smiled and handed Jackie the bag of alcohol.

"I'll be talking to you soon, Jackie Basile." He winked at her.

Melissa smacked Beth on the leg in excitement, and the three turned to leave. Once outside, they hugged their friend and got their jewelry tangled in her long curly hair. This made them laugh hysterically as they tried to untangle themselves.

The girls got back to the car, and they rode off. Susan remained silent about why she called a summit during the drive to The Boat.

They arrived, and she parked the car. Then she turned

around to face them all.

"I'm in so much trouble."

The panic in her voice was unusual for Susan and Beth knew it was serious. She and the others stared at Melissa, waiting for her to continue. Susan started sobbing.

Melissa and Beth looked at one another and said, "Uh-oh."

"Just tell us what happened," Lynne said in a calm voice.

Beth waited to hear her friend say she was pregnant, or had VD, or something equally as tragic.

"Tyler and I went out last night," she sobbed. "We went back to my house, and my mom and stepdad were in bed. We sat in the family room watching TV." Sniff, sniff, snort. "We took the afghan off the couch and laid on the floor. We were messing around and then we...we...fell asleep!" The crying reached a new level.

Jackie took over the conversation. "Did you get caught?"

"Not exactly." She wiped her eyes. "We never woke up, and this morning my stepdad got up early to go on a trip for work. I heard him making breakfast in the kitchen. He was slamming dishes around real loud."

A chorus of "Oh my Gods!" filled the car.

Jackie asked, "Did he see you in there?"

Susan nodded. "I'm sure he did! I'm sure of it."

"Did you have your clothes on?" Jackie asked.

Susan let out another sob.

"My pants were off and lying up on the couch!"

The girls looked at each other apprehensively.

"Sue! Oh my God! What are you going to do?" Lynne's eyes widened.

Are you sure he saw you? Beth asked.

"Yes!" Susan replied and began to cry again.

Lynne took in a sharp breath, and then Jackie said, "Susan, he won't bring it up. Do you hear me? Your parents will never talk to you about this, but if they do, you tell them nothing happened. You just continue to say nothing happened. No matter what they say. They might say they won't be mad at if you just tell the truth. Don't! They won't want to believe anything happened, and they will believe you—even if you lie."

All the girls stared at Jackie with gaping, awed expressions. She was a teenage genius, a Queen, really, when it came to dealing with parents and sex.

Susan finally calmed down after her third beer. The other girls drank the screwdrivers. Later, they ended up at Burger Chef eating fries and talking about Al Black, the bartender. Jackie filled in Lynne and Susan on the new developments with Al. Then the girls all spent the night at Jackie's. They smuggled the second six-pack into her house through the secret entrance up the tree and over the porch roof into her bedroom window. Beth was glad they could be a distraction for Susan. She shuddered. God, if she had been caught in a compromising position with a boy, her parents would ground her for the rest of her life.

CHAPTER 31

A week later, Beth went to the Valentine's Day Dance. She hated this time of year, but a boy from her grade had asked her to go, and she'd reluctantly said yes, even though he was only a friend. They triple dated with Jackie, Melissa, and their dates. None of the couples were romantically involved. They laughed, joked, and danced the night away. No drama at all. The group ended up in the basement at Melissa's house, watched *Saturday Night Live*, and cracked jokes until one in the morning. They vowed to be friends forever. Beth enjoyed the night way more than she thought she would.

A few weeks later at the lunch table, Kenny and the other boys who ate lunch with them were bragging about going to Highway 15 Drive-In the night before on "Penny A Pal" night. You only paid one regular admittance price, then everyone else in the car paid one cent.

"No way did they let you in! It's an X-rated theater," Beth said, her girlfriends shook their heads in disbelief.

"Well, we did, and we dare you to go." Kenny grinned broadly.

Beth slanted her head, not sure if he was serious.

"They won't go," Ron said.

"We'll bet that you won't go." Kenny raised his eyebrows.

Jackie chimed in, "What will you bet?"

The boys looked at one another and dug money out of their pockets. There was a total of $17.32 on the center of the lunch table.

"You're on!" Jackie smiled.

Beth and Melissa gaped at her. The other girls at the table squealed with delight.

"Oh no," Beth said. "Who's going to drive? None of us

have a car of our own, and we can't very well drive our parents' cars to an X-rated drive in!"

"You'll drive," Jackie said in a nonchalant manner. "No one will notice the car."

The girls started jumping in their seats and pleading with Beth to drive. She was stuck. Jackie always knew when Beth was nervous or afraid and then she forced her to face that fear, take the chance. She often made her miserable.

Beth looked at Kenny and gave him a dirty look. He laughed.

"You'll need to bring back the ticket stubs, so we know you actually paid and went in and...you need to go tonight," Kenny said.

They sealed the deal with handshakes all around. Beth shook her head in dismay and wondered what in the world she had gotten herself into.

That evening she got permission to use the car and headed around town to pick up her four friends and three more girls from the lunch table. Even in the station wagon, they were packed like sardines. Beth drove down Highway 15 about 8 miles south of their hometown and turned into the dirt lane. The potholes were severe, and the car rocked from side to side as they traveled down the lane. No one had alcohol in the car because Beth refused to allow it.

She drove toward the entrance, and a young guy sat in a small white booth up ahead. A wooden train track style gate ran across the path leading into the Drive-In.

Beth pulled up next to the booth. The fluorescent lighting didn't help hide the guy's acne as he ducked his head down to count how many people were in the car.

"Seven dollars. Are you all seventeen?" he asked them.

"Yes," Jackie lied loudly from the seat beside Beth.

"Good. You know you all have to be seventeen to go in?" The girls nodded.

Beth gave him their money. He handed her the ticket stubs and pushed a red button on the wall next to him. The gate went up, and Beth got nervous. She looked in the rear-view mirror at Lynne and Susan. They both appeared ashen like they might pass out. Jackie and Melissa laughed excitedly. Beth worked up her nerve and drove inside. The potholes were worse in the parking area than in the driveway.

Lynne fretted in the back seat. "Oh my God, I hope we don't get a flat tire."

The girls all yelled at her to shut up, and Beth got a sick feeling in her stomach. *I will get in so much trouble if I get caught.*

There were only five cars inside, and Beth pulled up to a speaker pole. The girls screamed and squealed as they reacted to what they saw on the screen. Beth was too busy dodging potholes to pay attention. She parked the car and turned the lights off. Damn it. She had parked too far from the speakerphone and couldn't reach it without climbing partway out the window. Beth refused to get out of the car for fear someone would see her and recognize her.

Jackie handed her the brown grocery bag that carried the snacks and sodas they'd purchased on the way. "Here, put this on."

Beth pulled the bag over her head, and the girls laughed hysterically, calling her "The Unknown Comic." She climbed out of the car, grabbed the speaker, and jumped back in the car screaming. The she hooked the speaker to the window and rolled the window up. She fumbled for the volume button. They girls carried on over what they were seeing. Finally, Beth turned the volume up. The woman moaned a lot, and a man's voice talked a streak of vulgarity.

"Oh my God!" the girls screamed.

Beth finally looked at the screen. The couple onscreen were having sex, and the sounds and language overwhelmed her. She wanted to die from embarrassment. They watched, and soon it was dead silent in the car. Each girl sat stunned and speechless. Melissa and Jackie laughed, falling into each other. Before long, the couple on screen switched positions.

The girls started to gag and scream. Jackie and Melissa were unable to recover from their laughter. Beth felt like she was going to throw up. She rolled down the window and threw the speaker on the ground next to the car.

Lynne yelled to her from the back seat, "We won the bet. We have the ticket stubs to prove it. Let's get the hell out of here!"

Everyone agreed. It was time to go.

Beth dropped off all the girls except Lynne, Jackie, Melissa, and Susan. Beth and her friends headed out to The Boat, stopping first at Chester Black's.

"I hate driving my parents' car here," Beth said while they waited for Jackie to return with two six-packs.

"Oh, you might as well let people see it at the seedy bar. They've already seen it at Highway 15!" Melissa said, cracking herself up.

Susan laughed, and Beth smiled but scrunched her brow as she looked out the window.

Jackie returned to the car more excited than usual.

"Guess what?" Jackie said as Beth took the bag from her hand and handed it over the back seat.

"What?"

"Al's cousin was in the bar tonight. I guess he saw you here one night and asked me where you were."

Beth smiled because Jackie was so thrilled about it.

"So, what did he say?" Susan asked.

"I was talking with Al, and this guy sitting at the bar next to me said, 'Where's your friend tonight?' I really didn't know which one of you he was talking about. Then he described you, Beth. He's really cute, too!"

Beth grinned as the girls batted their eyes and made kissing noises. They were so goofy.

That night at The Boat, Beth learned the details of each girl's sexual experiences, and they were surprised to learn she was still a virgin. They assumed she'd had sex with Rocky. While they munched on Doritos and drank, Beth finally told them what had happened with Rocky.

"I can't believe he did that!" Jackie said, her eyes wide. The other girls nodded and tsked.

Susan told her, "I'm glad you found out before you did anything. He wasn't right for you. You will know when the time is right. Don't settle."

"You sound like my mother." Beth laughed.

The other three chuckled at Susan, and she made a face at them.

The evening ended with the girls sleeping over at Jackie's. At 1:30 in the morning, Beth watched Jackie sneak out her bedroom window to meet Al. Her friend's nerve was never ending. She heard Al's car pull away from the house. In the morning, Jackie was sleeping soundly in her bed. Beth never heard her reenter the room.

On Monday, the boys at the lunch table were dying to know whether they followed through or not. None of them believed the girls had gone to the Drive-In and completed the dare. Jackie had kept the ticket stubs, but first she told the boys to put the money on the center of the table. They dug out their change and wrinkled dollar bills from their pants pockets and wallets. The girls maintained their somber faces.

"Okay, we've put our money on the table. It's time to prove it or lose it," Kenny said.

Jackie stood and searched through her wallet.

"I knew they wouldn't do it!"

"You are such babies!"

"Oh, come on!" the boys shouted as Jackie took her time.

She smiled sweetly and plopped the ticket stubs down onto the table. The girls screamed in victory, and the boys all moaned in defeat. Their loud shrieking caused quite a stir in the cafeteria. The assistant principal began walking toward the table. The group shushed one another.

"What's going on here?" the principal asked.

"Nothing, Mrs. Stackhouse. Everything's okay."

She glanced at Beth as if to ask "Really?"

Beth nodded.

The assistant principal gave a stern warning look to the boys. The table erupted in a flurry of silent giggles and shaking shoulders as she walked away.

CHAPTER 32

Spring would soon be upon them, and the seniors were out of control and more obnoxious with each day that passed. Rocky left Beth another note and tried to talk to her. Kenny Nixon kept reminding her what an asshole he was. A rumor spread around the school that a major event was supposed to take place in the cafeteria the day before spring vacation. No one knew what was going to happen, and Beth was anxious to find out.

The cafeteria served their Easter holiday menu of ham, sweet potatoes, corn, and pineapple pudding. No other lunch options were available. The tables were covered with white linens, lit candles, and centerpieces, and the jazz band was set up in the corner for entertainment. Most of the students groaned when they realized the jukebox would be unplugged. However, the cafeteria looked beautiful. Beth and the girls at the table enjoyed the atmosphere, but the boys were miserable.

Kenny joked with the other boys saying, "I can't believe they expect us to chew with our mouths closed!"

The assistant principal put the blinds down at the windows. The candles looked elegant on the tables, and everyone was on their best behavior. Beth's table talked excitedly about what was supposed to "happen."

There were several theories. Firecrackers, a bomb scare, a false fire alarm. They could hardly bear the excitement. It was difficult to hear the jazz band over all the voices, and when lunch was halfway through, everyone gave up on the idea of something big going down.

Suddenly they heard a flurry of commotion and screams from the back of the cafeteria. Students jumped up from their chairs and tables. The assistant principals and the cafeteria workers headed over to see what happened. In a wave, some students jumped up on their chairs while others ran through the cafeteria toward the Center. All those at Beth's table sat stunned and watched the confusion. Mrs. Stackhouse looked furious, and Beth was concerned.

"What in the..." Kenny said as they all stood.

A tide of screaming students headed toward them. The cafeteria manager pulled the fire alarm, and everyone left through the side exits. The student-packed parking lot buzzed with the news of what had happened. Someone let over fifty white mice loose in the cafeteria! The kids went wild with excitement.

The second assistant principal, Mr. Epstein, came outside, his face red. "I want to see the following people in my office immediately," he bellowed over the school's bullhorn. His list included Rocky Mulinero and his friends from the senior class. The shit was about to hit the fan, and Beth hoped he would get collared. Immediately, she felt remorseful about her mean thoughts.

Whatever the consequence, it would be worth it to the boys. People would talk about this for years to come, and it would be brought up at every class reunion thereafter. It was their claim to fame. The boys adamantly denied that they were involved, and the head principal became frustrated. Eventually, the principal went to the local pet store with a yearbook. The proprietor identified the mouse purchasers, and the boys were suspended from school for one week. The principal tried to get them kicked out of the graduation ceremony, but the school board members wouldn't allow that. Beth's mother and father thought it was a funny prank but understood the need for punishment. The school board agreed the prank was unacceptable but not hurtful.

CHAPTER 33

Beth was excited that Susan and her sister Janet were having a party on Friday. A large crowd had been invited. They took up a collection at the Center one morning to pay for the keg. Susan and Janet walked away with a basketful of dollar bills. Charlie and Mike came to see Beth at work and promised to be there. She had heard Rocky was coming but she hadn't seen him in a week due to his suspension. Thinking about all the screaming kids standing on lunch tables and chairs made her laugh out loud. She roared as she told Charlie and Mike about it.

Beth, Melissa, and Jackie went to the party together. Susan was coming with Tyler. Lynne was working that night. Graduation was less than six weeks away and everyone was jazzed up about finishing school or being a senior. Beth was thrilled to have only one more year left, but she got a little sad when she thought about missing the girls and the Boat.

The party started early. Beth saw Charlie, and they hugged. He now worked for the local post office. Mike quit college, too, and worked for the electric company. Hearing about their jobs make her feel young again. Neither one of the guys mentioned Danny.

After a couple of beers, she worked up enough nerve to ask about him, "So, do you guys ever hear from Danny?"

Charlie and Mike looked at one another. Mike told Beth he was still in California and having a great time. Charlie shot him a disapproving frown. Mike shrugged and raised his eyebrows.

"Good," Beth said. "I'm glad he's happy."

Charlie offered to get her a fresh beer as if he wanted to

change the subject.

She secretly hoped Danny would come home for the summer, but why would he?

Susan and Lynne screamed for her and Melissa to join them in the living room. Meat Loaf was playing on the stereo. Beth groaned. They were going to perform. At Jackie's insistence, the girls had practiced performing to the song, "Paradise by the Dashboard Light."

Their friends whooped and clapped as they finished, and they received lots of drunken hugs.

The party continued, and Charlie got drunk.

He approached Beth and asked, "How come you and I never went out?"

"Because I'm an idiot," she said seriously. The two placed their foreheads together and began to laugh.

"I think it's because I never asked you." Charlie's eyes were solemn.

"Why is that?" Beth flirted with him as she held her beer, which gave her a false sense of bravado.

Charlie bent his head up slightly and the two shared a small gentle kiss. Beth had never acted this way with Charlie, and she was drunk enough to enjoy it. She leaned in closer and began to kiss him again. It felt right, and she melted into him. He pulled away and took her by the arm, guiding her outside.

"Why are you kissing me like that?" he asked, his gaze serious and intense.

Beth stood stunned at his sudden foul mood. "What are you talking about?"

"You're drunk, that's why you're kissing me like that." He turned away from her.

Beth made a couple of snorting sounds. Shocked and put off by his comment, she moved in front of him and looked in his eyes with an equally serious expression.

"Come on, Charlie, we've known each other a long time. Why shouldn't we kiss?"

He stood and stared at her. She sensed she could read his mind. He knew why they shouldn't kiss, and so did she. She was in love with one of his best friends. She would never feel that way about him. He knew it, and she knew it, too. That's why they shouldn't kiss, and it pissed him off.

"You need to stop drinking if this is the way you act. This is a small town, Beth. It sucks around here. Everyone knows everything about everyone."

How dare he talk to her like that and act so superior! Why was it such a big deal to share a stupid kiss?

"Who in the hell do you think you are? I've never done anything to be ashamed of, and I certainly won't start now! Don't you ever act like my conscience again! You and Danny are so, so...so fucking pompous and conceited! If it's so bad around here, why don't you just move to California, too? I guarantee no one around here would miss you!"

Beth began to cry as Charlie's eyes flashed with anger. He turned and began to walk away.

"I didn't mean that. You know I didn't mean it," Beth said.

He slowly turned around and walked back to her. He held his arms out and pulled her into them. She cried because she wished she could be in love with Charlie. She was frustrated and angry that she couldn't make herself feel the way she wanted to.

"You know how I feel about you, Beth, but we both know the situation. It would never work out, and we would just wreck a great friendship."

Dammit. He was right. She nodded and smiled at him.

Melissa came outside looking for Beth to take her home. She hugged Charlie, and the two said "good night." Beth, Melissa, and Jackie headed home.

"I don't know why those guys keep coming around here anyway," Melissa said.

"Danny doesn't come around anymore." Beth pursed her lips.

"Danny is an asshole," Melissa and Jackie said in unison.

"Thanks, girls, that helps a lot," Beth said, irritated.

Great. Everybody was in a foul mood.

CHAPTER 34

At school, the guidance counselors pressured the juniors to make life-long decisions about what college they wanted to attend, and what they might want to major in. Beth and her friends signed up for the SATs and started filling out their college applications. The girls tried to make plans for their futures together, but it became increasingly obvious that everyone's parents had different ideas about where their daughters would attend college, if at all. Susan and Beth had plans to attend the University of Delaware located about an hour north of their hometown. At least they would be together. Jackie would go to an all-girl college somewhere in the state of New York at her parents' insistence. Melissa had yet to decide what she would do. Since Lynne had decided not to go to college, she would finish her business courses at the connection in town. She wanted to work for the telephone company. Her boyfriend, Joey, planned to go to the University of Delaware, so she would be up to visit often. Beth was relieved to know she would still see her.

On Monday, the counselors scheduled more meetings with the juniors. "What do you want to do with your life?" they asked repeatedly. Beth was in desperate need for spring break. Amongst the hubbub, the prom committee formed, and Beth and her friends were on it. The prom was considered a gift from the junior class to the senior class. It was a source of irritation for Beth to be working hard to plan Rocky's prom. She realized he had hurt her more than she wanted to admit to anyone, even to herself. He had betrayed her. She had believed they were friends, that he had cared for her. They had laughed a lot, talked all the time, and danced a lot. Beth didn't suffer a broken heart, but it surprised her to acknowledge she missed him and their friendship.

Rocky refused to even look at her after Beth didn't respond to his notes. He brought his dates into the store where she worked to parade them in front of her. Beth decided he was mean-spirited and tried not to let it get to her, but it did. Was he trying to make her jealous, or was he just being mean? Beth had mixed feelings about Rocky. She was angry that she had been so gullible, and she directed her anger at him. Now she had to deal with this Prom thing.

Beth secured a date for the Prom with a boy she had met at work named Jack. He attended college in her hometown and was originally from Virginia. He was a friend of her co-worker Debbie. She had asked him to go with her, and he'd accepted the invitation. Jackie decided to go with her friend Pete since Al was way too old to take to a high school Prom. Pete was in their class and was kind and sweet. Everyone loved him, and he liked hanging around with the girls. Jackie and Beth decided to double date. Lynne and Joey and Susan and Tyler were double dating as well. Melissa had to work that night at the Bowling Alley and wouldn't be attending.

Beth, Jackie, and their dates decided ahead of time not to go the Hudson House for dinner. Beth was especially grateful not to be going to the Mitchell family's restaurant. They planned on attending the After-Prom dance at the Fire Hall from 11:00 to 1:00. Beth was fairly sure she would not be going to the beach afterwards with her date.

The date started out okay. They got pictures taken at Jackie's house and then at Beth's. On the ride to the dance, Beth's date pulled out a pint of Old Granddad he'd hidden beneath his jacket. Their dates were up for it, but the two girls were anxious to get to the gym. They had worked hard on the decorations. The theme was "Still" by the Commodore's. Beth and Jackie exchanged irritated glances as they rode around for a half an hour. The two boys got smashed. The more they drank, the sillier they became. They laughed in high-pitched voices. Beth and Jackie looked at one another with concern. They finally made it to the dance and both girls breathed a sigh of relief.

Beth admired the beautiful gym decorations she had helped create. A gazebo covered with roses waited for couples to visit. Beautiful, garden style murals hung on all the walls. Balloons floated everywhere, and there was a large stage for the band. It looked nothing like the same gym in which the Pep Rallies and basketball games were held.

The boys asked the girls to dance. Beth glanced around for Rocky and hated herself for doing it. She briefly wondered why he hadn't come to his own Prom, and then focused on having fun.

Beth's date danced with her during fast songs but refused to slow dance with her. She couldn't figure out what the problem was, and she didn't know him well enough to ask him. Despite the fact her date was acting weird and didn't really seem to be enjoying himself, she liked seeing everyone dressed up.

The five girls ended up in the bathroom together as they freshened their makeup and checked their hair. Susan asked Jackie if she was having a good time.

"It'd be great if my date wasn't falling in love with Beth's," she said bluntly.

The girls fell silent and stared at one another in the mirror. Beth looked at Jackie, and the realization hit her all at once.

"Oh my God!" Beth blurted. "Yes! That's it!"

The girls fell into gales of laughter.

"Is that true, Beth? Is that true?" Lynne asked her.

Beth nodded and laughed so hard she couldn't speak. It was just her luck to be at the Prom with a date who was gay.

Jackie laughed hard.

Soon, all of them joined her and were wiping mascara from their faces.

"Yes, Yes, I believe Jackie has hit it right on the nail!" Susan said.

Eventually, the girls settled down and were able to go back out to the dance. When the last dance was over, everyone else was anxious to change into their casual clothes and head to the Fire Hall for the After-Prom Dance.

Susan and Tyler left with Lynne and Joey, while Beth and Jackie departed with their dates. In the car, Beth decided she was ready to go home, and Jackie agreed. Jackie and Beth announced to their dates that they wanted to call it an early night and asked to be taken home before the Fire Hall Dance.

Her date dropped Jackie off first and then Beth. He said it was on his way to take Jackie's date home last. Beth cracked up inside. Jack and Pete only had eyes for each other. The two guys laughed exaggeratedly at each other's jokes, stared at one another, and touched each other on the arm and leg.

They arrived at Beth's house, and Jack started to walk Beth to the door.

"No. Please, it's okay. Thank you for taking me," she said.

She left the car and headed into the house. Her mother greeted her with a relieved smile. Beth went to bed thinking the two guys were probably headed down to the beach together. At least the night wasn't a total loss for everyone.

CHAPTER 35

As Beth waited impatiently for spring vacation, she focused on the new summer line that had come out at work, and she created displays and helped plan the summer fashion show. She liked working, but she was excited to go to the party Susan's sister Janet and her boyfriend, Joe Cahall, were having at his newly rented home on Saturday night. Beth and Melissa decided to go together. Since Beth had to work late, and Melissa didn't get off until ten, Beth drove to the bowling alley at 9:15 to wait for her. If she went home first, her parents would question why she was going out so late. As it was, she didn't have to be home until twelve thirty.

Beth picked her up and they headed to Melissa's house. While Melissa changed her clothes, Beth freshened up. By ten o'clock, they walked in the front door of Joe's house. No other kids from the high school were there. They saw Charlie, along with Mike and Billy, who had come home for the Easter holiday. Everyone was happy to see the girls, and they were pleased at the warm reception.

Beth heard a familiar voice behind her, and she slowly turned around, her heart racing.

"Danny?" she said, peering up at his face.

His hair was cut shorter, but otherwise he looked the same. God, he was handsome.

Danny smiled at her, and she smiled back. The two stood that way for a long moment.

"Here, I got you a soda." He handed it to her.

She raised her eyebrows as she accepted it from him. "Isn't there any beer?"

"Yes, would you rather have that?"

"No, this is fine," she said, feeling like a small child. "I'm surprised to see you home again." She didn't look him in the eye as she sipped her soda.

"I try to get home on major holidays."

"Well, how's California?" she asked, not really knowing what else to say. Her heart was beating too fast, and her palms were sweating.

"California is awesome, Beth. I wish you could see it. The surfing is amazing there, nothing like here."

"I've never surfed," she said.

"Well, you have to try it!" he said excitedly. "I'll teach you!"

Beth smiled then, catching his enthusiasm despite her confusion.

She didn't want to waste time playing games. It never worked out when she tried to be cool and aloof. The two stood together for most of the night talking. Beth was now making eye contact and laughing often at Danny's stories about California. What was she doing? She didn't know, but it sure felt wonderful to be talking with Danny again. The others left them alone for the most part. Beth noticed Charlie spent most of the night talking with Melissa.

Beth's conversation with Danny was light and friendly. He genuinely seemed to be enjoying it as much as she was.

"I bet you're looking forward to your senior year," Danny commented.

"I'll just be glad when high school is over, to be honest." Beth felt acutely aware of how young she was.

"Are you still seeing Rocky?" Danny asked tentatively.

"No. Are you seeing anyone?" She realized suddenly that she didn't want to know that answer.

Danny shook his head but said nothing.

"Come with me." Danny placed his hand on her shoulder.

As always, she followed him without resistance. She set her soda on a table on the way out.

They left the party, got into his Mustang, and drove around town for a long time. Music played out of the car stereo.

"You got your radio fixed!" Beth exclaimed.

Danny laughed and said, "I thought you'd like that."

He turned the volume up, and they rode around and listened to the song on the radio. Tom Petty sang, "Oh baby, don't it feel like heaven right now. Don't it feel like somethin' from a dream? Yeah, I've never known nothin' quite like this, don't it feel electric now, might never be again. Baby, we should know better than to try and pretend. Honey, I don't want to go around talkin' bout this. I said, yeah, yeah, yeah. The waiting is the hardest part, every day you send one more card, you take it all in faith, you take it to the heart. The waiting is the hardest part."

Each was lost in the lyrics, and Beth felt connected to the song. She realized that it *did* feel like heaven to be there with him and that waiting *was* the hardest part. Danny reached over and held Beth's hand as the song repeated, "The waiting is the hardest part."

Beth looked at the clock on the dash. It was almost eleven. She still had an hour and a half before she had to be home. Beth made up her mind to stay out as late as she wanted tonight. She would deal with whatever punishment she might receive later.

Danny drove past the high school and down the street to the Old Mill Pond. He pulled in, turned off his lights, and turned the ignition key backwards, so the radio stayed on. "Thunder only happens when it's raining..."

He turned the volume down and said, "I want to know how you are, Beth. Are you okay?"

"I'm fine. Are you alright?"

"Not really," he said miserably. "My parents are pressuring me to come home and work at the restaurant, but that's not what I want to do."

"Do your parents understand that? Have you told them that's how you really feel?"

He shook his head.

An ache tore through her heart. Beth hated to see him unhappy even if she really wanted him to come home. She realized she still loved Danny. Tears formed in her eyes, and she quickly wiped them away so he wouldn't see.

"Danny, what *do* you want to do?" she asked gently.

He looked at her and let out a broken, pensive laugh that panged her chest. "I have no idea. What are your plans?"

"Well, I've applied to the University of Delaware. Beyond that, I'm not sure." She waited for him to laugh at her.

He didn't. Instead, he smiled at her.

"That sounds great, Beth. Really it does."

Beth took hold of his hand.

He leaned back in the seat. "I guess I should get you home."

She glanced through the windshield at the pond. Moonlight shone like glittering diamonds on the water.

Sighing, she focused on Danny. "I'm not ready to go home! Besides, I drove Melissa to the party. My car is back at Joe's."

"What do you want to do?" he asked.

"I don't know, but I don't want to go home."

"Okay." He started the car.

They drove around town looking at houses and pointed out the ones they would like to own one day. Around twelve o'clock, they headed back to the party. Numerous cars were still parked in front, indicating the party was still going strong. Beth leaned back against the seat, a wistful sensation flaming in her chest as Danny parked the car. Tonight, she and Danny acted like old friends. It was different and wonderful, but Beth's heart ached because she would never be able to just be friends with him.

"Beth, I have to say something to you," Danny said hesitantly.

Beth looked up into his eyes, waiting.

"I'm really sorry." He hung his head.

"Sorry for what, Danny?" she spoke softly.

"I'm sorry for everything, Beth. I know I hurt you and if it helps, that was never my intention. I was drinking too much the night I saw you kissing Rocky, and I lost my mind. That's not an excuse, honestly. I had no right. I'm sorry if I caused you pain. Drinking seems to get me in trouble a lot." He looked at her with sorrow in his eyes and whispered, "I'm sorry about Jackie, too."

Beth gaped at him. She didn't know what to say.

After several seconds, she said, "I know you're sorry. It doesn't matter anymore. Yes, you did hurt me a lot. But I forgive you. And I hope you go back to California and have a wonderful life, if that's what you want. Thank you for apologizing, Danny."

Beth moved to exit the Mustang. Danny leaned over in front of her and put his hand over hers to stop her. He hadn't made a move to kiss her all night. Beth turned to look at him as he leaned in and kissed her softly. She reached back with her right hand, touched his face and cheek, and felt the familiar softness there. She returned his kiss. Emotion overcame her, and the back of her throat tightened. His kiss was so warm and comforting. He knew how much pressure to put on her mouth and how to move his tongue with hers. Beth melted as he pulled her close to him.

"You know we can't keep doing this every time we see each other," he said between breaths.

"Why not?" she whispered.

He moved his lips down the curve of her neck and nuzzled the area between her neck and shoulder. Beth responded, and she began to glide her hand down his chest and to his thigh. Tingles coursed through her entire body. He should be the one to take her virginity. There could be no one else. The two kissed more passionately than ever before, touching one another more intimately over their clothes.

Beth pressed her body close to Danny's, and his breathing grew more ragged. He was so familiar. So right. Her body thrummed with blissful vibrations, and she wasn't afraid.

She wasn't even nervous. She trusted him completely. She sat on his lap as he reached his hands around her waist and tugged her sweater up slightly. He touched her softly, and his hand traveled up her stomach and sides. Beth felt a little embarrassed, but the excitement was more than she could bear. She leaned back onto his lap and looked in his eyes as goose bumps arose on her flesh. He stared into her eyes and caressed her at the same time. She was amazed by the thrilling sensations of heat and euphoria that seized her. Beth wriggled her body against his. Desire and affection softened the light in his eyes. He appeared ready to say what she so desperately wanted to hear. She could feel his erection, which caused strange but pleasant tingles in her pelvis. Instead of speaking, he kissed her intensely and touched her as she moved back and forth. Sensations that were raw and new rocked her to the core.

Condensation covered the windows in the car and blocked them from nosy eyes. His breathing became ragged as they worked up to a fevered pitch. Danny leaned Beth forward to remove her sweater. Tap! Tap! Tap! They froze, and Danny quickly dropped his hands.

"Hey, um... Danny?" Charlie called from the other side of the steamed window.

"Danny?" Charlie repeated in a shouted whisper.

"What?" Danny said with a slight whine.

Beth laughed quietly against his face as he continued to hold her close.

Danny pointed his finger at her face and whispered, "Don't start laughing, don't even start..."

He smiled. He knew her very well.

"Um, uh, is Beth in there with you?" Charlie asked.

Danny rolled the window down a little and gave Charlie a stern look. He peered around Danny and focused on Beth sitting on his lap and giggling.

"Oh, sorry, Beth, but Melissa made me come looking for you. She needs to go home. I offered to drive her, but she said she needed to see you first."

"I'll be right there, Charlie," Beth said shyly.

Charlie nodded. "Okay. I'll tell her you're coming." He turned to walk away.

Danny and Beth looked at one another and burst out laughing at Charlie's choice of words.

Danny groaned as Beth hauled herself off him.

"How long will you be home?" she asked.

"For three more days."

She leaned over and kissed him one more time.

"We're always getting interrupted." She frowned, adjusted her sweater, and fluffed her hair.

The two took a moment to compose themselves. Damn it. She really had to pee.

"One day, we won't get interrupted." He winked at her.

She smiled at him as she exited the car.

He leaned over. "I'll call you tomorrow. What time is good?"

"Six."

"Make sure you're there. I really don't want to talk to your mom or dad."

"Don't worry. I'll be there. Make sure you call."

He grasped her hand and pulled her to him. They kissed again, and then she left him. She went back inside the house with a skip in her step and a warm flutter in her heart. Could it work out between them this time?

CHAPTER 36

Beth was on cloud nine as she drove her friend home.

"Um, Beth?" Melissa asked hesitantly.

"Hmmm?"

"Charlie asked me out," Melissa blurted. "But I'm not going to go out with him."

Beth raised her eyebrows, then narrowed them. "Why? Charlie is the nicest, kindest guy I've ever known."

"I know," Melissa responded. "For one, I was afraid you would be mad. For two, I'm dating someone I met at the bowling alley. He's an airman at Dover Air Force Base. We've been seeing each other about a month."

Beth darted a quick glance at her. "How old is this guy?"

Melissa grinned and said, "He's twenty-four."

"What?" Beth's voice rose. "Tell me, tell me..."

Melissa spilled the beans. "Well, we met when he started bowling on a league on Wednesday nights. He asked for my phone number, but I wouldn't give it to him at first. I didn't want him to have to talk to my mother. Well, you know..." After a few moments she continued, "He talked to me a lot at the bowling alley, and we became friends. Finally, I told him about my mother. He really understood. His dad was an alcoholic and died from liver failure two years ago. He gets it."

"That's great, Melissa. Is he nice to you?"

Melissa smiled and said quietly, "Yes, very. Too kind sometimes. I'm not sure I deserve it."

They had reached Melissa's house. After Beth put the car in park, she hugged her friend. Words weren't necessary.

After Beth dropped her friend off, she drove home, and went right to bed where she dreamed of Danny and bowling alleys.

The next day, the phone rang at five fifty-eight p.m. Beth was in her room, and she answered the phone quickly. "Hello?"

"Hi Beth."

Hearing Danny's deep voice made her smile, and she could hear in his voice that he smiled, too. The two talked for a half hour. She made plans to meet him at Pippy's.

Beth told her parents she needed to use the car for an employee meeting at the store. They let her take the car, but she had to be home by nine thirty. By the time she got to Pippy's, it was already seven thirty.

Danny appeared disappointed and said, "I was really hoping we would have more time."

Beth nodded and furrowed her brow. "Me too. You know what my parents are like..."

He said, "Okay, okay. Let's order."

They talked and ate pizza. Danny ordered a pitcher of beer. The waitress embarrassed Beth by reminding him that she couldn't have any of it. Danny told Beth to ignore her.

He talked about California and made it sound like heaven. If he asked her to go with him, she would pack up and run away from home. Danny would never ask her, though. Before long, it was time to go. They kissed goodbye outside her car. It was nice to have a regular date with Danny. They made plans to see each other again on Monday night. Hopefully, Debbie would cover her hours at the store.

The next day, she called Debbie, and she agreed to cover for her. She could hardly contain her excitement until it was time for her date with Danny. She left her house before her parents could interrogate her and parked her car in the lot at Hannigan's. He met her there, and she got into his car. They were both quiet and serious. They sat in Dunkin' Donuts, drank coffee, and then parked at the lake.

"You know I'm going back," he said. "I have to leave tomorrow instead of Wednesday."

"Oh." Beth was silent for a moment, wishing she weren't

stuck in this town. "You're lucky. I hate being in high school."

Danny brushed her hair from her cheek. "Sometimes I wish I were still in high school. Life was simpler. I'll try to come home and visit more often."

Beth smiled at him, and her eyes began to tear up. They listened to music, and before either of them knew it, the clock indicated it was time to go. Back at the store parking lot, Danny exited his car and walked over to hers. The two stood and held one another for about ten minutes.

He finally let her go and leaned back to look down at her. "I don't think I'm going to be staying out there much longer, Beth."

She smiled and knew she shouldn't get her hopes up. Besides, he would be miserable if he came back here.

They kissed one last time, and she pulled away blinking back tears. Maybe she could change her plans about going to the University of Delaware and go to college somewhere near him.

He followed her home in the car. He flashed his lights at her one last time as she pulled into her driveway. Beth went in the house and straight to her bedroom. She ran to the window. He flashed his lights and then headed down the road. That was his final goodbye. Beth cried herself to sleep as she tried to figure out how in the world she would make it through another year here at home. Next year, she would be eighteen and could do whatever she wanted. But for right now, she was only sixteen about to turn seventeen.

CHAPTER 37

Spring break ended, and Beth returned to school. She was ready for the year to end.

Beth stopped going to the Center. The seniors were just too obnoxious. Rocky and his friends strutted about and showed off. They told off-color jokes loudly and laughed at themselves even more loudly. The senior girls came in just in time to go to homeroom and left exactly at dismissal time. It was clear they were done with school and their male classmates. Beth envied the senior girls.

On the last day of school for seniors, a girl in her class bounced up to Beth and her friends saying, "Aren't you guys excited? We're going to officially be seniors tomorrow!"

The underclassmen still had another ten days of school to attend.

Jackie looked at her and said sarcastically, "Oh yeah, I can hardly stand it!"

The rest of them laughed.

The final days of school passed quickly. Beth and her friends that worked took vacation time and headed to the graduation ceremony on Saturday afternoon.

The girls cheered for their senior friends as they accepted their diplomas. Susan cried as Tyler graduated. Melissa, Beth, Lynne, and Jackie comforted her with hugs. Soon the graduates tossed their hats in the air, and the ceremony was over.

Beth watched from the railing of the bleachers as Rocky approached his family on the football field. They took pictures of him, and he smiled broadly. He looked more handsome than she remembered. He looked up into the bleachers at Beth, smiled and waved. She returned his friendly gestures, letting go of her anger, allowing bygones to be bygones.

After the ceremony, Beth and Melissa drove to the graduation party held at Kelly and Kim Jenkin's house. They were Tyler's twin cousins, and Beth knew Kelly but not Kim. Before they left for a trip to Alaska, the twins' parents had set up a bar in the basement and had it fully stocked. They had also ordered a keg. What a cool graduation gift to their daughters. Beth couldn't wait to get to the party. Susan and Lynne had gone early to help set up.

Jackie and Al were coming later. Jackie was in love and spent most of her free time with Al. She and Al were no longer hiding their relationship and had been dating publicly about four weeks now. They were inseparable. He was tall and handsome. He and Jackie were a stunning couple. When Jackie's mother first met Al, she had refused to let Jackie date him because of his age. She had since realized the futility of that. Jackie didn't care what her mother thought and apparently, neither did Al. Jackie had no problem lying and sneaking around. Al didn't seem to mind the risks she took to be with him. Danny would have never gone along with that type of relationship, but Al was okay with it. He probably really loved Jackie. *Unlike Danny*, Beth thought. Beth felt a little jealous of her friend and wished Danny were more like Al.

As they drove to the party, Melissa asked Beth if she had heard from Danny.

Beth looked down and sighed. "I haven't heard from him since his last blow into town. No phone call, no letter. Once again, I'm a fool."

Melissa clucked her tongue at her friend, "No, you're not! He is!" She looked at Beth sympathetically.

Beth and Melissa arrived at the party. Lynne and Susan were with their dates so the two hung out together near the pool.

Beth said, "Tell me more about your airman."

Melissa wouldn't look Beth in the eye. "Well, we're still friends but not really dating anymore. I still see him at the bowling alley."

Beth narrowed her eyes at Melissa and wondered if it was because of Eric. She let it go. After all, with her history with Danny, who was she to give Melissa advice?

The two drank beer as they reclined in the lounge chairs and watched the boys do shots by the pool. The music blared and the windows and doors were wide open. Beth couldn't believe the neighbors didn't call the police.

Rocky approached Beth. "Can we talk?"

"I guess." This was the first time they had spoken face to face since the night she found the picture.

Melissa excused herself and went inside.

Rocky took the seat next to Beth. He smiled at her, and she lowered her head.

"Beth, I am so sorry about this year."

She saw sincerity in his expression. "It's really okay, Rocky. I was angry at the time, but I'm not anymore. It doesn't matter."

"Don't say it doesn't matter. She really was nobody. I was stupid and…"

"…a jerk?" Beth finished the sentence for him.

"I guess. Do you forgive me?"

Beth assured him she did, and he was relieved.

"Is there any chance you would go out with me again?" he asked her hopefully.

Beth smiled at him but shook her head. "No, Rocky. We do much better as friends, don't you think?"

Rocky grinned at her and said, "Well, it was worth a try." He paused and added, "I heard you and Danny Mitchell were back together. Is that true?"

"I don't know where you heard that. No, he's in California." Her voice choked a bit, and Rocky leaned forward to force her to look at him.

"You're really hung up on him, huh?"

Beth smiled forlornly.

"I don't know what you see in him anyway. He's an ass-hole. He thinks he's God's gift, really, Beth! I heard when he was home this last time, he was doing coke and hanging out at The Back Door."

Beth's nostrils flared and her eyes narrowed. How dare he talk about Danny like that! "Well, he doesn't think too highly of you either."

"I think you can do a lot better than him, that's all. Everyone thinks so, and no one can figure out the big attraction."

Beth had heard enough. She got up and marched away. Charlie came out the door and almost ran into her.

"Beth!" Charlie said as the two hugged.

Rocky stomped past her in a huff and entered the house.

Charlie narrowed his eyes. "What's up with him?"

Beth shrugged. It didn't matter anymore.

She and Charlie spent the next half hour talking and dancing. He asked if Melissa was dating anyone. Beth smiled at his interest in her friend. She told him she wasn't exactly sure.

Mike showed up a little later, and he asked Beth to dance. The two slow danced to "Lady" by The Little River Band. Beth was having fun. Mike was a good dancer, and the crowd was friendly and jovial.

He smiled at Beth. "I never thought you'd agree to dance with me."

"A couple of years ago, I wouldn't have!" She laughed, happy to be with the same group of people she'd been friends with since ninth grade.

Mike pulled her close and spun her around. Despite their rough start, she was glad they were friends. She caught Charlie smiling at her as she danced with Mike.

Lynne was there with Joey, unaware of anyone else around them. The two stayed by themselves and were very quietly whispering and smiling back and forth. Susan danced with Tyler. He paid extra attention to her, and she wore a happy smile. She had confided to Beth earlier, "... at least I don't have to worry about college girls where he's going."

People continued to pour through the front door. Jackie walked in with Al Black. He held her hand, and she was radiant and looked happy. Before long, more guys from the class of '76 showed up.

While Beth was dancing with Mike, Brian Knight entered. He waved at her, and she beamed, a flutter tickling her stomach. She waved back, genuinely glad to see him. He walked toward them, grinned, and told Mike to "take a hike." Mike feigned being upset, and Brian laughed at his dramatics.

Brian cut in and danced with Beth. "How are you, Gorgeous?"

"I'm good. How are you?"

"Great now," he said, flirting harmlessly.

They finished the song, and he asked her to walk with him to the keg. He followed her down to the basement bar filled with people. Jackie drank a beer as Al poured a cup from the keg. She formally introduced Beth to Al providing real names to go with the faces he'd seen so many times in the bar. He greeted her pleasantly.

The moment she and Al spoke, a guy standing behind him came around, stuck his hand out and said, "Hi, I'm Greg Black."

Brian and Al laughed at their friend's not so subtle attempt to get her attention. Beth looked up into his face and held her hand out. She had seen him before. He was the guy at the bar who had nodded at her when she had gone into Chester Black's Bar with Jackie the very first time.

He was about six feet tall and had dark brown, almost black hair. His eyes were a beautiful shade of light gray she'd never seen before, and the area around them wrinkled when he smiled at her. She was dumbstruck. He had a perfect face.

His nose was straight, and his jaw was square and muscular. His lips were full but not large. He was clean-shaven and had a deep, dark tan. Beth trembled as he took hold of her hand.

Brian spoke to Greg over Beth's head, "This is Beth O'Brien."

Greg smiled and held her gaze. "It's nice to meet you."

Beth had seen handsome before, but this guy was extraordinary. His dark hair touched his collarbone in a sexy way that caused a flutter in her stomach.

Greg continued to hold her hand.

Jackie nudged her friend. "Well, Beth, are you having a good time?"

Beth looked away from Greg to her friend, realizing she was staring. "Uh-huh, it's been a lot of fun."

Greg continued to hold her hand, and she looked back up at him.

Beth smiled and said, "Uh, it's nice to meet you, too."

He freed her hand, and she felt as if it floated in mid-air. Things moved in slow motion.

Greg began talking to Brian. Brian told her that the two of them played football together the year C.R. won their first state championship.

"I graduated a year ahead of him," Greg said.

That meant he was a graduate of '75 and had to be twenty-two years old.

Jackie joined in the conversation, telling Beth, "Greg and Al are cousins. Greg's father is Chester Black. Al's dad owns Black and Sons Roofing Company. They work for the roofing company during the day. Al bartends for his Uncle on weekends."

Beth listened halfway, still thinking about how handsome Greg was.

Greg continued to watch Beth as he drank his draft.

Jackie looked up at Greg and told him, "Beth and I go to school together. We've been friends since ninth grade."

Greg nodded and smiled at Beth.

She could feel the heat in her face as she shyly smiled back.

Al began to tell Brian about their current roofing project. Brian was interested, and the guys talked amongst themselves momentarily. Jackie and Beth moved away for a chance to speak privately.

Jackie tried to be discreet, so she turned her back to the three guys. Beth continued to stare at Greg.

"Oh my God, did you see the way Greg looked at you?"

"Uh huh."

"Beth!" Her friend called her to attention. "He's the one who asked me about you that night at the bar. Remember?"

Beth leaned into Jackie's ear and said, "Yeah, I figured. He's the most handsome guy I've ever seen in my entire life!" She laughed as she said it.

"He's not as handsome as Al," Jackie said.

Bullshit! Everyone had to see this guy was an Adonis, and she had only seen his face. He stood behind the beer keg with Brian. She wanted to look at the rest of him, but she didn't dare.

Melissa came down the stairs, her beautiful auburn hair hanging down past her shoulders. She joined Beth and Jackie by the beer keg. Beth waited to see if Greg introduced himself to Melissa in the same way he did to her. He didn't. As a matter of fact, he didn't seem to notice her. He nodded at her absently and turned back to the boys. This made Beth happy. He looked over at her often, nodding or smiling. She was staring, but she couldn't stop herself. Whenever he looked at her, she glanced away. She was embarrassed by the way her face became warm and her palms were sweating. What *was* this? The only time she ever remembered feeling such attraction was in the car with Danny.

Charlie jumped down the steps. "Beth! Get your ass up here and dance with me."

Beth smiled at Charlie, and she headed toward the stairs. As she turned to climb up, she glanced at Greg. He wasn't looking at her this time.

She studied him momentarily. He was two inches taller than Brian. He had on a pair of faded blue jeans and a white cotton button-down shirt with the sleeves rolled up just below the elbows. The muscles and veins showed on his forearm as he lifted his plastic cup to his lips. Beth didn't want to leave the basement, but she had to. It would not be a good thing for her to get too close to this guy. He was way too old for her. Her folks would absolutely croak!

Charlie dragged her into the living room, and they danced to Bachman Turner Overdrive's "You Ain't Seen Nothing Yet."

The rest of the girls joined her in the living room. She danced near her friends, and they smiled, laughed, and butt bumped each other. When the song was over, they were sweaty, so they headed outdoors to cool off. Beth turned to follow Charlie out the door. Greg came upstairs, stood alone by the side of the room, and watched her. He didn't smile. Beth suddenly felt like a caged bird. She smiled nervously, and he smiled back but narrowed his eyes. What was up with this guy? She wasn't getting a good read. Did he like her? Did he not like her? She passed him as the girls stepped outside. He followed them out. Greg knew Tyler Jenkins slightly, and the two began to talk.

Lynne approached Beth and told her Greg Black used to date a girl she knew and worked with at Arthur Treacher's. She was from St. Mary's. They dated a couple of years, and she broke up with him when she left for Europe over a year ago. It apparently left him devastated. Lynne rarely said anything bad about anyone, but she did tell Beth she didn't like his old girlfriend. According to Lynne, she was mean and snotty. Beth felt strange. She soaked up information about this guy like a sponge, and she wanted to know more about him. Beth couldn't believe she had that familiar tingle in her stomach over him. Only Danny had ever been able to make her feel this way.

Greg literally took her breath away. *Sorry, Danny, but you shouldn't have gone off. You should have called me or written me.* Maybe Greg was just the guy to help her get over Danny. She talked herself right into flirting with him.

Brian leaned over from behind her and whispered, "Go for it."

Beth wondered if he could read her mind.

She jumped and looked back at him. "Really? What about Danny?" she whispered.

"Danny? What the hell are you talking about? Do you think Danny Mitchell isn't dating anyone else while he's away? Come on, Beth!"

She felt as if she had been punched in the stomach.

Brian softened his tone and voice, "Beth, Danny doesn't deserve you and Greg probably doesn't either. I can tell you that Danny is not being celibate in California. I know that for sure."

Her eyes filled with tears. She didn't know what celibate meant, but she was sure it meant he was screwing other girls. She knew it but didn't want Brian to confirm it.

"Come on now, don't cry about that. You need to stop sitting around waiting for a guy who may or may not decide that he wants to be with you."

Beth nodded in agreement.

Brian jerked his chin toward Greg. "Besides, Greg is here in town. He's single and looking for someone. He dated the same girl for a couple of years. This is the first time I've seen him act like this about anyone in an awfully long time."

"He's too old for me. My parents would have a fit," Beth said chewing the right corner of her bottom lip.

"No, they wouldn't. They let you go out with me."

"Why is that, Brian? Why didn't they ask about your age and refuse to let me date you?"

"Probably because I wasn't Danny!" He laughed.

Beth smiled at her friend and said, "And I didn't tell them how old you were!" She turned and looked at Greg.

"I don't know." She bit the bottom part of her lip.

Brian took her by the shoulders and turned her around. He gently pushed her forward and said, "Go for it."

Smiling from ear to ear, Beth felt like she had just been given permission to be very, very bad.

Greg walked towards her. Beth got nervous as he came closer, and her knees wobbled. She dodged to the left and headed back inside.

What on earth is wrong with me? Beth winced at her actions.

Jackie caught up with her inside the house.

"What is wrong with you?" She grabbed Beth by the arm.

"I don't know. He makes me nervous. I almost can't breathe when I look at him. Jackie, I feel guilty feeling this way."

"Guilty? For what?" Her friend stared at her with a deeply furrowed brow. "Don't even tell me this is about Danny. If you tell me that, I'm going to kick your ass right here, right now!"

"I can't help it." Beth drew her brows together.

"Yes, you can, God damn it," Jackie said in a loud whisper. She lowered her tone and continued sarcastically, "Oh, I see, Danny Mitchell breezes into town and pays a little bit of attention to you, and you get hearts and stars in your eyes. Has he called you since Easter, Beth?" She shook her head. "Has he written you one letter since he's been in California?"

"No but stop. You're making me sound like a complete idiot!" Beth pursed her lips.

Jackie put her arm around Beth's shoulders.

"You are when it comes to him, but we all have someone we act like a fool over." She let out a lighthearted laugh, Beth chuckled, too.

"What am I going to do?" she asked Jackie.

"You are going to live your life! You are going to date as many guys as you can. You are going to stop whining over Danny and let him do his thing. You are going to have one hell of a senior year! For starters, you can stop running away from great looking guys like Greg Black."

Lynne, Melissa, and Susan approached with curious expressions. After hearing what Jackie said, they all chimed in their agreement. Beth started to laugh and cry all at the same time.

"I have to get back to Al. Now, go in the bathroom, get yourself together and when you come out, you be ready to have a great time!" Jackie pushed her friend towards the restroom door.

Beth entered the restroom and quickly shut the door. She sat on the edge of the bathtub trying get up her nerve to go back out to the party. The door burst open, and she jumped up.

Greg stood in the doorway and stared at her.

"What are you doing?" she asked him, not sure if she should be angry at him for barging in.

"Are you alright?" he asked. "I was worried about you."

"Uh-huh, yes. Yes, I am." Beth stammered. "Why wouldn't I be?"

"I was getting worried. You seemed upset when you came in here."

Beth knew then that he had been watching her when she was talking to her friends.

"Thank you. I'm really fine," she said, squeezing past him towards the door.

She opened the door slightly, and he gently took hold of her arm.

"Don't go yet."

She froze at his touch, and he shut the door behind them. Beth's mind whirled. Why are we talking in the *bathroom*? *Should I leave?*

He turned Beth to face him. Confused, she obliged and looked up at him.

"I think you're beautiful. I remember the first time I saw you with Jackie at my dad's bar. I can't believe I've never met you before," he said as he admired every inch of her face.

"Are you dating anyone?" he asked, cutting to the chase.

Beth shook her head, and he smiled.

"Do you think maybe you'd like to go out with me?"

Beth stared at him and blinked. Her mouth was dry, and she couldn't breathe.

"I don't know," she mumbled, and she darted her gaze around the room. Her palms started sweating again.

"Why are you so nervous?" Greg asked.

Beth had acted like a lunatic ever since she met him, and he deserved to know why.

She took a deep breath and said, "Look, I think you're very handsome, and I'm sure you're nice, too. I've been a little hung up on someone for a very long time, and I'm not sure that I'm over him." There. It was out.

Greg smiled at her and told her he felt the same way about his ex-girlfriend.

"I can't guarantee you if she walked in that door right now that I wouldn't walk off with her. But I can promise you this. I haven't met anyone else since she left that I thought I might want to spend time with until I saw you in the bar."

Beth smiled and looked down at her feet, embarrassed and unnerved by his compliment. She relaxed a bit, though.

"I'm going to be a senior in high school next year," she said.

Greg nodded. "I'll be working for my uncle next year." He spoke as if the one fact equated with the other, as if her being in high school was no big deal.

His response was interesting and curious. Beth took a deep breath. It came out jagged and jumpy when she exhaled.

"Come here." Greg guided her to the edge of the bathtub, and they sat side by side.

After taking hold of her hand, he traced the outline of her fingers, thumb, and wrist. He didn't talk, and Beth couldn't think of anything else to say either, so they sat quietly while he touched her hand softly.

"Do you like that?" He ran his finger lightly across the tender flesh of her wrist.

She nodded. He moved onto his knees in front of her and began to touch her arms in the same way.

Sensing his intentions, Beth wanted to run from him as much as she wanted to stay. She was mesmerized by the anticipation of what was next. He glided his hands down to her legs.

Greg stared into her eyes. "Do you like this?"

"Uh-huh." Beth held his smoldering gaze.

Warmth grew in her stomach. She had never felt this way with anyone but Danny, and it fascinated her. Unable to looked into Greg's eyes, she focused on his lips. He leaned in with his hands on the sides of her legs, kissed her gently and pulled away. They stared at one another, each waiting for the other to react.

After being rejected time and time again by Danny, it felt great to be wanted by someone. Greg was uncomplicated in that way. It was obvious he wanted her. He didn't hide it. Greg kissed her again, and Beth closed her eyes and kissed him back. Their caresses were deeper and longer this time. She leaned back and opened her eyes. He sat still with his eyes closed. After a few moments, he slowly opened them and reached his hands up to her face. He used his fingertips to trace the features of her face.

"You are fascinating and stunning."

Beth melted at his flattery. No one had ever talked to her like that. Closing her eyes, she enjoyed the gentle way he touched her, and she felt his face near hers. She opened her eyes.

"Look at me," he said as he leaned in and kissed her, keeping his eyes locked on hers.

He gently slid his tongue into her mouth. She very weakly tried to draw back. He leaned forward, moving his tongue in circles slowly as the two continued to watch one another intently. Despite his request, she closed her eyes, overwhelmed by the reaction he pulled from her body. He held her close, and they kissed passionately again and again.

"What am I doing?" she asked herself over and over as Greg overwhelmed her mouth and touched her body through her clothes while she enjoyed it all.

Greg stood and pulled her up, too. He reached over and locked the door. Beth turned her back to him and tried to regain her senses. She felt incredibly drunk, but it wasn't from the two beers she'd had. He kissed her neck from behind. Beth leaned into him as he wrapped his arms around her. He placed his right hand on her stomach and slid it down inside the front of her jeans. Beth's eyes widened. Even Danny had never done that before! She grabbed Greg's hand and pushed it away. He was strong and resisted her attempts to stop him.

"Please, stop." She pushed away from him. Suddenly, she was frightened.

Greg pulled his hand away and turned her towards him. He collected himself and pulled back.

"I'm sorry. I got carried away," he said.

Beth turned sideways toward the door to exit the bathroom. She was in a daze and didn't know which direction to go. Her heart was racing. She had behaved ridiculously. Greg was handsome, and she was strangely drawn to him. She had never felt that way before, so why was she freaking out?

Greg reached his left hand up to her face and cupped it under her chin. He applied gentle pressure to turn it up towards him, and he kissed her one last time. Greg slipped his tongue inside and caressed hers. She hesitated at first. Why was she acting so afraid? Then, as arousal tickled her stomach, she returned his kiss with equal passion.

Greg bent down slightly and reached underneath her with one hand in front, the other under her backside. He clasped his hands together and lifted her up so he could kiss her more deeply. The pressure of being lifted in that way caused a rush of pleasure, and Beth exhaled a small moan into his mouth. Embarrassed by her reaction, she pulled away from him. He put her down and smiled. Beth swallowed hard and tried to collect herself.

"You're a virgin, aren't you?" he asked.

Beth wanted to die. Great! Now guys could tell how inexperienced she was just by kissing her. She closed her eyes, wincing, and dreaded opening them again.

"It's okay. I wasn't expecting it, but I'm really glad to know you are."

She felt so humiliated...like a child.

Greg moved her chin up and forced her to look at him. Beth opened her eyes and made eye contact with him, and he smiled down at her. Why did he look so happy?

"Maybe we should get out of this bathroom, huh?" he suggested and chuckled slightly as he tapped her playfully on the nose.

She turned to check her reflection in the mirror. He placed his hand behind her head as he stared into the mirror behind her.

He said, "You look beautiful."

Beth smiled, and her breath caught in her throat. She looked at him. He was even more handsome than before.

"I'm embarrassed," she whispered, lowering her head.

"Don't be. I shouldn't have..."

They stared at one another through the mirror.

"Well, we should get out of here. There's probably a line in the hallway. I'll check it for you. I know you don't want anyone seeing us coming out of here together." He chuckled.

"Oh no, I don't!" Beth hadn't thought about that.

He laughed harder at her panicked expression as he opened the door.

Thankfully, no one waited outside.

Greg let her go out first. "I'll wait here for a couple minutes," he said.

Grateful for his discretion, she returned to the party. The good Lord knew she didn't have any.

What am I doing? she thought, berating herself.

She came around the corner to the living room. Jackie and Al kissed passionately as they danced.

Brian Knight said, "There you are! Come dance with me."

He led a sluggish Beth to the dance floor, and they danced to "Sara" by Hall and Oats.

"Are you feeling alright?" he asked her.

"Yeah, I'm fine."

"You're sure? You're not drunk, are you?" He grinned at her.

"Have you designated yourself my guardian or what?" she asked.

"I would be if you needed it. You know that, Beth," he said seriously, though he still smiled.

"Thank you," she said.

Beth saw Greg shake hands with Al, and he looked as if he were getting ready to go.

She left Brian and ran to Greg. "Are you leaving?"

Greg looked at her darkly. "Yep. I sure am."

He turned his shoulder and walked past her, throwing the front door open as he left.

Beth turned around in confusion. Why was Greg so angry?

Brian rushed around Beth and headed out the front door, leaving it wide open.

Beth walked out onto the front steps.

Brian ran after Greg. "Hey! Black! Wait up!"

Greg stopped, and Brian caught up with him. They talked, but she couldn't make out what they were saying. While Brian spread his arms out dramatically, Greg shook his head and pointed back to the house. Brian shook his head and put his hand on Greg's shoulder, turning him towards the house. Greg held his two hands out in front of him and shook them back and forth. Brian put his head down, and Greg shook his head again. Their confrontation ended with a handshake. Greg got in his car and drove away. Brian returned to the house.

"What's going on?" Beth asked.

Brian rubbed the back of his neck. "You shouldn't have agreed to dance with me at that particular moment."

"Oh no, oh no!" She panicked as the realization hit her. "Oh my God, did he tell you what happened?" She winced, and her cheeks heated. "In the bathroom?"

"Yep," Brian said with irritation. "He said nothing really happened. He also said he thought you were still a virgin." He raised one eyebrow.

"Oh my God." Mortified, she hid her face in her hands.

"Take a walk with me, Beth." Brian directed and pulled her by the right hand.

As they walked, he told her about the perils of being a virgin and making out with guys you don't know in a strange bathroom. He treated her like a child telling her things she already knew. She knew she'd made a terrible mistake, and his fatherly tone was a little too much for her to handle.

"You're the one who told me to go for it!" she yelled at him.

"Well, I didn't mean to get down and dirty in the fucking bathroom!" he yelled back.

"Oh, I wasn't going to get 'down and dirty' in the bathroom! It wasn't like that," she added quietly.

"Yes it was, Beth. It could've been a disaster. If you had been with the wrong guy, it really could've been," Brian said in a soft, concerned voice.

"But I wasn't," she insisted.

He stood quietly for a moment and looked up at the night sky.

Beth stared at her feet and asked, "He's not going to call me, is he?"

Brian threw his hands in the air in frustration. "I don't believe you, Beth! No, I really don't think he's going call you. I mean, a guy meets a girl he thinks is gorgeous and special, she acts like she's really into him one minute, and then she goes off acting hot to trot with another guy…"

"Hey! I was not acting 'hot to trot,' and I *definitely* wasn't going off with another guy! Damn you, Brian!"

"Okay, okay. I know that and you know that, but that's not how it looked to him. Can you blame him? You must think, Beth. You have to think, think, think!" he said loudly, tapping the side of his head.

Beth huffed and kicked the ground. She was done with this conversation.

"Let's go back in. I need to get Melissa and go home." She walked past him.

"Alright, but please…" he continued.

She twisted her head toward him. "Don't say anything else, Brian. I get it, okay? I get it!"

"I certainly hope so, my beautiful virgin." He gave her a reassuring, teasing smile.

"Oh, shut up," she said as he grabbed her shoulders from behind and shook her back and forth.

Dammit. Now everyone was probably going to find out she was a virgin.

CHAPTER 38

Beth worked at the store the next day. Greg occupied her mind, and she couldn't stop thinking about the episode they'd shared in the bathroom. She thought of the reaction her body had toward him, and heat crested over her cheeks. It puzzled her that she could get so worked up with some-one other than Danny. She convinced herself it was pointless for her to have encouraged Greg. Her parents would never let her date a guy who was twenty-two. He'd become frustrated with her curfews, and they would have to sneak around just like she and Danny had done. Eventually, they would have to end it, and she would suffer a broken heart and quite pos-sibly, a horrible reputation. Thank God their relationship ended before it ever got started.

Thankfully, the store only had few customers. Beth wasn't really in the mood to work. Andrew and the girls stood around and talked to one another at the large entrance between the two departments. The front door jingled, sig-naling a customer was entering. The workers separated to take their spots.

Jackie rounded the corner and entered Beth's area.

"Hi Beth," Jackie said shortly.

Recalling the events of last night, Beth dreaded her visit. "Hey Jackie, did you need to do some shopping?"

"No, I came in here to see what in the hell happened last night!"

Beth pulled Jackie back towards the bins so no one could overhear their conversation.

"Greg was totally into you, and now he apparently thinks you are a huge slut, which I happen to know person-ally that you aren't. I tried to convince Al, but he said he didn't think he would be able to convince Greg of that fact."

It made Beth furious that Greg thought she was easy. How could she convince him otherwise, and why was she even concerned about what he thought? She hardly knew him anyway. How dare he call her a slut? She had told him she was a virgin!

"What a dick! Did he actually call me a slut?" Beth asked wide eyed, fists clenching in anger.

"Yeah, he did," Jackie replied, and the two stared at each other.

"Jackie, do you know what happened between us in the bathroom?"

"*Yes*! He told Al, and Al told me. Al said Greg hasn't been with a girl in over a year, and it was too bad for him that you turned out to be such a cock tease. Did you deliberately dance with Brian to make Greg jealous so he would leave you alone?"

"No!" Beth scowled at her. "Why would I do that?!"

Jackie arched one eyebrow.

"Honest to God, Jackie! I didn't do it intentionally. I wasn't thinking. I never dreamed he would be jealous of Brian! Everybody knows Brian and I are just friends," she said.

"Everybody but Greg. Brian is a great looking guy, Beth, and he cares for you so much. You know that. Imagine how it looked to Greg, who just happens to be the one guy who's knocked your socks off since Danny Mitchell!"

Beth lowered her head and felt ridiculous. "I don't think I did it because of that. I really think I was just stupid. I wasn't thinking. I didn't want anyone to know we had been in the bathroom together, so I overcompensated trying to be normal. I feel terrible. I really do."

Jackie compressed her lips. "Well, Al and I don't want you guys at odds with each other. Do you think you could be nice to Greg when you're around him?"

"I don't know, Jackie. He's an ass," Beth replied, silently

hoping she would never have a reason to see Greg Black ever again.

She was humiliated. Why had he thought she was a virgin one minute and a slut the next? Then she remembered how she had acted in the bathroom. Oh my.

"Jackie?" Beth asked softly.

"Hmmm?" she said as she checked out the corduroys on the table next to her.

"How come he asked me if I was a virgin?"

"What?" Jackie snapped her head around to look at Beth.

"In the bathroom, he asked me if I was a virgin. Would there be a reason why a guy would know something like that just from kissing a girl?" Beth asked.

Jackie started to laugh. "Sometimes you are so stupid it blows me away!"

Beth became irritated again and said puckishly, "Well, there had to be a reason why all of sudden he asks, 'You're a virgin, aren't you?'"

Jackie took a deep breath. "A guy can tell because a girl won't go too far. He probably made a move and you stopped him, right?"

Beth nodded.

"Well, that's what clued him in. It doesn't have anything to do with the way you kiss. Apparently, you must have been doing something right in that department. He was very hot and bothered about you dancing with Brian."

"Okay then, if that's the case, why does he think I'm a slut now?"

"He thought you were rejecting him for Brian," Jackie replied. "Geez!"

The two stood quietly looking at one another. Beth tried to process everything. She sensed Jackie doing the same.

Jackie finally broke the silence. "By the way, the girls are going to the beach tomorrow. I'm driving. You want to go?"

"Yeah, I'm off tomorrow," she said, still preoccupied with thoughts of Greg.

"Isn't tomorrow someone's special day?" Jackie flashed her a sly smile. "Birthday girl."

Beth grinned happily. The girls remembered.

CHAPTER 39

Beth hopped into Jackie's parents' white station wagon, joining Lynne and Melissa. They picked up Susan, and the girls were off to the beach. The radio was loud, and the girls sang and danced in the car all the way. The sun was shining, and Beth was thankful the weather wasn't too hot. They arrived, and the surf looked rough. Beth didn't want to go in the churning ocean water, so she lay on the beach blanket while her friends dared to swim. Jackie's top popped off from a rogue wave, which caused a stir among a group of teenage boys.

At noon, they went up to the boardwalk and ate lunch at Nicola Pizza. After, they walked around the shops for about an hour. The girls each bought a box of Dolly's caramel corn to take home, and then they went to play skee ball and air hockey in the arcade. A fierce competition broke out between Susan and Melissa at the "Shoot-out at O.K. Corral" game. Susan won and rubbed it in the rest of the day.

The girls headed back down to their spot on the beach. The radio played the only station they could pick up. Susan and Beth sat in low beach chairs and started to bop their knees up and down in time with the music. Melissa, Jackie, and Lynne started moving their feet up and down as they lay on the blanket. They started to sing along to the radio, and the lifeguards watched them. They laughed at the girls having fun.

Jackie lowered her sunglasses and said, "Hey, that lifeguard is really cute!"

Before long, she and Melissa stood at the bottom of the lifeguard stand. There were two of them on duty. Both looked tan and gorgeous in their red trunks, and their noses were slathered with white sunscreen. They wore sexy mirrored sunglasses. One of them twirled his whistle around his finger one way and then the other. Beth, Lynne, and Susan laughed at their two friends and shook their heads.

The afternoon sun turned hot, and everyone decided to go in the water. Beth walked in thigh high, rinsed herself off, and then got right back out.

"Beth, you are such a wuss!" They yelled to her, and she flipped them the bird.

Her friends squealed with laughter.

She returned to the beach chair and listened to the radio. Bored, she picked up a magazine Lynne brought and leafed through it as the sun dried her skin. She stopped at an article about long distance romances and thought about Danny.

Lately, her friends got frustrated with her if she even brought up his name. They were right. What was it about him? She had a fantastic couple of days with him two months ago and she hadn't heard from him. Not one letter. Not one phone call. Why was he like that? Maybe she was too easy to rely on to care about him. That had to be it. He wanted her when she was around but forgot about her when she wasn't. What was up with that? She began to question everything again. Had he ever really cared about her at all? Why couldn't he just be like Al and deal with the problems of dating a high school girl? She threw the magazine down and crawled over near the radio.

Beth sat on the blanket by herself and tried not to be hurt that her friends had not even wished her a happy birthday. She was feeling a little sorry for herself, so she turned the volume up on the radio. There weren't many beach goers on the sand today. She liked it when they could spread out and not worry about being overheard. After what seemed like a five-minute commercial, the music began. "Hello, yeah it's been awhile. Not much, how 'bout you? I'm not sure why I called, I guess I really just wanted to talk to you, and I was thinking maybe later on, we could get together for a while.

It's been such a long, long time and I really do miss your smile. I'm not talking 'bout movin' in..."

Beth lay down near the radio and closed her eyes. She was deep in thought about Danny when the girls ran back to the blanket. They chattered and shivered and wiped off with their towels as the song finished. Beth moved back to the chair and brooded. Her friends glanced at one another. The song droned on, deepening her sour mood.

"I won't ask for promises, so you don't have to lie, we've both played that game before, say I love you then say good-bye. I'm not talking 'bout movin' in, and I don't want to change your life. There's a warm wind blowin' the stars around, and I'd really love to see you tonight." The radio announcer finally cut in to introduce the next tune. Lynne turned up the radio when she heard "Your Momma Don't Dance and Your Daddy Don't Rock and Roll."

They danced and bopped around again. Beth shaded her eyes from the sun and watched them solemnly.

Melissa stopped dancing, "What's wrong with you, Beth?"

"Nothing."

"Yes, there is. What is it?" asked Susan.

"I know what it is...she's having a 'Pining for Danny Mitchell' moment!" Jackie said sarcastically.

The girls went into a dramatic response of gasps and fake fainting spells.

"Not that! Oh my gosh, someone call an ambulance."

Beth had to laugh at their gyrations. In a hushed hiss, she said, "Screw you all!"

"Oh no. Screw you!" Jackie squirted Beth with white Coppertone.

Beth screamed at the mass of white slime on her stomach.

"Yeah, screw you all!" Melissa said, imitating Beth.

They roared with laughter. Each girl grabbed her suntan lotion and pointed it at Beth, walking toward her slowly, threatening her.

"Come on, you guys! Don't you dare!" She jumped up from the chair and backed away.

They chased after her toward the water with their Coppertone and Bain de Soleil bottles. Beth screamed and laughed as she ran into the water.

Beth waited until they gave up and walked back to the blanket. They laughed and bumped into one another, and she was so proud they were her friends. They were willing to make complete asses out of themselves just to make her laugh. What would she ever do without them? Even if they did forget her birthday, she loved them. She rinsed herself off in the water and strolled back towards the blanket.

A lifeguard hopped down off his stand as she walked past.

"What was that all about?" he asked.

Beth was taken by surprise. "Oh, we were just playing around."

He lowered his mirrored glasses and looked her in the eye. "Exactly how much playing around do you girls do together?"

"You're disgusting!" she said and walked back to the blanket.

She told the girls about the lifeguard's comment. Susan and Lynne were grossed out along with Beth. Jackie and Melissa thought they should torture the lifeguards with a suggestive display. Luckily, the steam wore out on all the ideas they had. The afternoon passed quickly, and clouds rolled in. The girls packed up and headed back home.

Jackie drove Melissa home first.

As Melissa climbed out of the car, she said, "I'll pick you guys up around six tonight."

Everyone except Beth shouted approvals.

Beth bunched her brow together. "What's going on tonight?" Again, she felt a pang because they didn't remember it was her birthday.

"It's your birthday!" the girls shouted in unison.

"We have major plans for you, girl, and we're not telling you what they are," Susan said.

"At least tell me what to wear." She cheered up considerably.

"Jeans and a sexy top," was all Jackie would say.

Beth got home and took a shower. The water felt so good. She washed her hair with Herbal Essence shampoo and used her father's shaving foam to shave her legs. She couldn't wait for tonight, and her thoughtful friends filled her heart with love.

She got out and dried off, noticing her slight sunburn that would change to a tan soon enough. Beth put on blue jeans, white espadrilles, and a sleeveless white soft-spun cotton blouse. It had a round collar and buttoned up the front. The color of her tan was striking against the blouse. Briefly, she thought about Greg and how handsome he'd looked in his white shirt, and then she put him out of her mind. She put on a small gold chain necklace, bangle bracelet, and gold stud earrings. After a quick perusal, she decided she didn't need to do her nails. They looked perfect after the day at the beach. She sprayed on her Grass Oil perfume and headed downstairs to the kitchen.

Her birthday gift from her parents sat on the table, and she tore the package open while they watched. She hugged the new purse and an outfit from Hannigan's to her chest. Debbie must have helped them pick the gifts.

"Thank you. These are just what I wanted." Beth was touched. She set her gifts on the table and hugged them both.

She had been getting along so much better with her parents lately. They had begun to relax now that she had a job and her grades were good. Her mother asked about Rocky often. Beth didn't share the details of what had happened so her mother maintained a good impression of him.

"What are you girls doing tonight?" her father asked as Beth waited for her ride.

"I have no idea—big birthday secret."

Her father remained silent.

Beep! Beep!

"There's my ride. See you later." Beth jumped up, grabbed a pink sweater, and ran out the front door.

Everyone was in the car and had beautiful tans from their day at the beach. Beth was dressed casually like everyone else, and she relaxed.

"Where are we going?" she asked.

Melissa said, "Right now we're going to Captain John's for dinner. That's all you get to know."

The girls laughed at Beth while she begged for more details. They arrived, had a great meal, and the waitresses brought over a piece of cake and sang "Happy Birthday" to her. Susan asked the host to take their picture. The girls crouched together, and the special moment was preserved for eternity.

They left the restaurant at seven thirty. It was still light out as Melissa drove down the country road to The Boat. They made Beth close her eyes as they pulled into the dirt lane that led to their secluded spot. After they parked, her friends helped her out of the car.

"Okay, you can open your eyes," Melissa said.

Within the circle of logs, a blanket was spread on the ground, and a small cooler sat nearby. Small bouquets of flowers stuck out of the holes on the boat, and a bunch of multicolored balloons with Happy Birthday on them floated on the back of it. Beth was overwhelmed and began to cry at the effort they made for her. This birthday started a tradition of decorating The Boat for all future events.

Jackie told her to look inside the boat. When she approached, she could see beautifully wrapped gifts arranged in the bottom. They climbed in one by one, and Beth opened her presents. Susan gave her a candle for her bedroom. Lynne gave her a Richard Pryor album. Melissa handed her a brown paper bag with a bow on it. Beth smiled, opened the bag, and found a pint of premixed screwdriver. The girls shouted their approval. Jackie gave Beth a beautiful friendship bracelet. Beth fought back happy tears.

"Don't cry yet. That's not the best gift!" Melissa said loudly.

All the girls started to bounce up and down with anticipation.

"What? What is it?" Beth could hardly contain her excitement.

Jackie handed her a shirt box wrapped in beautiful paper. Her friends were barely able to contain themselves. Beth was nervous as she tore the bow and paper off and pulled the lid open a little bit, peeking inside.

Lynne bounced in her seat. "Open it!"

Beth saw a picture of something inside and pulled the top all the way off. She almost fainted as she stared at the June 1979 issue of *Playgirl*.

"Oh my God!" she exclaimed.

A rush of hands grabbed the magazine, and the boat rocked back and forth. Amid screams and laughter, they hopped out, grabbed the gifts, and skipped back to the blanket. They squeezed closely so they could all look through the magazine together. It was close to eight o'clock, and they began to share the fifth of screwdriver mix. The magazine mesmerized them. Beth had only seen a naked man on the screen at the Drive-In, and that was so disgusting she couldn't even recall what he'd looked like. She was sure she mentally blocked it from her mind. Phil Donahue had done a show about repressed memories, so she was sure it was possible. These guys didn't look disgusting at all. They were quite handsome. Beth and her friends each picked their favorite guy, and the conversation degenerated as the screwdriver level in the bottle lowered. After looking at each page, the girls spread out on the blanket. Of course, Jackie continued to flip through the magazine.

"So, if you could see anyone in the world naked, who

would you want to see?" Melissa asked Jackie while braiding her long blonde curls.

"I don't know. I guess maybe Superman, Christopher Reeve."

The girls agreed he was an excellent choice.

"Who would you pick?" she returned the question to Melissa.

"I think I'd want to see John Travolta." She finished weaving Jackie's hair and undid the braid.

"Oh yeah!" they yelled in agreement.

"How 'bout you, Lynne?" Beth asked.

"Probably Chachi."

The girls laughed hysterically.

"What's wrong with Chachi?" she asked, highly offended at their laughter.

"Nothing, nothing at all," Beth replied with a slight smirk. "He's a definite cutie pie."

Lynne turned to Susan. "What about you?"

"I just like to see Tyler."

They all groaned at her lack of imagination.

Melissa looked at Beth. "Do we even need to ask you?"

"No," Jackie said, and they all replied in unison, "*Danny!*"

Beth laughed at them, and then she widened her gaze. "Oh my gosh! I wasn't even thinking about Danny."

Jackie perked up. "Who were you thinking of?"

They all looked at her, and she said sheepishly, "Greg."

Jackie hooted, and immediately the girls all high fived one another. They were happy she no longer dwelled on Danny.

"Well, you might actually get the chance to lose your virginity with Greg. At least he's around town," Jackie added.

"Too bad he absolutely hates me!" Beth pursed her lips.

Lynne said, "Can you believe he thinks she's a slut?!"

Melissa was drinking the last swallow from the fifth, and overcome with laughter, she spit it out. She hadn't heard this about Greg. They cracked up as Jackie relayed the story to Melissa. Beth laughed slightly, but she wasn't really amused. Her virginity had become too much of a joke with them.

Beth grabbed a Fresca from the cooler, and the girls cleaned up The Boat. She wanted to leave the balloons and flowers.

"She probably hasn't felt that pretty in years," Beth said as they looked at it.

"She needs a name," Susan added.

Choosing a name for The Boat was too big a task to be done in one night. They gave themselves an assignment. Each girl had to think of a name, and they would vote on it when they went out the next time. Soon, they were off to the next secret birthday location.

CHAPTER 40

Beth was shocked when Melissa pulled out on the highway and headed uptown. Melissa turned left and pulled in the 'The Club' parking lot.

Beth arched her eyebrows. "We're not going in there!"

"Oh yes we are!" Melissa parked and turned the ignition off.

"Don't forget these." Jackie proceeded to hand out fake IDs to everyone.

"Where did you get these?" Beth asked nervously.

"Some of Al's friends let us borrow them. *Do not* lose them."

They divided up the IDs as best they could.

"We'll never get in." Beth worried her bottom lip with her teeth.

"Yes, we will," Jackie said with determination. "Let's go."

The girls strutted toward the club, Jackie leading the way.

A bouncer sat on a stool in front of the entrance. He was a large guy wearing glasses with a long ponytail that hung down the length of his back. His eyes were glassy, and he looked pretty wasted to Beth. There was a $1.00 cover charge, and the girls dug out their wallets. He quickly glanced at each ID and waved them in. The music was deafening, and thick cigarette smoke choked the air. The band performed an Allman Brother's tune "No Way Out."

It took Beth a moment to adjust her eyes to the darkness. They had entered the world of adults, and it was impressive and exciting. Jackie seemed to know exactly where she was going.

She led them toward the bar located in the back. There

were tables in the front part of the club, and a large dance floor stood before the band. No one danced because the band was performing its floorshow.

The girls got excited as they looked around and pretended to be nonchalant. Jackie strutted up to the bar and ordered five Michelob Lights in bottles. She turned around to collect the money. Once the beers were opened, she turned back to pass them out. None of them spoke to one another. They were all fascinated to be in the hottest bar in town.

They turned toward the stage, and Beth saw Al stand up and wave his hand to Jackie. He sat at a large horseshoe-shaped table in front of a high wall. The seats were covered in black vinyl. Two tables left room for the customers to divide up the booth or to gain easy access to the dance floor, no matter where you positioned yourself at the table.

The girls followed Jackie down a few steps towards Al and the table. Beth walked directly behind Jackie and turned to make sure the rest of the flock followed her. This was not the time to lose anyone. Jackie made a sharp turn around the wall and walked up to Al who stood and smiled at her. The two kissed, and he motioned for her to let the others sit in the booth first so she could be next to him. Jackie's face lit up at Al's attention. She was truly in love with him. Beth had never seen Jackie in love with anyone before. She turned to slide into the booth, and she stopped frozen in her tracks.

Greg glared at her from the opposite side of the booth. She smiled weakly and decided to move forward, swallowing the lump in her throat. He turned his face away and watched the band. He said nothing to any of them. Beth became exceedingly uncomfortable seated at his left, and she focused on the band. She thought they were good, and the lead singer finished the song. As the drummer banged out the final beat, the stage went black. The crowd clapped, cheered, and whistled.

Greg sat quietly staring at the dark stage. He turned to Al

and said, "I'm going to get a drink."

Beth felt like an idiot. Of course, everyone knew he left to get away from her. Susan, Lynne, and Melissa pointed out people they knew in the crowd as the band took a break. Fleetwood Mac's "Rumors" album played through the speakers, and the volume was low enough for people to talk. Beth saw quite a few people she knew from work and some former graduates from C.R. A constant stream of people stopped by the table to say "Hello."

Nervous jitters kept Beth frozen in her seat. She was afraid someone would approach them and tell them to get out. Jackie didn't seem to care if she got caught. She and Al traveled around the room talking to his friends.

Beth looked back towards the bar. The back of the booth was too high for her to see over. She took the chance, stood slightly, and peered over to see if Greg was still there. He drank a shot of something and took a gulp from the draft beer in his hand. He didn't see her watching him, and she was grateful. Beth turned her attention to the crowd. Mike Crowley was there with a date, and Brian Knight was with a girl Beth had never seen before. It seemed odd to see Brian with a girl. He was usually alone, and she never understood why.

Brian came over to speak to them, but there were no hugs or kisses on the cheeks like normal. Beth observed the guys' dates. They were older, of course, but not exceptionally beautiful like Beth would have imagined. The only thing they had over her and her friends was the freedom to go with the guys to the places they wanted to go, which was apparently quite important to young men in their early twenties. Beth envied that freedom and was convinced that when she turned eighteen, she and Danny's relationship would flourish once she was free to drink, travel, and have sex. What else was there?

Greg returned to the table and twisted slightly away from her as he sat facing the dance floor. Lynne leaned over and asked Beth if she were okay.

"I'm fine. This place is just a little overwhelming, don't you think?"

Lynne and Susan nodded. They seemed as nervous as Beth about getting caught with fake IDs. Melissa talked to someone a couple of tables over and eventually sat there. Al and Jackie returned to the table. Al tried to engage his cousin in a conversation, but Greg wouldn't participate. He acted like a big bear—quiet, sullen, and very anti-social.

Al ordered more beers for the girls. "These are on me," he said.

Beth hadn't even finished her first one. She tried to pace herself.

The band returned to the stage, and the dance floor opened up. They began with The Stones "Brown Sugar."

The dance floor filled quickly. Before long, all the couples danced and left the singles to size each other up. Melissa accepted an invitation to dance. Susan refused a dance, as did Lynne. Beth was glued to the seat next to Greg. No one approached her, and she hoped it was because she was seated next to Greg. He watched the crowd and didn't turn his head to speak or even look at her. If he gave her the opportunity, she wanted to explain her actions at the party.

Finally she couldn't take the tension between them anymore, and she touched his left arm. He turned his head toward her but didn't look her in the eye.

She asked, "Do you want to dance?"

His eyes locked with hers and he simply said, "No." He narrowed his gaze and looked away.

Beth felt like she was going to throw up. He smirked, rose, and then strode back to the bar and ordered another shot.

What a dick! Beth was ready to go. She was fed up with this guy and his mistaken ideas of her. Greg remained at the bar the entire music set.

Around ten o'clock, Melissa came back to their table and said, "I need to go in a few minutes. Jackie's going to stay here with Al. He said he'll take you guys home if you want to stay, but I'll take anybody who's ready to go now. Give me about five minutes. I have to make a call."

Beth, Susan, and Lynne decided they would go with Melissa. It wasn't all that much fun dancing with strangers, and the only guys they knew were there with dates.

Greg returned to the table. He sat down and watched the crowd with glassy eyes, apparently drunk.

"Hey man, you better lighten it up a little," Al said to his cousin.

Greg only stared at him with a hateful scowl on his face. Beth watched the exchange and decided it wasn't worth it to hang around here. She was ready to go if Greg was going to be mean and nasty the rest of the night.

Melissa returned. "Okay, let's go."

Greg watched as the girls got up to leave.

"Where are you going?" he asked Melissa.

She explained that she had somewhere else to be.

"Do you all have to go?" he asked and then looked toward Al.

"I'll take anybody home who wants to stay," Al offered again.

Susan and Lynne said thanks, but they needed to go. Beth didn't respond. She seemed to irritate him, and he obviously didn't like her.

The girls said their goodbyes to Jackie, hugged her and walked past Greg one by one. Beth was the last one to pass him. He reached out and grabbed hold of her wrist with a firm grip. She was startled and paused to look down at him.

He tried hard to focus his eyes on her, and he said simply, "Don't go."

Beth didn't know what to say. She looked back at Al and Jackie with wide eyes.

Al said, "Come on and stay with us."

Beth watched the other girls walk towards the exit. When they reached the door, Melissa looked back at her and paused. Beth turned back to Greg.

"Please? I think we ought to talk," he said.

Beth agreed and nodded. She really wanted him to know her behavior in the bathroom was not typical, and she was not easy.

"You'll have to quit with the shots, okay?"

Greg nodded and smiled.

Beth waved to Melissa, signaling her to leave without her. She returned to her seat.

"Do you need a beer?" Greg asked her.

"No, I'm fine. Thanks."

Brian walked by their table again and said "Hello." He didn't greet Beth with his usual "Hello, Gorgeous." Instead, he was stiff and polite when he spoke. Beth assumed it was because he didn't want to upset Greg again.

Once he was far enough away from the table, Greg looked at her and said, "There goes your boyfriend."

Beth responded quickly. "Brian is my friend and has been incredibly good to me over the past couple of years. We tried dating when we first met, but it didn't work out. We've been close ever since. I can assure you he's not my boyfriend."

"Did he break up with you?" Greg asked.

"No." Beth smiled at the pathetic look on his face. "It was me."

Greg nodded.

Beth continued, "I know you were upset with me for dancing with him at the party. I heard you called me a slut. I think you owe me an apology. You jumped to conclusions. If you had let me explain, I would have told you that Brian is like my big brother. I had no idea it would upset you. I only agreed because I felt weird about having been in the bathroom with you and I didn't want anyone else to know."

Before Greg could respond, the band took the stage again, and that was the end of any real conversation. It was difficult to hear one another over the loud music. Greg tried to sober up and ordered a soda from the waitress. Al and

Jackie went to dance and left Greg and Beth alone at the table. Greg continued to have his body positioned towards the stage, and Beth sat next to him feeling ignored and awkward. He was drunk, and she wondered why in the world she agreed to stay.

"Hey you!" Mike Crowley yelled as he slid into the booth next to Beth. She was relieved to have someone to talk to.

"Hi Mike," she yelled over the music.

"Hey Greg, how are you?"

Greg nodded a silent hello and turned to drunkenly position himself towards Beth and Mike.

"What are you doing in here, girlie?" Mike teased Beth, poking her in the side.

"Jackie hooked us up. It's my birthday present."

"Today's your birthday?" Mike asked.

Beth nodded.

"Well, Happy Birthday, sweetheart."

"Thanks," she said smiling.

"Who's the girl you're with?" Beth asked Mike.

"She's a girl from work. Brian's here with her friend. Did you see Brian?" He nodded his head in Brian's direction. Beth nodded and Mike continued, "The girls are in the bathroom now. They are okay. I saw Lynne here with you." He shrugged and gave her a small smile.

"Mmm hmmm." Beth smiled at his awkwardness.

"I hear she's pretty into this boyfriend. I saw them at the last party. She looked in love. Is she happy?"

Beth nodded and said gently, "I think she's very happy."

"Good. That's good." He looked down at his hands folded together on the table.

What was wrong with these guys? Beth wondered if there were just too many girls around, and they couldn't make up their minds.

Mike continued to sit with her, and he told them both about a party at Joe's house the next weekend. His date exited the bathroom doorway, and he jumped up. "I better go. Bring Lynne to Joe's next weekend." He smiled, waved, and walked toward his date.

Beth glanced toward the table where he and Brian sat. Brian was alone and smiled at his date as she approached him. He stood and held her chair out for her. The band finished their song.

Greg had sobered a little and looked at Beth.

She confided to Greg, "I will definitely 'not' bring Lynne to that party. I'm not going to let him mess up her relationship."

He smiled at her.

"That's probably smart," he said.

Beth was glad he hadn't turned his body away from her again after Mike left the table. She tried to continue with a normal conversation, but Greg wasn't talking much.

They locked gazes with one another. He was still the most magnificent creature she'd ever seen. There was nothing wrong with him anywhere. She glanced down at his hands on the table. They were perfect. She studied the outline of his fingers and the way the veins traveled up to his wrists. His hands were strong, and she knew how they could affect her. She boldly touched his hands and turned them over for further inspection. Beth's face grew warm, and he laughed at her.

"What's so funny?" She let go of his hand.

He stared at Beth, and she became uncomfortable. "You want to go to Joe's party with me?" he asked.

Beth felt a lump in her throat.

"Sure," she said.

He picked up his glass of soda and tapped her beer bottle in a toast.

"Good. You be ready, little girl," he warned and winked at her.

She smiled with embarrassment and averted her gaze from him. He was so good looking it almost hurt to look at him.

He reached his hand under the table and placed it over her knee, and her breath quickened. She shot a wide-eyed stare at him. He moved his hand slowly up and down her leg and gently squeezed the inside of her thigh.

Oh God... Beth thought.

Greg moved his hand up with no intention of stopping. He continued to stare at her as she faced forward expressionless. She placed her right hand over his to push it away. Beth applied pressure, but he refused to move. She pressed even harder, and he ignored her attempts. His strength easily overpowered hers. Greg's hand reached its destination, and Beth gasped, quickly taking a deep breath. Her shocked gaze swept his face. He stared at her intently.

Oh God... she thought again as he touched her.

He leaned into her right ear. "Happy Birthday," he whispered and kissed her slowly on the ear and neck.

Beth trembled. "Please stop." She turned her face to meet his.

He silenced her easily with a kiss, and to her shock, she surrendered to him.

Beth was stunned. Greg was able to assault all her senses at one time. He didn't wear cologne, but he smelled clean and earthy. She liked his scent and inhaled deeply when they kissed.

The band began to play "The Best of Your Love" by the Eagles.

"Let's dance," Greg said as took her by the hand.

She allowed him to lead her to the dance floor. In fact, it dawned on her that she allowed him to make all the decisions—when to touch her, when to ignore her, when to smile, when to kiss, and when to dance. She had never once stopped Greg Black from doing anything. That needed to change.

They danced together, and he held her loosely with one hand around her waist, and the other held her right hand up close to his chest. Beth loved being held like that. He looked down at her and sang softly with the song.

What is wrong with me? I'm acting like an idiot, staring at him like I am totally in love. She was seriously attracted to this guy, but she wasn't in love. Also, if they had any chance of a real relationship, she would have to get her nerves under control. Once again, she would have to lie to her parents. She took a deep breath and tried to relax.

Greg pulled her body in close to him, and he continued to sing to her as she closed her eyes and drank in his smell, sound, and touch. At the end of the dance, they shared a long, deep kiss.

The band started up a driving beat and began to deliver "Tush" by ZZ Top. Beth and Greg stayed on the dance floor and danced the entire set. Greg had sobered up by the time they returned to the table. He smiled and behaved pleasantly. This made Beth happy. Al and Jackie were ready to go. It was obvious what their plans were because they couldn't keep their hands off one another. Beth was slightly jealous.

The four left The Club and headed to Beth's house. Greg paid attention to the directions so he could pick her up on Saturday for the party at Joe's. He kept his hands to himself the entire ride home, and Beth felt grateful.

"Thanks for the ride," Beth said to Al.

Jackie said, "Bye, Happy Birthday."

"Catch you later," Al called to her.

Greg exited his side of the car. Beth seriously hoped her mother wasn't watching out the window. If she caught sight of this guy, Beth would be placed under lock and key in her room.

Greg was a gentleman as he walked her to the door. "I'll pick you up Saturday around eight. Is that okay?"

"That'll be fine."

"Okay, sweetness. I'll see you."

Sweetness? Who actually says that to someone? Beth's cheeks flushed, and she gave him a demure smile.

"See you Saturday."

"Bye," she said in a breathy tone, embarrassed as she turned to go in the house.

CHAPTER 41

Beth worked on Tuesday night. Brian came into the store, and she was surprised and happy to see him.

"Hey Beth," he said tentatively. "I know it's none of my business, but I saw you and Greg the other night. You guys looked really into each other."

Beth raised her eyebrow and asked, "And?"

Brian shifted uncomfortably. "I really like Greg but just be careful, okay?"

She narrowed her eyes. "What do you mean?"

"I don't know." He shifted from one foot to the other. "I just like you both, and I don't want either of you to get hurt."

"Thanks, Brian. You're a good friend. I know about his girlfriend and what she did to him. I promise I won't hurt him."

Brian looked at her intensely. "It's not him so much I'm worried about."

"I have to get back to work." Beth laughed, blew him a kiss, and went back to restocking the shelves. She wasn't sure what Brian was talking about. She knew he wasn't jealous. Or was he?

She turned around and watched him leave, a strange warm sensation growing in her chest. Beth brushed it off and stocked the shelves.

Earlier, Beth had learned Melissa was seeing Eric again. She was disappointed because she thought Melissa had finally gotten over him when she began dating Chuck. While chatting on the phone, Melissa explained that she couldn't stay away from Eric, and it sounded very much like Beth's feelings for Danny. Beth understood too well but had hoped her friend was over him.

"Just be careful," Beth had advised.

"I will be, I promise." Melissa had replied.

Why did falling in love have to be so painful?

~

On Wednesday night, Greg called to say hello and finalize their plans for Saturday. He didn't have much to say, and Beth wished he would talk more. Susan called on Thursday and said Tyler was leaving for boot camp Friday morning. She was down and out, and Beth convinced her to go to Joe's party on Saturday. They made plans to go to Burger Chef for dinner and then out to The Boat Friday night. All the girls agreed to go to support Susan. Lynne admitted to the girls that she was in love with Joey and then Jackie told them how much she loved Al. Jackie's spunk and independence seemed to have gone right out the window. The girls had never seen her this way. It was all about what Al thought, what Al said, where Al went. Nobody said it aloud, but they were concerned Jackie was in for a hard fall if Al changed his mind about her.

At the Boat on Friday, Susan was a sobbing mess. The girls offered support and understanding. They took Susan's mother's car because it had a cassette tape player. They played Elton John's Greatest Hits tape and sang along.

"Can you believe he's bi?" Jackie drank from the wine bottle.

"Who in their right mind would go public with something like that?" Lynne asked.

"I don't know. I think David Bowie said he was, too, didn't he?" Susan asked.

Melissa chimed in, "Didn't his wife catch him in bed with Mick Jagger or something like that?"

The girls screamed and laughed out loud.

"Can you imagine?" Beth yelled. "Honey! I'm home! Honey? Why are you in our bed with your best friend? Poor girl."

"Poor girl? Who knows what she's into? Maybe she hopped in there, too," Jackie added.

Everyone paused to ponder that comment and then burst into gales of laughter. Jackie held her sides as she laughed. Susan and Lynne flopped onto their backs, laughing hysterically. Beth and Melissa laughed at the others.

"Well, you can talk about those guys all you want, but nobody better tell me Steven Tyler is gay. If he is, I will truly die. I'll be mortally affected forever more!" Beth added dramatically as she put one hand to her forehead and swooned.

"I think he is," Lynne said.

Beth gave her a dirty look.

"Well, seriously I do. Don't you? He looks like it to me with that hair and those lips! He gyrates around on stage like the rest of them." She got up and imitated him, walking around and gyrating.

The girls roared with laughter.

"Lynne, you better shut up or I'm gonna kick your ass," Beth said lightheartedly as she put up one fist.

"Why do you suppose so many guys are gay?" Susan rolled her eyes and looked confused.

"Because men are R.B.T.R. You know, Ruled By The Rod. They don't care where they stick it," Melissa said with a nonchalant shrug.

The girls stared at her with wide eyes for a split second and then burst into uncontrollable laughter.

"My Dad told me that the guy from *Macmillan and Wife*, Rock Hudson, is gay," Lynne said.

"No way!" Beth replied shocked.

"I don't believe it either, isn't he married to Doris Day?" Susan asked.

"No, they aren't married. They just do movies together. Anyway, Dad said it has been a rumor for years," Lynne added, smiling smugly.

"We'd probably be shocked about all the guys who are

queer," Jackie said.

"Well, I do know Steven Tyler isn't. It's all about faith," Beth insisted.

"Okay, Okay! It was just my opinion." Lynne rolled her eyes.

"Well, I don't know how he could write a song like "Walk this Way" and "Sweet Emotion" if he were gay," Beth added.

"Yeah, but he says, 'Some sweet talkin' momma with a face like a gent.' Sounds a little Lola'ish to me," Melissa said.

"That's true," Lynne agreed.

Beth frowned at them.

"I know David Lee Roth isn't," Melissa said to change the focus.

"Definitely not!" they each agreed.

"He'd be on my list of 'Guys I'd Want to See Naked.'" Jackie twirled her blonde curls.

There was a chorus of "me, toos!"

Susan said, "I know the guys from AC/DC aren't."

"Oh, hell no!" Melissa chimed in. "They aren't very good looking, but when they sang "Girls Got Rhythm" at the concert, it sent me over the edge. Tyler got lucky that night!"

The girls giggled with approval and she laughed.

The trip to The Boat had done what it was supposed to do. Susan was happy and relaxed. She thanked the girls for cheering her up and hugged each of them.

When Beth returned home early, her mother asked her if everything was all right.

"Yeah, Susan was down because her boyfriend, Tyler, left for basic training. We just hung out and tried to cheer her up," Beth replied.

"I mean with you, Beth. Lately you seem sort of edgy."

"Really?" Beth hadn't been aware her mother could see through her so well.

Her mother nodded, and Beth said, "I'm fine, really."

"You'd tell me if something were wrong?" her mother questioned further.

"Of course, I would," she said, knowing full well she probably wouldn't. Her mother would tell her father.

"Mom?"

"Yes?"

"I was asked out on a date for tomorrow night," Beth said hesitantly. She could barely look her mother in the eye.

"With whom?" Her mother's gaze narrowed.

"His name is Greg Black."

Her mother paused and asked, "Is he related to Janine and Frank Black?"

Beth smartly dodged the question. "I don't know. I didn't ask him his parents' names."

She knew better than to tell her he was the son of Chester Black who owned the seedy bar in the next town over.

Her mother pursed her mouth and raised her eyebrows. She wanted more details.

"We are invited to a party at Joe Cahall's house...Janet Pallace's boyfriend? You know, Susan's sister?"

Her mother finally nodded.

"Does Greg go to C.R.?" she asked.

Oh great. Here we go again!

"He did. He graduated already," Beth said, holding her breath.

"When did he graduate, Beth?" she asked, clearly annoyed.

"He never mentioned it," she said, avoiding a lie. "You'll like him, though."

Her mother looked at her intensely. "Well, okay. I guess you can go. But I want to meet him first."

Relieved, Beth hugged her mother. "Okay, no problem. He's coming to pick me up, and I'll tell him to come early."

~

Beth had to work on Saturday from ten to three. She planned to buy a new outfit for her date with Greg. Debbie was also working that day, and she helped Beth find a delicious ensemble. She was excited to wear it, but she began to get the jitters as it got closer to the end of her shift.

When Beth got home from work, she needed a distraction to help pass the time until Greg came to get her. Why was she so nervous? She told herself she was being ridiculous, then she called Melissa's house. Thankfully, Melissa answered the phone, so Beth invited her over.

Melissa arrived, and Beth's mother let her in. She bopped up the stairs to Beth's room.

"Hey," she said, and the two got comfortable on the bed.

Beth confided in Melissa about the advances Greg had made under the table at The Club.

Melissa smiled at her. "He really likes you."

"I'm not sure."

"Why wouldn't he?" Melissa asked.

Beth said she felt incredibly attracted to him.

"Who wouldn't be? He's gorgeous! There are a lot of girls who would love to be you! Have fun with it. Enjoy it!"

Beth was glad she asked Melissa over. She felt more confident and relaxed.

"You know, I'm not on the pill," Beth told her.

Melissa shook her head. "Why not? Geez! You never know, and you don't want to be pregnant. They'll kick you out of school!"

"And my parents will kick me out of the house, too!" Beth added.

"No, they wouldn't," Melissa said.

"Yes, my father would, and you better believe it." Beth said sincerely.

Melissa told Beth she needed to get on the pill if she thought she might have sex. "Just call the clinic and make an appointment. It's really not that big of a deal."

The idea of going to get a pelvic exam scared the hell out of Beth. She really couldn't bear the embarrassment of being examined by a male doctor.

Melissa reached for her purse, opened it, and took two condoms out. She placed them in Beth's hand.

"Here, these are for you. I bought them for you the night we were at The Club for your birthday. They had a machine in the bathroom. I figured part of your problem was birth control, so here you go."

Beth laughed, and her face flushed with embarrassment.

Melissa ignored her immaturity. "I'm going to show you how they work."

Beth fell over on her side of the bed cracking up.

Her laughter was contagious, and Melissa began to laugh, too, and then whispered seriously, "Look, you really need to know, Beth!"

"Okay. Okay." She sat up and tried to put on a serious expression while her eyes danced with laughter and her mouth twitched.

Melissa opened the box and pulled out a large balloon that was rolled up flat. She handed it to Beth. She took it in her fingers.

"It's slimy!" She made a face.

"It's *lubricated.* Here, pretend these two fingers are a guy's 'you know.' You put the pointy tip on the top and roll it down over it with your hand." She motioned the proper technique without unrolling the condom. "Mom said a guy is more likely to use one if you offer to put it on for him." She paused to make sure Beth paid close attention.

"Your mother told you that?" Beth gaped at her.

Melissa nodded.

"Go ahead, try it." Melissa nodded toward her fingers.

"Now?" Beth asked incredulously as she looked at her friend's fingers holding an unrolled condom at the tips.

"Yes, now," Melissa said.

"On your fingers?" Beth asked, horrified.

"Oh Beth, for God's sakes!" Melissa rolled her eyes and looked around the room, but there was nothing suitable to use.

"Yes, just do it, Beth." Melissa held her index and middle finger up in the air.

Beth placed the condom on the tip just as instructed. "Now roll it down over my fingers with a firm grip."

"Like this?" The condom slid quickly down the length of her fingers.

"That's perfect!" Melissa smiled.

The condom was now appropriately placed over Melissa's fingers. She bent them as if it were a puppet, causing Beth to laugh. She grinned, feeling proud of herself.

Melissa pulled the condom from her fingers and said, "Do you think you could do it again?"

Beth nodded with confidence.

Melissa slanted her head. "Are you sure?"

"Yes! Don't treat me like a baby."

Melissa laughed at her and said teasingly, "You *are* a baby! Here, put this one in your purse."

Beth opened her purse and unzipped the compartment that carried her tampons and Tylenol.

"Do you think you're going to use it tonight?"

"God no, not tonight. I really like Greg or rather, I'm really attracted to him, but I don't want to sleep with him yet. I'd like to be in love with whoever I sleep with the first time." She paused. "And it really should be Danny."

Melissa took hold of Beth's hands. "Beth, Danny is gone. Come on! The last time he was home he got you all worked up and then left with no further contact. What is that all about? That should convince you he's just playing around. He comes home feeling like a failure and a waste. I mean what is he doing? Hanging out, that's all, and here you are looking at him with adoring eyes. That's some heady stuff for a guy."

Beth never thought about it that way, but Melissa could be right.

Still, there was something about when she and Danny were together that no one else understood. Hell, she didn't even understand it.

"I always wondered if maybe he was using me. I thought that couldn't be because, well, you know, we weren't doing it. Maybe he just uses me to build up his ego. He acts so different around other people. He tries to make himself out to be a big shot."

Melissa nodded and said, "People don't like that, Beth."

"I know, but he doesn't act like that with me when we're alone. It drives me nuts when he acts that way."

Melissa shrugged, and the two fell silent for a moment.

Beth slapped her hands on her lap, snapping them to attention. "Well, anyway... I'm not going out with Danny tonight. I am going out with Adonis, I mean Greg. I'm having enough trouble keeping composed while putting the damn rubber on you. I can't imagine saying to Greg, 'Honey, could you please use this condom? I'll put it on for you,'" she said in a breathy, idiotic tone.

Melissa bent over laughing hysterically. "You're too much! Just make sure you use it if you guys do go at it. You understand?"

"Yes, yes, yes!"

They went downstairs, and Beth's mom asked Melissa to stay for dinner, and she accepted the offer. Beth's dad had a lodge meeting so it would just be the three of them. The time passed quickly with Melissa there. Beth found it easier to talk with her mother when her father wasn't around. After they finished eating, the girls cleaned the dishes and headed back upstairs.

"Thanks for the help, girls!"

"You're welcome," they called back.

The phone rang. Beth ran up the steps and grabbed the phone in her room. It was Greg. Her face grew hot as she spoke to him, and Melissa smiled. When Beth got off the phone Melissa said, "Your mother's going to totally lose it when she sees him."

Beth made a nervous face, bit her bottom lip, and smiled.

"I know."

The two talked about Eric a lot and what was going on between him and Melissa. He pretty much stayed at Melissa's house full-time now. Her mother was still cool with it. Melissa was a little concerned because Eric had been drinking a lot more, and now her mother had a drinking buddy in the house. Eric got along well with her mother and that made it easier, but it bothered Melissa. She was sure they were smoking dope together after she went to bed at night, though she couldn't prove it. Melissa told Beth that she and Eric wouldn't be at Joe's party. He didn't care much for that crowd, so he would never agree to go. Beth pouted at her friend.

Melissa changed the subject. "Show me what you're wearing to the party."

Beth showed her a pair of black Chino's with a pastel lavender pullover cotton shirt with quarter-length sleeves. The shirt had thin, black swirl designs and a low neckline, and she liked that a lot. Beth retrieved her black thong sandals with platform heels from the closet. Then she showed Melissa a plain gold chain with a black onyx pendant, a beautiful gold watch with a mother-of-pearl face, and gold earrings with light purple crystals. Beth liked the plain but elegant style.

Melissa said, "It's the perfect outfit. Greg will love it."

The two decided to paint their nails. They applied Sally Hansen's Pearly Lavender Fields to their finger and toenails while listening to Janis Joplin and talking non-stop throughout the entire process. When they were finished, Beth dried the polish with her blow dryer.

The clock read six thirty. Melissa said she needed to go, and Beth walked her out. The fiery sun began to set, and the weather was gorgeous. The stars would shine bright tonight. She imagined leaning back into Greg's arms as they sat outside staring up at the night sky. It would be so romantic.

"Wow, your nails look great, Beth," Melissa said from the

driver's seat of her mom's car.

Beth returned the compliment, and they waved good-bye.

"Have a great time. You'd better call me tomorrow with *details!*"

The two smiled at one another and waved again as Melissa pulled out of the driveway.

Beth raced up the steps two at a time and headed for the shower. She shaved her legs and armpits and took extra time as she washed every square inch of her body twice. By the time she finished, it was ten after seven. She twisted the towel around her head and threw on her robe. The phone rang as she entered her bedroom. It was Jackie and she was crying. Her brow furrowed with concern, Beth asked what was wrong. Jackie said Al called her and cancelled their date for tonight.

"Did he say why?"

"He said he worked all day on a roof down at the beach and was badly sunburned. He wasn't feeling much like going out tonight," she sniffled.

"Well, that sounds reasonable," Beth replied

"Yeah? Well, then I offered to come over to his apartment and hang out for the night, and he said, 'We'd better do that another time.' He said he was exhausted. I said I was going to go to the party without him, and he said that would be fine."

Beth took a deep breath. "Jackie, I'm sure he's telling you the truth. I saw how he looked at you when we were at The Club. He cares for you a lot," she reassured her friend.

"Well, I'm going to that party without him," she stated stubbornly.

"I don't think there's anything wrong with that either," Beth added.

"Do you think you and Greg could give me a ride? Mom won't let me have the car."

Beth felt a wave of disappointment. She wanted to be

alone with Greg. But she couldn't say no to Jackie.

"Sure, we can give you a ride."

"You don't think Greg would mind?" she questioned.

"I can't imagine he would. I've got to get going, though. I don't even have my hair dried yet. We'll be there as soon as we can," Beth told her.

"Okay," Jackie said pathetically.

Beth felt badly for her, but the girl was freaking out before she had a reason to. This was so unlike Jackie. She was in love with this guy, and if Al was indeed blowing her off, it was going to be interesting to watch how Jackie handled it.

"Lord, help us all!" Beth said out loud.

Beth was dressed and ready ten minutes early. Her hair bounced and shined from the blow dryer. She had grown it out since her freshman year, and it now fell midway down her back. Her makeup looked good, too. The lavender top was a little snug but not too tight. She admired how great her feet looked in the high heels with the polish she'd chosen. Pleased, she sat on her bed and watched out the window for a car. She didn't remember what kind of car Greg drove. A burgundy Camaro came down the road. It slowed down as it approached her house. Beth was certain it was him. The car pulled into her driveway, and she jumped off the bed and raced downstairs.

Beth reached the bottom of the steps and halted.

Her Mother was peeking out the window and turned to Beth, her brows lifted. "Is that him?"

Beth nodded and joined her mother at the window.

"My Lord, Beth!" she said, her eyes widening.

Beth grinned at her mother.

Greg stepped out of the car and paused to adjust a pale-yellow button-down shirt in the back of his Levi's. His shirt was rolled up over his forearms, and the color complemented his amazing tan. He was tall, gorgeous, and built like a Greek god with broad shoulders, narrow hips, and muscular legs hugged loosely by his jeans. They both admired him as he walked up the sidewalk.

"Move! Don't let him see you staring out at him!" her mom whispered, gently pushing her toward the front door.

"Stop, Mom!" Beth laughed as her mother's touch tickled her sides.

The doorbell rang. Beth looked at her mother, shook her hands out in front of her, and took a deep breath to settle her nerves.

Her mother grinned. "You're going to be fine."

Beth opened the door, and Greg entered the foyer. She introduced him to her mother.

He said, "Hello" and shook her mother's hand when she extended it.

She watched her mother examine every detail of Greg's face as he spoke. Greg and her mother chatted a minute more about the weather and where they were going.

"We'd better go," Beth said, and the two of them walked out of the house.

Greg opened the passenger door for her, and she slid in. He walked around the front of the car. When he was out of sight, Beth stuck her tongue out at her mother who she knew still peeked out the dining room window. She smiled and waved at the window, knowing her mom smiled, too.

Greg got in and gazed at her. "You look beautiful."

"Thank you, you don't look bad yourself."

What was she saying? He truly couldn't have looked any better.

"There's something I want to show you before we go to the party, is that okay?" He started the car and pulled onto the street.

"Sure," Beth said. "Oh, by the way, Jackie called and said Al cancelled on her tonight. She wanted to know if we could give her a ride."

Greg pressed his lips together and glanced at her. "I suppose you told her yes."

Beth gave him a guilty shrug.

He tightened his grip on the steering wheel. "Damn! I wanted to be alone with you tonight. What did Al tell Jackie?"

"He said he was exhausted and sunburned from working at the beach today," Beth replied.

"Where does Jackie live?" he asked.

"Turn here. What did you want to show me?"

"My apartment," he said sullenly. "We won't be able to go there now."

Beth smiled nervously, and her stomach flipped. Suddenly, she was grateful her friend needed a ride.

Beth directed him toward the highway. They were about to pass Burger Chef when he quickly cut the car into the parking lot and drove to the rear of the restaurant. He stopped the car with a jerk and threw his right arm up on Beth's seat as he turned toward her, startling her in the process.

"Are you trying to get out of being alone with me?" He narrowed his eyes at her.

"Why would I do that?" Beth was taken aback.

He looked forward and said, "I can't believe you told Jackie we'd pick her up. Why didn't you tell her to find her own ride?"

Beth could not believe this god of a man was feeling insecure.

Greg stared at her, and she traced his facial features with her gaze.

"I think you're the most handsome guy I've ever seen," she spoke softly and honestly. "I'm very attracted to you and that scares me a little. Okay, that scares me a lot. I would love to be alone with you, and I didn't plan for Jackie to ride with us. She asked me, and I could not very well turn her down. It's just a ride there and home. I didn't think it would be a big deal."

He looked at her intently as if he were deciding whether to believe her or not. Finally, his features softened.

"Sometimes I get the feeling you're playing around with me." He stared at her mouth and leaned in to kiss her.

Beth gently pressed her hand to his chest to stop him. "Greg, I don't want you irritated with me over little things all the time. So far, you are either all over me or mad as hell. You make me jumpy because I don't know what to do to make you happy."

He smiled at her and said, "Look, I went through a really bad split with my ex-girlfriend, and I think she did some serious damage. The only thing you can do to make me happy is to not lie. Don't ever lie to me." His face was still close to hers.

Beth placed her hand on his cheek and said sincerely, "I have *never* lied to you." She hoped that would end his feelings of insecurity and convince him she was *not* a tramp.

She leaned in and kissed him on the lips, soft and quick. He sat perfectly still for a moment. Beth wondered what he was thinking. He still seemed stiff and unsure. She hoped he believed her. He moved in and kissed her on the mouth.

"Let's skip the party and go back to my apartment," he suggested.

"What about Jackie?"

"She's not invited." He smiled at her.

Beth laughed and was happy to hear the humor in his voice. He laughed, too, and turned to take hold of the steering wheel.

Rolling his eyes dramatically, he said, "Let's go get Jackie."

The three arrived at Joe's around eight thirty. The party was already in full swing. It appeared several of the guys had been there for a while. They swayed in their seats in the kitchen and drank shots. This was Greg's old football crowd, and he was glad to see them. He looked down at Beth as if to ask permission to leave her and go to the kitchen. She nodded at him. He quickly brought back two beers—one for her and one for Jackie.

Mike Crowley danced his way over to talk to the girls. He hugged Jackie and then Beth.

He was very drunk, and he almost knocked Beth over as he tried to kiss her cheek. "Hey girlie."

Wham! Greg was immediately at her side, grabbing Mike by the back of the neck and pulling him away from Beth.

"Not tonight, cowboy. Tonight's my turn."

Mike, Jackie, and Beth looked at Greg wide-eyed.

Mike held up his hands and backed away, heeding the warning. No sooner had Mike walked away, then Billy Englehart came around the corner. He saw Beth, ran up to her, and gave her a tight hug. He was a little drunk, and Beth thought it was funny. She laughed as Billy pretended to kiss her on the neck, bending her over backward. Beth's gaze flew to Greg who was looking at her with a cold stare. She tried to stop Billy, and then Jackie grabbed Billy and pulled him away from the imminent "Greg" explosion.

The three of them stood alone momentarily.

Jackie saw Greg's expression and tried to diffuse the situation. "Oh, come on, Greg! Those guys have been our friends for years! It's nothing!"

He ignored Jackie, sent Beth a hard stare, and stalked into the kitchen.

Beth and Jackie watched as he picked up a bottle of vodka and began to drink right from the bottle.

Jackie looked at Beth. "Maybe this isn't such a good idea."

"What are you talking about?"

"Greg," Jackie said.

"It'll be okay. He seems to have this idea that I'm jerking around with him. I'm not sure why or what that's about. He can be funny and very charming at times. I'm not sure what's up with him."

As friends entered the party, they inevitably came over to greet the girls.

"Hey, Hey!" Rocky said as he entered the front door.

Beth cringed and hoped he wouldn't say or do anything

to make Greg angrier than he already was.

Trying to ignore the fact that the date was going downhill fast, Beth talked with the girls for about a half hour. They wanted to spread out and socialize, but Beth asked them to stay with her. Another half hour passed. She watched Greg as he sat sullen and quiet in the kitchen amongst a bunch of his friends who laughed and acted silly around him. He continued to drink from the same bottle. He stared at Beth, his lip curled with distain, and then looked away. He appeared as if he wished he hadn't brought her.

Beth finally had enough of his dirty looks and boldly walked toward him and asked if he wanted her to leave.

"I'm apparently making you very unhappy tonight," she said.

Greg took her by the hand and hauled her onto his lap.

"You're not making me unhappy." He slurred his words and tried to hold his eyelids open to look at her.

"Well, I don't understand at all," she said to him.

Totally trashed, he swayed back and forth in the chair. She grew concerned he would fall off the chair at any moment, possibly taking her with him.

Brian and Joe came over, their brows furrowed with worry.

"Hey man," Brian said to Greg. "Let's go downstairs and shoot pool."

Joe added, "Or maybe outside to sober up."

"Nope, I'm staying right here and keeping an eye on this one," he slurred poking his index finger into Beth's arm. She rubbed her arm. He held on to her tightly with the other. Beth was unsettled by Greg's behavior, but she couldn't get away from him without making a scene. She was becoming increasingly uncomfortable.

Brian laughed uncomfortably. "Come on, man, she'll be alright. It's you I'm worried about right now."

Greg jumped up from his chair, knocking Beth to the floor. She wasn't hurt, but she was angry.

"What the fuck is that supposed to mean?" Greg puffed up, ready to throw a punch if anyone threatened him.

The guys turned immediately sober and formed a line behind Brian. Mike reached down and grabbed Beth by the arm, pulling her up off the floor and out of the kitchen to get her out of harm's way.

Joe stepped forward. "Greg, man, everybody's having a great time. You've been hitting that bottle hard for almost an hour. Come on in the basement and work some of the alcohol off."

Greg relaxed his posture and looked at his lap and then around the floor.

"Where's Beth?"

The guys separated just enough to let him see her.

She stood in the living room with her arms crossed. She was fuming when her girlfriends gathered around her for support. Greg looked off to the side as everyone waited for his reaction.

He held his head down. "Shit," he said quietly.

Brian stepped forward. "It's alright, man. Let's just get you busy. We'll take a walk."

Four of them walked around him as he staggered slightly towards the front door.

He passed Beth and said, "Don't leave, don't leave. Please, I'm sorry. I'm sorry."

Joe guided him out the front door.

"What the hell?" Beth threw her arms up in exasperation. She didn't understand his behavior and neither did her friends.

"Do you think he has a drinking problem?" Susan asked.

Beth shrugged. She really didn't know him that well.

The music started up again and "Black Betty" barreled from the speakers. Mike brought Beth a shot of Peach Schnapps.

"Mike's answer to everything. A good ole shot, sayeth the Shot Man!" he said.

Beth took the offer, drank the shot, and finished her beer quickly. The alcohol went straight to her head.

Jackie and Mike did shots together and danced. Mike played with Jackie's long blonde curls.

Beth continued to drink beer and shots of Schnapps for about forty-five minutes and waited for the guys to return with Greg. Finally, Brian came through the front door. He pointed to Beth and curled his finger, beckoning her toward him.

She glided forward and felt exceptionally light and airy. She weaved a little on her path to him.

"Oh Lord," Brian said. "You're drunk. Anyway, here's the thing, Beth. Greg has been through a tough time this past year. He says he really likes you a lot. He's sobering up now, and I think he'll be alright."

Beth blinked slowly and swayed. Shit, she was trashed.

Brian slanted his head. "I'm thinking you should let me take you home, though. Do you want to stay with him or let me take you home?"

"It'll be alright. I can't go home now anyway." Beth weaved forward towards him.

"Do you know how handsome he is?" she asked.

Brian laughed at her. "Yes, he's very handsome," he said sarcastically.

He put his hands on her face to steady her. "I am so jealous."

"You are too sweet. I love you!" Beth drunkenly hugged Brian. Oh Lord, thank God Greg didn't see that.

Beth exited the house with Brian and saw some figures walking up the driveway. "Greg!" she called out as she staggered towards him.

She jumped up onto him as if he were a long-lost friend. He held her up as she wrapped her legs around his waist. She threw her arms around his neck, and he staggered a bit but managed to keep himself steady.

"I'm so sorry, Beth," he whispered in her ear.

The rest of the guys went inside and left Greg to deal with his drunk date.

Brian said, "Take care of her."

Greg nodded. Beth heard the exchange, but she didn't react. He still held her, and she leaned back to look at his face.

"Exactly what's wrong anyway?" she asked him.

He only kissed her. She didn't care what was wrong after that. She laid her head on his shoulder. Greg walked her to his car and placed her gently in the passenger's seat.

"I want to go home," Beth said, feeling the world spinning around her.

"I can't take you home like this. It'll be okay. It's early," Greg said. "Stay here. I'm going inside for sodas and to find Jackie."

Beth nodded and leaned back against the seat.

A few minutes later, Brian approached the car.

She groaned as she shifted to roll down the window.

"How are you doing?" he asked.

"A little better now that I'm sitting down." She managed a weak smile.

"Good."

Greg and Jackie emerged from the house.

"I'll see you later, Beth."

"Thanks, Brian." She watched him walk away.

He really seemed to care about her.

A wistful sensation pressed into her chest.

CHAPTER 42

Beth watched with a slightly amused grin as Greg struggled to get a drunk Jackie in the car while juggling two soda cans. He slammed the back door, went around, and climbed into the driver's seat.

"Bethy, what happened to you? You look like you are going to puke." Jackie leaned over the front seat.

Beth groaned.

"Same thing that happened to me earlier, and now to you." Greg set the two sodas in the console, started the car, and pulled onto the street.

"Where are we going?" Jackie asked.

"I'm taking you home."

"No! I can't go home! My mom will kill me if I go in like this! Take me to Al's. I can get straightened out there."

Greg glanced at her in the rearview mirror. "Nope. Can't do that."

"Why not?"

He cut his gaze to Beth. She sensed he was hiding something from Jackie about Al, but she decided not to say anything.

"I'm going to be sick," Jackie said weakly.

Greg pulled the car off the side of the road.

Beth turned, and Jackie was hanging out the window puking, her hair a wild, tangled mess of curls.

With raised brows, Beth glanced at Greg.

"How do you feel?" he asked.

"Okay, I guess. Better than her." Beth nodded towards Jackie.

Greg handed her one of the sodas. Beth set it between her legs, glad she was starting to sober up.

Jackie finally pulled herself in the window. "I'm okay now, Glen."

Beth laughed as she realized Jackie was calling him by the wrong name.

"Where are we going?" Beth asked him.

"To my apartment."

"What time is it?" she asked, panic in her voice.

"It's only ten thirty-five," he answered.

Beth sighed with relief. He reached over and patted her forehead. She smiled at him nervously.

"I'm sorry I got drunk. Is there anything else I should be sorry for?" she asked as she adjusted her seat to a straight position.

"No, but there's a lot I have to make up for. I'd like to start now." He wrapped his arm around her.

She leaned into him and rested her head on his shoulder. Beth was grateful he was taking care of her and Jackie. She nodded and closed her eyes.

After a few minutes, they pulled into the parking lot of Greg's apartment. He had a hell of a time getting Jackie inside. Beth was unstable herself, but at least she could walk by herself. She slung her purse over her shoulder and clutched both unopened soda cans.

Jackie threw up again outside the apartment building.

"Greg, she's going to vomit all over her hair," Beth said.

"This is just great," Greg muttered as he held Jackie's hair back. Finally, he got her inside and deposited her in the bathroom where she proceeded to vomit some more.

Beth groaned, set the sodas on the kitchen counter, and pressed her fingers against her pounding temples.

"Can I get you some aspirin?" he asked.

Beth stared at the unopened soda and frowned. "I can't take aspirin. It upsets my stomach. I have some Tylenol, but can I please have some water?"

She placed her purse on the counter and fumbled awkwardly to find it. First, she pulled out two tampons, then the condom, then a small metal container of Tylenol.

Greg looked down at the contents lying on the counter as he handed her a glass of water.

"You're not on your period, are you?"

"No, no, no." Beth swallowed one tablet. "Why would you ask me that?"

"I knew you weren't a virgin," he said.

Beth gulped to swallow the second Tylenol. "What are you talking about?" she asked as Greg pulled her to him roughly.

"I'm going to make you feel things you've never felt before. You'll forget about every other asshole you've ever been with." He kissed her intensely, hurting the inside of her lips.

"Greg, stop!" She pushed him away and tried to steady herself, but he continued to press into her.

"Look, we don't have a lot of time. She'll be out of there soon, and I need to get you home in a couple hours."

Beth's body went rigid.

"Do I need to use this?" he asked, taking the condom off the counter.

"Oh shit!" Beth said.

"It's okay. I don't mind." He gripped the condom in one hand as he pulled her by the arm towards the steps that led to his bedroom.

"Oh no, wait! Hold on a minute! You don't understand." She yanked her hand back in a panic. He didn't let go.

"Come on, Beth. It'll be great, I promise."

"No, no. No, I can't! Wait!" she pleaded loudly as he tried to forcibly drag her by the arm up the steps.

Jackie yelled pathetically from the bathroom, "Greg, you leave her alone!" She continued to wretch.

Beth's adrenaline kicked in and she held on to the banister with all her might. "No!" she screamed.

Greg let go of her and said, "Okay, okay. Okay."

His quick release sent Beth to the floor. She began to cry

as she dragged herself up.

"Settle down now," he said. "Don't cry. I'm not all that bad. I could make you feel good, and I'm willing to do whatever it takes to do that."

Greg scooped her up off the bottom step, holding her in his arms, comforting her.

"I don't know why you like to tease me the way you do," he said.

"I'm not trying to," Beth said weakly.

"I don't understand why you don't want to have sex with me when I promise it'll be great. I'll do whatever you want. I care about you. If you want to be boyfriend and girlfriend, that's fine. Whatever you want." He took her face in his hand and kissed her again.

Beth let him kiss her despite her terror. She hoped it would keep him from getting angry again. Her body was shaking, and her mind was racing. How was she going to get out of this? She decided to be forthright.

"Greg, I've never done it before and I'm really nervous about it. I'm just not ready." Her voice quivered.

"You've got to be kidding me," he said snidely as he narrowed his eyes at her.

He grabbed her tightly by the wrists and yanked her close to his chest. "Do you think I remotely believe that bullshit when you've dated Brian Knight, Danny Mitchell, and Rocky Mulinero? You're a fucking liar. Those guys wouldn't date a girl who didn't put out. Don't treat me like I'm an idiot!"

She flinched at his anger. That wasn't the reaction she had hoped for. She would have to be nice to him. If she were nice, he would care a little more about whether he hurt her or not. Right?

"I can treat you better than any of them if you'd only let me. I can show you." He kissed her roughly.

She pulled away, but he was too strong and held her close to him.

He put his hand between her legs and rubbed her. "See? I won't hurt you."

Pleading with him to let her go, she twisted and turned her body against his.

Jackie yelled from the bathroom, "Stop it, Greg! I mean it. You let her go!" Then she began to wretch again.

Beth and Greg were involved in a major struggle. Her heart was pounding, and she struggled frantically to push him away. She used every ounce of strength she had. Even as she continued to struggle, she was terrified and felt helpless. He picked her up and carried her to the couch.

She fought to breathe. "Please don't do this, please."

He held both her wrists together in one hand, pulled her shirt up and undid her bra with the other.

Beth was screaming and twisting, but she was unable to stop him. He pressed his mouth hard against hers, and she couldn't breathe as he pinned her on the couch. Her screams and cries were muffled as she continued to do her best to fight him.

"It'll be alright, just relax, Beth."

She continued to scream and protest.

He placed his hand over her mouth. "Stop screaming!"

She looked at him, tendrils of dread shuddering through her body. He only focused on her exposed chest.

"Relax," he said repeatedly and kept his hand over her mouth as he used his left leg to hold her one arm down.

With his other hand, he held her right arm, and she pushed her body against him with all her might. His body pinned her legs down on the couch cushions.

"You have to stop screaming, Beth. I don't want to hurt you, but you must stop screaming. I'm going to remove my hand, okay? Don't scream. If you do, so help me God. You won't scream?"

Beth shook her head.

She didn't scream, but she did continue to fight against him, begging him to stop. He kissed her so hard, her lips cut into her teeth. His body weight was on her knees, and his one hand again held both her wrists up over her head. Greg reached down and undid the button on her pants and then pulled the zipper down. He yanked them down with her underwear. She screamed again, and he clamped his hand over her mouth.

"You're beautiful, you know that?"

Beth's eyes widened. He was crazy! He'd lost his mind. He was raping her for Christ's sake. How had she let this lunatic get so close to her? No, she couldn't believe this was happening! She sobbed and struggled against him while berating herself mentally.

Her entre body trembled as her muscles grew tired from the battle. She was convinced Jackie had passed out in the bathroom. Otherwise, her friend would be helping her.

Greg touched her body roughly. Beth shook her head from side to side and screamed as loud as she could.

"Leave her alone, Greg!" Jackie yelled again. Her voice echoed and was muffled from the toilet.

He flipped Beth over on her stomach and pressed her face into the sofa cushion. She struggled to breathe through the fabric as he pulled her pants the rest of the way off. He flipped her over again and quickly covered her mouth with his left hand. Beth gulped for air and feared she would pass out or suffocate from lack of oxygen. She forced herself to breathe deeply through her nose. Her legs were secured by his, and he gripped her wrists with his right hand. He kissed her breasts and then her stomach.

"Jesus, Beth! Relax, you will enjoy it. I promise. Just relax!"

He continued kissing her stomach and moved his lips downward.

Oh God! Beth struggled and felt the pressure of his hand lessen on her mouth. She seized the moment, quickly turning her head and screaming as loudly as she could. Greg was on top of her in an instant.

He grabbed the back of her hair and pulled her head close to his. "Stop it. Stop it right now, or I *will* hurt you."

The bathroom door flew open, and the light poured into the living room.

Jackie stood over them. "Get off her, Greg. Now!"

Beth had never heard Jackie use that threatening tone before. She thanked God Jackie was able to come to her aid. The light from the bathroom illuminated her friend's wild, tangled hair. She held a hairbrush high over her head as if she were ready to strike Greg.

"Get off her. Now!"

Greg glanced at Jackie and then looked down at Beth. He released his hold on her hair, sat up, and moved to the end of the couch near her feet.

Beth gagged and sobbed as she ran across the room, trying to button her shirt with shaking hands. She wouldn't dare go near her pants because they lay at his feet.

"Give her the pants," Jackie commanded, still clutching the brush.

Greg sat bent over with his head in his hands. After a few moments, he picked up her pants and tossed them to her, keeping his head hung low.

Beth fell into the wall as she struggled to put them on in a rush. Her sandals were at the bottom of the stairs, and she quickly retrieved them and slipped them on. She saw the condom on the floor. Oh my God! Beth shook uncontrollably. She was freezing and her teeth chattered violently.

She grabbed her purse and ran toward the front door. "Please, Jackie, let's go. Please! Please!"

"Give me your car keys," Jackie said to Greg.

He reached in his pocket and tossed them to her on the floor at her feet without looking up at her.

Jackie scooped up the keys and threw the brush at him. It hit him hard in the chest, but he didn't even flinch.

Clutching the keys, she ran to Beth at the door. Beth grabbed her arm, trying to pull her out of the apartment.

"Al can come and pick your car up from my house tomorrow," Jackie said as they ran out the door and towards the car.

Beth called out hysterically, "Unlock the doors, unlock the doors!"

"It's alright, he's not coming. It's alright!" Jackie said as she unlocked the doors.

Beth jumped in, slammed the door behind her, and pressed the lock down. After Jackie climbed into the driver's seat, she clawed her way over Jackie to lock her door, too.

Greg stood outside watching her, and Beth started screaming again.

"It's locked! It's locked! It'll be alright. You're alright, you're alright," Jackie said as she held on to her. "Jesus! Jesus!" She rocked Beth back and forth.

"Thank God you were there! He was trying to kill me. I couldn't breathe!" Beth cried.

"Oh my God, was he actually able to...?" Jackie questioned.

Beth shook her head.

"Thank God, Beth. Thank God for that!"

"What have I done? What did I do?" Beth's body shook.

"You didn't do anything. It isn't your fault. It's not your fault!"

Beth slumped into her seat. Thankfully, Jackie had sobered up and was able to drive.

During the entire ride home, Beth stared out the window and shivered. Jackie pulled into Beth's driveway, took out some tissues from her purse and helped Beth remove mascara from her face.

"Here. Brush your hair and fix your bra."

Beth did as she was told.

"Go in now, and go straight to bed," Jackie instructed.

Beth walked into the comfort of her home before eleven thirty. Her mother had fallen asleep on the couch while waiting for her to come home.

"I'm home, Mom," Beth said quietly. She forced herself to stop shaking.

"Did you have a good time?"

"Not really. I'm afraid Greg turned out to be a bit of a jerk. I don't think I'll be seeing him again."

"I'm sorry you didn't have fun. I'm going to bed now. If you want, we can talk tomorrow." Her mother got up and headed towards the stairs.

"I'll be up in a minute, Mom. I'm going to get a drink first."

Her hand trembling, Beth fixed a glass of Diet Pepsi and went to her room. She tried not to think about what happened, but that was all she could think about.

CHAPTER 43

Jackie came over to visit Beth early the next morning. They hung out in her bedroom because she didn't want her parents to know about what Greg had done to her. Melissa showed up a little later and learned about what had transpired at Greg's the night before. Beth made them swear to never tell anyone. Not even Susan or Lynne. The two tried to convince Beth that it wasn't her fault, but she wouldn't accept it. She recalled how she'd acted with Greg in the bathroom the first time they'd met and then again last weekend at The Club. She had jumped up onto him at Joe's party, and the condom had been blatantly resting on the counter.

"I led him on! I really did."

Melissa tried to tell her all those things didn't matter. She had said "no," and no decent guy would force himself on a girl if she weren't willing.

Beth knew that was true, but she still felt guilty.

Jackie said Al came to her house earlier with his brother to pick up Greg's car. Beth wanted to know if Al knew about what happened.

Jackie shook her head. "I didn't say anything to him about it, although I wanted to. I really did. Greg needs to be arrested or, at the very least, beaten to a bloody pulp."

Beth said, "No!"

"Okay, okay," Jackie continued. "Apparently, Greg told him that he got too drunk to drive home, so I drove you and him home. At least that was the impression I got from Al."

Melissa added, "Greg's not going to tell anyone what he did. He'd be an idiot to do that."

"I don't ever want to see him again. Never, you understand? Never." Beth's body begin to shake again.

"You don't have to," they both assured her.

The three of them listened to music the rest of the day, and Beth felt a little better having her friends with her.

~

Jackie continued to date Al for about two weeks until she found another girl's maxi pad in his bathroom trashcan. He confessed he had been seeing someone else. She was much older than Jackie, even older than Al. Jackie was devastated and vowed to get even. Beth was disgusted by both him and Greg.

Beth didn't do anything except work and stay in her bedroom. She was jumpy all the time and wouldn't go to any parties with the girls. Melissa finally talked her into going out to The Boat with them on the Fourth of July. They would hang out there, and then go see the fireworks downtown. Beth agreed to go.

Melissa brought firecrackers and sparklers, and Jackie brought cigarettes. Lynne brought two six-packs of beer her boyfriend had gotten for them.

Susan demonstrated the art of belching. She then obliged the girls and taught them the technique she'd learned from Tyler. They laughed at the very activity they always turned their noses up at when the guys were around. Susan laughed so hard beer came out of her nose, and they lost control of themselves.

Beth was on her second beer before she finally relaxed. The girls discussed the names they came up with for The Boat. Melissa offered up "Beeline." She said if it were seaworthy, she would beeline it out of town, fast. Susan liked the name "Miss June" since that was the month they first found it. Lynne wanted to call it "Clarisse" after Colonel Roberts' wife. Jackie liked the name "Secret Keeper." Beth wanted it to be called "Pint-Sized Paradise" since this was the one place they could go and really be themselves.

They couldn't come up with a winner because the girls all voted for their own choice. Jackie took out a tube of lipstick, and each girl wrote her name choice on the boat somewhere. Susan brought a battery-operated radio, and they listened to a rock station out of Philadelphia. As they reclined and relaxed leaning on the logs, Beth realized her neck had been tense for weeks, and it felt wonderful to feel safe and normal again. She asked about gossip from the parties she'd missed these past few weeks. Lynne and Susan asked her why she hadn't been around lately. Jackie and Melissa shared a secretive look, and then glanced at Beth with raised eyebrows.

Beth glanced down at the ground and was silent for a few moments.

"What happened?" Lynne whispered.

Susan touched Beth's arm softly and asked with concern, "Beth?"

Beth began to cry out of shame for what had happened and for her gratitude for her friends. She looked at Jackie. "Can you tell them?"

She cried quietly while Jackie relayed the awful story.

Lynne and Susan listened intently and cast sympathetic looks at Beth as Jackie talked.

The girls hugged her and reiterated repeatedly, "This was not your fault."

Beth couldn't shake the responsibility weighing heavily on her shoulders, but she hugged her friends and accepted their love. She was relieved that all her best friends knew about the "Greg incident" and didn't blame her even if she blamed herself.

She was also relieved to hear that Greg had not been to any of the parties they'd been to. Earlier that week, Brian had called her on the phone to see where she had been. Charlie and Mike had both come to see her at work. Charlie had asked why she had been hiding at home "under her bed." Beth had laughed at his comment but didn't explain. She only said that she had been working a lot.

Jackie lit a cigarette and took a long drag.

"Let me have a cigarette," Beth said to Jackie.

Beth had tried cigarettes in junior high school and had coughed endlessly. Jackie had been sneaking her mother's cigarettes and bringing them to The Boat for months. Beth was ready to try smoking again.

Jackie handed her one from her pack of Kools. After the third inhale, Beth felt sick and dizzy. Gagging she tossed it into the pond.

"It's always like that at first. You get used to it. Try it again later," Jackie said, and then took a drag of her cigarette.

Beth made a face. Lynne and Susan fussed, "Don't start doing that!" Melissa just laughed at her.

Melissa told the other girls she and Eric were back together. Beth had known for a few weeks. There were a lot of concerned questions and then cautious happiness from the other girls for their friend.

Susan was happy she was receiving letters from Tyler and shared several of them with the girls. She looked over at Beth and said quietly, "Charlie's brother asked me if you were dating Greg."

Beth's neck tightened. Jackie lowered her eyes to watch the cigarette she stubbed out in the dirt. Melissa stared at Beth as if willing her to handle this well.

"Why was Joe asking?" Beth asked.

The girls fell silent and glared at Susan.

"I really don't want to say," she said softly and looked at the others sheepishly.

They rolled their eyes and began to mumble and groan.

"What's going on?" Beth demanded.

"You might as well tell her now," Lynne said with frustration.

Susan looked back at Beth.

"What? Tell me. What?" Beth narrowed her gaze.

"Danny's back," Susan blurted.

Beth's stomach churned in knots, and she took a moment

to calm her nerves.

"What do you mean 'Danny is back'?" she asked, sitting straight up.

Everyone stared at her.

Lynne said, "He's moved back home from California."

"How do you know?" Beth arched her eyebrows.

"His mom plays Pokeno with mine, and she told my mother," Lynne said.

"How long has he been home?"

"About a week," she replied.

Beth got up and walked towards the embankment of the pond.

"Crazy Little Thing Called Love" came on the radio. Beth turned around and let out a loud, "Woo hoo!" and jumped in the air. She began to dance.

"Turn it up!" she yelled, and Susan complied.

The excitement was contagious, and they all started to dance. They sang at the top of their lungs, spinning and twirling. The song ended, and the DJ came over the waves. Beth hugged everyone.

"I've got to see Danny."

Advertisements started to play over the radio, and Lynne turned the volume down.

Jackie narrowed her eyes at Beth. "Sweetie, keep it together, okay?"

"Do you know how long I've been hoping he would come home? Maybe now that I'm a senior my folks will let me see him. How can they refuse? Oh, now it's finally possible." Beth grinned at them excitedly.

"Settle down, Beth. You shouldn't get your hopes up," Lynne said.

"Tell me everything!" Beth said, and she dragged Susan over to the log to sit down.

Beth caught Jackie rolling her eyes at Melissa and Lynne as if to say, "Here we go again!"

Feeling giddy, Beth ignored her and listened to Susan.

"Okay, apparently he ran out of money in California, and his dad wants to retire from the restaurant and move to Florida. They want Danny and his sister to run it. Danny agreed to take some classes at the community college. His parents will pay for them if he lives at home. Apparently, his parents were worried about what he was doing out there and wanted him to come home." Susan paused. "That's pretty much it."

Beth looked at Jackie and Melissa as if it were Christmas morning. "When do you think I will get to see him?"

"Joe's having another party at his house this weekend," Susan said.

Beth immediately chewed the bottom right corner of her lip and glanced at Jackie. She wondered if Greg would be at the party.

"Greg won't be there," Jackie said, reassuring her.

"You're sure?" Beth asked.

Melissa grinned. "I think we should all go."

Beth shook her head. "I'm not sure..."

"After all that jumping around, you're definitely going if I have to club you over the head and drag you there!" Jackie said.

A hopeful feeling grew and warmed Beth's chest. She could see Danny again.

"Okay, let's go to the party."

~

Beth worked at the store all day Friday. She drove her co-workers crazy trying to find an outfit to wear that night. In between waiting on customers, she shopped for herself, running around the women's and casual departments. Debbie and Ann helped her and showed her over twenty different outfits. She settled on a pink halter top with small white polka dots and a V-neck. She would wear the white Bobbie Brooks slacks she had at home. On her break, she went to the shoe department and bought a pair of high-heeled slide-on

Candies with a pink leather strap that went over the top of the foot. She clocked out at six and headed home.

Susan said she would pick her up at seven thirty. She showered and dressed quickly. Her nails looked good and didn't need mending. She wore her hair down and used hot rollers and the blow dryer. Her hair turned out bouncy and full. She carried a pink sweater with her and a small white clutch purse.

Susan arrived to pick her up, and the two of them went to Pippy's for pizza, and then they picked up Jackie. Jackie was still getting ready when they arrived, so they went inside and hung out on the couch in her room listening to The Knack while Jackie did her hair.

It turned out Melissa had to work late at the bowling alley and wouldn't be coming to the party until later. Lynne and Joey would meet them there.

It took an eternity for Jackie to "diffuse" her unruly head of blonde curls. Beth and Susan started to moan about the wait. Eventually, Beth went into the dressing area of the bathroom and stood next to Jackie. She looked at her friend in the mirror.

Jackie turned off the diffuser, and Beth asked again, "Are you sure Al and Greg won't be there tonight?"

"I'm sure. They never went to any of these parties before Al and I dated. Why would they go now that we've split up?"

It made sense to Beth, and she was reassured.

"Do I look okay?" Beth asked, and the two studied one another in the mirror.

"You look beautiful. I hate you because of your hair. It's perfect. I wish mine was straight and dark."

"No, you don't. You look gorgeous. I wish mine was naturally curly and blonde, like yours." Beth pursed her lips then asked, "Do you think Danny will be there?"

Jackie said it was a definite, and Beth smiled broadly. Her friend smiled back at her and shook her head. After ten more minutes of diffusing, the girls were in the car headed to Janet and Joe's party.

They arrived, and a Boz Scaggs album played on the stereo as they walked in. Friends ran up to greet them. It was the regular crowd. Beth was afraid to look in the kitchen. The last time she was here, Greg had been drinking vodka at that same table. Her body shuddered when she replayed that night in her mind.

From behind, someone placed his hands on her bare shoulders and whispered, "Hello, Gorgeous."

Beth was startled, let out a gasp, and whipped around. Brian threw his hands up in the air and indicated he was sorry to have startled her.

"Oh Brian," she said, relieved, but she darted her gaze the party.

"What's going on?" he asked.

"Nothing, nothing's going on," she said nervously. "Who's in the kitchen?"

Jackie approached and handed her a Michelob Light. "Here I brought you this from the kitchen. All's well, drink up," Jackie said.

Beth looked deeply into her friend's eyes.

"Really, there are no boogeymen in the kitchen, only one that you might want to see." Jackie giggled.

Beth's legs wobbled as if they were going to give way underneath her. She wasn't sure if she was more excited over the fact that Danny was there or more relieved that Greg wasn't.

"Do I get my hug or not?" Brian finally asked.

Beth smiled and leaned in to hug him. Brian was tall and muscular like Greg, and that made her a little tense.

Brian gushed over the girls and how pretty they looked. Jackie and Susan giggled and smiled at his flattery. Charlie and Billy were there and came over to say hello. Billy hugged Beth for an extra-long moment. He was always so sweet to her, not much taller than Beth and on the thin side. Beth could feel herself relaxing as he held her close to him.

"How the hell are you?" He smiled.

She flashed him a grin and said she was good.

"I bet you are." He wiggled his eyebrows up and down at her and grinned like a Cheshire cat.

Beth laughed at his stupidity and realized why she liked these guys so much. They were plain corny. She loved their sense of humor.

Charlie hugged her next and ogled her halter top. He laughed as Beth blushed. Mike ran over with a toy water gun in the shape of a mobster machine gun.

"Okay, you dirty rat, open up," he commanded and swayed back and forth on his feet doing his best James Cagney.

Beth raised her hand over her face and closed her eyes. "No, Mike!"

"Don't be a sissy, missy! I'm makin' you an offer you can't refuse," he continued.

Everyone laughed at them, and he proceeded to squirt Peppermint Schnapps into Jackie's and Susan's mouths. Beth watched and laughed as it dripped down their chins and shirts.

"You sure?" Mike asked one more time in his regular voice.

Beth shook her head. "No thanks."

Danny came out of the kitchen and approached the group.

Her friends and his moved back, and she was alone with Danny.

"Hi Danny," she said. Caught off guard by his sudden appearance, Beth smiled, her stomach fluttering.

Her voice snapped him to attention. He gulped down his mouthful of beer.

"Hey Beth, how are you?" he asked, a little reserved. "Did you get shot by Mr. Cagney?"

Beth shook her head.

"It's good to see you," he said.

His words and his body were both rather stiff. What was wrong with him? Did he have a date with him?

"Are you alright?" she asked and looked around to see if there was a girl nearby.

He shook his head and smiled but didn't make eye contact with her.

"I heard you've moved back home," she continued.

"Yep, the old man is retiring, and I had to come home."

He put on a brave face, but she suspected he felt miserable about it. She decided not to go into that right now. He acted like he didn't want to talk to her. Beth didn't need a two by four to hit her over the head.

"Well, it's nice to see you again." Beth returned to the living room, feeling disappointed.

"You too," he called after her.

She glanced back. Brian leaned over to Danny and said something that made Danny yell, "I have no fucking idea what I'm doing...Hey Cagney! Bring that gun over here and shoot me!"

Scrunching her brow, Beth turned away, unhappy with the reception she'd gotten from Danny. She had hoped he would see her tonight and immediately start apologizing for not keeping in touch. He could have told her he couldn't write because his hands had been in casts or that he couldn't call her because he had a terrible case of laryngitis. Now, she was sure he didn't care about her at all.

Feeling glum, Beth passed on drinking more beer. The guys didn't congregate in the kitchen, and everyone laughed, danced, and joked around in the living room. A Cheap Trick album played as they told jokes. The guys were feeling no pain but were jovial. They showed off and generally acted goofy and fun.

Danny commanded a lot of attention from some older girls she didn't know. Beth felt jealous but was determined not to show it. People continued to come and go throughout the evening. "I Want You to Want Me" came on, and Danny walked up to Beth, singing and dancing. He was seriously buzzed. She laughed at him. He took her by the hand and danced her out to the kitchen where they were alone.

"I really, really, really need to tell you something," he said, unsteady on his feet. "I have to work full time in the restaurant and take classes at the tech college. It sucks big time. You understand?"

Beth nodded. She understood he wasn't happy about his responsibilities.

"Good. Now, I know what you want from me, but I can't be that for you, at least not now."

She frowned and lowered her head.

"I'm a total asshole, Beth."

She cleared her expression, peered up at him, and nodded and forced a smile.

"I just can't get involved with anyone right now. Give me some time. Can we please be friends?" He stared at her with a hopeful glimmer in his eyes.

Unable to say anything, Beth nodded again and walked out of the kitchen.

Brian met her in the doorway. The two looked at one another.

"Are you drunk?" she asked.

"No, I don't think so," he answered with a furrowed brow.

He didn't look like it to Beth, either.

"Can you take me home?" she asked.

"Sure, give me a minute."

Beth went to retrieve her purse and sweater. She told the girls she was leaving. They were concerned something had happened, but Beth assured them she was fine, just very tired from working all day.

Brian walked her out the door and to his car.

"Are you going to tell me what's wrong?" he asked as he drove her home.

"No, not really," she said.

He took hold of her hand and patted it.

"Danny Mitchell is crazy," he said.

She smiled and thanked him for being such a good friend. Then she took hold of his hand, and they held hands the entire drive home. For the umpteenth time, she asked herself why she wasn't in love with Brian Knight.

CHAPTER 44

For the next month Beth focused on working and going to the beach with her friends. She seemed to run into Danny everywhere: the gas station, the grocery store, the record store, and in restaurants around town. He was always stiffly polite. His crappy attitude toward her made her depressed and easily agitated. She claimed she was too tired to go out to any parties, and she stayed home often. Her friends were worried but unable to help her. As the summer began to wind down, she was anxious to get through her senior year so she could leave this godforsaken town.

The five girls spent the last long weekend of the summer at the beach.

Tourists and locals jammed the roads, the shops, and the beach. Everyone was trying to pack in the last bit of summer fun. The girls enjoyed getting on the beach early and stayed until five or six at night each day. Their evenings were spent at The Boat listening to music, sharing secrets, celebrating birthdays, and hanging out.

On Labor Day morning, they headed to the beach at eight o'clock. They parked two streets north of Rehoboth Avenue. The meters were cheaper there. Loaded down with bags, coolers, towels, and a radio, they headed toward the beach. Beth spotted a few runners on the beach and several morning bike riders on the boardwalk.

Some construction guys worked on a new condominium building nearby, and they cat-called to the girls as they walked by. Jackie flipped them the bird, which only invited more lewd comments.

"Come on, baby, I can make you squeal!"

"I'll be the best lay you ever had!"

Beth began to have an anxiety attack. Her hands and legs shook as she tried to ignore the crude comments. Her heartbeat quickened, and the adrenaline worked overtime throughout her body. She wanted to run to the beach. She walked faster and faster, leaving the girls far behind her.

"What's the rush, sweetheart?" one of the guys yelled.

"Come on back here, and I'll make you feel really good!" another guy called to her.

"Shut the fuck up, Neal," one of the guys said.

Neal began to run off a string of obscenities to his coworker.

The girls ran to catch up with Beth.

"What's the matter with you?" Jackie asked.

"Nothing, I just want to get on the beach, that's all. I missed yesterday because of work. I want to get in as much sun and fun as I can today."

"I need cigarettes," Jackie said. "I'll catch up with you in a minute."

The rest of the girls went down the steps to the sand and set up their beach camp. Melissa and Susan nursed sunburns from the day before and decided to rent an umbrella from the rental shed. The boy carried it over to their spot, pushed the pole into the sand and rocked it back and forth to secure it.

Beth's hair was already damp and sticking to her neck at nine in the morning. She pulled her long strands up and secured them into a bun on top of her head. Beth decided to keep her shorts and T-shirt on so she wouldn't attract any attention. She sat in a beach chair in the sun and put lotion on her arms, legs, and face. The rest of them took off their shirts and shorts to apply lotion. Jackie joined them on the blanket once everyone was settled.

Melissa and Susan sat in beach chairs under the umbrella. Lynne was already lying on her stomach tanning her back in the early morning sun. Jackie plopped her sandals and bag down on Susan's blanket. She yanked her shorts down and pulled her T-shirt off.

"Beth, why are you still wearing your clothes?" she asked.

A wave of embarrassment swarmed her, but she said, "I just feel really fat in this bathing suit. I don't even know why I wore it." That was a lie. Beth thought it was too skimpy, and she was afraid of unwanted attention. She couldn't explain that to the others because their suits were skimpy, too.

Jackie asked how much money she had. Beth had brought about twenty-five dollars.

"There's a huge sale at that shop on the corner up there. It says up to seventy-five percent off. I'll go with you if you want to buy a new one."

Beth didn't need a new suit. She just didn't want to be parading around for everyone to see. This was a developing problem this summer since the night of... *Don't think about it*! Beth told herself.

"Well?" Jackie asked.

The other girls looked at her with raised brows.

Beth thought maybe she would feel better if she wore a different suit. After announcing that she and Jackie were going shopping, she rose, and the two of them headed up to the boardwalk.

Surprisingly, she found some beautiful one-pieces. Jackie tried to talk her into buying a bright yellow one that opened on the sides and laced up the back. Beth absolutely refused. She settled on a basic black suit with a halter top. Her stomach was fully covered, and the suit had a beautiful coral-colored Hibiscus flower on the bottom left side. The back came up to her waist. She thought it looked pretty and not sluttish. Jackie said it was pretty, but she should show herself off a little more. That was exactly what Beth didn't want to do.

The suit cost her eighteen dollars. She asked the saleswoman if she could wear it out, and after getting her approval, Beth changed in the dressing room. She felt a lot better, like she could take her clothes off on the beach and not be worried about guys staring at her.

After she returned to the beach with Jackie, Beth read *The Other Side of Midnight* by Sidney Sheldon while the girls chatted. A group of guys on a blanket not far from them flirted with them. The guys flexed their muscles as they threw a football around. Beth ignored them and continued to read. She purposely placed the radio nearby so she could pretend not to hear what was going on around her. The girls soon complained they were hot and decided to go for a swim. The guys followed them to the water.

Beth put the book down and glanced around. A lot of families with small children played in the sand. She smiled at them.

"Hi," a male voice said.

Beth jumped and looked to her right. A boy squatted down to her eye level. He was way too close to her, and Beth almost fell over as she tried to move away from him. He stood up and moved back.

"Hey, I'm sorry. I didn't mean to startle you."

Beth forced herself to relax. She was acting foolish. Her heart pounded, and her pulse beat against her temples.

"I'm sorry, do I know you?" She straightened herself in the chair.

He squatted near her again. Beth bristled. She didn't like that he was so close. He wanted to chat. She didn't. He was cute, but it didn't matter. Beth didn't want to chat with anyone. She was short and distant as he tried to draw her into a conversation.

Finally, he got the message and said a pleasant "goodbye," walked away and headed towards the water. Beth realized he was one of the guys that had been throwing the football around.

Her heart slowed down a bit. She rolled her head from side to side and tried to get her neck to unwind. She picked up her bag, retrieved her shorts, and promptly tugged them on to cover herself. Then she got up, went over to Jackie's bag, and pulled out the cigarettes. She lit one, sat back down in the chair, and closed her eyes. The cigarette made her feel grown up. It gave her a false sense of security. Besides, if anyone tried to touch her while she had a cigarette in her hand, she could use it to burn their eyes out.

Beth sucked in a small amount of smoke and remembered what had happened the last time she tried it. She didn't want to get sick, so she inhaled slowly and waited. Nothing happened. No dizziness, no sickness. Her pulse began to settle. She took in another small amount and inhaled deeply.

She started to relax. This was a good thing. Sweat ran down her neck and back. Beth refused to get up out of the chair because she didn't want anyone to look at her. She was becoming neurotic. *What am I going to do?* She stuck the cigarette in the sand to hide any trace of her thievery. Beth began to cry, a little at first, and then she put a towel over her face. She sobbed quietly into it and hoped no one noticed.

"Honey? Honey? Are you alright?" a lady's voice came from beside her, and she placed a hand on Beth's shoulder.

Beth stopped crying and sniffed deeply. She raised her tear-stained face from the towel to look at the lady. The woman appeared to be about her mother's age.

"I'm fine, thank you." Beth sniffed.

The lady leaned down. "Sometimes it feels like the whole world is going to fall apart, and there's nothing you can do about it."

Nodding in agreement, Beth sniffed again.

"Well, you need to remember something. All things pass. Five years from now, whatever it is won't seem nearly as important as it does right now."

Beth smiled at her and thanked her for her kindness.

"You go have fun with your friends," the woman added as she turned and walked away.

Beth allowed her breathing to return to normal and put

the towel down.

The girls ran back to the blanket.

"The water feels great, Beth. You should go in," Melissa said.

Beth had sweated so much the canvas on the beach chair was soaked with her perspiration.

Jackie took her hand. "Come on. I'll go in with you."

Beth let Jackie pull her up. She reached down to remove her shorts and turned to look for the lady who had spoken to her, but she was gone.

Jackie dragged her toward the water. Beth ran and dove into a wave.

"Isn't it great?" Jackie called to her.

"It's fantastic! I was so hot!" Beth yelled with exhilaration.

Jackie smiled at her, and the two bounced above the waves for about ten minutes.

Jackie waded toward Beth, and they treaded water close to one another.

"So, is this mood you've been in about Danny or about what happened with Greg?" Jackie asked.

"I guess a little of both," Beth replied honestly.

"That night really freaked me out. I can't imagine how you must feel about it." Jackie regarded her with solemn eyes.

"I know. I don't know if I ever really thanked you for being there," Beth told her.

"I'm just glad I was."

"Oh my God, I can't even think about it." Beth treaded water and narrowed her gaze. "You want to hear something stupid?"

"What?"

"I really liked Greg a lot. I probably would have slept with him eventually if he had bothered to be...you know, decent, a gentleman. I feel stupid for being so wrong about him."

Jackie swam closer to her. "Are you still feeling responsible for what happened? Good Lord, you have taken it all on yourself, haven't you? Beth, most guys aren't like him. You just have to be careful not to get into situations where those kinds of things can happen."

"What happens if I run in to him again?" Beth asked, treading water.

"You hold your head up high, that's what! You didn't do anything wrong, and you don't have anything to be ashamed of. He does! He should've been arrested for what he did." Jackie treaded water in front of Beth, and the two smiled at one another.

"I love you, Jackie," Beth said.

"Oh Geez! You're not even drinking! I love you, too, dipshit. Let's go eat some lunch," she said and splashed water at her.

Beth followed her onto shore, and the girls hit Nicola Pizza for lunch.

Finally, Beth pulled out of her sour mood. After their meal, they walked out of the restaurant, and the heat of late summer fell over them like a wet blanket.

"Ugh!" Lynne said. "Let's go back down to the water."

It had gotten too hot for shopping, and the shops were too crowded at this time of day anyway.

They walked down the main street toward Dollie's Candy Store. Jackie, Beth, and Lynne walked in front of Susan and Melissa. A couple of guys worked on the roof. Jackie stopped dead in her tracks. The rest of the girls stopped and looked to see what had captured Jackie's attention. Beth saw Al, and then a guy moved to stand up next to him. Greg stared down at her.

Beth suddenly couldn't breathe. Her heart hammered in her chest, and her legs felt like jelly "Let's go. Let's go, let's go!" She grabbed at Jackie's arm.

Melissa, Lynne, and Susan looked at her with alarmed expressions.

Both guys headed towards the ladder. Beth was unable to breathe.

Jackie turned to Melissa and snapped, "Get her out of here!"

Melissa grabbed Beth's arm and began to pull her away. Al was on the ground, and Melissa was able to get Beth past the ladder before Greg could make it down to the pavement. Greg jumped down from the last few rungs on the ladder.

"Beth!" he called out and ran up to her and Melissa.

Beth froze, and Melissa halted beside her. He stood in front of them, looming in the sunlight. Al talked to Jackie earnestly.

"Can I talk to you? Privately?" Greg asked Beth.

Beth couldn't answer. She relived the terrible night in his apartment again in her mind.

"There will be no more private moments for you with Beth, *ever!*" Melissa yelled the last word at him for emphasis. She positioned herself between Beth and Greg protectively. Greg looked at Melissa.

"I understand," he said contritely. "It's just, I want to apologize for what happened."

"Nothing happened," Beth said quickly.

"Beth, I was a class A pig, and I am really sorry about it. I was hoping you'd forgive me."

"Oh please!" Melissa rolled her eyes.

Jackie finished her talk with Al and walked up behind Beth and said, "Get away from her."

Greg looked at the girls and hung his head.

"You may not believe me, but I'm sorry about what happened," he said it this time to all of them.

"Fine. You apologized. Get the hell out of the way." Then Jackie pushed him aside.

Melissa put her arm around Beth and guided her past him.

Lynne and Susan followed behind them. Beth dared a glance over her shoulder. Al had gone back up the ladder to work. Greg turned and climbed up, too. After reaching the top, he grabbed his hammer and began pounding the nails into the roof.

The girls walked down to the blanket on the beach. Nobody said anything for a few minutes.

Beth sat down. "Give me a cigarette, Jackie."

Jackie laughed and grabbed her bag. Beth chuckled at her friend's amused expression as she lit two cigarettes and handed one to her. They all huddled close together.

"Can you fucking believe we saw him here today?" Melissa said. "I just can't believe it!"

Beth laughed, and the girls looked at her as if she'd lost her mind.

She stopped laughing and said, "You don't understand. This is the very thing I have been terrified of for weeks. Now it's happened. It's over. Nothing bad happened. What's the worst thing that happened? He apologized. He looked pathetic. He didn't seem near as big and tough today, did he? Not up against all of us!" Beth let out another round of strained laughter. She continued to smoke the cigarette until she felt calmer.

"What did Al have to say for his sorry self?" Susan asked Jackie.

Jackie narrowed her gaze and exhaled some smoke. "Can you believe he wanted me to 'stop by' tonight? What a joke. I asked him if he was still seeing that woman. I could tell by the look on his face that he was. I wonder what she would think of him if she knew about me. Anyway, I told him to go to hell."

The girls nodded and murmured their approval.

"What did he say to that?" Beth asked.

"He got this pathetic face and said, 'Come on Jackie, don't be like that. You and I are really good together...' Fucker!"

The girls laughed.

"I'm going to pay him back."

"What're you going to do?" Lynne asked, opening her

eyes wide.

Jackie smoked her cigarette and looked out at the ocean. "Don't you guys worry about what I'm doing."

Beth didn't really want to know. She didn't want to be an accomplice in any way.

The rest of the day Beth sat and nervously looked around to make sure Greg wasn't lurking on the beach somewhere. Soon, to her relief, they were headed home. The first day of school was tomorrow. In the car, the girls all expressed excitement about the first day of their senior year. Beth would get through it with the help of her friends. God, she loved them. They would never tell a soul her secrets. Guys could clearly not be trusted, but she trusted her friends with her life.

When Beth returned home from the beach, she went upstairs to take a shower. She finished and entered her bedroom. On her bed lay several bags from J.C. Penney. Inside she found a new bedspread—one of those new comforter style bed covers with a white dust ruffle. The pillow shams matched the comforter, the latest height of fashion for bed linens. The colors were a dark royal blue, gold, and white. They matched her high school colors! Thrilled, she ran downstairs to thank her mother.

Beth redecorated her room that evening for her senior year and pulled out every high school memorabilia item from her closet. She had several jerseys and T-shirts tacked up on the wall. She laughed as she read through a pile of old notes and letters she had received over the past three years. Some were from Rocky, some from her girlfriends, and some were from Danny. Feeling nostalgic, she made some picture collages of her and the girls doing crazy things at the beach, the ball games, dances, and at The Boat.

Beth planned to hit the school store Tuesday after school to shop for new items for her room. She had covered her bulletin board with school spirit buttons for every possible function held at the high school from 1976 through

1979. Next, she rearranged her furniture and hung new white lace curtains at the windows. She stepped back and admired her changes, feeling good that she had impressed her mother.

Class of '80 stickers decorated her mirror. She used to be embarrassed to be in the class of 1980 because it sounded so babyish. Now she was proud and happy to be a member of a class full of such wonderful people.

After finishing the room, Beth got her clothes ready for school the next day. Hot weather was predicted. With no air conditioning in the school, she decided on a light blue sundress with small pink and yellow daisies and a pair of flesh-tone sandals. She would pull her hair up in a ponytail and use a light blue hair tie. Her plain gold watch, necklace chain, and cross earrings completed the outfit. Her neighbor called her at eight fifteen that evening and offered to drive her to school again this year. Beth accepted and offered the same three dollars a week for gas money.

She was relieved that the price of gas had gone down the past couple of years as the recession improved, and the gas lines disappeared. The state mandated a rule for fueling your car on even or odd days. It depended on the last digit of your license plate number. That finally ended, too. Things seemed to get better each year regarding gasoline prices.

Beth sat on her bed and read through her old notes once again. She saved the best for last. A note from Danny dated February 12, 1977. In the letter, he teased her about baby-sitting too much and having to be home too early. He wrote a stupid four-line poem about love. Beth smiled, then cried, and then wondered what in the world she could do to help herself feel better. She had given him time like he'd asked, but it became apparent to her that all the time in the world would not be enough.

CHAPTER 45

Senior Year
1979-1980

Love

Love is anterior to life,
Posterior to death,
Initial of creation, and
The exponent of breath.
Emily Dickinson

The school day began exactly like every other day for Beth in high school. She headed to the Center looking for friends. A collection of people gathered there. The guys she had known since elementary school were now the head honcho jocks. The freshman and sophomore girls acted giddy, falling all over them. Beth laughed. She had acted exactly like them a few years ago. Same play, different cast of characters.

Beth walked over to her four best friends, and they all hugged and smiled at each other.

She asked, "Can you believe we finally made it? We're *seniors!* I wonder what the year will be like."

Jackie nodded toward Donald Jackson. "He's kind of interesting. I might like to get to know him better," she said as she wiggled her eyebrows up and down.

Beth groaned. "I think I'm doomed. There's not a single guy I want to date."

Susan, Lynne, and Melissa just laughed at Jackie and Beth. They were all still in relationships.

Jackie wondered out loud, "Do you think there will be any decent parties?"

The other girls shrugged. After wishing each other well, they parted ways to get to their new classes.

Beth had an easy daily schedule. She carried a lot of electives this year—much more interesting and more fun. She had the B scheduled lunch for the fourth year in a row. Kenny Nixon and Beth had the same homeroom again this year and shared a locker. The homeroom teacher didn't know whether she could allow it or not because of a boy/girl share. Beth explained they weren't a couple, just good friends, and the teacher relented.

At lunch, she entered the cafeteria with Jackie to find a huge crowd at her normal table. Finally, this year all the girls had the same lunch period. There was no way they would all fit! After ten minutes of re-organization, the group spread out and occupied three tables. Soon, she and her friends sat together along with Kenny and the regular crowd of boys from last year. The jukebox played "Carry On My Wayward Son" by Kansas. Beth looked around and noticed the freshmen right away—they looked like babies. She couldn't believe she and her friends once looked like that.

A couple of weeks into the school year, Beth realized her mistake in sharing a locker with a smelly, large football player. Kenny started hanging pictures of models in the locker. Cheryl Tiegs was the most annoying of all. Beth couldn't stand it. She hung pictures where she could of handsome guys. Neither of them visited the locker at the same time during the day, and they often left stupid notes for one another taped to the inside of the door. Most of her pictures were of Billy Joel in a black leather jacket holding a switchblade knife or standing under a New York street sign. Beth thought he looked adorable. Kenny didn't have the same feelings, and the two teased one another relentlessly about the photos.

"I look like a fag standing at my own locker with pictures

of Billy Joel in it, for cripes sake! It's so not cool!"

She refused to budge. If the girls stayed, so would Billy.

Beth continued to work about twenty-five hours a week at the store. She and a few coworkers had now become quite close, even though they attended different, rival high schools. A time-honored tradition consisted of large crowds, pep rallies, and spirit day whenever the two high schools met on the football field. Dullard High School held the longevity title for most wins, but C.R. had won the past four games. The most important night of the year? The Dullard vs. Colonel Roberts football game. Whole families turned out to root for their alma maters. The local police patrolled the crowds and broke up fistfights between boys who were aggressive.

It was the second month of school and the big game would be played next week. Beth expected to see a large crowd of people she knew at the game and looked forward to attending several parties. Hannigan's always gave the night off to the kids who attended either of the two rival schools. People all over town placed bets in barber shops, dentist offices, laundry mats, and hardware stores. They sat around the radio and listened to the action if they couldn't attend the game. At Hannigan's, the staff got caught up in the action, and the girls placed bets. Debbie and Beth had become good friends. Debbie had graduated from Dullard a couple years ago, and the two bet a friendly five dollars on the game.

Blue and gold signs adorned the school hallways. The school scheduled a Pep Rally for the last period of the day. The football players wore their jerseys on the day of the game, and the cheerleaders wore their uniforms. Buttons were sold in the school lobby for fifty cents for large ones, twenty-five cents for small ones. Melissa and Lynne both cheered on the varsity squad this year. The Pep squads yelled out cheers, and the cafeteria workers served blue and gold cake.

At the lunch table, Kenny told Beth, "I feel too sick to

eat."

Beth wasn't sure if it was because he was nervous about the game or if he didn't have any lunch money again. She had teased him several days before about owing her about a hundred dollars, and he hadn't borrowed money from her since. Finally, he admitted, "I'm worried about the game."

"You have to eat something," Beth said.

He refused again and she insisted, placing her food on his tray.

Finally, he whispered loudly in an irritated voice, "I have diarrhea, okay?"

Beth started to giggle, and the whole table began to laugh. The other guys at the table admitted they did, too. This was their big night, their huge moment. As seniors, they had to beat Dullard or live with defeat the rest of their lives.

The girls tried to soothe their nerves.

"You guys will be great!"

"You can do it!"

"Tomorrow you will be sitting on top of the world."

Beth left Kenny a note in their locker after lunch that read "You are the Big Guy—You can do it—You will do it—No worries! C.R. is Number 1! X O X O, Beth."

CHAPTER 46

The entire student body squeezed into the gym during the last period of the day. The noise was deafening and came from four different sections in the gym. Bleachers had been pulled out from opposite walls. The freshman class of 1983 sat on the far-left corner. The sophomore class of 1982 sat in the section next to them. On the far opposite wall was the junior class of 1981. Next to them, the senior class of 1980 sat closest to the doors. The faculty and staff sat in folding chairs on the gym floor at the opposite end under the basketball hoop. Under the opposing net stood four rows of empty folding chairs reserved for the football team.

The JV cheerleaders took center stage on the gym floor and did a dance routine to "I Feel Like Dancing" by Leo Sayer. They did a fantastic job, and the crowd was pumped. The kids sang along with the song and clapped their hands. The cheerleaders smiled broadly, happy to see the entire school responding to their routine. When the dance was over, the girls skipped, bounced, and cartwheeled off the floor to sit on the sidelines.

The varsity cheerleading squad headed out on the floor next. The crowd stood, and they applauded the girls as they took their positions. Catcalls and whistles erupted. Beth, Susan, and Jackie screamed and clapped for their friends Lynne, the cheerleading captain, and Melissa. The two smiled, and their cheeks were red with embarrassment. They took their marks, huge blue and gold pom-poms held still at their waists. The room grew quiet as they waited for the music to begin. The volume was turned up louder than before and "Dancing in the Street" began. The entire student body and faculty clapped, sang, and danced along with the girls. When their routine ended, the crowd enthusiastically applauded. They hugged one another and laughed. The vice-principal introduced the senior cheerleaders, giving them special recognition.

The principal took the podium and made a few comments. The crowd grew restless, so he introduced the football coach. The kids applauded wildly. He was a nice guy and a great coach, and he taught driver's education. Beth and most of the girls thought he was handsome as well. He made a few humble comments, embarrassed by the attention and applause he received. Finally, he introduced the team players. The girls cheered for their friends as the boys received personal recognition for their efforts on the team. The boys looked stunned as they sat in the metal chairs. Excitement filled the air. Since this game was a huge deal in town, the local newspaper covered the Pep Rally. After dismissal, the girls met in the Center to make plans for attending the game.

That night at dinner, Beth bet her father ten dollars on the game. She thought she would be in deep shit if C.R. lost. Ten dollars was a lot of money to her. She was hoping her dad wouldn't make her pay. Beth's father graduated from Dullard and liked to tease her every year. Beth, Susan, and Jackie went to the game together in Beth's parents' car. Lynne and Melissa had to report early for cheerleading warm-ups.

It was an unusually cold fall night. C.R. hosted this year's game, and the bleachers filled up a half hour before the scheduled start. The band was already there in the stands playing "Sir Duke," and the crowd was fueled with excitement. People crowded around the field near the chain-link fence. Dullard fans packed the visitor section.

Beth, Susan, and Jackie walked to the fence to talk to Lynne and Melissa and wished them luck before they started cheering. The press box filled with local radio station and television announcers. People wrapped themselves in blankets to keep warm on the metal bleachers. More graduates returned to the high school for this game than for the yearly homecoming game. It was that big a deal.

"We'd better go get a seat," Susan said and again wished Lynne and Melissa good luck.

The three managed to get a seat near the fifty-yard line, but they had to squeeze together tightly.

Beth searched the crowds near the fence for Danny. She felt certain he would be there, but it became impossible to find him in the growing crowd. She did see Joe and Charlie Cahall standing with Mike Crowley. Brian Knight stood a little further down with several guys from his graduating class. She saw Greg Black standing with Al, and she let out a shudder.

"Are you looking for Danny?" Susan asked.

Beth smiled and nodded.

"He's over there," Jackie said and pointed toward the thirty-yard line.

Beth spotted him and flashed a smile at her friend. "Thanks."

He talked with some guys she recognized as former C.R. graduates, but she didn't know their names. She didn't notice any girls with him.

"Are you going to go talk to him?" Susan asked.

"Nope, he wanted me to give him time and space, so I am." She lost track of everybody when the game started.

C.R. won the coin toss. The crowd roared as if they had scored the winning touchdown. The first half of the game was a nail-biter. The teams alternated control of the ball and the scoreboard. At halftime, the two teams headed to the lockers, bruised and bloody. The band took the field for the halftime show. The girls left their seats to go buy hot chocolate and visited briefly with Lynne and Melissa at the fence.

The two frozen solid cheerleaders cried with thanks as Beth and Jackie handed each of them a Styrofoam cup full of hot chocolate.

Danny approached Beth and said, "Hi Beth. It's nice to see

you."

She returned his greeting and was polite, but she wasn't going to hang around and chat. He wanted space so she would give it to him.

He arched his eyebrows when she said, "Well, I'd better go. I'll see you later."

She turned around to leave but almost ran smack into Charlie Cahall. The two were genuinely glad to see one another and hugged. Danny narrowed his eyes at them, but he smiled at Charlie and stuck out his hand.

Beth had to give him credit for being nice to Charlie.

Brian approached her from Danny's left. He leaned in past him saying his usual, "Hello, Gorgeous."

Beth hugged him, feeling Danny's arm touch hers as she held on to Brian. She leaned back as the two let go of one another. Tears welled in her eyes.

"What's this all about?" he asked.

She sniffed. How could she possibly explain that Danny made her feel rejected, ugly, and miserable whenever he was near? To be called "gorgeous" in front of him by a great guy touched her deeply. Or maybe she was just getting ready to start her period. Either way, she felt very thankful to Brian for the comment.

"I'm just glad to see you." She chatted with Brian for several minutes.

"I thought you had somewhere to go?" Danny interrupted, anger lacing his tone.

Beth was startled by his comment. She turned to Brian, "I was going to look for you." She laughed as he smiled down at her. Danny walked away from them.

Beth watched him with a pensive ache in her heart. Why did they always play head games with each other? She turned around, and Greg Black approached her. She moved quickly to wrap her arm around Brian. He instinctively placed his arm around her in return. Jackie and Susan shifted closer to her.

Feeling protected, she looked up at Greg, and he nodded to her. "Hello."

Beth said nothing. Brian turned to look down at her, a puzzled crease on his brow. He had never seen her be rude.

"How are you, Beth?"

"I'm fine," she said through clenched teeth as she held a death grip on Brian's arm.

"I'm glad to hear it. I really am." He put out his hand to shake Brian's.

Beth held on tightly to Brian while he shook Greg's hand.

Al tapped his cousin on the shoulder saying, "Come on, man, we got to go."

Greg bowed slightly to Beth. She didn't know whether he was being polite or sarcastic.

Brian asked her what happened between the two of them. She only said, "It just didn't work out very well."

"Well, looks like he still wants to take you out."

Beth shook her head emphatically and removed her arm from his, no longer needing his protection.

She couldn't see over the crowd gathered around her. Once Greg had gone, Jackie and Susan had left to talk with Lynne and Melissa at the fence. The Dullard High School band had taken the field and performed for the crowds. She wanted to talk to Jackie and see if Al had spoken to her. She was fearful of running into Greg again, but she figured she was safe in front of all these people. She said goodbye to Brian and walked over to where the cheerleaders were huddled watching the band. Jackie and Susan were deep in conversation with Lynne and Melissa.

"Did you see Al?" Beth asked Jackie, touching her arm.

"Yes, he told me he's miserable. He's not dating that woman anymore, and he wants me to meet him at his place after the game." Jackie had an excited twinkle in her eyes.

Her excitement floored Beth. Jackie never acted giddy like this. Beth narrowed her eyes at her friend.

"Are you sure that's what you want to do?" Beth asked

with sincere concern.

"Yes. Beth, I love him. He's nothing like Greg," she reassured her.

Beth smiled at her and shook her head.

"I know you love him, but he cheated on you!" Beth thought her friend had lost her mind.

Jackie moved her gaze up over Beth's head, and her eyes widened with concern and surprise. The startled look on her face sent a chill up Beth's spine.

"What do you want, Greg?" Jackie asked curtly.

Beth whirled around. "Excuse me..." She tried to move past him.

Greg moved to block her escape. Beth stood perfectly still, refusing to look at him. She stared at the ground instead. He wouldn't budge and stunned her by dropping to his knee in front of her and forcing her to make eye contact.

Jackie said, "Oh my God."

Beth gaped down at him as he took both her hands in his.

"I need you to forgive me Beth," he said, attempting to look into her eyes.

Beth stood stock-still and continued to stare at the ground.

Al walked up on the scene. "What the fuck?"

"Please, Beth," Greg said quietly.

Beth began to glance around frantically, her cheeks heating. Al, Jackie, Brian, and Joe watched the exchange with gaping expressions, and others were starting to stare. Greg was causing a scene. Tears formed in her eyes.

"Get up, man." Al took hold of Greg's arm.

Greg pulled away from his cousin and wouldn't budge.

"Please, Beth, I'm so sorry. I should have never done that. I'm sorry if I hurt you."

As he stared up at her, Beth said quietly, "Please get up."

"You won't even look at me," Greg said, holding her hands tight.

She tried to pull away, but he wouldn't let go. The movement caused her body to pitch back and forth slightly.

"Let go. Please! Get up," she continued, her voice louder but steady.

"Tell me you forgive me..." He continued to tightly hold her hands.

"Okay, Greg. I forgive you. Please get up." She wanted him to go away. Dammit, now Danny was here watching this. She wanted to crawl under a rock. She was so mortified.

"Really? Do you really?" He stood.

"Yes. Okay?" This was too much! How dare he play the victim in this! She felt like screaming *Just get away from me you lunatic!*

Greg put his hand on her face and leaned in as if to kiss her.

Beth jerked back, her heart crashing against her ribcage. "Just let me go!"

"What the hell is going on here?" Danny asked. He placed his left arm protectively in front of her.

"What's going on?" he repeated to Beth.

Greg still had hold of her hands, visibly angered by the intrusion. She made eye contact with Danny, and he saw her fear. Danny physically removed Greg's hands from hers and yanked her away. Greg's face twisted with anger, and he turned his attention to Danny.

Beth trembled at the malicious glint in his eyes as he started toward Danny with his chest puffed out and his hands clenched into fists.

Al stepped in front of his cousin, blocking him from Danny.

"What in the hell is going on? What does she need to forgive you for?" Danny asked Greg

Greg froze. He stared at his cousin for several seconds before he turned and marched away from the field. Al followed closely after him. The rest of them stood there looking at each other in bewilderment.

Danny walked Beth over to the refreshment stand. The

second half of the game began. Thankfully, the crowd stopped staring at her and focused on the game.

"Beth? What the hell was that all about?" He spoke in an angry and frustrated tone.

Beth said, "It's nothing, really. Thank you for getting me away from him. He really embarrassed me!" She let out a deep, jagged breath and widened her eyes.

"Was he *proposing*" Danny asked her.

Beth let out a short snort. "Hell no! He was apologizing." She refused to look Danny in the eye.

Danny took her chin in his hand and turned her face to his, making her look at him "What was he apologizing for?" he asked ominously.

Beth ignored the question and said, "He's just an ass, Danny!"

"Did he do something to you?" Danny was not about to let this go.

"You don't need to stay with me, Danny. I'm fine. Go on, go back to the game. This is not your concern." Beth could not tell Danny! Ever!

Danny whirled on his heel, shook his head angrily, and stomped away.

Beth felt like she was going to throw up.

CHAPTER 47

Susan and Jackie ran up to her as Beth walked toward the restrooms and leaned against the brick building. They wanted to talk to her, but she wasn't ready yet. Her legs gave way beneath her. She sat on the ground for a few minutes and allowed her body to settle.

She said, "I'm fine. Can we talk about it later? I'm just not up to it. Go have fun. I'll meet you at the car after the game."

The girls tried to object, but Beth was firm. Reluctantly, they moved away, giving their friend some space. Beth sat on the ground several more minutes. She was angry at Greg for causing such a scene. She was grateful to Danny for coming to her aid, but she wondered what it meant. Did he care for her or not? She sat there feeling miserable and confused for several more minutes. After recovering somewhat, she got up, left the game, and went to the car. She listened to the game on the radio and waited for Susan and Jackie to meet her there afterwards.

C.R. won the game 24-12.

"Good for you, Kenny!" she said aloud to herself as the crowd screamed and cheered in the stands.

It seemed to take forever for Susan and Jackie to reach the car. Lynne and Melissa arrived with them.

"We've been looking for you everywhere!" Jackie shouted. "Why didn't you tell us you were leaving?

"I'm sorry, really I am." Beth sounded so pathetic that the girls' anger at her evaporated.

"Tell us what happened," Lynne said in a quiet voice.

Beth started to cry. Between sobs, she poured her heart out to her friends, giving them details of her encounters with both Greg and Danny and telling them how confused and miserable she was. Her friends offered no advice. They just listened sympathetically and hugged her when she finished her story.

Beth went home and right to bed. After a fitful night, she got up and forced herself to go to work on Saturday. Mike Crowley came in to visit her on his lunch break. Beth sensed he wanted to know what happened with Greg at the game, but she didn't offer any information, so they had a pleasant but awkward conversation.

Shortly after that, Brian Knight came in. Camouflaged in the back behind a table of corduroys and stacks of wooden bins, Beth grinned from ear to ear as her coworker Ann almost fell over when he entered their department. She had never seen him before. The effect he had on girls never failed to amaze Beth. Ann anxiously approached to welcome and wait on him. He looked around the store for Beth.

"May I help you find something?" Ann asked.

"I'm looking for Beth O'Brien," he said.

Ann's face fell with disappointment, and Beth giggled.

"She's back there," Ann said, slightly irritated, and pointed her thumb toward the back.

Brian searched for her and met her gaze. He walked towards her as she waved.

"How are you, Beth?" he asked.

"I'm fine." She beamed brightly at him.

He narrowed his eyes and focused on her face. "Are you going to tell me what happened?"

Beth knew if she told him, there would be a big "to-do," and she wanted no more made of it.

She shook her head and replied, "No, I'm not. It's all over now, and I don't want to talk about it."

"Did he hurt you?" he asked, his lips in a firm line.

Beth looked at him and said, "Please, Brian, let this one go, for me. Please?"

His gentle gaze swept her face. He kissed her on the forehead and whispered, "Okay, but if you ever need me, I'm here."

Beth was relieved and grateful.

Brian had been a super friend to Beth. Since she met him, he had never had a girlfriend. She only saw him with a girl once at the nightclub that night on her seventeenth birthday. He deserved a nice girlfriend.

"Come here a minute," she said and pulled him towards the front of the department.

"Ann?" Beth called to her coworker.

She would introduce these two to one another. Ann was nice and she was cute. Beth thought they would make a nice couple. Smiling, Ann walked towards them. Beth made the formal introduction. Brian spoke to Ann, and the two had a short conversation, which pleased Beth. When he was ready to go, Beth walked him to the front door.

"What do you think of her?" she asked him.

Brian looked at her and smiled. "Are you trying to fix me up?"

"She would be a good person for you to date."

Ann was already out of school and old enough to drink in Maryland and New Jersey where the drinking age was eighteen. Delaware's drinking age was twenty but most of the eighteen and nineteen-year-olds hung out at a club located just on the other side of the state line.

"How about if I get her phone number? Would you call her?" Beth pushed him a little further.

He tightened his lips and rubbed his chin. "I suppose I could do that," he said.

Beth jumped up and down with excitement.

Brian rolled his eyes at her. "Settle down, Gorgeous." He kissed her on the cheek and agreed, "Get her number."

Beth turned around, clapped her hands together and skipped back to her department.

Ann was excited about the prospect of going out with him. She tormented Beth with questions about him for an entire week. Brian finally called Ann and asked her out.

CHAPTER 48

Beth had a new admirer at work. For the past few weeks, a young guy came into the store often, asking for Beth. He bought jeans the first time she waited on him. The next few times, he came in to chat with her. Tom Henry attended Smythfield High School and knew Joey Griffin, Lynne's boyfriend. Before long, he asked Beth out on a date. Beth accepted, to Tom's and her friends' surprise. He was painfully shy and could barely bring himself to kiss her on the cheek. Beth liked that a lot. He was safe, and Beth was happy with that.

She continued to run into Danny around town.

At the gas station, he talked to her like she was his buddy. "Hey Beth. How're you doing? I need to buy some jeans. I will come in and get them from you very soon."

Beth was cold and distant as he spoke to her. Rolling her eyes, she answered, "Yeah, Danny, whatever. That will be fine" clearly not meaning it. He stared at her with his mouth hanging open, and she turned and walked away.

Beth's feelings were so conflicted when it came to Danny. She wanted to be nice to him and be friends with him on one hand, but on the other, she wanted so much more. It made her mad at him all the time. Beth wasn't sure she had it in her to be *just friends*. She felt bad about being rude to him, but she couldn't help it. Once in the car, she snuck a peek at him. He looked furious, slamming the hose into the gas pump, slamming the door, and zooming away without a glance at her.

She tried not to think about Danny and decided that maybe dating Tom would help. She went with Tom to her Homecoming Dance. He was a perfect gentleman and nice to her, but there was no chemistry between them. Beth watched all the other couples kissing romantically and despite her best intentions, she longed for Danny or at least the kind of relationship she'd had with him. Beth wore a cream-colored long gown. Tom wore a brown suit that complemented her attire. He looked nice, and they made an attractive couple, but she didn't feel an attraction to him. The guys in her class seemed to like him, including Kenny who liked anyone provided they weren't Danny Mitchell or Rocky Mulinero.

Al Black brought Jackie to the dance. Some of the guys grumbled at how old he was and made snide comments about "cradle robbing." Susan went with a friend from their class, and Lynne came with Joey, of course. Lynne was the homecoming queen, and Joey was proud to be with her, beaming from ear to ear. Of course, Lynne enjoyed the attention. Melissa did not come to the dance. She was spending time with Eric somewhere else.

The dance ended at eleven. Tom and Beth went back to Beth's to change into jeans and headed out to Pippy's to meet the girls and their dates for pizza. Al came with Jackie, but they didn't stay long. He was making a greater effort to be nice to Beth and engage her in conversation whenever possible. Beth speculated that he probably knew what had occurred between her and Greg, and he felt bad about it.

After the pizza, Tom drove her home. Awkward silence filled the car.

Beth fidgeted with her hands in her lap, cleared her throat and then said, "Thank you for taking me. It was fun." She didn't know what else to say.

He smiled at her but said nothing. They pulled into her driveway. After parking the car, he cleared his throat, took off his class ring, and asked. "Will you wear this?" His face was crimson.

Beth was touched but knew she shouldn't accept it. He was such a sweet, sweet guy but... *But what? You idiot, take it!*

"Yes." Beth smiled and accepted the ring.

Tom leaned in to kiss her. He didn't know where to put his hands to hold her, and his mouth tensed and felt slobbery. Beth tried not to be judgmental, but he really couldn't kiss well. She pulled back to get away from the misery. He smiled at her. Oh shit. Now what would she do?

She said, "I really need to go in now."

He fumbled for his door handle and told her to wait. Like a gentleman, he opened her car door and walked her to the house. He tried to kiss her again, and Beth placed her hand on his chest.

"Um. Tom? I think I'd better not take this just yet." She handed the ring back to him. She hated herself right now. "I shouldn't have agreed to take it. I think we need a little more time, okay?"

"Sure." He took the ring back and put it in his coat pocket.

"Call me tomorrow, okay?" Beth said, trying to be polite.

Tom did not call her the next day. She wouldn't hear from him ever again.

What the hell is wrong with me?

CHAPTER 49

Beth wished she had not introduced Brian Knight to Ann. Ann often thanked Beth for introducing them, and more than once, she tried to share intimate information about their relationship. Beth would always stop her. She couldn't listen to stuff like that about Brian. Brian came in the store to see Ann now, not Beth. She was always so dramatic about her "baby" coming in to say hello. Whenever he showed up and Ann started gushing over him, Beth would roll her eyes and keep busy organizing the clothing racks.

On Tuesday evening, Brian came in to visit. Ann was in the break room, and Brian and Beth had a chance to talk alone for the first time in a while. He told Beth there would be a party at Joe's house on Friday.

Thank God, Beth thought. It had been a while since she had gone out with her friends. She hoped Greg Black wouldn't be there.

That night, she called the girls to let them know about the party. Susan and Jackie said they would go with her. Melissa would be working late at the bowling alley. Jackie assured her Greg would not be there. He and Al had had a huge falling out recently anyway. Their relationship was very strained. Beth felt certain the problem had to do with her and Jackie, but she really didn't care.

On Friday, Jackie picked Beth up at eight thirty and then they went to pick up Susan.

When Susan opened the car door, she said, "You aren't going to believe this!"

"What?" Jackie and Beth said in unison as Susan hopped in the back seat.

She continued breathlessly, "Well, there's a party next

weekend at Donny Jackson's farmhouse. His dad is totally cool with it and...it's a party to celebrate the return of one of our old junior high school friends. Guess who?" she said excitedly.

"I have no idea," Jackie said.

"Me either. Who?" Beth asked, curious.

"Guess! Guess! Guess!" Susan did not let their lack of enthusiasm hinder her own.

"Oh, just tell us for Christ sake!" Jackie rolled her eyes.

"Chris!"

Beth and Jackie looked at one another with narrowed eyes.

"Chris. You know, Chris Kneeland!"

"Oh my God, I remember him," Jackie said.

"Do you mean Christian?" Beth asked.

"Apparently, he doesn't go by Christian anymore. Now it's Chris."

"Oh, all grown up," Beth said sarcastically. She paused, thinking about the boy, and smiled. "I used to have a crush on him in fifth and sixth grade."

"Really? I didn't know him until junior high. We had a make out party in my basement, and he and I hooked up there," Susan said seriously.

Beth and Jackie laughed and exchanged knowing looks. Susan at a "make out" party was an amusing thought.

"Should Tyler be made aware of this?" Jackie asked, still chuckling.

"Shut up. Here's something else you should know. It's going to be a toga party!"

Jackie and Beth grinned devilishly and said, "A toga party?"

"Yep," she said. "Cool, right?"

"Well now, that could be very interesting, couldn't it?" Jackie said to Beth.

"Most definitely... I can't believe Christian is back in town."

Christian Kneeland had been an adorable little boy with big dark eyes, long eyelashes, and dark reddish-brown hair. Beth recalled when he'd played with Lynne and her on the playground at Haley's Elementary School. Whenever Beth went to Lynne's house to play, Christian and his buddy Ron hung around. They ran around her neighborhood walking Christian's Great Dane that dragged them through yards, dangling on the end of his leash. She remembered him in Junior high. He had been cute and funny. It had seemed like such a big deal when he'd announced his dad would transfer to his company's home office in Atlanta. On the last day of eighth grade, Christian had run up to Beth as she'd headed out to the bus and kissed her on the lips. She had been shocked and embarrassed as he'd said, "Bye" and ran away. Beth had laughed and smiled. She figured he had been running around the school kissing all the girls goodbye. That would be classic Christian. Beth smiled as she recalled those innocent childhood days.

"Did he kiss you on the last day of eighth grade before he left?" Beth asked Susan.

"No. Why?"

She directed the same question to Jackie. "How about you?"

Jackie shook her head no.

"Did he do that to you?" Jackie asked.

Beth nodded as she looked out the window.

"You never told me that!" Susan said.

"I thought he kissed everybody!" She laughed and pinched Susan on the arm.

"Ow!"

Beth looked out the window and smiled. *Well, son of a gun, Christian Kneeland is back in town. This could be interesting...*

CHAPTER 50

People were packed into every square inch of Joe's house. Most people were home from college for the Thanksgiving holiday. Billy Englehart looked fantastic. He was in his junior year at the university and doing very well. He had begun to fill out and looked more like a man than the scrawny Billy from high school. Danny was there, too. Beth ignored him as she headed into the kitchen to get a beer.

Charlie stood by the refrigerator. "Beth!" he shouted drunkenly when he saw her.

"Charlie!" she yelled back, smiling.

He came over and hugged her.

"I can't believe I never see you anymore," Charlie said a little too loudly. "I always had a thing for you, you know?"

"Oh, please, Charlie, you're drunk." She laughed.

"Yep, I am really drunk, but I always thought you were A-Okay, Beth," he slurred.

He turned to Brian and Ann who stood near him at the kitchen counter. "Isn't she great?"

"Shut up, Charlie." She smiled at him again as she reached around him to get a beer out of Joe's refrigerator.

"How come you never went out with me?" he asked her.

"Because you never asked." She removed the cap from her beer bottle.

"Oh, I know that's bullshit. I know I asked you out at some time, didn't I?"

Beth laughed at him.

"No, Charlie, you never did." She tapped her hand gently on the side of his face.

"Well then, I'm asking now. You want to go out?"

Beth gave him an uneasy smile, uncomfortable with the

question.

"Charlie, be serious."

"I'm as serious as a fuckin' heart attack! Give me your answer. Do you want to go out?" he asked her again.

He sounded determined. Beth wasn't quite sure what to say. Brian and Ann laughed at her unease.

"I'll tell you what, Charlie. You sleep this one off and call me tomorrow night. If you ask me tomorrow, I'll go." She leaned in and kissed him on the cheek.

"Aw, you won't go tomorrow. You won't go ever, because of Danny Mitchell. Isn't that right? Tell the truth now," he said, slurring his words.

Beth smiled tightly, trying to be polite.

"I knew it, I knew it. Didn't I tell you guys that a minute ago?" he asked and pointed dramatically at Brian and Ann.

They nodded with amused grins on their faces. Everyone enjoyed Charlie's performance.

Beth peered around Charlie, and her heart skipped a beat. Danny was standing in the kitchen doorway, and he was frowning. Charlie continued to talk, oblivious to his surroundings. Beth closed her eyes and took a deep breath. She wasn't sure if he could hear or not.

"He's a flippin' idiot, Beth. Can I tell you that? He's one of my best friends." He leaned into the refrigerator to steady himself. "But I can't believe how stupid he is. I mean, he could be with you instead of that ugly and I mean ugly..."

Charlie was about to tell her something she really didn't want to know.

She interrupted him. "Well, Charlie. It's nice to know somebody really cares about me like you do. I really care about you, too. Danny is lucky to have a good friend like you and so am I."

She reached over, took hold of his hand, and looked him in the eye. "Maybe you ought to lay off the beer for a while, huh?"

"I love you, Beth," he said again.

"I know you do. I think you love everybody right now."

She turned to Brian and gave him a beseeching look, signaling him to take Charlie outside to sober up. He guided Charlie out the kitchen back door.

"Thank you," Beth mouthed to him.

Brian winked at her and said, "You're a good girl, Beth."

Ann followed Brian out the door, rolled her eyes at Beth, and smiled. Beth watched them through the window. Brian sat Charlie in a lounge chair. Beth turned to walk back to the living room.

Danny leaned against the doorjamb and stared at her, blocking her passage.

"Oh, hello Danny," she said flippantly, preparing to walk past him.

"How come you're so nice to him?" Danny asked calmly but with a serious tone.

"Charlie?" she asked.

He nodded.

"Because he's always nice to me and never says things to me he doesn't mean."

"You think he meant that when he said he loved you?"

Beth glared up at him.

"I think he meant it at that moment. Besides, he's a nice guy. He's always glad to see me, and he keeps in touch with me."

"Is that right? How has he kept in touch with you other than moving back to Dover and seeing you at parties?" Danny asked snidely.

"For your information, Charlie wrote letters to me when he was away. I got one from him every week. Since he moved back to town, he comes to visit me at work." She pursed her lips and crossed her arms.

Danny put his head down and blinked with irritation.

"Oh well, yes, I guess that proves it. He must really love you!" he said nastily and walked away from her.

Exasperated, Beth stomped her foot on the floor. She and

Danny ignored one another for the next hour.

Beth felt no pain after her third beer and a shot of Peppermint Schnapps. The girls had fun, and Billy came over to dance with Beth. She watched Danny brood out of the corner of her eye, and she rubbed it in as much as possible. Mike approached Beth and asked where Lynne was.

"Sorry, Mikey, you lost out on that one. Hell, we hardly see her anymore," Jackie said, answering for Beth as she came to stand beside her.

"Are you still seeing Al Black?" he asked Jackie.

She nodded and snapped her fingers as if he were out of luck.

"Beth, are you dating anybody?"

"Don't even come to me third in line, Mike!" Beth laughed.

"Oh, I'm sorry, Beth...really I am." He hugged her and forced her face into his armpit.

She began to spit and sputter dramatically. Mike cracked up, and the three laughed.

"Could I talk to you for a minute?" Danny interrupted their fun.

Beth stopped smiling and glanced down at her beer. "Is it important?" she asked coolly, more than mildly annoyed as she raised her gaze to him.

Danny rolled his eyes upward and looked at her.

"Oh, alright!" Beth said, agitated, and she walked quickly back towards the bathroom. Recalling her last encounter in a bathroom, she halted before the doorway.

She spun toward Danny. "What do you want to tell me?"

He sputtered as if he didn't know where to begin. "I wanted to tell you I really have grown up a lot since I went out to California."

"Is that so?" Beth replied.

"Yes! It is. I'm trying to tell you something here," he said, raising his voice.

Beth waited while he stood there saying nothing and

fidgeting. He looked at the floor. She lost her patience with him.

"What, Danny? What is it you want to tell me? How about this, Gee Beth, I don't know how I feel about you. How about, I think you're nice, but you're just not good enough for me."

"Don't be ridiculous," he interjected.

"Well, what is it then? You have a girlfriend? I know that. Charlie pretty much spilled the beans in the kitchen. I thought you needed time to get settled in? I guess that wasn't it, huh?"

Danny stared at her for a moment and said, "You have no idea how much I care about you. Jesus, Beth, you're still in high school!"

That was all she needed to hear him say. "Go back to California. You need to grow up a little more!"

She marched away, spotted Billy, and danced her way up to him. After she set her beer down on a table, he swung her around to "Do Ya Know What I Mean?" Beth forced herself to have fun despite Danny. And surprisingly, she did.

CHAPTER 51

Work and school passed by in a blur for Beth that week. She got ready for the big toga party at Donny's. Her mother thought the party concept sounded fun and helped Beth make her toga.

It was early Saturday evening when Melissa pulled into her driveway unexpectedly. The party was still a couple of hours away.

By the melancholy expression on her friend's face, Beth could see something was wrong. The two went to her room and sat on the bed.

"What happened?" Beth asked.

Melissa told her she and Eric had broken up again, this time for good. Apparently, he had developed a relationship with another girl who was much older. He had been two-timing them both, and when Melissa asked him to choose one or the other, he chose the other. She was beside herself. She was more angry than sad, and that worked in her favor.

"We have really screwed ourselves up with these older guys," Beth said, and Melissa nodded. She didn't even cry. She seemed relieved that it was finally over.

"Do you want to go to the toga party tonight to welcome Christian Kneeland back to town?"

"Absolutely." Melissa smiled at her.

"Yahoo! Melissa is back!" Beth hollered.

"There won't be any older guys there, only the guys in our class," Beth told her.

"Even better!" Melissa sighed, pulling her auburn hair back in a ponytail.

Beth recruited her mom to help make a toga for Melissa. They dressed in their togas, and Melissa drove them a mile and a half past The Boat toward the other side of the farm. Music by The Cars blared loudly from the farmhouse as they pulled up the long driveway. A large banner welcoming Christian home hung on the front door. The girls parked behind a row of cars, got out and entered the house.

All the senior kids they had known for years were milling about, dressed in togas. This was their first party together as a class. About twenty-five people attended, and everyone fit nicely in the extra-large kitchen. Donny's dad provided a keg, and the boys drank heavily. The group told jokes and reminisced about elementary and junior high days while lounging around the large farmhouse table.

Beth was in her comfort zone.

Kenny Nixon came over and hugged her. "I'm so glad you came."

Donny called the girls to the keg across the kitchen and poured them each a beer. Beth was the last one served. She was relaxed as she turned and headed over to the table. Fred and Ron from her lunch table told a story about some prank they played on a teacher in junior high.

"Hello, Elizabeth."

Beth turned to see Christian, the guest of honor. He stood up from the chair, smiling at her. She would have known him anywhere. He walked over and hugged her.

"Oh my Gosh! Christian, you look the same. How are you?"

"Good." He grinned at her. "And by the way, no one calls me Christian anymore, it's just Chris."

"Oh, okay. Well, no one calls me Elizabeth either. It's Beth," she told him.

They looked at each other intently. Beth felt comfortable, like no time had passed at all since they saw each other last.

"You look great." He wrapped his arm around her shoulders and hugged her to him.

"You do, too." She smiled.

His hair was still red but a darker shade. He had filled out and had a nice physique, tall and handsome. Everyone at the table smiled as they watched Beth and Chris greet each other.

Fred clapped his hands. "Well, I've been waiting for this moment all night." He pulled their eighth-grade junior high school yearbook out from under the table.

Everyone started to groan at the same time.

"I haven't seen any of you since then," Chris said, adding, "except Beth."

She jerked her head up to look at him. Everyone else stopped to listen.

"I haven't seen you since junior high," Beth said.

"Yes, you did. It was the summer after my freshman year in Rehoboth Beach with my folks on vacation, and you were there, too. Remember we saw each other at Jolly Time?"

Beth gaped at him. She had forgotten about that night! The two ran into each other on the rides and had spent about an hour together before Beth had to leave with her sister. She searched his face again while she tried to recall details.

"I even remember what you were wearing," he said.

Beth smiled, embarrassed by the comment. "I also remember a note you wrote to me in fifth grade. You had written my name and yours all over the entire piece of paper."

Her friends roared with laughter, and heat crept up her cheeks.

"I kept that thing for ages. I don't know where it is now, though."

Beth shook her head. "I don't recall doing that."

"It's true, I swear," he insisted.

"Well that wasn't very smooth, was it?" she smiled ruefully.

He laughed at her as she blushed.

Beth got a glint in her eye. "You know what I remember?"

"What?" he still smiled.

"I remember the last day of eighth grade at dismissal

time..."

"Oh no! Don't tell that!" Chris widened his gaze.

Everyone begged her to finish.

She slanted her head. "I'm going to tell."

"Go ahead." He nodded.

"I was walking out to my bus, and Christian called to me. He came running up to me on the bus line and kissed me on the lips!"

Everyone roared with laughter. The guys slapped high fives at him, and the girls laughed.

"What happened then?" Kenny asked.

Beth grinned at Chris. "He ran away."

More gales of laughter erupted.

"That's not true at all. I really laid her out, right there on the bus line. She tried to ram her tongue down my throat." He laughed impishly.

"That is definitely not true!" Donny shouted with laughter, slamming his empty beer cup on the table.

The night went on in the same fashion. Each person had a tale they wanted to tell. A real bonding took place. No jealousy. No upset. No expectations. No hurt. Simply good friends reminiscing and having fun. It was all so easy, and Beth forgot about her troubles for a little while.

Donald Jackson had a fifth of vodka, and Chris did way too many shots. He wasn't looking too good by the end of night.

Beth watched as he staggered out the back door. Nobody else seemed to notice him leave. Beth knew he was going to get sick, and she felt sorry for him. She grabbed a handful of paper towels and walked outside to see if she could help.

He stood behind a tree. "Please don't come over here," he said to her.

"It's okay. I've been there myself," she said, wanting to help. He vomited again.

"It's best to get it all out. Here." She handed him a couple paper towels.

"Thank you." He moaned as he wretched. A few moments passed.

"Are you going to be okay?" she asked as he tried to collect himself.

"I think so." He blew his nose.

"They were trying to get you drunk," she said.

"Well, I sure let them, didn't I? Thanks, Elizabeth."

"You're welcome." She turned to go back in the house.

Beth instructed Donny to make sure Chris didn't try to drive home.

"Yes, Mother," Donny said, teasing her lightly.

CHAPTER 52

The next few weeks passed slowly as Beth and the other seniors waited impatiently for Christmas vacation. Work got crazy right before Christmas. The Saturday before the holiday, Beth clocked in and headed toward the jeans department. She walked in the door and saw Danny. Beth was instantly excited. He never came to see her at work. Maybe the cold shoulder routine had worked and now he wanted to see her. She descended the three steps to her department and began to walk around the tables in his direction. He leaned on a clothing rack as if waiting for her. The dressing room door in front of him was closed, and she realized he could have been waiting for someone to come out. She paused and wondered whether to approach or not.

Danny wouldn't be cruel enough to come in here with a girl, would he? The door opened and indeed, a girl walked out. Beth quickly moved behind the counter. She watched Danny and the girl.

"Done? Good, let's get out of here," he said impatiently.

Danny turned toward the cash register and saw Beth standing there. He looked uncomfortable and wouldn't make eye contact with her. The girl brought the pants up to the counter. She must be the girlfriend Charlie had referred to at Thanksgiving. Beth pursed her lips. The girl looked older and dressed as if she had a lot of money, but she also had a big nose. Danny didn't speak to Beth. She ignored him as the girl paid for her purchase.

Beth was livid as she watched them leave the store. How dare he come in here with a girlfriend? There were plenty of other places to shop. He never came in alone, why now with a girlfriend?

She managed to finish her shift despite her agitation. She couldn't wait to see her friends. That night the girls headed to Pippy's for dinner. Beth told them about Danny coming into the store with "Miss U. R. Ugly."

"I hope you told him to get fucked," Melissa said as they waited for their pizza.

The rest of them laughed at her use of the word "fuck."

"I felt like it. Can you imagine me taking Rocky into the restaurant when we dated and making him wait on us?" Beth sipped from her Diet Coke.

"You should do it," Jackie said. "You know those two hate each other. That would set him off."

"Even worse, start dating Mike or Charlie," Susan suggested.

Their pizza arrived, and they all paused to grab a slice.

After a few moments of eating silently, Lynne said, "Beth, I think you should start dating Chris Kneeland."

The girls paused and looked at her with creased brows.

"How would that get to Danny? He doesn't even know Chris," Susan said.

"It wouldn't. I just think Beth and Chris should date. They have known each other forever and had crushes off and on. You should ask him to the Winter Dance in January."

Beth stared at Lynne.

This was coming from out of the blue. "Are you serious?" she asked.

"I am," Lynne said, biting into her pizza.

"I saw him vomit. That does not make me want to date him." Beth chuckled.

"Don't talk about vomit while I'm eating." Lynne grimaced.

The girls giggled as she took a huge bite from her slice of pizza.

Jackie changed the topic and told them she found out Al had been seeing the older woman again. The girls were stunned. Al seemed so into her. They couldn't believe it.

Jackie told them his lady was a divorced bank teller. She wouldn't say how she knew they were dating again, just insisted it was true. Jackie confided that she hadn't confronted Al yet because she wasn't ready for him to dump her. Then she broke down in tears, shocking her friends. Usually she had it all together. She got herself under control quickly.

"I have to do it soon, though. It's either her or me. Otherwise, I'm going to lose my mind. He has to make a choice," she said, swiping her eyes with a napkin.

Melissa spoke from experience when she said, "Be careful about issuing an ultimatum. Be prepared for the choice you don't want to hear."

The girls shook their heads and focused again on their pizza.

After a few moments of tense silence, Melissa asked, "Sue, when is Tyler coming home?"

Susan's face lit up.

"He has leave in February. He'll be here then. I can't wait! He won't be here for Christmas, though."

Everyone smiled sympathetically at her. Elvis's "Blue Christmas" started playing, adequately describing the general mood at the table.

CHAPTER 53

The Christmas holiday came and went without much excitement. Beth spent it quietly with her family. She and the girls visited each other throughout the week, and they went to the movies a couple of times. No surprise, Jackie and Al broke up. The ultimatum did not work out in her favor and resulted in Jackie's very first summit at The Boat. It was too cold to stay long so they ended up going to Jackie's, climbing up the tree to the porch roof and into her bedroom window. Armed with a bottle of wine, they spent the night there with their friend, helping her through her heartbreak.

The Fire Hall hosted a big New Year's Eve Dance, and the girls decided to go. Lynne got mad with Joey for flirting with another girl at work, and she broke up with him. Beth and the other three girls agreed the breakup wouldn't last, but for tonight, Lynne didn't have a boyfriend. With the New Year looming, Beth decided to develop a new attitude. She would go to this dance and try to find someone new to date. She spent a long time getting ready, choosing a pair of black chinos with a lightweight red sweater over a white button-down shirt. Beth pulled her hair up in a barrette and let the rest hang down in curls. She spent extra time on her makeup and nails.

Jackie arrived to pick her up and honked the horn.

"Be home by one fifteen," her mother said.

"Okay," she said as she kissed her mom goodbye.

She climbed into the car, grinning at her friends. The general atmosphere in the car thrummed with excitement. This was the first time in a long while that each of them was single.

"Here's the rule for tonight, ladies. Dance with everyone

who asks you. You can't turn anyone down." Jackie flipped her curls.

"No way." Melissa scrunched up her nose.

"I think it's a good rule. You guys are way too picky. There are a lot of nice guys you could meet," Susan said, being rational and kind.

Beth looked at Melissa. "Come on, let's do it!"

The girls agreed to the rule, and then agreed they would each pay five dollars to the girl who had the worst dance partner of the night. They would have to stay sober and keep an eye on each other. Rule number two was they had to meet in the bathroom at twelve unless they had someone to kiss.

They arrived, and the dance was packed, due in part to the local band, The Travelers. They covered a myriad of dance and rock tunes. The girls quickly scoped out a table. Beth saw Brian Knight and Ann at a table across the room. Neither of them looked happy. Hmm, were they about to break up? The prospect didn't make Beth entirely unhappy. Truth be told, she was a little jealous of Ann. She shifted her focus. After all, tonight was all about having fun.

Several of the guys from their class came and sat with the girls at their table. Charlie, Mike, and Danny were there without dates. To Jackie and Beth's dismay, Al showed up with his older girlfriend and Greg. Jackie enlisted the aid of "Shot Man Mike" to help her hide her misery. He was more than willing to supply Jackie with shots, and he played with her long blonde curls in a tender way that surprised Beth.

Lynne moped because she missed Joey. Beth experienced a sympathetic pang for her friend. She glanced at the doorway. Rocky Mulinero entered with a few of his buddies. Beth wondered why all the guys came here alone. Then it dawned on her—they came to get drunk.

Rocky walked toward her and said, "Hello."

Beth decided to stand for a while.

They spoke briefly and caught up on the details of each other's lives. He said he worked at a car dealership in a town north of Dover. He told her he was also taking classes at the technical school in town. He had a couple of classes with Danny Mitchell. He added that Danny was "still an asshole." Beth smiled at him and agreed wholeheartedly.

Danny approached them and said, "Hello."

He offered a hand, and Rocky shook it as they nodded a greeting to each other. Beth was surprised at how friendly they acted toward one another.

Beth felt uncomfortable standing there between them. She was delighted when Charlie appeared out of nowhere. He hugged Beth and said hello. He then introduced her to a guy she had never seen before. His name was Frank Kneeland.

"Nice to meet you," she said. "Are you related to Chris?"

"Yeah, he's my little brother."

Beth nodded pleasantly as Charlie provided her with information she already knew. Frank's parents had just moved back to town. They grew up across the street from him and his family, blah, blah, blah.

The band started to play "China Grove."

"You want to dance?" Frank asked her.

Adhering to the rules she had agreed to with her friends, Beth said, "Yes."

The girls smirked at her. She sent them a brilliant smile, letting them know she was perfectly happy to be dancing with him, stupid rule or not. Only a few couples went out on the dance floor. She felt a little self-conscious because he was a better dancer, but she rolled with it. He looked a lot like Christian except he had blond hair and dark eyes. As they danced, he smiled at her.

Before long, Susan was out on the floor with Fred from their class. Beth laughed. Fred was a bit of a nerd. Her friend would not have accepted his invitation had it not been for "the rule." Susan scrunched her face up at Beth. The song ended, and Beth thanked Frank for the dance.

Beth ran up to Susan, imitating her earlier remark, "Yeah, you guys are way too picky anyway."

The two laughed and teased each other. Beth walked over to greet Ann and Brian at their table. Brian had glassy eyes and a goofy grin on his face. He was massively drunk. Beth had never seen him that blitzed. Ann frowned and sat stick straight in her chair while he talked loudly and dramatically.

"Hey, Gorgeous!" he called to Beth.

Ann gave her a dirty look, and Beth flinched. *He should stop calling me that.* He stood up and knocked the folding metal chair over and grabbed her in a big bear hug.

"I need to talk to you," he whispered soberly into her ear. "Meet me in the parking lot."

She nodded and glanced toward the dance floor. Melissa danced with Charlie, and Jackie worked it with Mike, most likely for Al's benefit. Susan and Lynne danced with guys from their class. Beth walked out the door towards the parking lot. Brian came outside a few minutes later.

"Ann's pregnant," he blurted out.

Beth's stomach lurched and she raised both eyebrows. "What?"

Brian explained that Ann refused to get an abortion. He said she told him she had been on the pill and claimed the pill didn't work. Beth asked what Ann wanted to do. He told her Ann wanted him to marry her.

A wave of dizziness hit Beth, and she had to take a deep, steadying breath. *Marry* her! No way!

"What are you going to do?" she asked.

"Looks like I don't have much choice, do I?"

"Do you want to marry her?" Beth searched his face for the truth.

He shrugged the question off. "It doesn't matter, does it?"

Beth hugged him, knowing he was miserable and not nearly as drunk as he had appeared inside the dance.

"Do you think she did it on purpose?" Beth asked and Brian nodded.

"I'm really sorry," Beth said.

"Yeah, me too. There's not much else to do now, though, is there?"

They stared at one another pathetically. Brian turned away.

"You'd better go back in. I need to be alone for a few minutes," he said to her, and Beth noticed tears glistening in his eyes.

"No, I won't leave you like this." Beth touched his shoulder.

"Beth, everything is going to change. I am getting married. *Married!* I can't be out here with you in the parking lot. I can't drive you home anymore from parties, and I can't call you on the phone or visit you at work. I'll be married." Tears spilled over onto his cheeks.

An ache tore through her chest, and she started to cry.

"I'm not trying to be mean to you, and I don't want you to cry. Please," he said.

She realized now how much she would miss him and his friendship.

"Go in, please," Brian begged her quietly as he wiped his eyes and walked away from her.

She wiped her face and silently went back inside and headed to the restroom.

Beth stared at her red-rimmed eyes in the bathroom mirror and splashed cold water on her face. Wow. That was a harsh blow to absorb. Brian was getting married. Shit. Brian was going to be a father. She composed herself and left the bathroom.

Ann approached her in the hall. "Did he tell you?"

"Yes, what happened?" Beth asked, wanting details.

Ann told her she was on the pill, but it didn't work because she was now six weeks pregnant. She said they had an appointment with the Justice of the Peace on Saturday to get married. Smiling, she grabbed hold of Beth, hugged her, and told her how happy she was.

Beth stared at her in disbelief. "You're happy about this?"

"Yes." Ann held her chin up in the air. "Very happy."

Saturday? Brian didn't tell me he's getting married on Saturday! She couldn't believe the two completely different reactions her friends had to the pregnancy and marriage. Unsure how to react to Ann, Beth gave her a reassuring smile.

"I'm sure everything will work out," she managed to say, but a knot twisted in her gut.

A stunned Beth returned to her table. Frank asked her to dance again, and she danced in a daze. Soon afterwards, the band took a break. Charlie and Melissa had danced the entire set together.

Danny approached Beth and said, "It looks like Charlie and Melissa are having a great time together."

She ignored him. How dare he speak to her after bringing his girlfriend in the store?

Beth?" he asked, and she looked at him.

They stared at one another for several moments. She was still reeling from her conversation with Brian. The back of her throat tightened and burned. Danny Mitchell was the last guy in the world she needed to get in a nasty conversation with right now.

"Remember when we used to get along?" Danny asked with a surprisingly gentle manner.

"I remember," she said calmly, looking down at her feet. "Where's your girlfriend?" she ground out between clenched teeth.

He raised one eyebrow. "Come outside with me, will you? I want to talk, and it's quieter out there."

Beth felt a lump form in her throat, but she still followed him out the door.

Danny turned to her. "Look Beth, I'm sorry, I really am. I didn't think you were working that night."

Beth looked at Danny, unshed tears stinging her eyes. "It doesn't matter, Danny. You have a right to see whomever you want and shop wherever you want."

"But I care about you. I really do," he said, his voice

cracking. Danny hung his head. "I'm sorry, Beth. I'm sorry for everything. I didn't think you would be working that night. I didn't intend for you to see us. I'm not even dating her anymore."

"What are you saying, Danny?" Beth searched his face.

"I care about you, I really do. I'm just not ready for a serious relationship, I guess." Danny shrugged.

Anger flared Beth's nostrils. "What do you want from me, Danny? First you want me, then you don't. Sometimes I'm what you want, but then not exactly what you want..." She stared into his eyes, searching for an answer as she blinked back tears.

He pinched the bridge of his nose, closed his eyes, and then pulled her into his arms.

She looked up at him. He leaned down and kissed her softly and at length.

"I want us to stop fighting," he said as his breath passed into her mouth. "I hate to see you crying because of me."

"I don't want to fight either." She leaned into him again as the passion began to rise like an electric current between them.

He reached down and pressed his hand into the small of her back. She could feel his instant response to their kiss.

"Get your things. Let's get out of here," he said as Beth drew away from him.

"Did you say you're not seeing that girl anymore?"

"No, we broke up," he said happily.

"When?" Beth asked.

"What does that matter?" Danny narrowed his eyes.

"Just tell me, please."

"We broke up today."

Beth laughed in disbelief as she put her head down.

"What?" Danny asked.

She peered up at him and shook her head. "I don't want to be your "instant ego repair kit" anymore. That's not fair to me."

414

Danny let out a frustrated sigh. "Beth, it's not like that."

"I cared about you so much, Danny," she said and walked back into the hall.

Beth went to find "Shot Man Mike" and take some of his medicine. Before long, Beth laughed and flirted with false happiness. She was about one inch away from a breakdown. Her heart broke for Brian. Whenever she looked at him, she saw the unhappiness on his face. Then there was Danny. Also, Charlie Cahall acted like he was totally into Melissa, and then there was that stupid rule, so she had to dance with all kinds of idiots. She found herself asking Mike and Rocky to dance a lot to avoid being asked by any other guys.

She stood near the table, and the band began to play "Against the Wind" by Bob Seger. The music plucked her nerves, and she felt the room sway. Her eyelids moved slowly as she blinked. She had gotten herself officially drunk.

Greg approached Beth and asked her to dance. Melissa shook her head at Beth to let her know she didn't have to dance with him. The stupid rule didn't include Greg Black. Beth looked across the room. Danny watched the two of them. She wanted to piss him off, badly.

Greg again said, "Dance with me, Beth. You are the boss from now on." He leaned into her ear and whispered, "I'm so sorry."

Beth's mind, muddled from the alcohol, told her it might be okay. Her thumb went up, and she bit her nail as she considered it. He was still incredibly handsome, his apologies seemed genuine, and he had made her feel good when they'd kissed in the bathroom so long ago.

I am being stupid, but I don't give a damn right now.

Then Jackie approached. "Go away, Greg." She stepped between them and turned to point her finger at Beth.

"Don't you dare," Jackie said. Beth focused on Jackie's face, stared her in the eyes, and nodded.

"Get out of here, you fucking bitch!" Greg barked at

Jackie.

Beth tilted her head up to look at him. He was a little out of focus, but she managed to stare him in the eyes. The cruel way he spoke to Jackie jolted some sense into her.

"Please just go away," she said.

He gave Jackie an angry glower and stormed back to his own table.

Instead, Beth danced with Mike, enjoying the angry scowl on Danny's face. The song ended, and she staggered slightly as she walked with Lynne towards the bathroom.

Beth exited the bathroom with Lynne, shocked to see Danny standing there with her belongings.

He handed her the purse, helped her on with her coat, and said, "Come on, Beth, it's time to go."

Danny took her by the hand, and she let him walk her out the door.

Lynne stopped him briefly. "You be nice to her, Bam Bam."

Beth and Danny drove to Burger Chef and went through the drive-through. Danny bought her a Coke and a small order of fries. Beth ate the fries slowly as they sat silently in the parking lot. It was cold, so Danny turned the car on and off several times to run the heater. Beth began to sober up. She thought about Greg asking her to dance and shuddered when she remembered she had considered it. Her mind replayed the night of the near disastrous exchange between the two of them. She shuddered again and remembered her face shoved into the couch cushions. Beth set the rest of the fries on the dashboard and pulled her coat close around her.

"You're cold?" Danny asked, breaking the silence between them.

"No, I'm fine, thanks."

He asked if she felt well enough to go home. Beth shrugged. It really didn't matter.

"Well, we can just sit here for a while longer," he said, making the correct call.

Beth picked up and handed him the half empty bag of fries, and he ate the rest of them. He had his own drink and took a deep gulp. Beth watched him as he drank. His face looked dark in the shadows. He stared out the front window and glanced at her. They smiled at each other and looked away.

What am I going to do about you? Beth stared out her side window.

Danny turned the radio on. Beth leaned her head back on the seat, beginning to feel sleepy as the alcohol effects began to subside.

"Are you going back to the dance?" she asked.

Danny shook his head. "Nah, I'll just head home."

She nodded. He lived less than a mile from Beth.

He reclined his seat back a little and relaxed as he waited patiently for her to be ready to go home. Beth stared out the front window at the streetlights. The radio commercials ended, and the announcer said he was getting ready to play a "rock block" of Fleetwood Mac. "Listen to the wind blow, watch the sunrise. Run in the shadows, damn your love, damn your lies, and if you don't love me now, you will never love me again. I can still hear you sayin' you would never break the chain."

"Look Beth," Danny said, not looking at her but staring out the window. "You know I'm attracted to you. I always have been. But you are still in high school. Sometimes I think we should start dating again, but there is such an age difference, you know? But still...maybe we should try it again."

He reached over, taking her hand in his. The music continued, "If you don't love me now, you will never love me again, I can still hear you saying you would never break the chain..."

Beth pulled her hand away. "Don't, Danny," she said stiffly. "I may be young, but I have feelings. You seem to hurt them all the time. It's always about what you want..."

Danny cleared his throat and rubbed the back of his neck.

Beth waited for him to speak, her heart pounding. They stared at one another, an electric current charging the air between them. Danny focused on her lips, and a flutter tickled her stomach.

He placed his hand behind her neck and kissed her. Beth wanted to pull away, but she couldn't. She wasn't ready to lose this part of her life yet, and she responded to his kiss.

Danny kissed her gently at first then leaned in to heighten the intensity. Beth felt him come across the seat toward her. His kiss deepened, and she melted into him.

The song on the radio continued. "Chain, keep us together, chain, keep us together, runnin' in the shadows…"

He moved his body, and his mouth pressed a little too hard on hers, causing the inside of her lips to press against her teeth. Beth's mind instantly flashed back to Greg's apartment. Images came to her of Greg with his hand over her mouth as he roughly pressed his mouth against her chest and stomach. Unwittingly, she began to pull away from Danny and shook her head. Her body trembled.

"What's the matter?" Danny kissed her softly on the neck.

Beth's temples pounded with adrenalin. She was on the verge of having a panic attack. *Calm down, damn it!* She closed her eyes and forced herself to breathe deeply. *This is Danny, he really won't hurt you. Relax, just relax.* She tried to calm herself. Beth opened her eyes and looked at him as he continued to kiss her ear and neck. She took hold of his chin and moved her mouth to his, trying to force herself to overcome the irrational reaction her body was having to him.

"We're not going to stay here. Let's go somewhere else," Danny said.

Beth had a moment to collect herself.

He started the car, pulled out of the parking lot, and looked at her. "Where should we go?"

"Turn here," she said.

Beth directed him out to The Boat—telling herself she

418

had to do this. The girls would be totally pissed. The one rule they all adhered to was no guys allowed, ever. However, Beth had to go there with Danny. She had to do it once and for all to get over this stupid fear of having sex, and she had to do it so Danny wouldn't think of her as a little girl anymore. She had to. She desperately wanted him to want her in his life all the time. They wouldn't be interrupted at The Boat, and she felt comfortable with the privacy there.

Danny smiled as they glided into the small patch of woods. "How do you know about this place?"

She shrugged, not giving up information about the girls' secret place.

"I've never been here before," he said.

Beth only smiled.

"Is it cool here?" he asked.

She nodded. Beth swallowed hard, nervous jitters eating at her.

He reclined his seat, and she did the same. This was it. She would lose her virginity to Danny tonight.

He kissed her gently and hauled her over on his lap. They kissed and held on tightly to one another. Her body trembled on and off, and he asked if she was cold.

"I can turn the heat on if you need me to," he said.

Beth didn't want him to talk, she just wanted to have sex with him before she panicked and lost her nerve.

"I'm fine," was all she said.

Danny pushed Beth up so he could pull her blouse up out of her pants. He reached up her back to unhook her bra. She began to tense and couldn't hear the radio. She cleared her throat in a nervous manner and felt as if she might throw up.

"Relax," Danny said. "I won't hurt you."

At those familiar words, Beth was once again transported back to the couch with her face pressed down in the sofa cushion, suffocating. She couldn't breathe, and her eyes widened with fear. She started shaking her head back and forth and pushed his hands away from her saying, "No, no,

LAURA MCWILLIAMS HOWARD

no!"

Danny stopped touching her and peered at her, concern creasing his brow. "Beth?"

She looked at him conveying panic and terror in her eyes.

"It's okay. No big deal. We don't have to do this," he said quietly.

He eased her off him and over to her seat, and she curled her knees up to her chest. Her whole body shook.

"What's wrong?" He scrubbed his hand through his hair.

"Nothing," she replied as she turned away from him to look out the window.

"Why won't you talk to me?"

She remained quiet, mad as hell at herself.

Danny let out an exasperated sigh and started the car.

The entire tense ride home, Beth screamed at herself in her head. *You idiot! No wonder he thinks you're crazy! You are!* The self-recrimination continued all the way back to town until Danny pulled into her driveway.

"I guess you're not interested in talking to me anymore?" He put the car into park with a jerk.

Beth shook her head "no," meaning not right now, not tonight.

He didn't offer to walk her to the door.

Why would he? Beth thought as she got out of his car. *You're pathetic!* God, she hated herself right now.

Danny peeled out of her driveway.

Beth flinched and opened the front door. *Why can't I tell him what happened?*

420

CHAPTER 54

Beth was not surprised Danny didn't call her that week. She thought about him constantly and wondered if she should have told him about what happened with Greg. Beth knew that doing so would escalate the situation and she didn't want that. She wanted to forget about it. Forgetting didn't seem to be working either, though. She agonized over the situation, but she tried her best to focus on school. Thank goodness, she liked her class schedule this year and the kids in her classes.

Two weeks passed and the Winter Dance was approaching. The girls asked the boys to this dance, a time-honored tradition. A type of Sadie Hawkins dance. A conversation took place at the lunch table between Beth and her male and female friends over the role reversal and how they all felt about it. The girls didn't like having to ask for a date, and the guys worried if they would even get asked. It gave them all some real perspective on what the opposite sex normally had to deal with. Beth had never had the nerve to ask anyone to this dance in the past.

Susan asked Kenny to go. Melissa asked another boy from their class, Todd Meredith. Lynne would take Joey because, of course, they were back to boyfriend/girlfriend status. Jackie had plans to go with Donald Jackson. Fred from Beth's lunch table suggested that Beth ask Chris Kneeland, but she wasn't sure. She heard that he hadn't been asked yet. He was new to the school so no one else felt they knew him well enough. After some pressure from her girlfriends, Beth agreed to ask him, but she was nervous about it. She caught up with him in the Center on Monday before the dance and suggested they go together since neither of them had a date yet. He smiled and accepted.

"Great! I'll talk to you about it more later then," she said and walked away smiling.

At lunch that Thursday, Chris suggested they double date with his friend Ron and his date, Nancy. She was a junior. Beth really didn't want to and would have preferred to double date with one of the girls, but Chris would be more comfortable with his friend there. Beth reluctantly agreed.

Tradition dictated the girls pick the boys up and treat them to dinner at Pippy's or Burger Chef. The four decided to skip it. Ron and Nancy picked up Beth. The three of them drove to Chris's house. As Beth exited the car and approached the door, she was surprised how nervous she was feeling. She wasn't nervous about meeting his parents, she felt foolish about picking a guy up on a date. Before she could reach the house, Chris exited the front door and ran towards her. They greeted each other with a "Hello" and walked back to the car. Ron suggested they head over to the baseball field for a minute.

"What for?" Beth asked.

Ron held up a pint of something.

Beth took a deep breath and hoped they would hurry up. She wasn't eager for them to start drinking. Ron and his date, Nancy, drank from the bottle first. The two of them were drunk before they even parked the car. Apparently, they had already polished off a bottle before they'd picked up her and Chris.

Nancy leaned into Ron, kissing and hanging all over him.

Beth leaned back against the seat, stared out the window and the night sky, and wondered if she had made the right choice for her date. Chris didn't even tell Beth she looked nice, and he seemed more interested in drinking out of the liquor bottle than talking to her. Perhaps he was not as interested in her as she had thought. *This is going to be a long night.* Beth declined the bottle he offered. She felt like a babysitter and wasn't having fun at all. Did all guys her age act like this?

They finally reached the dance. Surprisingly, Chris held her hand as they entered the Center to pay admission. They saw several booths. One was a "Tunnel of Love" you could walk through to kiss your date in private. Of course, you had to go get married by the "Justice of the Peace" first. Beth thought about Brian and Ann. They had been married a week ago. A wave of sadness rushed over her, but she shook it off.

At the dance, a "Judge" charged each couple twenty-five cents to marry. He stood behind a podium and required them to say a bunch of ridiculous things to one another. He handed out to each couple cheap fake gold rings and a pink marriage certificate. To end the ceremony, he slammed his gavel down hard and announced the names so loudly that everyone at the dance knew who had just gotten married. The marriage certificate was required before you and your date could enter the Tunnel of Love. Beth had no intention of doing either.

"I hope you like to dance," she said when they found a seat at the table with her friends.

There was nothing worse than being at a dance with a guy who didn't dance. He assured her he did and promptly asked her to go out on the floor. They danced to "Love Stinks." They laughed and began to have a good time. Beth enjoyed herself more as the night wore on.

As they danced, Chris brought his face close and made eye contact, singing the song to her. Pleasantly surprised by his flirting, she wondered if she could feel an attraction to him. She thought it might be a good possibility because he made her laugh. The two danced non-stop the first hour.

During a slow dance, Chris whispered, "You have beautiful eyes."

Beth smiled, and he kissed her. Short, sweet, and nice.

"Do you want to get married?" he asked in her ear.

Beth nearly choked. She leaned back and looked at him. She had been sure they would not participate in any of that nonsense. However, she was beginning to like him, so maybe she would.

"We've known each other a long time. I think everyone would approve," he teased.

She put him off a few times as he tried to convince her.

The next slow dance brought an even longer kiss.

"Let's get married. It'll be fun," he said again.

Beth had enjoyed the kiss, and she was having fun with him. She looked in his eyes for several moments and shrugged, smiling. "Sure, Why not?"

They headed over to the Judge, Beth's former homeroom teacher and Chris's basketball coach. Since he knew the two of them, he really beefed up the routine and embarrassed them. They exchanged rings and signed the marriage certificate. He banged the gavel loudly ten times and made the announcement. Beth's friends and their dates clapped and hooted at them.

"Come on!" Chris ran over to the Tunnel of Love.

Beth was mortified as the chaperone told them to maintain their dignity inside. Chris walked her in. It was dark, and the floor was covered with white batting for a soft cloudy atmosphere. Several other couples sat in small cardboard boats. She and Chris climbed into one. Beth felt stupid and wished she hadn't agreed to this. She didn't want to give him the wrong impression. Although she liked him, she wasn't sure it would be a big romance.

"I'm going to kiss you now," he announced.

Chris kissed her several times. He crushed her mouth with the right amount of pressure and no slobber. Beth was pleasantly surprised. Maybe she could change her mind about the possibilities here...

The chaperone rang a bell and signaled that the ride was over. They exited and danced to a few more songs.

Ron and his date danced near them. Ron and Chris had been friends in elementary school and throughout junior high. It was obvious they had picked up where they left off. Nancy acted drunker than she had in the car. She must have snuck something inside. Beth warned her to be careful. She could get kicked out of the dance and suspended from school for a week. Nancy flirted with everyone else's dates, and it angered most of the girls. Ron didn't seem too worried about it so neither was Beth. She tried to avoid the girl as much as possible. Beth excused herself from Chris to use the restroom.

Jackie came in the restroom. Beth noticed her cheeks were glowing and her eyes were sparkling.

"It looks like someone is having a great time." Beth grinned.

"I am, actually," she said. "It looks like you and Chris are doing well, too. Getting married? Really, Beth!" Jackie giggled as Beth's face grew hot. Suddenly, she felt a little childish.

"Can you imagine Al or Danny doing something like that?" Beth asked.

"No way! It's an awful lot of fun, though!" Jackie said as she checked her makeup in the mirror. "Who cares what they would think?"

Beth agreed and felt more comfortable.

Melissa came in. "I've been looking all over for you guys."

She narrowed her eyes. "What's up with Ron's date? Is she drunk?"

"Uh, she's definitely drunk. She's been drinking nonstop since before we got here." Beth rolled her eyes.

After she brushed her hair and fixed her lip gloss, Beth said, "Got to go!" She smiled and opened the bathroom door.

Beth returned to the dance and sat down at the table. Chris wasn't there. She assumed he had gone to the restroom. A few minutes went by and he still hadn't returned. Beth searched the dance floor, but he wasn't there either. The warm air in the cafeteria caused a lot of people to step out into the Center. The doors to the Center were propped open to allow a breeze to flow in. Beth walked out there and looked outside. He wasn't there either. She had flashbacks of looking for Danny at the Fire Hall dance a couple years ago. This was totally different, though. Chris was her date and they were having a good time. He would return in a minute. She headed back to the table and waited.

Her friends returned to the table. People walked back and forth to the dance floor as the songs came and went. Twenty minutes had gone by, and Beth became concerned. She couldn't find Ron or Nancy either. Maybe they all went out to the car to drink more. She really didn't think Chris would leave to go get more liquor without telling her. Maybe he got sick in the bathroom. She got up and headed out to the Center to check near the bathrooms again.

Ron walked in the doors from the back parking lot, his face twisted into a scowl. "Hey Beth," he said, anger in his voice.

"Hey, can you check the bathroom for me to see if Chris is in there? I think maybe he got sick or something," she said.

"He's not sick," Ron said, his jaw clenching in anger.

Concerned, Beth nibbled on her bottom lip. "Did they get kicked out?"

Maybe one of the chaperones discovered Nancy drinking and threw Chris out, too.

Ron shook his head.

"What is going on?" she asked.

Ron looked down at her. "It appears our dates have left us and gone off with each other."

Beth widened her gaze, but she didn't believe him.

"What? That's ridiculous," she said, trying to soothe Ron's pride.

"That is exactly what's happened, Beth."

Jackie walked out to the Center with Donald. They approached Ron and Beth. Beth had not accepted what Ron told her.

He said, "I saw them leave together. They're gone."

Ron turned and shared the news with Jackie and Donald.

Jackie's eyes flew open wide. "Oh my God! That can't be

426

right," she said, looking at Beth.

Beth just shrugged. She was stunned. She didn't know what to say. She'd been through so much lately. This was just the cherry on top of a very sickening teenage cake.

Donald and Jackie gaped at Ron, apparently at a loss for words.

"That's pretty fucked up, man," Donald finally said to Ron.

"Tell me about it. I'm out of here." Ron walked out the door.

Stunned, Beth didn't remember in that moment that he was her ride home. Jackie guided Beth to the bathroom. Soon, the girls rallied around their friend.

"I feel like such an idiot," Beth said calmly. "I thought we were having a good time. God, I am a total idiot!"

The girls couldn't believe it either. It had appeared to them like Chris was having a good time, too.

"I really, really want to go home," she said.

Susan said she and Kenny would take her home. When they exited the bathroom, a crowd of about twenty people waited for her to come out. The news had traveled like lightning. Chris had left her with no date, and Ron had left her with no ride.

Her lunch table friend, Fred, ran up to her. "Do you want us to find him and kick his ass? We will, you know. You just say the word and we're gone."

Beth looked at her friends, people she had known her whole life. She smiled at them and tried not to get emotional.

"No," she said, sounding casual. "It's no big deal. I really don't care. I don't even really know him all that well." Her voice cracked, and her cheeks burned with embarrassment.

Donald chimed in, "I think we need to go find him."

Melissa, Jackie, Susan, and Lynne nodded at the boys. They began discussing their plan.

Beth held up her hands. "No! Please, I would really like

for this night to just go away. Any more attention on what has happened will just make me more embarrassed. Please?"

They all nodded at her. They did understand how she felt despite their anger at what Chris did to Beth.

Kenny said, "We'll give you a ride home, okay?"

Beth nodded. Everyone hugged her goodbye, telling her Chris was an idiot. She certainly seemed to pick an awful lot of idiots. She needed some serious psychological help.

She was quiet the entire ride home. Kenny and Susan didn't talk either. Apparently, Chris had ruined the night for all of them. In her driveway, Beth got out and thanked Kenny for the ride.

"Sorry you had to drive me home," Beth said.

"Hey, it's not a problem. I just wish I could do something else."

Beth smiled at him. Susan took hold of Beth's hand and squeezed it in a mini hug gesture.

"Thanks, guys." She stepped back, shut the car door, and went inside.

She walked into the family room.

Beth's mother sat on the couch. "Who brought you home? That wasn't the same car you went in. Did you have a good time?"

Beth stood in her family room in front of her mother. She hadn't needed her mother's arms around her for a long time, but tonight she did. After all the events in her life lately, the humiliation came out as anger. Beth fumed, telling her mother about it.

"The funny thing is I don't even care about him at all. I just felt mortified! You should have seen everybody's face when they looked at me!" She began to cry.

Her mother stood and hugged her. "They are your friends, Beth. They wanted to help and probably didn't know what to do."

"The guys wanted to go find him and beat him up," she said, chuckling through her stuffy nose.

"They should have." Her mother smiled as she stroked her hair.

Beth hugged in close to her mother again.

"It'll all be okay. I promise," she said, comforting Beth.

"I'm not going to school on Monday, Mom."

"Oh yes you are, and you will be fine. You didn't do anything wrong," her mother said.

"I'm still not going," Beth said again with determination.

"We'll talk about it tomorrow."

CHAPTER 55

"Beth. Get up. Wake up," her father said, invading her sleep.

She sat up, rubbing her eyes. "What's the matter?"

Her father sat next to her bed in the chair by her desk. Dread tightened her gut. He had woken her up this way when he'd told her she couldn't see Danny. Her stomach flipped over.

"Nothing's wrong, but I need to talk to you," he said.

Beth stared and blinked at him, waiting to hear horrible news.

He clasped his hands in his lap. "Well, you're probably going to be mad at me but that's okay. I did what I had to do as your father."

Beth looked closely into his face. A deep scowl distorted his features, and her pulse quickened.

"Your mother told me what happened with that Kneeland boy last night."

Beth swallowed hard.

He cleared his throat. "I called his father this morning and told him what I thought of the way his son had conducted himself last night. His father agreed and said he would be punished."

Beth's eyes widened in disbelief and horror. She had an out of body experience at that exact moment. Her father had ruined her entire life! She would never be able to live this down or go to school ever again.

"His father said he will be coming over here today to apologize to you."

"Oh my God! Dad!" Beth threw herself back on the bed, covering her face with a pillow.

"Well now, I know you're upset. But the boy needs to be

taught a lesson."

There was no point discussing it with him further. It had been done, and he thought he had done what was right. It didn't matter that all the kids would laugh at her on Monday because her father threw a fit to protect his pathetic daughter.

"I just thought you should know." She heard her father get up from the chair, but she kept the pillow over her face. "His father is upset with him, by the way, and he should be," her father said as he left her room.

She remained with the pillow over her face for some time after he had gone.

Beth did not have to work that Sunday, and she stayed in her room all day. She called the girls and told them what her father had done. They all expressed their sympathy for her. Beth wasn't really all that mad at her father. She was mostly angry with her mother. She should not have told her dad what happened. She should have known he would go berserk.

Her mother called her down for dinner.

"I'm not hungry," Beth called back.

"Yes, you are. Get down here," her father said.

Beth stomped down the steps. She still wore her pajamas and had not brushed her hair all day. They ate in silence.

"I'm sorry you're angry with me, Beth," her father said.

"Well, you should've just left it alone. I don't even care about the stupid guy anyway! It was embarrassing, that's all," she said, daring to raise her voice to her father.

"I know that. That's why I called his father. Eat your dinner," he said.

Beth quickly ate her food and asked to be excused. Her mother nodded to her. As she walked up the steps, her dad called to her, "You'd better get dressed because he is supposed to come over here to apologize."

Beth went to the bathroom and promptly threw up.

The phone rang around six thirty. It had been oddly

quiet all afternoon. Usually, the phone rang off the hook. Beth didn't answer, and it rang out over and over. She heard her mother answer and call to her father. The call wasn't for her, and she was relieved. She didn't want to talk to anyone anyway. After a minute or two, someone tapped on her bedroom door.

"Beth, it's me," her father said, and he opened the door. "That boy is on the phone. He wants to talk to you."

She wanted to jump out the bedroom window and fall to her death. The least her dad could've done was given the guy the opportunity to apologize to her on his own. What good was a forced apology?

Beth picked up the phone. "Hello?" She heard the receiver hang up downstairs, thank God.

"Beth? It's Chris."

Unsure what to say, she remained silent.

"Look, I am really sorry about leaving you at the dance last night."

"Thanks for the apology, Chris, I'll see you."

"Wait a minute! Don't hang up, Beth."

She hesitated and remained on the line. "I'm still here."

"I got in a lot of trouble for that," he said.

"I'm sorry." Beth sighed.

"Well, don't be sorry. I'm the one who's sorry. Really, I am. God, what I did was stupid and wrong."

"Look, Chris, we don't even really know each other. I was just kind of embarrassed, you know? I've never had anything like that happen to me before." She fidgeted with the phone cord.

"I know. I don't know what else to say except that I really am sorry," he said, sounding sincere.

"Well, I hope nobody brings this up tomorrow in school," Beth said.

"They probably will. You don't have anything to be worried about. I'm the one everyone is mad at."

Beth smiled, comforted that he took ownership of the

mess and was worried about going to school tomorrow, too.

"Okay, Chris. I'll see you later. Tell your dad you did your punishment now," she said, throwing in one dig before she hung up.

She spent the rest of the day hanging out in her room, reading and listening to music.

On Monday morning, Beth stayed away from the Center. No one said a word, but she knew everyone was talking about what Chris had done to her.

At lunch, Fred finally said, "So! I heard your dad called Kneeland's dad and told him that Chris bailed on you at the dance. I heard the shit hit the fan at his house, too."

Beth wanted to die as everyone stopped eating to look at her. "How do you know that?" she asked.

Jackie and Melissa squirmed in their chairs as she shot them an irritated frown. "I'm pretty sure Chris didn't tell you." She looked pointedly at the girls.

The girls hung their heads.

"Sorry, Beth," Melissa whispered. "I thought it was a cool thing your dad did.

"Let's not talk about it," Kenny Nixon said, seeing Beth was upset.

Everyone gave Fred a dirty look for bringing it up.

"What? I also think it's great he did that. He should've gone over there and kicked his ass." Fred furrowed his brow.

Beth smiled weakly at Fred then glanced around the table at her friends. All she saw was love and support. They all smiled back at her.

Donald Jackson said, "I'm with Fred. I think it's cool your dad did what he did. My dad would've done the same thing if he'd done that to my sister."

Kenny and the rest of the boys all chimed in, voicing their respect for her father. Once the boys finished, it got silent again.

Finally, Ron spoke, "I wish my dad had called his dad."

Beth raised her brow and shot him a knowing look, and

he smiled at her.

The entire table broke into amused laughter at Ron's comment. Beth's anger toward her father dissipated, and she started to feel a little proud that she had a father who cared about her so much.

Todd told them all what happened at Chris's house Sunday morning. Apparently, Chris's dad flipped out on him. Beth cringed, but everyone else seemed to delight in telling all the different versions they had of the "flipping out."

By Tuesday it was old news, and Beth's life returned to its usual mundane routine.

CHAPTER 56

In the middle of February, Beth attended a party at Susan's to celebrate Tyler's return home on leave. The girls were happy to see Susan head over heels in love again.

At the party, Jackie drank way too much. She asked Beth to go to the bathroom with her.

As Jackie primped in front of the mirror, she said, "I've been seeing Al off and on, even though he's still seeing that other bitch."

Stunned, Beth sat on the closed toilet lid. "I didn't know you were still seeing him."

Jackie turned away from the mirror and leaned against the sink. "I'm an idiot." Tears glistened in her eyes. "He just told me he can't see me anymore." Her voice cracked, and she spoke through her sobs. "He's going to marry that divorced bank teller! What does he see in her anyway?"

Beth got up and put her arms around her friend. "Guys are stupid. It's his loss."

Jackie sniffed and swiped at her eyes. "I guess you're right. Thanks, Beth. God, I can't wait until we graduate and get out of this crappy town. We will all be better off when we get away from these guys."

Beth yanked a handful of tissues from the box on the bathroom counter and handed them to Jackie.

"Do you want me to take you home?" she asked.

Jackie shook her head as she wiped her eyes and blew her nose.

"I'll be alright, you go on out there and have fun." She tossed the tissues into the trashcan.

"I'm not leaving you. How about a summit to The Boat?"

She shook her head. "You know what else? My dad is

adopting his girlfriend's kids. My brother and I haven't seen him in six months." Jackie didn't cry this time, but Beth wrapped her arms around her anyway.

"Really, I need to be alone, just for a minute," Jackie said pathetically. "It'll be okay."

Beth exited the bathroom and shut the door behind her. Susan was sitting on Tyler's lap, smiling from ear to ear. At least one of her friends was happy in a relationship.

Rocky entered the party with some of Tyler's other friends from school. He walked over and said, "Hi Beth. Would you like to dance?"

Beth looked at him for several moments then said, "Sure, Rocky. Let's dance."

She enjoyed dancing with him. As always, Rocky was charming, and he made her laugh. She found herself enjoying his company.

Rocky twirled her around the dance floor then pulled her close. "I miss you, Beth. Do you think we could be friends again? I'd like to visit you at work and hang out some time. You think that would be okay?"

"That would be great." Beth didn't see why that would be a problem. She could let bygones be bygones. Rocky was a fun person, just a sucky boyfriend.

"Thanks," he said. "If you ever need anything, you know you can call me, right?"

She nodded as she smiled and danced to the music.

Some of the guys from Beth's class were there, too. They had played on the varsity football team with Tyler. A short time later, Kenny approached Beth at the beer keg as she waited to fill her cup.

"Tell me you're not going out with Rocky Mulinero again," he said. "I saw you guys dancing."

"Don't worry, we're just friends," she assured him.

Relief softened his features. He nodded and walked away to talk to someone else.

A little while later, Chris Kneeland came in with several

other classmates. He and Beth had seen each other once since the Winter Dance. In the school library, he had walked up to her and apologized again.

Chris approached her at the keg, "Hey Beth. You look nice tonight."

Beth smiled at him, thinking *not in a million years, buddy.* She simply said, "Thank you." After filling her cup, she joined the main gathering in the living room.

Beth noticed that Charlie Cahall and Melissa had spent about an hour talking to one another, and they appeared quite chummy. Later at the party, Melissa told Beth that he had asked her out. She had accepted, and they had gone out the night before. Beth was happy for them, ignoring a small, selfish twinge of jealousy. Charlie needed a good girlfriend, and Melissa needed a decent boyfriend. He would be good for her.

Danny showed up a bit later. Beth tried desperately not to think about the last time they were together. He got a beer and greeted her briefly.

When he walked away, Chris said, "So that's the guy, huh?"

"What?" Beth asked.

"Everyone told me that Danny Mitchell is the big love of your life. So that's him, huh?"

Beth grew tired of Danny being called the "love of her life," but she was unable to deny the fact.

"I guess." She drank some beer from her cup.

"You could get him, why don't you try? He'd be lucky to have you," he said quietly, extending his apology once again for the Winter Dance fiasco.

"You're sweet to say that, but you don't know the whole story. We've dated each other before."

"So, what's the deal now?" he asked.

"I have no idea," Beth said truthfully.

"Maybe he needs someone to make him jealous. Can I help out with that?"

Beth shook her head and smiled at him. "I thought we were going to be just friends."

"Whose idea was *that*?" Chris asked, teasing her.

"Oh, go away..." she said and pushed him gently as she walked away with a grin.

Beth hung out with her friends and managed to avoid Danny.

Jackie asked Beth to stay over at her house, and the two left the party early. They stayed up late smoking Jackie's cigarettes and watching *Saturday Night Live* in Jackie's room on her small TV. They kept the window open so her mother wouldn't smell the smoke.

Jackie said, "You know we will be graduating in less than four months.

Beth couldn't believe it. "Before long we will all be split up at different colleges."

They both stared at each other.

"We definitely need to make sure the rest of our time together is a blast! No more moping around, right?" Jackie said and clapped her hands together.

"That sounds great to me!" Beth agreed.

They fell asleep with the TV on, and Beth went to work from Jackie's house on Sunday.

When Beth got off work at three, the girls all headed to The Boat, stopping first at Burger Chef to pick up food. Tyler was visiting his grandparents, so Susan came with them. Even with a jacket on, Beth's skin prickled from the cold, but the sunshine warmed the car. They liked to take Jackie's mom's car to The Boat in the winter because there was more room to spread out in the station wagon.

Melissa filled them in on the details of her date with Charlie. He had picked her up at her house. Her mother had been sober, thank God, and slightly charming. He had taken her out to dinner at the beach. They had walked the boardwalk and ended up at the movies and watched *Raging Bull*. Beth hoped this worked out for her.

Melissa was in the back of the station wagon leaning forward to talk to Beth. Beth and Lynne sprawled out in the back seat while Jackie and Susan sat up front and manned the radio.

"We wish you and Danny would get together so we could all double date," Melissa said.

"Jesus, Melissa!" Jackie barked. "Don't say that to her!"

Beth took a deep breath and decided to be silent.

Jackie changed the subject. "You guys know that Al is getting married, right?"

Beth knew but the other girls didn't. She had respected Jackie's trust and hadn't said a word.

"Oh no, Jackie! Are you okay?" Lynne asked.

Melissa and Susan clucked their tongues in sympathy.

"Don't worry," she said. "I have a plan to pay him back!"

The girls looked at each other with concern.

"What are you going to do?" Susan asked.

"I'd rather not say, but it will work. It will piss him off big-time," Jackie replied

"Just be careful, Jackie," Beth said. "He's not worth it."

Jackie had been so angry lately. Beth knew that part of the problem was Jackie's father adopting his new wife's kids, but she didn't think the others knew about that, so she didn't bring it up. She had an uneasy feeling about Jackie's plan. She was worried her friend would do something she would regret.

To change the subject and liven things up, Beth told the girls about bringing Danny out to the Boat.

Jackie grinned. "What did you do out here? Do we need to play Truth or Dare?"

They all looked at Beth and waited.

"I panicked," she said, embarrassed. They groaned at her.

"This is becoming a real problem for you, Beth. Maybe you should go talk to someone about it," Melissa said seriously. Then she grinned. "Do you still have the condom? You'd better buy a new one. That one is getting pretty old, don't you think?"

They laughed at her as she stuck her tongue out at Melissa.

"Why don't you just go to the clinic? They will give you six months' worth of birth control pills. Six months' worth for free!" Jackie said. "I think that's why you haven't done it yet. You're afraid you'll get pregnant."

Beth remained silent. She didn't even know what to say to her friends. They were right. She didn't know why she was so afraid.

Melissa distracted them from Beth's problems when she announced, "I think I'm going to sleep with Charlie.

They all screamed with excitement. Beth told Melissa she had to spill every detail. Melissa agreed but said it wouldn't be for a while.

Beth felt seriously left out of the whole sex thing. Everyone was doing it, everyone except her! Beth told them about a talk she had with her father a few days ago.

"He waited up for me which he never does. He asked me why I dated so many different boys. I didn't know what to say!"

The girls said, "No Way!" and "Oh My God."

She continued, "He said when he went to high school, they had names for girls who did that. I wanted to die."

Lynne's eyes widened, and she sat up. "I hope you told him you weren't like those kinds of girls! God! What did you say?"

Beth said, "I felt like crying, but it seemed so absurd. Me, the last virgin in the entire school, and my dad thinks I'm slutting around! I almost laughed at him. I told him that I didn't do anything wrong, and that nowadays boys don't want a girl that doesn't put out. He got really uncomfortable with the whole conversation and told me to go to bed."

They all got silent as they pondered how awful it would be to have that conversation with their fathers.

Soon they talked about the upcoming Spring Dance. No

one wanted to go. Beth said the Winter Dance fiasco put an end to her attendance at any more high school dances. Melissa said she would not ask Charlie to take her to a high school dance.

"I know what we could do," Jackie said. "We could go to the beach and spend the night in my folks' beach house. Maybe I can talk my mom into it. Do you think your parents would let you go?"

Beth said with a groan, "No way will my dad let me go."

Lynne nodded in agreement. "Mine either."

"I think I can talk my mom into it, maybe." Susan pursed her lips.

Melissa could do whatever she wanted so it was no problem for her.

"Well," Jackie said with a wicked gleam in her eyes. "Shall we try? The answer is always no if we don't ask." She grinned at her friends. "It will be so much fun!"

The girls were skeptical, but they all agreed to ask. All for one and one for all. If one girl couldn't go, then none of them would go. Beth and Lynne were sure they wouldn't be going but it felt exciting to think about it for the moment.

CHAPTER 57

The Spring Dance was only three weeks away, and everyone at school talked about who would be asking who. Since she and her friends had decided to skip this dance, Beth avoided those conversations.

Jackie called Beth on Thursday night. "Guess what? You're not going to believe it! My dad said it would be okay to use the beach house! He feels so guilty now, he will agree to anything. Maybe I should tell him I really need a car. Anyway, he's going to write down the instructions on how to turn the hot water on and off."

"Oh my God, Jackie! I can't believe it! I don't think my parents will be cool with it, though." She frowned.

"Well, think of something because Lynne, Susan, and Melissa all have permission, too."

"What?" Beth thought she would faint. She never dreamed the plan would get this far.

She called Lynne later and asked how she got her parents to agree to let her go.

"I just told them all the guys in our class were being jerks and asked younger girls to the dance, so we wanted to get away. Pretty much, that's what I said."

After a call to Susan, Beth learned that the same story worked for her.

Beth would have to go directly to her father. If she tried to go through her mom, it just wouldn't work.

That evening at dinner, Beth played with her food before finally saying, "Dad, you know Jackie's folks have a house at the beach."

"Uh-huh," he said, drinking his iced tea.

"The girls and I wondered if we could go down there the

night of the Spring Dance. Jackie's folks said it would be okay and so did Melissa's mom. Lynne's and Susan's parents also agreed." She took a breath and glanced at both parents.

"You mean to spend the night?" he asked as he stabbed his food with a fork.

Her mother continued to chew as she regarded Beth with raised brows.

Beth focused her attention on her father as he looked up at her.

"All their parents said it was alright to spend the night?"

"Uh-huh." Before he could say anything, Beth went on to explain, "Well, the Spring Dance is coming up and none of us really want to go, especially me after what happened at the Winter Dance." She maintained eye contact with him as she spoke. "The guys in our class are being jerks and asking all the younger girls, and we don't want to be embarrassed because we have no dates."

He looked at her mother with a questioning gaze. Her mother shrugged, indicating it was up to him.

Her father turned to Beth. "Is there a working phone there?"

"Yes, and we have directions on how to turn the hot water on and off."

"That shouldn't be too hard to do," he said.

Beth couldn't believe it. It was working! She tried to stifle her excitement.

"What are you girls going to do all night?" Her father wiped his mouth with his napkin and studied her.

"They have a TV and stereo. We'll probably just hang out."

"*Talking,*" her mother interjected. "I have never heard girls talk more than that bunch!"

"You'll stay at the house all evening?" he asked.

"Well, we might go get pizza or go to a movie or something."

"I don't see why not, do you?" he said to her mother.

"No, I think it will be okay."

"There won't be any boys there, correct?" he asked.

"Dad, no! We are trying to get away from them!"

He laughed and told her to have a good time. Beth's insides jumped up and down. She could barely wait to call her friends. After she helped her mother do the dishes, she got on the phone with Jackie to tell her the good news.

The following Monday at school, Ron asked Beth to go to the Spring Dance. She said she was sorry, but she would be out of town that day. No way was she going to miss out on a fun trip with her friends. She could hardly wait to get out of this town.

~

A few weeks later, on the day of the dance, the girls headed to the beach. They were overwhelmed with excitement. Lynne and Susan decided to share the bedroom in the loft. Beth and Melissa would be in another bedroom downstairs next to the master bedroom. Jackie had her own room, which seemed only fair since it was her parents' home. There was one bathroom across from the master bedroom they would all share. Once they put their suitcases away, they were in the car driving south to Ocean City, Maryland to buy two six-packs of Michelob Light, a fifth of slow gin, and a couple six-packs of soda.

They also stopped and picked up a couple of large pizzas. Lynne's dad sent a dozen homemade chocolate-covered donuts for them to eat for breakfast. They changed into their sweats and T-shirts, played the stereo, talked, played Gin Rummy with cards they found at the house, ate pizza, and got stinking drunk.

By one in the morning, everyone had gone to bed. Lynne passed out at ten, and they laughed as they heard her snore from the loft upstairs. Beth heard Jackie in the bathroom brushing her teeth before she fell asleep.

At four thirty in the morning, Beth heard a noise and woke up with a start. Someone had gotten up, and she hoped no one was sick. She got out of the bed, shuffled in her over-sized T-shirt and socks to the door, opened it, and walked out to the hallway.

Jackie headed towards the bathroom. She had a sheet wrapped around her, and her hair was disheveled in mounds of golden curls.

"Are you alright?" Beth whispered.

Jackie snapped at her, "Go back to bed, Beth."

"What's wrong?" Beth asked, eyes narrowed.

"Nothing's wrong, go back to bed," she said sternly.

Beth heard a noise in the master bedroom, and she walked towards the door.

Jackie stepped in front of her. "Don't go in there, Beth."

Her friend looked dead serious, and Beth stepped back.

"Everything is okay, but do not go in there. Do you hear me?" Jackie tightened her mouth.

Beth nodded and returned to her room. She stood on the other side of the door listening, trying to figure out what was happening. Someone, presumably Jackie, entered the bathroom and started the shower.

What the hell? Beth realized Jackie must have someone in the bedroom with her. Her mind started to race. *Why doesn't she want me to know who it is? What's the big fucking deal?* There was only one person Jackie wouldn't want Beth to see in her bed.

Beth began to get a pain deep in her throat and chest as the reality hit her. *It can't be! It just can't be!* She had forgiven Jackie, but she had never really forgotten. Beth walked out into the hallway. Jackie was still in the shower. Beth tip-toed into the hallway and opened the master bedroom door a crack. There was someone in the bed, but Beth couldn't really see. She opened the door a bit further and saw dark curly hair. She was ready to let out a primal sob, and her hands began to shake. She held herself together as she opened the door all the way.

She saw Jackie's suitcase on the side of the bed. Pretending she needed to retrieve something from the suitcase, she walked in the room. The streetlight streamed in through the window onto the bed. It was still hard to see, but she was determined to find out who Jackie was sleeping with, even if it killed her. She approached the bed not sure what she would do if she came face-to-face with Danny. If it were him, there would be a scene like none of them had ever known. Major shit was going to hit the fan all over the place. Whoever it was, he appeared to be sleeping. She stood next to the bed and looked down.

Greg Black turned and peered up at her. He sat up quickly, startling her. "Beth!"

She almost fell over as she scrambled backward away from him.

"I'm sorry, I didn't know anyone was in here. I'm sorry." She backed up and stumbled.

"Wait! I didn't know you were here. I..." He glanced around the room. "If I had known you were here, I would have been with you."

Beth ran out of the room and back to her bedroom. She shut the door, locked it, and lay on the bed. Beth shook violently for fifteen minutes. She heard Jackie leave the bathroom and shortly after that, two sets of footsteps treaded down the hallway. A few minutes later, a car started and drove off. Following that, Jackie headed back down the hallway, and the door to the master bedroom shut. Beth got up and opened the door softly. She crept back up to the master bedroom door and pressed her ear to the wood. Jackie was sobbing.

So, this is Al's payback.

Beth left the closed door and sat on the couch. She sat in stunned silence for a few moments. The she started to cry for the turmoil her friend must be feeling after her revenge sex. She cried about leaving her friends when they graduate.

She cried about the Polaroid picture she'd found in Rocky's car. She cried about the terrible night Greg had tried to rape her. She cried about the humiliation of being left at the Winter Dance. She cried about Brian getting married, and finally she allowed herself to cry about Danny. Beth cried harder and more deeply than she had ever cried before. She couldn't breathe through her nose by the time she finished.

Beth got up and used half the napkins in the napkin holder on the table in the dining area. She walked to the kitchen to wash her face. The cold water refreshed her. She found a mug and instant coffee. Upon further inspection, she discovered nondairy creamer and Sweet'N Low packets. She filled the teapot on the stove with water and turned on the burner. With a sigh, she plopped down on a kitchen chair, sinking into the big cushion. Once the water heated, she poured a cup and slowly sipped her coffee. Outside the kitchen window, the sun rose over the Delaware Bay. The sight warmed her soul, and she felt hopeful.

CHAPTER 58

The next day, Beth and Jackie didn't discuss their meeting in the hallway the night before. Jackie wouldn't find out that Beth had gone into the master bedroom unless Greg decided to tell her. Beth would never bring it up. She was even more convinced that Greg Black was the devil in disguise. On the ride home, she didn't have much to say to Jackie, but nobody seemed to notice.

On Monday, the girls told the guys at the lunch table where they had been on Saturday night.

With a hint of jealousy, Fred asked, "What did you girls do?"

Beth replied, "It's a secret and none of us will ever tell."

Kenny said, "I suppose there were older guys there?"

"Not a one. Girl's Night only." Beth glanced at Jackie.

She kept a straight face and avoided Beth's gaze as if pretending not to hear.

"You wouldn't believe what happened..." Melissa said with a smirk, taunting the boys further.

"What? What? Tell us!" Fred demanded.

They laughed at him.

Kenny shook his head at Beth then stuck out his elbow. She elbow-wrestled him and made him laugh out loud.

The week passed by without any major drama for Beth, and she looked forward to the Fire Hall dance on Saturday.

~

Beth drove herself to the dance and scanned the room. Thank God, Al and Greg weren't there. What would happen between the two cousins if Al ever discovered that Greg had slept with Jackie?

Ann and Brian entered the hall. The two were married now, and Ann looked very pregnant. Beth walked over to greet them. She hadn't seen Brian since the last dance. She missed him.

He forced a smile, hugged her slightly, and said, "Hi, Beth" not "Hello, Gorgeous," and she felt a little disappointment.

Beth sat beside Ann and talked with them about trivial stuff for about fifteen minutes. Soon, Ann left the table to talk to some friends. Brian and Beth sat in comfortable silence for a few moments, and then joked about some of the awkward dancers. Beth kept the conversation light. She didn't know what to say to him about his marriage.

Melissa and Charlie walked in holding hands. On the phone earlier that day, Melissa told Beth that Charlie had been understanding about her mother and that things were going well. They hadn't had sex yet, though.

Danny came in with Mike. Danny waved to Beth from across the room. She smiled at him, and he looked surprised that she had responded.

Brian nudged her leg with his. "Hey, I think he likes you."

"Ha ha, very funny." She rolled her eyes at Brian.

Beth decided perhaps she should stop being so angry at Danny. If he didn't want her as a girlfriend, it was okay. It hurt, but she just wasn't what he wanted. She felt calmer and more comfortable after her decision to forgive him. She enjoyed the peace of mind it gave her.

Danny walked over to her, and Brian pulled a chair up, an invitation to Danny to join their conversation.

Danny engaged her in a trivial conversation about the band and the number of people in attendance. Beth made eye contact with Brian. He grinned at her and winked, letting her know he realized Danny was trying.

Leaning forward in his chair, Danny said, "You look nice tonight, Beth."

This surprised her because she had not gone to much

trouble getting ready for the dance. Her hair, pulled back in a ponytail, hung straight. She wore a pair of Levi's with high-heeled black loafers and a short sleeve, black knit pullover. Her gold necklace had a black onyx pendant, and she wore matching earrings. She'd worn this outfit a million times. She was sure he'd seen her in it before, on more than one occasion. Her nails weren't even painted tonight.

"Thanks, Danny, so do you," she replied.

It felt so relaxing to be nice to one another. Beth turned to watch Melissa and Charlie dance.

"Looks like our friends are hitting it off pretty good, huh?" she said.

Danny looked at them, nodded, and then returned his gaze to Beth.

"How are things at the restaurant?" she asked.

Danny shrugged. "Alright, I guess. My sister and I have been thinking about adding on a bar and an outside deck."

Brian and Beth agreed that sounded cool and profitable. Beth suggested he hire "Shot Man Mike" to bartend. The three smiled at the idea and continued to make small talk. Being around Danny was friendly and easy for a change.

Brian relaxed in his chair with his legs stretched out in front of him. Beth leaned forward with her elbows on her knees, legs apart slightly. She slouched a little. Danny's hips were turned toward her, and he rested one foot across the knee of his other leg. His arm lay lazily across the back of her chair.

From behind, strong male hands clamped down on Beth's shoulders. Surprised, Beth sat upright.

Mike leaned over. "Hey girlie, let's dance."

Danny immediately looked at the floor. Brian caught Beth's eye, squinted at her, shaking his head slightly.

Beth turned around and said, "Thanks, Mike, but I'll have to catch you next time."

Mike looked at Danny and then at Brian.

"Sure, sure. Okay, come get me when you're ready," he

said.

"I will."

He squeezed her shoulder, gave them a knowing smile, and walked away.

Danny continued to smile and chat with her. He asked her how her senior year was going. She rolled her eyes, smoothing her hair back and said she couldn't wait to be done. Brian told her not to be in too big of a hurry to get out there in the world.

"She's going to college," Danny told him. "Right?"

Beth nodded. "That's the plan."

Rocky Mulinero walked over to say hello to Beth. Danny and Rocky didn't like each other, and she suspected it was about her. However, Rocky and Danny greeted one another politely. As soon as Rocky walked away, Danny turned to Brian and said, "I cannot stand that guy!"

Brian chuckled and said, "I don't really know him well."

"Beth dated him. He's an ass, isn't he?" Danny asked.

Beth smiled at Danny. "Well, I actually like Rocky a lot. He's a lot of fun. He didn't make the best boyfriend, but he really doesn't bother me otherwise."

Danny cleared his throat and shook his head as if he didn't see it.

Beth narrowed her eyes at him. "What?"

"Nothing," Danny muttered. He seemed ready to drop the subject.

Brian stood. "I'd better go check on my wife."

Danny and Beth widened their eyes at each other. It was weird to hear him refer to Ann as "my wife."

The band played a slow song. "Hello girl, it's been a while, guess you'll be glad to know..."

"Do you want to dance?" Danny asked Beth.

She stared at him for a moment to contemplate the hurt factor involved in dancing with him to this song.

"Sure."

He stood and offered his hand. She accepted, and he led

the way to the dance floor. When he turned to face her, Beth placed her left hand on his right shoulder. Danny took her right hand in his and held it up to his chest. Beth was surprised how calm she felt. The two moved in time as the song played on.

The band continued to play "I Go Crazy," and the singer belted out the lyrics. "I go crazy, when I look in your eyes, I still go crazy. No, my heart cannot hide that old feeling inside, way deep down inside."

It was the first time in four years that Danny and Beth danced together. Their friends grinned at them.

Danny said, "I feel like we're on display."

He seemed nervous, edgy, but Beth was calm.

"Are you going to yell at them and tell them you don't need seven or eight coaches?" she said, referencing their first date at the basketball game at Smythfield High School.

Danny looked down and smiled at her.

The song played on. "I realize that I was blind, just when I thought I was over you, I see your face and it just ain't true, no it just ain't true."

Neither of them had been drinking. There were no muddled or confused feelings. She looked up at him. His smile got wide and genuine as he gazed down at her.

Beth's heart tugged. *Be careful, Beth.* She tried not to listen to the lyrics of the song. Danny pulled her closer to him. He hummed along with the words, and Beth's legs got weak. The song was over much too soon.

The band began to play "Lay Down Sally," and the two stayed on the dance floor. After the song ended, Danny followed her to her table, keeping his hand on her back.

Charlie and Melissa were sitting at the table. Danny and Beth joined them.

A few moments later, Danny turned to Beth. "My cousin is getting married on Saturday. I'm house sitting for him in his apartment while he goes on his honeymoon. I have some friends coming over Saturday night. I'd like you to come."

He turned to the rest of the table and invited them, too. The group acknowledged the invitation and agreed to be there. Beth hadn't responded yet, and Danny waited for her answer. She smiled and tried to remain relaxed and comfortable. She knew from experience to never get her hopes up when it came to Danny.

"I'm not sure yet. We'll see, okay?" She tried to sound nonchalant.

"Will you dance with me now?" Mike said to Beth as the band began to play Elton John's "Saturday Night's Alright for Fighting."

Beth glanced at Danny with a question in her eyes.

He smiled at her and said, "Go, please shut him up!"

She smiled and headed to the dance floor with Mike.

Melissa and Charlie were making out at the table.

Beth watched them and realized she wanted a loving relationship like that. She wondered if her life would be different if she had gone out with Charlie years ago. She sighed, feeling a little wistful.

She missed Brian's friendship, she was envious of Charlie and Melissa's relationship, and she felt mostly confused by Danny's behavior. Once again, she wondered what Danny wanted from her. With a pang in her chest, she decided it was time for her to go home.

Beth claimed she had to work inventory at the store and report in early, so she left the dance before it was over. Danny kissed her on the cheek as she said her goodbyes to everyone and reminded her to come to the party next weekend.

CHAPTER 59

At school on Monday morning, Chris Kneeland approached Beth in the Center and said, "I heard you were hanging all over Danny at the dance Saturday night."

She rolled her eyes. "I wasn't hanging all over him. I danced with him. It was nothing."

Oddly, a few other people also mentioned it to her as if they were excited for her.

That evening, Danny came into the store to see Beth. She was surprised to see him there. They had a pleasant conversation. He was friendly, and he flirted with her. She made him laugh as she teased him about his white restaurant uniform.

She didn't work again until Thursday night, and Danny came to visit her again. This time he was there during her break. They walked across the street to the deli and ordered coffee. He watched her carefully and sat close to her at the table. Beth was relaxed and playful. She had forgotten how witty he could be. He behaved differently, too. She couldn't quite figure it out. He seemed settled, calm. Or maybe she imagined it.

He walked her back to the store, and they hung out a little longer. He bought a shirt from her to justify being in the store so long. Beth insisted he didn't have to, but he asked her to help him find something. He laughed as she picked out shirts that looked like those worn by John Travolta in *Urban Cowboy*. Beth told him he would look fabulous if he ever wanted to ride a mechanical bull. She teased him further by picking out a pink shirt and told him the store sold concert tickets to see The Village People.

She got serious with the next choice and held it up for

him to see. It was a light blue Izod polo shirt. Danny liked it and bought it on the spot.

Before Danny left, he asked Beth hopefully, "Have you decided if you're coming Saturday?"

Beth said, "I don't know, Danny. I'm still undecided."

She felt they were doing okay as friends. Maybe they shouldn't mess with their new relationship. On the other hand, he wasn't asking her to be his date so maybe he just wanted to be friends, too. There were always mixed signals with Danny. She just didn't know what to do.

"Please come, I'd love to see you there," he said pointedly, then turned and left the store.

She scrunched her brow, feeling uncertain about his intentions.

CHAPTER 60

We outgrow love like other things
And put it in the drawer,
Till it an antique fashion shows,
Like costumes grandsires wore.
-Emily Dickinson

Friday night Beth and the girls went out to The Boat. They sat in the boat and chatted as they passed around a bottle of Boone's Farm. Beth and Jackie shared a cigarette, handing it back and forth. There was a sense of calm and familiarity. Despite the jacket she wore, Beth shivered from the chilly air. She stared up at the clear sky sparkling with stars and smiled at its beauty for several moments.

Talk of the Prom brought her back to the present. She didn't join the conversation because she didn't want to go. Instead, she listened as they chattered on about their dates, their dresses, and the after-Prom party.

"Are you guys all going to Danny's party Saturday? Melissa blurted out in an eager voice. She was clearly psyched to go.

Before the other girls could answer, Beth sighed and admitted, "I'm not going. Danny has been nice to me lately, and I've started thinking about him way too much. He's let me down so many times, you know. I just need to put an end to it."

The girls gaped at her. Clearly, they did not recognize this Beth. Usually, she jumped at any chance to see him.

Susan said, "Well, we want you to come but we do understand. Danny has been nothing but trouble for you."

"If I go, I'll do the same thing I've always done. Get my

hopes up. I'm leaving for college in September, and I don't want to go with a renewed crush on Danny or worse yet, a broken heart."

The girls all nodded their understanding.

"I think it's best to leave it alone. He has been coming around the store, you know. Being sweet. I don't know what he's doing. Maybe he knows I'm getting ready to go off to college and doesn't have to worry about any long-term commitments or expectations from me."

"Oh, I don't think that's it. I think he has grown up some. You've wanted him for so long and here he is trying. You're the one holding back now because you're scared," Lynne said gently.

Beth blinked at her, stunned.

Jackie took a drag from the cigarette and exhaled a cloud of smoke. "She's got a right to be nervous where Danny is concerned. One minute he loves you, and the next minute he's got a girlfriend or is going off to the other side of the country."

Beth appreciated that her friend came to her defense. She sent Jackie a grateful smile as Jackie handed the cigarette to her.

Melissa added, "Well, I want you to go to this party lady. If not for Danny, then go for me. All of you!" She looked around at them all, her eyes imploring. "I'm uncomfortable going to this party with Charlie without you there."

Jackie, Susan, and Lynne agreed readily. Beth stared at Melissa a few moments, and then took a drag off the cigarette.

"Please?" Melissa said.

Slowly, Beth nodded her head in agreement and released a plume of smoke. She couldn't let her friend down.

Beth was scheduled to work until four that day, and Melissa would finish work at two. They all made plans to go out shopping until Charlie picked Melissa up at six for dinner before the party.

Her friends chattered on about what they were going to wear to the party, and Beth remained silent for most of the night. She was still anxious about going to Danny's party.

The next day the five girls hung out at Melissa's house after their shopping trip to Pappagallo's on Saturday. Melissa's mother wasn't home, and they didn't watch the time as they chatted on the couch in the front room.

The doorbell rang, and Melissa jumped up.

She let Charlie in. "Oh my goodness, you're early. Let me run and get ready. We lost track of time."

Danny came in behind Charlie, surprising the girls. Beth stared at Danny. He looked so handsome in his gray suit.

Charlie explained that he gave Danny a ride home from the wedding reception so he could get things ready for the party tonight. Gazing into her eyes, Danny reminded Beth to come over for the party.

Everyone except Beth headed to the kitchen where Melissa and the other girls deposited their empty iced tea glasses. Jackie, Lynne, and Susan stayed in the kitchen, giving Beth some space, while Melissa went to her room to get ready. Beth stayed on the couch in the living room. Danny stood in the kitchen doorway and regarded her with a pensive expression. She swallowed hard. Damn! He looked good.

He walked over and sat next to her. "You will be there tonight?" he asked.

She nodded.

He smiled broadly. "Good." Then he leaned in and kissed her tenderly.

She raised one eyebrow, surprised by his bold move, but she didn't object. He drew back, his eyes smoldering and focused on hers.

Her stomach fluttered pleasantly, and warmth spread across her cheeks. He moved in again. This time he used his tongue to explore her mouth. Beth surrendered to the passion of the moment. They broke away, and Danny's eyes looked a little cloudy.

"It's been a very long time since I've been kissed like that," Beth said softly.

Her lips still tingling, Beth watched him as he got up off the couch.

"I need to go prepare for tonight. See you later." Danny smiled softly at her. "I'm so glad you're coming."

"Come on! We have to go!" he yelled to Charlie. He jumped up from the couch.

Melissa rushed out of her bedroom. The others came out of the kitchen, and Beth stood up on shaky legs. Charlie, Melissa, and Danny got in Charlie's car while Beth moved towards her own. Jackie's car was next to hers, and Lynne and Susan rode with her.

"Oh wait!" Beth shouted, and her friends turned toward her. She asked Jackie, "Can I spend the night at your house?" She didn't want to lie to her parents about where she was going.

Jackie motioned with her arm. "Why don't you all stay? My mom won't care."

Beth, Susan, and Lynne agreed to meet at Jackie's around seven.

When she arrived home, Beth had nervous jitters up until it was time to leave for Jackie's.

The girls minus Melissa gathered at Jackie's with their bags, putting on makeup and doing their hair. Beth wore a black spring V-neck sweater with quarter-length sleeves and matching black chinos. She had chosen a silver jewelry set, which included her charm bracelet, a bangle style watch, dangling earrings with small black beads, and a choker with seven chains connected by a black bead clasp worn in the front. She wore high-heeled black loafers with silver buckles on the sides. Her hair was down, parted in the middle and curled under. For tonight, she had chosen a French manicure. Her makeup was natural looking with a light blush, eyeliner, mascara, and pale pink lip-gloss.

After waiting for Jackie to finish her hair, they all complimented one another, borrowing perfume, and using last minute hair spray shots.

Beth wished she still had Grass Oil perfume, remembering how Danny liked it. The company quit manufacturing it a long time ago. She borrowed some of Lynne's Jovan Musk. Jackie drove them all in her station wagon, and they headed over to the apartment around nine o'clock. Beth glanced at her three friends. They all looked magnificent.

Danny welcomed them in and appeared flustered as he said hello to Beth.

Mike fell over himself as he spoke with Lynne. Billy was there, and he made a beeline for Jackie. Charlie and Melissa came over to greet them. There were five other guests there.

As everyone chatted and got themselves drinks, Danny leaned towards Beth and said quietly, "You look beautiful tonight."

What is up with him? Beth decided to just go with it.

Danny played the gracious host, making sure everyone had drinks and circling the room to chat with all the guests. Eventually, he returned to Beth and sat next to her on the couch. He reached over to put a wayward strand of hair back behind her ear and stared into her eyes. She stared back and suddenly it felt as if they were the only two people in the room. They sat together and talked most of the night. By eleven, only a handful of guests remained. The girls caught Beth's eye periodically and smiled or nodded their approval. Danny was attentive and sweet. She was a goner once again.

The other guests left them alone. Maybe they were hoping they would find a way to get it right this time.

Danny asked to see her senior picture. Beth didn't carry around her own picture, but Jackie offered to show him her copy.

He stared at it and then at Beth. "Jackie, can I keep this?"

This side of Danny embarrassed Beth. He acted like he wanted her, but why now? In four months, she would be going away to college. He knew that. Her doubt did not stop her from enjoying his attention, though. The attraction to Danny had a strong drug-like effect on Beth.

It was close to twelve o'clock when Jackie came over to Beth, Danny, and Charlie who were standing together in the kitchen, and she said to Beth, "We need to go. My mom will have the cops looking for us if we're late." She laughed.

Melissa walked over to Charlie. "I need to get my bag from my house. Can I borrow your car?"

Charlie nodded. Melissa and Charlie were staying in the guestroom for the night.

Beth said, "Jackie is ready to go, too, and I'm staying at her house, so I'll see you guys later."

As Beth turned to leave, Danny grabbed her arm and said quietly, "Will you stay with me, Beth? Please?"

Heat crested over Beth's cheeks.

"I don't know," she stammered. "All my things are at Jackie's."

Danny took Beth by the hand and pulled her closer to him.

"Get Melissa to bring you back when she comes."

"I don't know, Danny." She looked around. Did everyone know what they were talking about? Melissa and Charlie were kissing, and no one else seemed to be paying attention. "I'll see," she said.

Danny pulled her close to him and kissed her in the way that only Danny could. She was so in love with him. He knew it, she knew it, everyone at this party knew it, her family knew it, the entire school knew it, and God in heaven knew it, too.

Charlie told Melissa to hurry back and tossed her the keys to his car. Jackie jingled her keys to get everyone's attention.

"I'm leaving!" she announced.

Jackie, Susan, Lynne, and Beth walked out the door. Beth looked back at Danny one last time. He stared at her intently and drank from his beer bottle. She stared back as she followed Susan out the door. They walked out to their cars, and Beth grabbed Melissa's arm. "Can I ride back with you? Can you pick me up at Jackie's after I get my stuff?"

Melissa grinned broadly, with complete understanding. "Of course."

Beth, Jackie, Lynne, and Susan rode together in the station wagon. In the car, Beth had a silent panic attack. What should she do? She didn't speak for the entire ride to Jackie's house. She tried to breathe calmly. When they got upstairs to Jackie's room, Beth stood in the doorway with her eyes wide, ready to hyperventilate.

"What's the matter with you?" Jackie asked.

"Danny asked me to come back."

Everyone stopped moving and turned to look at her and then each other.

Jackie's eyes widened. "Oh my God, Beth! This is great!"

She hugged her friend. The other girls came towards her all talking at once.

Beth stood in a daze.

"You *are* going, aren't you?" Susan said.

"I don't know. I don't know what to do. Tell me what to do!" Beth said, taking small, quick breaths.

"Go!" they all shouted in unison.

Beth pulled Lynne into the bathroom. "Look, you are my oldest friend. Tell me, should I go?"

Lynne grasped Beth's arms. "Beth, honey, if you don't do this, you will regret it for the rest of your life. You have a chance to make love for the first time with Danny. Danny! You have loved him forever! He loves you, too. I know it. Why would he still be like this with you after all these years? Your first time will be in a bed, not in a tacky car, and you know he would never hurt you."

"But I'm not on the pill."

"When did your last period end?" Lynne asked.

"Yesterday," Beth replied.

"Oh my God, that is perfect timing. Go! Go!"

Beth smiled, and they exited the bathroom.

Melissa had made her way to Jackie's. She stood in the doorway, holding her overnight bag. Susan, Jackie, and Melissa stared at Beth with expectant expressions.

"I'm going to Danny's," she said.

Jackie hugged her and looked intently in her eyes. "It will be okay."

"Let's go," Melissa said.

Beth grabbed her bag.

"Here's the number if her mom calls," Melissa said, giving a small paper to Jackie.

Beth hadn't thought about that and looked at Jackie in a panic. "What if my mom calls?"

"It's okay! I'll say you're in the shower, and I'll call you. You can call her from there."

Panic rolled over Beth's shoulders, and she was sure she looked like a deer in headlights.

"For God's sake, Beth. In all these years, has your mother ever called for you this late at night?" Melissa said, trying to rush her friend.

That convinced her. "Let's go," she said and smiled at her friends.

Both anticipation and fear gripped her.

CHAPTER 61

Consecration

Proud of my broken heart since thou didst break it,
Proud of the pain I did not feel till thee,
Proud of my night since thou with moons dost slake it,
Not to partake thy passion, my humility.
-Emily Dickinson

On the ride back over to the apartment with Melissa, Beth kept asking, "What if I get scared and can't do it?"

"You won't," Melissa answered each of the ten times Beth asked the question.

"Beth, you make sure you tell him to pull out, you hear?"

Beth nodded. "I just finished my period. Lynne said I'd probably be okay."

"You can't be sure, though. Make sure he pulls out. Promise me," Melissa said firmly.

"I promise." Beth frowned. She hoped he would just do it and she wouldn't have to ask.

Melissa glanced at her before refocusing on the road. "Are you sure about this?"

"Surer than I've ever been," Beth said, her voice becoming calm.

"You know it's going to hurt, right?" Melissa said.

"Uh-huh." Beth didn't want to think about that.

She started to remember Greg and the fiasco at his apartment and forced herself to put it out of her mind.

"I swear it only hurts the first time." Melissa flashed her a reassuring smile. "Usually, if the guy is careful, it will start to feel pretty good after a bit."

"Please, Melissa! You're starting to freak me out." Beth

clasped her hands in her lap.

"Okay, sorry. Just tell him to be careful. Tell him you're a virgin."

"I'm sure he already knows that." Beth rolled her eyes.

"Don't bet on it. You tell him before he starts. Swear to me you'll tell him," Melissa ordered.

"There are an awful lot of directions you're telling me to give him. Be careful, pull out, tell him I'm a virgin!" Beth said, her voice rising.

"I'm sorry. I'm sorry." Melissa took a deep breath. "I want this to go right for you."

"If I tell him I'm a virgin, he probably won't do it." Beth sighed.

"Yes, he will. You just have to tell him! You have to!" Melissa said, raising her eyebrows. "Shit! I don't want to be worrying about you while I'm in the other room with Charlie!"

Beth narrowed her gaze at her friend. "Don't talk to me anymore, Melissa. I mean it. Don't say another word."

"Alright, I'm sorry. I'm sorry," she said quietly.

The two girls drove the next three minutes in silence.

"Charlie has to be at the Post Office by seven thirty. I need to get the car back to him before it's time for him to leave. I'll knock on the bedroom door when it's time to go, we'll meet in the kitchen, and I'll drive you back to Jackie's. She'll let you in the window. You just climb up the tree out front and onto the porch roof. Knock on the window, and she'll let you in. You got it?" Melissa gave her directions as if they planned a bank heist.

"I got it, Melissa. Geez! I've done this before."

Melissa pulled Charlie's car into the lot and parked in front of the building. They exited the car in silence and walked up the steps. Melissa pressed the buzzer and looked at Beth with a here-we-go expression. Charlie buzzed back, letting them in the building door. They climbed two flights of steps to the second floor. Beth began to feel sick to her stomach. Melissa took hold of Beth's hand as they reached the wooden door.

"Ready?" Melissa whispered.

Beth nodded.

Knock. Knock. Knock.

Charlie opened the door. He raised his eyebrows at Beth, and then lowered his head, avoiding eye contact with her.

"Come on in," he said. "Wait here. I'll go get Danny. I'll be right back."

Beth heard Charlie knock on Danny's bedroom door. It opened, and Charlie said, "You've got a visitor, man."

Then Charlie and Danny spoke in voices too low for her to hear. Her palms started sweating and she wiped them on her pants. What were they saying?

When Beth saw Danny, she lost track of what Melissa and Charlie were saying and where they went. Danny wore a pair of gray sweats and a navy-blue T-shirt. He had obviously already been in bed. She felt like she was going to throw up.

Beth waited for him to say *What are you doing here? Go home, Beth.*

He didn't, he only smiled and took her hand. She followed him as he led her down the hallway to the back bedroom. He glanced at her reassuringly as they made their way to the door.

"You look beautiful," he said. "I'm glad you came back."

Danny brought her in the room and sat her on the edge of the bed. He knelt in front of her. "This is okay?" he asked her.

She smiled at him and nodded. He took her bag and the purse she held tightly in her lap and placed them over by the door.

"I think I need to use the bathroom," she said.

"Sure, sure." He walked her to the door across the room.

Thank God she didn't have to go out to the hallway to use the restroom. She didn't want to see Charlie again tonight. Beth walked into the bathroom. Danny turned the light switch on for her and shut the door. She emptied her bladder and stood in front of the sink. Her mind returned to Greg's apartment, her pants being pulled off forcibly, her face getting smashed into the couch cushions. Reliving that terrifying moment when she couldn't breathe, she turned on the faucet, pressed cold water to her face, and tried to settle her stomach. She was having a full-blown panic attack. Beth looked in the mirror and forced herself to take deep breaths and to remember that this was Danny. He would never hurt her. *Breathe, breathe.* She calmed as much as possible and exited the bathroom.

He had turned off the bedroom light, and the light from the bathroom shone on him where he sat at the end of the large bed. Danny had removed his shirt but still wore his sweatpants. He stood and met her at the bathroom door. He turned off the light, took her by the hands, and guided her to the edge of the bed.

"You're shaking." He knelt in front of her and began to kiss her.

She tried extremely hard not to think beyond the kissing. Instead, she focused on his breathing like she had done so many times before when they'd kissed in the car. His breath came evenly. Hers did, too, unless she breathed too deeply. Then it became jagged.

He kissed her softly and slowly while he gently touched her face. He glided his lips to her neck and wrapped her hair through his fingers. Beth sat perfectly still, trying to hide that she was ready to jump out of her skin.

"Relax," Danny said softly.

Wham! There was Greg in her mind, screaming, "Relax, goddamn it!"

Beth pulled away from Danny momentarily.

"Please don't say that anymore, please..." she whispered.

"Okay." He kissed her on the forehead.

Dany brushed his lips against her cheeks and then back to her mouth. She had perspiration on her forehead, and he wiped it away. He grasped the bottom of her sweater and gently pulled it up.

Beth tried hard to stay calm. *I will not be a baby tonight. I will not!* She raised her arms as he tugged the sweater slowly over her head. He set it on the floor at her feet.

He kissed her deeply and reached behind her to remove her bra. Beth was rooted to the spot. Danny removed it quickly then held her in an embrace. He lowered her on the bed and admired her necklace against her bare skin. With desire brightening his eyes, he caressed and kissed her. Beth watched as he used his tongue, lips, and fingers to create sensations she'd never felt before on her bare skin. It fascinated her, and she couldn't tear her gaze away. She gently held his head and played with his hair around his ears and neck. He was being extremely gentle.

He won't hurt me. His soft touch was nothing like Greg's rough strokes.

Her legs still hung off the end of the bed, and Danny straddled her and kissed her again on the mouth, caressing her as he did. Beth relaxed beneath his soothing touch. She wished he would talk to her a little. Just reassure her that it would be okay.

He reached to undo the button and zipper on her pants. She flashed back to Greg pinning her hands over her head as his mouth crushed hers.

It's Danny, it's Danny, it's Danny, she told herself over and over as she forced herself to breathe deeply and let him remove her pants. He knelt on the floor again as he undressed her and placed her pants on the floor. Danny ran his hand over her legs and stomach, and pleasant tingles rippled through her body. Beth had never been touched intimately before, and she worried about how she would feel to him. He stood and removed his pants. The sight of Danny's erection shocked Beth. She became embarrassed and frightened. She forced herself to breathe deeply.

Danny positioned himself on the floor in front of her. He kissed the top of her right thigh and worked his way to the inner part of her leg. Beth shuddered in response. Danny touched her other leg softly with his right hand. He wasn't hurting her, and Beth enjoyed the delightful sensations. Danny climbed onto the bed next to her and guided her up towards the pillows. Her entire body was positioned on the bed, her head on the pillow. She glanced to the side, and her hair fell in dark contrast to the white pillowcase.

Beth ran her fingers along the outline of his upper arms and back. He shivered beneath her hands as her nails lightly tickled his sides, hips, and back. She touched him lightly along his thighs and over his hard planes, trying to memorize every part of his body. Beth kissed him deeply and moved her body against his. She felt his passion against her skin and tried not to be afraid. So far, so good.

Danny trailed his hand down her stomach and traced around her sex. She sucked in a sharp breath but surrendered to his touch.

Don't be a baby, Beth! Don't you dare! she told herself. She forced herself to move her hips up toward his hand, letting him know it was okay to continue. Feeling the movement of her hips, he did just that. She never imagined he could touch her like this, make her feel so wonderful. Beth reached down to touch him. He pulled his hips away from her.

"Not yet," he whispered in her ear, using his mouth to focus his attention back to her breasts.

She relaxed, and her breathing grew heavy as his caresses filled her with bliss. He removed his hand and held himself over her again. His breathing remained deep and steady, and he licked his way down toward her stomach. He kissed her, glided his tongue across her flesh, and moved his mouth close to her center. Beth was overwhelmed with all the new sensations.

"No! Please don't," she begged when he got too close, not ready to handle that kind of intimacy.

He didn't say anything but pulled himself back up and separated her legs with his knee. She felt him slowly easing into her body, and there was no pain. He wouldn't hurt her. She breathed out with relief. Then suddenly, he pushed into her with a force Beth had never known. Pain ripped through her stomach and took all the breath from her body. In shock, she closed her eyes tightly and clenched the bed sheets with tight fists.

Danny moaned and thrust back and forth, causing her to grimace in pain.

"Are you on the pill?" he asked her breathlessly.

Beth was unable to speak, unable to breathe. She shook her head.

"Don't worry, I'll pull out," he grunted.

She couldn't respond.

Danny slammed into her body, racking it with pain. Beth slipped into fear and despair. She couldn't take a breath, certain if she tried, she would scream aloud in pain. She didn't want Melissa or Charlie to hear her, and she didn't want Danny to know he was killing her. Beth grew lightheaded and thought she was going to pass out. She had to take a breath. He kept slamming into her with no reprieve. Beth scooted her body up the bed to get away from the full force of him.

"Move with me, Beth," Danny instructed.

Beth wanted to die. He found fault with her now? She was dying from the pounding, and if she didn't take a breath soon, she would truly die. He wanted her to move her body underneath him? Was he crazy?

She ignored the comment. *Breathe, Beth. Breathe!* she thought. Beth let her breath out and gulped in another, holding it as long as possible, trying to brace against the pain. She continued to creep up the bed until finally her head was up against the headboard.

Melissa had said it would hurt but this was unbearable. *Tell him you're a virgin, tell him! No! I will not be a baby* she thought with conflicted emotions. She squeezed her hands into the pillows next to her head. Quickly, she placed them on the headboard to relieve the pressure on her head.

He continued thrusting, repeatedly, never ending.

Beth worked up the courage to ask him to stop, the pain more than she could bear. She convinced herself she was going to hemorrhage. Then she would have to go to the hospital. Her parents would know exactly what she had done, and she would want to die.

"Danny? Danny?" she finally gasped as she looked up in his face.

He was lost in an expression of rapture. Danny reached his hands underneath her and pulled her down the length of the mattress, slamming his body deeper into hers.

Beth finally called out in pain as he pressed into her with great force. He mistook her sound for passion and moved deeper and with more force. Finally, he removed himself from her and quickly released onto her stomach. It was over. Thank God. Thank God, it was over.

He held her close to him, and his body jerked involuntarily when she tried to move. Finally, he shifted off her and lay to her side. Sweat glistened on his skin, and she wiped moisture off her brow. She turned to her side and drew her legs up to her chest, easing the worst cramps she'd ever experienced. Slowly, she raised herself off the bed and reached into her bag. She tugged a nightgown over her head and walked slowly toward the bathroom, convinced she was bleeding terribly. The light assaulted her, and she quickly checked for blood with toilet tissue. There wasn't any. Thank God! She sat on the toilet and cried. She tried to be quiet and hoped he wouldn't hear.

Beth began to smile. She felt so happy! She had faced her worst fear and gotten through it. Everyone had told her Danny wouldn't hurt her, but he had. He'd hurt her a lot. Did he realize that? Beth got her emotions under control and finally exited the bathroom. However awful it was, she and Danny could be together as a couple now. Her parents would have to come around. She would make them. Beth crawled into the bed. Danny lay on the opposite side of the bed with his back to her.

Beth leaned over and touched his shoulder. "Danny?"

Warmth bloomed in her chest. She would tell him she loved him. Surely, he would say the same in return.

"Danny?"

He didn't move. His breathing was deep and steady. He was asleep.

Beth lay awake for four hours trying to figure out why he just went to sleep and wouldn't talk to her. Why would he be so cruel and turn his back to her? Her tears fell silently onto the pillow. She wanted to leave and wished she had never agreed to come back. If she wanted to be treated like this, she would've just let Greg have his way with her. She wanted to yell and scream at Danny.

A knock finally came at the door. It had to be Melissa, thank God! Beth jumped up and opened the door.

"We need to get ready to go. Can you be ready in ten minutes?" Melissa asked.

"Yes, I'll meet you in the kitchen," she whispered.

Beth tormented herself as she dressed. *Why would Danny fall asleep on me like that? Maybe having sex with me was so awful he can't stand me? He told me to move, but I couldn't bear it with the pain. Surely, he would understand that if he would just talk to me, I could learn to do better. Why won't he talk to me?*

Once ready to leave the room, she crawled across the bed to him one more time.

"Goodbye, Danny," she said in a regular voice. No response. "I'm sorry." She apologized for being a disappointment to him. He never moved.

She left the room feeling frustrated.

Melissa and Beth ran to the car and headed back to Jackie's house.

"I have to have Charlie's car back to him in fifteen minutes or he'll be late for work."

Melissa shot a worried look at Beth. "Are you okay?"

"It hurt." Beth turned and stared out the window.

Melissa seemed to sense she didn't want to talk about it and turned on the radio for the rest of the ride.

She dropped Beth off at Jackie's house.

"We'll talk later, okay?" Melissa said, giving her a faint, reassuring smile.

Beth nodded, got out of the car, climbed the tree, and tiptoed across the porch roof. Jackie opened the window at her signal, and Beth slipped in. She was aware she looked like hell.

"Are you okay?" Jackie asked Beth.

"Uh-huh."

"Did you...?"

"Uh-huh."

"Come on." Jackie pulled her to the bed. "Get some sleep."

Susan and Lynne sprawled on the floor on sleeping bags. There was nowhere to sleep except in Jackie's double bed. Beth lay her head down on the pillow next to her friend's and curled up on her side. Jackie turned her back to Beth just as Danny had done all night.

Jackie reached back and patted Beth on the knee. "It will be alright."

Beth began to cry quietly. Danny could've at least said that to her. She deserved that much. Eventually, Beth fell asleep.

Sometime later, she awoke to Jackie shaking her. "Beth, my mother said your mother is on the phone."

Beth blinked hard and glanced around. What time was it? It was still dark outside. Then it hit her, and she jumped up and out of bed, panic setting in. Why was her mother calling?

All the girls started to wake up. Jackie told Beth to relax. There was no way her mother knew what happened.

Beth walked to the phone and picked up the receiver. "Hello?"

"Beth?" her mother said.

"Yes?"

"I'm a little concerned. Danny Mitchell called here about fifteen minutes ago looking for you. He seemed surprised that you weren't home and acted quite determined to speak with you."

"What?" Beth drew her brows together.

Why would Danny call her this early in the morning?

Her mother spoke again in a more agitated voice, "Why would Danny Mitchell be calling here looking for you at this hour of the morning?"

"I don't know. Did he say what he wanted?" she asked.

"No, he didn't," her mother said, her voice laced with anger.

"Well, I can't tell you, Mom. I don't know."

Jackie stood next to her, offering her silent support. Susan and Lynne huddled together behind her. They nodded their approval as Beth spoke to her mother.

"Beth, have you been seeing that boy again?"

"I saw him last night at Melissa's house. Melissa has been dating his friend Charlie Cahall. We had a terrible argument. It ended badly. Maybe he called to apologize," Beth said, lying and feeling like shit about it.

There was a long pause on the phone. Her mother didn't say anything. She probably didn't believe any of this crap.

"Well, I still feel the same way about him. You're not allowed to see him."

"I know, Mom. I know. Did you need anything else?"

Her mother said no, and Beth quickly got off the phone.

The girls looked at Beth with raised brows.

Beth sighed. "Danny just went to sleep after. I didn't get to talk to him at all."

The girls crawled back into their beds. Beth now believed when Danny woke up and discovered she'd gone, he'd desperately wanted to talk with her. He would probably ask her out tonight to say all the things he wanted to say last night. Beth smiled and fell sound asleep.

CHAPTER 62

Beth returned home around noon. Her mother was in the kitchen making a pot of soup. She avoided looking at her mother, sure she would be able to tell she wasn't a virgin anymore just by her appearance. It wouldn't take much to figure out who she had done it with.

"Did Danny call back?" Beth asked as she searched the refrigerator for a soda.

"No." Her mother smacked the metal spoon on the side of the pot.

She grabbed what she wanted from the refrigerator, quickly left the kitchen, and went up to her bedroom.

Beth felt thankful she didn't have to work today. For the first time in years, she waited for Danny to call. She stayed in her bedroom all day reading and listening to music.

By dinnertime, it was obvious Danny wouldn't be calling her for a date tonight. Maybe he had to work late or something. By eight thirty Beth was beside herself. Why had he called her this morning but not called her back? Maybe he was still at work. The phone rang several times, but first it was Melissa, then Jackie, then Susan, then Lynne. Never Danny. She couldn't stand it another moment.

She called Jackie. "Give me that phone number Melissa gave you last night, please."

"You're going to call him?" Jackie sounded surprised.

"Yep, I think he owes me some kind of explanation, don't you?"

Jackie read off the number. Beth thanked her and hung up. She checked upstairs to make sure her folks were downstairs, and for the second time in her life, she called Danny Mitchell.

He answered the phone.

"Hi Danny, it's Beth."

He said hello and asked if her mom told her he called. Beth said she had.

"She had a feeling something was going on when you called so early in the morning," Beth said.

"Well, where were you anyway?" he asked.

"I was at Jackie's. I was supposed to be spending the night at her house last night."

"I see."

Beth waited for him to say something else, anything.

"Well? What did you want this morning?" she asked impatiently, but as sweetly as possible.

He took a deep breath and exhaled. She waited, excited.

"Beth, I'm really sorry about what happened last night," he began.

Beth's mind started reeling. *No! Don't say that, Danny, please. That's not what you're supposed to say.*

He continued, "I feel terrible. I took advantage of a situation and I shouldn't have. I'm sorry."

Beth sat on her bed, stunned. She took in a deep breath. He fell silent.

"Don't worry about it, Danny," she said lightly as tears welled up in her eyes.

"Well, I feel bad, and I'm sorry it happened."

Stop saying that!

"I'm not sorry. I'm glad it happened, so you don't need to feel bad." Tears poured from her eyes as her heart broke in two, but her voice gave no indication of her feelings.

"That's why I called you this morning to say I'd made a mistake," he said in a flat tone.

"Okay, I understand. I guess I'm sorry, too, then. I'll see you," she said and gently returned the phone to the receiver.

The pain in her throat welled up unbearably. She held her face into her pillow so her parents wouldn't hear the sobs as she cried herself to sleep.

She awoke at two in the morning. She was still fully dressed, and the light was still on in her room. The phone still lay on her bed. She got up and changed, putting on her nightgown. Beth checked her underwear again for signs of blood but found none. She lay down to sleep again and put on an America album. She moved the arm up to the right so the album would repeat itself. She turned the volume down low and listened to the song. "Mary, have you seen better days, will you find different ways, and does he really mean that much to your heart? Carry all of the weight you can, find another man, and lead him directly there to the source..."

Beth stared at the green light from the stereo as it played the album again and again. She never closed her eyes to sleep and never moved from the position on her bed. Tears poured out of her eyes onto the pillow. She couldn't stop them.

Beth couldn't concentrate all week at school or work. All she could think about was losing her virginity to Danny and not doing it right. If she had been able to move with Danny when he'd told her to move, he would have wanted her again. She convinced herself that if she were prettier, thinner, blonde, or more experienced sexually that he would want her. She also convinced herself she must have looked totally disgusting naked.

Beth gave herself no breaks. She tormented herself by replaying his words to her. *I'm sorry about what happened. I feel bad. I'm sorry it happened. I made a mistake.*

She didn't tell anyone the things he'd said. Instead, she told her friends they had decided not to see one another after all. She got depressed and moody, and it didn't help that the Prom was only a short time away. Beth had already decided not to go.

At The Boat on Saturday evening she told her friends she was definitely not going to the Prom.

"You'll change your mind when someone asks you." Lynne said.

"You have to, it's our last one, ever." Susan pouted her lips.

Melissa just gave her a sympathetic look.

Beth drew in the dirt with a stick. She wouldn't change her mind.

The girls told her about a party at Joe's that they'd gone to the night before. Since both Danny and Beth hadn't been there, most people had assumed they were together.

"I can't wait to get out of here!" Beth threw the stick into the pond.

"God, you're in a foul mood," Susan said to her.

Beth apologized and said she knew she wasn't fit to be around.

"I think I want to get drunk," she said.

"Brian and Ann are having a party tonight. We're going. You're welcome to go with us if you want," Susan offered.

Beth agreed. It was better than moping at home.

They all left The Boat and drove to Brian and Ann's house. Beth had mixed feelings about going there, but she didn't want to be alone tonight.

The party wasn't out of control, but there was still a large crowd. Danny wasn't there, thank God! Rocky was there and poured on the charm.

"We're friends, right?" Beth asked him.

"Absolutely," Rocky said.

"Remember when you told me to call you if I ever needed anything?"

"Uh-huh. What is it?" he asked.

Beth stated with a nonchalant shrug, "My Prom."

Rocky's eyes lit up.

"You want me to take you to your Prom?" He smiled at her.

"Well, yeah. I guess I do."

"I would be happy to," he said.

"Thanks."

They spent most of the evening together talking. Rocky had her laughing before the night ended. Beth needed him, his flattery, and his attention even if it wasn't real. She sensed the girls were happy she decided to go to the Prom, but they weren't thrilled she planned to go with Rocky. He was such a player.

Several of the girls wanted to see the baby's room and all the supplies Ann bought. Ann was happy to oblige, and the girls headed to the back of the apartment.

Beth hung back, and Brian approached her.

"Got a minute?" he asked.

"Sure."

"Let's go for a walk," he said.

He led the way out the door, and she followed.

Beth and Brian walked down the street.

He let out an exasperated sigh. "Beth, I've never been so miserable. What a terrible situation this is."

Beth looked at him sympathetically. "I feel so responsible for this. I wish I hadn't introduced you two."

"Oh my God, Beth. This is not on you. We made our own mess." He glanced at her. "How are you and Danny doing? Why isn't he here with you?"

Beth started to cry.

Brian put his arm around her shoulder. "Beth, what happened?"

Tearfully, Beth told him everything. She told him about Greg Black, about being a virgin and waiting for Danny for all these years, about the night in the apartment and how he told her to move with him but it hurt so badly she was unable to breathe let alone move. She told him all the awful things Danny had said to her on the phone the next day and confided to him all her fears about being ugly and miserable at sex.

Brian gaped at her while she told her story then pulled her into a big bear hug.

"You are hurt, Beth, but you're not foolish. Danny *should* have apologized to you. He knows how you feel about him. He shouldn't have made love to you if he was only playing around. You know?"

Brian's anger at Danny didn't make her feel any better.

"It won't hurt the next time. You know that, right?" He gave her a lopsided grin. "Did he know you were a virgin?"

"I don't know. He probably does now. I'm apparently pretty bad at it." She frowned.

"Sounds like he didn't know. Was there blood on the bed?"

Beth's eyes got wide, and her face grew hot. "I don't know. Oh my God! What if there was?"

"What if? It's no big deal, Beth."

She rolled her eyes, but a part of her relaxed. She wasn't sure why she had spilled everything to Brian, but he was so easy to talk to.

"Beth, tell me either you are on the pill or he used a condom."

She shook her head. "No to both."

"Did you tell him you weren't on the pill?" he asked.

"Yes, he asked me that."

Brian arched on eyebrow. "He knew that and didn't use a condom?"

"We did something else, you know," she said.

"He pulled out? That's what you two did? Jesus Christ!" Brian rubbed the back of his neck. "He knows better than that! That doesn't necessarily work, Beth."

"It worked. Okay?" she said quickly.

"Thank God for that. You'll find someone else one day, you will. It will be someone who will appreciate you completely."

Beth smiled at him. "Thanks."

They walked a while longer and returned to the party.

Greg was there, and he approached Beth.

"Get out of here, Greg," Brian said, standing in front of

her, scowling and blocking her from him.

Greg looked at her and then at Brian. After a brief, tense standoff between the two males, Greg turned and left.

Beth gazed at Brian, a strange warmth spreading through her chest. He cared about her and was her protector. Why hadn't she seen that before?

CHAPTER 63

The week before Prom, Rocky called Beth to make final arrangements. Could he wear a suit instead of a tux? Beth could have cared less what he wore. Did she want to go to the After-Prom Dance at the Fire Hall? Yes, she did. Did she want to go to the beach afterward? A long pause. Yes, she wanted to do that, too. Satisfied with her answers, Rocky ended the call. As she hung up the receiver, she wondered why he seemed so stoked that she wanted to go to the beach with him. She put it out of her mind and focused on school and work, only slightly excited about the Prom.

Prom night arrived, and Rocky picked her up in a brand-new T-Top Camaro. She had to hand it to him, he knew how to pick great cars. Her parents took loads of pictures. The two were all smiles, and Beth had to admit she was glad she'd asked him to take her.

She was a little concerned about her period not coming, though. She would try not to think about that tonight. It was her Prom night, after all. The two walked on the promenade and sat with her friends and their dates. He even agreed to pay for their formal pictures.

As they danced to a slow song, Rocky kissed her. Beth thought, *Oh God, what if I'm pregnant? Don't think about it, don't think about it!*

"Beth, I have always cared about you. Let's take tonight and really do it right, romance and all." Rocky's eyes glimmered in the dim, romantic lighting.

"Maybe." Beth smiled but inside she cringed.

Rocky had always been there whenever she wanted him. Even when he'd tried to make her jealous, all she would've had to do was call him and he would have been right there.

Rocky would probably marry her if she got pregnant. Danny wouldn't. He would probably tell her to go get an abortion. When her mother had Beth's sister, she was only eighteen. How upset could her parents be? Hah! At least she would be out of high school when she started to show. If she were pregnant, she could go stay with her aunt and uncle in Texas and start a new life there. She would never even have to tell Danny. She wouldn't want him to pity-marry her like Brian did with Ann. Danny would hate her guts if she let that happen.

She tried to hide her worries. Rocky acted goofy during the next dance song, and he smiled at her with a playful sparkle in his eyes. He was a good friend. As the night wore on, Beth became increasingly worried about being pregnant. She just couldn't stop thinking about it. She began her period when she was thirteen and it always came every twenty-eight days. Every month, every single time, never late. She was now four days late. Nobody seemed to notice her anxiety, not even her girlfriends. That was good. She knew she was over the top and wanted everyone to have a good time.

A thought occurred to her. If she slept with Rocky tonight, then maybe he would accept the baby as his own. She pictured him sitting in a chair in a white T-shirt watching football and drinking Schlitz as she cooked Sunday dinner. Their son would be lying on the couch with his girlfriend stoned out of their minds. No way! She dismissed that thought. *Stop it, stop it.*

After the Prom ended, Rocky and Beth went back to her house, and she changed her clothes for the next dance. Rocky asked her why she was so quiet in the car, but she told him she was only tired. He brought his clothes and changed in the downstairs bathroom. They arrived at the venue and danced for a while. Rocky kept looking at her with concern and asking her if she were okay. At around twelve thirty, she had had enough. Her obsessive thoughts about Danny and a possible baby had taken its toll.

"Can we skip the beach trip, Rocky? I'm beat. How about we go home to sleep for a while and head down there early in the morning?"

"Okay." Rocky regarded her with a bunched brow. "If you're feeling that tired, then let's go now."

They said their goodbyes to their friends.

Beth became suspicious when Rocky made a wrong turn. He drove her out to a housing development that was under construction.

She narrowed her eyes at him. "What are we doing here?"

"I just want to talk to you."

He parked the car and said, "I know I screwed things up between us. I want you back. Please let me make it up to you."

She watched his eyes and listened intently. He looked at her adoringly. Rocky cared more about her than Danny ever did. Maybe Rocky was the special guy Brian referred to. She reached up and touched Rocky's cheek, and he cleared his throat.

"Take this tie off," she said, loosening it with her hand.

A tic pulsing in his jaw, he unbuttoned the top button of his shirt and stretched his tie out to relieve his neck.

Beth gaped at the purple mark on his neck. Was that a hickey? She peered closer, squinting as he went on and on about how they should show how they feel about one another, blah, blah, blah. Yep, it was a hickey for sure.

He was in mid-sentence when Beth said, "You have a fucking hickey on your neck, Rocky. Take me home."

"Shit. Okay." Rocky rubbed the back of his neck, put the car in drive, and took her home. He did not say another word as he drove her home.

He pulled up in front of her house, his hands tight on the steering wheel. She climbed out and slammed the car door. Rocky peeled away from the curb, and Beth marched into the house.

She went up to her room, got undressed, put on her nightgown, and then crawled in bed and dreamt about babies, Texas, and running from a knight chasing her with a jousting pole.

The next morning, Beth awoke to sunlight pouring in through her bedroom window. She jumped from the bed and ran to the bathroom. Quickly checking herself for signs of a period, she found none. Now she was five days late.

Oh God...Please God, don't let this happen, please!

She went downstairs to the kitchen and fixed a cup of tea. Her mother sat at the table reading the Sunday newspaper. She asked Beth if she had a good time with Rocky. Of course, Beth said it was wonderful. She would never risk another "father to father" call again in all her natural born days.

"I'm glad you had fun. Rocky is a nice boy. I really like him," she said

As she turned towards the counter dunking her tea bag, Beth rolled her eyes at her mother's comments.

"Yeah, he's great." She worked hard to keep sarcasm from her voice.

"I'm glad you two are dating again."

Beth told her mother they weren't dating again. They were just friends who went to a dance together.

Beth pondered what she was going to do today. She had asked for the day off because she thought she would be hanging out with everyone at the beach. Furrowing her brow, she decided she should keep herself busy. All the girls had gone to the beach with their dates. Melissa and Charlie had not attended the Prom but had planned to go to the beach early this morning.

After carrying her cup to the table, she sat down next to her mother. She asked about her sister and grandmother and the latest family news. She asked how long it had been since her aunt had written or called. Each summer, her aunt and uncle visited for a couple of weeks, and Beth figured when they came in July, she would be about three to four months along. She could ride home with them for a visit and figure out what to do then.

"Are you alright?" her mother finally asked.

Beth nodded and told her mother she was exhausted from the lack of sleep she'd been getting lately.

"I definitely need to find something to do today," she said. "Maybe I'll go visit Ann Marie. Can I use the car?"

"Sure, honey."

It had been awhile since she had seen her sister, and this was a great time to do that. Or maybe not. It was too much effort to visit anyone.

Eventually she decided to go back to bed. She slept until one in the afternoon. She felt crampy and ran into the bathroom to check for her period. Nope, it just wasn't going to happen.

Beth finally got up and showered. She read a book for a while, and then went downstairs to see her mother. She offered to cook dinner that night, and her mother looked pleased to have help in the kitchen.

Beth tried desperately to stay busy. "Did anybody call for me today?" she asked nonchalantly as she peeled potatoes.

Her mother shook her head. Beth felt like an outcast. Where the hell was everybody anyway? After dinner, she helped wash the dishes and then she asked permission to use the car. She headed out to The Boat. She needed to think about why relationships seemed so hard for her. It felt creepy being there alone, so she headed over to Rocky's house. She was just going to ask him, damn it! He was outside in the driveway, washing his car. She pulled up to the curb and turned off the ignition. Rocky looked surprised to see. He dropped the oversized sponge in the bucket, grabbed a towel, and dried his hands as he walked up to her car. Beth sat there, wondering what she was doing.

"Hi Beth," Rocky said sheepishly, leaning in the window.

Beth turned and peered up into his face.

"What's wrong with me, Rocky?"

He stared at her and put his head down.

"There is nothing wrong with you, Beth. I'm sorry about last night. I think I have a real problem." He tossed the towel in the driveway.

Beth didn't want him to apologize for the hickey or the infamous Polaroid picture of the bimbo he'd cheated with, or anything else. She wanted an answer to her question.

"That's not what I'm talking about at all. I want to know what's wrong with me."

Rocky stared at her with a furrowed brow.

"Why would someone not want to be with me? I want you to be honest. Tell me whatever it is. I want to know. I need to know," she said, looking at him intently.

Rocky arched both eyebrows.

He rubbed the back of his neck. "Is this about Danny Mitchell?"

Beth looked away from him and down into her lap.

"Beth, it's not you. It's him. He's an asshole. I keep telling you that, but you don't listen."

She took a deep breath. Beth remembered this was Rocky she was talking to.

"Maybe he thinks you are too good for him." He glanced down at his feet.

Beth lifted her gaze to his face. Truth reflected in his eyes. She smiled at him. "That's what *you* think, Rocky. I think Danny thinks I'm not good enough for him."

He shook his head. "He's an ass."

She paused before asking, "Is there any way we could go back to being friends again?"

Rocky nodded. "I'm dating someone, you know. She put the hickey on me. I told her I would be taking you to the Prom and she wasn't happy. She did it on purpose."

"You shouldn't have agreed to go with me if you were dating someone."

"I know, but I had to go."

488

They gazed at each other, and Beth saw emotion in his eyes. It hit her hard that they would never be able to be just friends. He couldn't do it.

"Sounds like the same girl who planted the picture in your car," Beth said laughing slightly, trying to lighten the situation. Rocky didn't laugh.

"It *is* the same girl, isn't it?" She couldn't believe it! Beth just shook her head at him. "You are a mess. She must absolutely hate me!"

"It's all my fault," he admitted. Finally, he was being honest with her.

Beth turned the ignition, said her goodbye, and drove away.

She arrived home and hung out in her bedroom, only coming out for dinner. At eight o'clock that night, she drove to Melissa's house. Her friend was putting groceries away and had made iced tea. She offered some to Beth, and they each sat down with a glass. Melissa's mother was napping before her shift at work so the two talked quietly while drinking their tea, then went for a walk around her neighborhood. Beth told Melissa her period hadn't come, and she was now over five days late. Melissa told her she needed to make an appointment at the clinic but added that they wouldn't be able to tell if she was pregnant until she was at least two weeks late. Her friend assured her that it could just be the stress causing her to be late.

Beth was convinced it wasn't just stress.

"Until you know for sure, try not to freak out, okay?" Melissa gave her a reassuring smile and patted her shoulder.

Beth forced a smile, but inside that nagging feeling that she might be pregnant gnawed at her.

CHAPTER 64

On Monday, Beth went to the nurse's office at school.

"I need to make a private phone call. Can I use your phone?" Beth asked.

The nurse allowed Beth to use the small office area and closed the door.

She called the phone number Melissa had given her. A lady answered, and Beth made an appointment for a pregnancy test at the clinic for the following Friday. She was six days late, and she was in a terrible state, worrying all the time. Having to wait that long for an answer would be torture, but the lady said it couldn't be done any sooner if she wanted an accurate result.

Would Danny even care if she were pregnant? It was just her dumb luck to have sex the very first time in her life and end up pregnant. She grimaced and wondered how painful childbirth would be. Conception was more painful than she had ever imagined. Beth decided she was never going to have sex again in her life. She left the nurse's office and entered the cafeteria for lunch.

Melissa and Susan ran up to Beth.

"Did you hear what the senior boys are doing?" Susan asked.

Beth hadn't heard any gossip lately, so the girls filled her in.

The senior boys were taking up a money collection to pay a girl to sleep with Fred. Apparently, he was the last virgin among the guys in their class.

"They are running around asking every girl in our class to sleep with him!" Melissa said, followed by a snicker.

Beth shook her head in disgust.

Jackie approached them. "Those guys just offered to pay me to pop Fred's man cherry. Can you believe that?" She pursed her lips.

Beth decided not to point out that Jackie was kind of a slut sometimes.

"They are such assholes," Melissa said. "But you aren't the only one they asked."

Beth and Susan giggled.

"Still, those guys are jerk offs." Jackie tossed her long blonde hair over her shoulder and asked playfully, "What are you going to say when they ask you, Beth?"

Instead of delivering a funny quip, Beth sighed and said, "I don't know. I know I'm never going to have sex again in my lifetime."

Her friends raised their eyebrows and looked at each other but let the subject drop.

By the end of lunch, the offer of almost two hundred dollars had been made and declined by every girl at the lunch table. Poor Fred. He had no idea what was going on.

Beth continued to be in a solemn mood. Her humor was gone, her nerves spent. She got home and went straight to the bathroom and stared at her reflection in the mirror. Her skin was sallow from not sleeping well, and she had dark circles under her eyes. She was barely functioning at work. Beth had scheduled herself to work until nine p.m., but she was so tired. She debated whether to call in sick for the first time ever. She went to her room and picked up the phone but decided she didn't want to use her sick time yet because she might need it later, and she hung up.

She dragged herself into the store.

Debbie narrowed her eyes at her. "You look pretty rough. Are you sick?"

Beth shook her head.

Debbie told Beth to perk up because she had good news. They would be adding a new department to the store. In two weeks, they would be selling wedding and bridesmaid dresses, as well as renting men's tuxedos.

The store was also having another fashion show in three weeks.

"We have to wear wedding dresses?" Beth asked incredulously.

"Yes." Debbie slanted her head. "Is that a problem?"

Beth couldn't believe the amount of salt constantly being rubbed in her wounds. Sure, let's get the pregnant, unwed mother to trot down the runway in a couple of beautiful wedding dresses! Beth's face contorted, and she burst into tears.

"Beth, are you okay?" Worry lines formed on Debbie's brow. "You should go to the bathroom and compose yourself."

Beth nodded, entered the restroom, and continued to sob as she relieved herself. She finished and stood to flush before washing her face in the sink. The red toilet water caught her eye. Beth dropped her pants and sat down again. She checked herself with more toilet tissue. Her period had arrived like gangbusters! Beth found some female supplies located in the bathroom cabinet and took care of things. She washed her face and dropped to her knees in the bathroom and thanked God for allowing her to be back to normal. She swore to God she would never do that ever again, and she thanked him repeatedly.

She exited, and Debbie was walking towards the bathroom.

"What's going on? Why were you freaking out?" she asked.

"Nothing." Beth sent her a wide smile. "Just hormones I guess."

Debbie watched in amazement as a beaming Beth sauntered past her.

That night when she got home, she called Melissa. The girls celebrated over the phone. They made plans to go out to The Boat on Friday. Melissa would call the others. Beth intended to drink a beer, maybe even two, or three, or four, or five! Yahoo!

She turned on the stereo receiver in her bedroom. Gloria Gaynor belted out "I Will Survive."

Beth silently mouthed the words and danced around her room as the weight of the world left her shoulders.

After she undressed, she headed to the bathroom in her robe, turned the knob, and stepped into the running shower. She stood in the streaming hot water and turned the shower massage dial to "hard." The pulsating spray massaged the back of her neck and upper shoulders. She contemplated all the thoughts and worries from over the past weeks. Leaning against the shower wall, she was sure she'd never be able to cry again. She had already cried enough for a whole lifetime.

Beth placed her hand on the lower half of her stomach and contemplated what might have been. She allowed herself to envision one last time her graduation ceremony from Texas A& M University. Her friends attended with their spouses. Her aunt and uncle approached her as she stood in her black cap and gown. The most beautiful five-year old boy with brown eyes and dark curly hair smiled as he ran toward her to give her a congratulatory hug. She lifted him up into her arms, spun him around, and kissed him on the cheek.

Beth opened her eyes immediately, and the vision evaporated. She felt the sting of the water. Surprising herself, she began to cry for the baby she would never have. Which was worse? Beth didn't know. She refused to allow herself to contemplate that question and certainly never allowed herself to picture that small boy ever again. It had turned out for the best. Grinning as she shampooed her hair, Beth was happy to be her old self again.

CHAPTER 65

On Monday morning, the principal announced that the seniors needed to see their class advisors to order their caps and gowns. The seniors' last day of school would be on May twenty-fourth. All underclassmen would attend until June eighth. The announcement sent Beth and her friends into a tailspin of excitement. The girls went out to Pippy's that night to celebrate.

Lynne told them Donald Jackson had a friend who worked at the Ramada Inn, and he gave him a key to a room there. The guys invited the girls to go up and check it out on Friday. They decided to stop by the room before they headed out to The Boat. Beth started to get nervous as Jackie drove them up to the hotel on Friday night. She was afraid someone would see them and tell her parents. The girls knew they would look ridiculous walking through the hotel as if they were guests. They were all underage. Of course, the boys had booze. Somehow, they managed to calm their nerves and get into the elevator undetected. The elevator stopped on the second floor. They searched the hallway for room 214.

"We're here!" Jackie pointed to the door just beside Beth.

Melissa knocked on the door, and Ron opened it.

"Get in here," he said sharply, pulling Melissa's arm.

The girls walked in. The guys were sitting on the bed and in the only two chairs. There were a couple of six-packs on the table, and only two beers remained. The girls got jumpy and eyed each other warily as they sat on one side of the bed. Beth sensed they were thinking what she was—they would all get caught underage drinking.

No music played, and they sat and stared at one another, quiet as church mice. Beth began to giggle. Ron yelled at her to be quiet.

"Don't tell her that, she'll only get worse!" Susan said, smiling at her friend.

They continued to sit and stare at each other. Beth thought how childish this all was. This was just stupid and entirely boring.

"I'm leaving," she said, and the rest of the girls nodded in agreement.

The girls left the hotel, piled in the car, and headed out to The Boat.

Jackie stopped at Marsteller's Market to buy gum, soda, chips, and cigarettes. She insisted that Beth pitch in for the cigarettes because she would end up smoking half of them anyway. Jackie wanted to go to Chester Black's Bar where Al worked. The others convinced her to go to the liquor store they'd been using since she and Al split up. It wasn't nearly as far away. Jackie agreed after whining a little about not being able to see Al. She bought Bacardi, and the girls mixed it with their sodas. They sat in the station wagon, Jackie and Susan in the front, the rest of the girls in the back, drinking their alcohol.

The radio played Jackson Brown's "Doctor My Eyes," and the girls sang along, tapping their hands and feet to the beat.

When the DJ interrupted the ending of the song, Susan said, "I've got something else for us to try."

Everyone turned to look at her.

Beth chewed a large wad of cherry-flavored bubble gum and had blown a huge bubble as Susan held up a joint. The bubble popped, and the girls all stared at one another.

"Where did you get that?" Melissa asked.

"My stepbrother sent it to me from college," she said.

"In the mail?" Jackie gaped at her.

"Yep." Susan smiled and appeared unfazed.

"Jesus Christ, Susan! Do you know how much trouble you could get in for that?" Beth shook her head at her friend. Usually, Susan worried about getting in trouble.

Susan just continued to smile at them.

"You guys want to try it or not?" she asked.

"I'm not!" Lynne said. Then a chorus of "Okay, but you can never tell," and "holy shit'" came from inside the car.

"Everyone, out. My mother will flip out if she smells pot in the car," Jackie said.

They poured out of the station wagon and followed Susan over to the logs.

After they all sat, Jackie handed Susan her cigarette lighter. Susan showed them how to take the smoke into the lungs and hold it in as long as possible, and then let it out slowly. She took a few drags, demonstrating the technique. Then she passed it to Lynne who shook her head no and passed it on to Melissa. Melissa inhaled and began to cough uncontrollably. She passed the joint to Jackie who followed Susan's instructions. She passed it to Beth. Beth did the same and returned it to Susan.

The joint worked its way around the second time. This round Melissa managed to inhale without all the gagging and coughing. Lynne took it back from Melissa, looked around at her friends, giggled and inhaled, mimicking what Susan had shown them. She opened her eyes wide as she held the smoke in her lungs. The other girls laughed at her.

By the third round, Susan was unable to continue smoking. She rolled on the ground laughing uncontrollably. The joint continued to be passed from one to the other, and the girls laughed so hard they could barely breathe. Lynne tried to maintain her dignity but fell into fits of laughter like the others.

"Hey Lynne, Miss Goody Two-shoes, how ya feeling?" Jackie yelled and laughed hysterically.

Beth said, "Hey! Where'd my gum go?"

The girls searched the ground on their hands and knees looking for Beth's wad of cherry bubblegum.

Melissa laughed again and said, "What the hell are we doing?"

They went into hysterics again imagining what a sight they must be, crawling around in the grass and dirt looking for a large pink wad of chewed gum.

Jackie laughed so hard when she spoke that no one could understand what she said. This caused them to lose all sense of control and dignity.

Susan jumped up. "I'm going to pee my pants, I swear to God." She ran over toward the car and squatted on the other side for privacy.

Tears of laughter rolled down Beth's face. Her sides hurt from laughing so hard.

Eventually, the unsuccessful search for the gum ended, and they lay against the logs feeling very relaxed and content.

"I'm hungry," Susan said.

The girls all agreed they were starved, but no one could move enough to get up and go to the car. Jackie said she needed more time to collect herself.

"I'm glad I brought this jacket. It's chilly out here." Beth pulled her jacket tighter around her.

They sat in silence while they slowly sobered up. One by one they followed each other back to the car. The bag of chips was gone in less than sixty seconds. Susan passed out some cinnamon Trident gum.

Lynne suggested, "Let's go to Burger Chef. I'm still starving."

They all cheered the idea. Jackie insisted she felt fine and she drove them into town.

It took twice as long as usual to get there. Jackie said the speedometer must be broken. They flew down the road, but the dash only read 35 mph. The girls watched the speedometer in amazement. When they parked at the restaurant, they moved slowly out of the car and headed inside. Soon, the table was full of chocolate shakes, large fries, cheeseburgers, and cherry pies. Beth looked around the table at her stoned friends.

Not one of them had straightened their clothes, hair, or makeup since they had crawled on the ground on all fours in a wild search for her gum. There was grass in Melissa and Lynne's hair. Beth touched her strands and pulled out a grass blade that must have gotten there when she had rolled on the ground laughing. Lynne and Jackie had grass stains on their bare elbows and the knees of their pants. Mascara had smudged under their eyes, and all other traces of makeup were gone. Lynne had potato chip crumbs around her mouth. Beth could only imagine how she must look, but it was too much of an effort to go to the bathroom and fix herself up.

Brian walked in with Joe and walked over to their table. "Hey girls!" Brian said, and Joe nodded.

The girls all said a quick "Hey" and virtually ignored them as they continued to focus their attention on the food. Brian looked at Joe and raised his eyebrows. Joe shrugged, grinning. The boys hung there for a few moments, eyeing the girls with suspicion. Beth became warm and removed her jacket.

Brian looked at her with one arched eyebrow. "Beth? Did you lose your gum?"

The girls paused and gaped at him as if it were an incredible miracle that he knew.

"How did you know I lost my gum?!" Beth asked as Jackie made the sounds from *The Twilight Zone*.

Brian pointed towards her chest. Beth looked down at the huge wad of cherry bubblegum smeared across the front of her sweater. It covered her left boob as if it were a shield.

Beth peered up at the girls, her eyes widening. A loud burst of laughter erupted from around the table. Jackie fell off her chair, and Susan's Coke spurted up through her nose. Once again, it proved difficult for them to regain their composure.

Brian and Joe narrowed their eyes at them, shook their heads, said goodbye, and left.

Beth put her jacket back on to cover up the mess and snorted with laughter as she did. The gum had fallen out of her mouth without her knowledge. She wasn't going to be smoking pot anymore.

CHAPTER 66

Beth worked from noon to four o'clock on Sunday. After her shift, she drove to the bowling alley to visit Melissa. Her friend was busy and unable to talk, but the two made plans to meet at Beth's house after work. A guy was standing at the counter, and Melissa introduced Beth to Chuck Weismann. Her friend wasn't helping him with anything. He just stood there and visited while she worked. Hmm. Melissa had dated this guy before, and she wondered if Melissa was thinking about doing so again. She went home and listened to music in her bedroom until her mom called her down for dinner.

Melissa arrived at her house later, and they grabbed a couple of sodas and headed up to Beth's bedroom.

"You're not seeing Chuck again, are you?" Beth asked.

Melissa nodded and made a nervous face.

Beth scowled at her. "What about Charlie?"

Melissa explained that she really liked Charlie and hadn't broken up with him because she didn't want to hurt his feelings. She couldn't help the way she felt about Chuck, though. She was in love with him, and she would have to let Charlie know they were through.

Beth looked at her dumbfounded. "Why didn't you tell me this before?"

"I thought you would be mad at me," Melissa said sheepishly. "I know you have a soft spot for Charlie."

"I'm not mad, Melissa, but geez. I feel bad for him."

Melissa put her head down as if she were ashamed.

Beth's heart broke for Charlie. He really cared for Melissa, but she didn't feel the same about him. There was nothing he could do about it. He'd have to wait out the heartache of rejection. Just like Beth would have to get over Danny. People say the pain goes away in time. It might take her an exceedingly long time to get over the rejection from Danny. She hoped Charlie didn't suffer the same way.

"I was hoping you would be happy for me," Melissa said. "I wish I hadn't told you now."

Beth didn't know what to say. She wanted to be happy for her friend, but Charlie was her friend, too. She nodded and changed the subject. The conversation was strained after that.

~

On Monday Beth and the other seniors made plans for "Senior Skip Day." Most of their friends planned on going to Ron's parents' mobile home at the beach. It was the only thing happening, and a ton of people would be there. The idea and general purpose of "Senior Skip Day" was not to get caught. It was a tradition for the principal, his two assistant principals, the attendance lady, and a handful of coaches to go in search of the students and their cars at the beach. They would write down tag numbers, and then those students got suspended.

Beth talked with the girls in the Center and suggested they do something else. The principals and teachers would be out searching, and the most likely place to find a couple hundred seniors on "Senior Skip Day" would be at the beach. The girls agreed with her. The party at Ron's had gotten a lot of talk and it was only a matter of time before a teacher found out about it. Inevitably, a jealous junior or other underclassman would tattle on them. The principals offered rewards to the canaries and boy did they sing!

The girls got permission from their parents to skip. Their older brothers and sisters had been allowed to do it. Beth and her friends planned to hang out at Melissa's house. She would go around and pick up everyone early in the morning so there wouldn't be a lot of cars parked at her house.

On Senior Skip Day, they watched *Phil Donahue* and painted their fingernails and toenails while Melissa's mother slept all day. They calmly discussed their plans for freshman year at college, and everyone smiled and appeared happy.

Melissa waved her hands to dry her wet nails. "My plans might change."

Beth and the other girls sat at attention.

Melissa announced, "I'm in love with Chuck, the guy at the bowling alley."

The girls all nodded, looking at each other in bewilderment. Beth was the only one who knew Chuck was back in the picture.

Melissa blew on her wet nails before continuing. "Well, I'm probably going to stay close to home so I can be near him. I'll take classes at the local junior college."

Lynne said softly, "I thought you wanted to get away from your mom? And what about Charlie?"

Melissa shrugged, "I care about Charlie a lot and I'm having a hard time breaking up with him. But..." She looked at Beth.

Beth narrowed her eyes at her. "You should do it soon. It's only fair."

Melissa nodded, her expression pained.

Jackie and Susan seemed to have little to say. Beth sensed shock from the other girls at Melissa's sudden announcement, but everyone concentrated on their toes as they painted their nails.

The girls watched *Days of Our Lives* and jumped when the doorbell rang. Melissa got up and looked through the peephole. Her eyes got wide. She put her finger to her lips and tiptoed back to the couch, whispering, "It's one of the assistant principals!"

Beth and the other girls exchanged worried glances. They sat stock still as the doorbell rang several more times. Thankfully, Melissa's mother continued to sleep and never came to answer it.

At the dinner table that night, Beth discussed Senior Skip Day with her mom. Her mother would have to write a note saying she was "out sick" for her to avoid suspension. Beth's mother didn't understand why the high school made parents lie about their child's absence. It seemed a harmless tradition. She would write "Beth O'Brien had my permission to be absent yesterday."

Beth insisted she had to write "out sick" or it would be an unexcused absence. Her homeroom teacher had been very clear.

Her mother fussed about it because she didn't want to lie. Beth listened anxiously. She hoped her mother would relent and just write the damn note so she wouldn't get a suspension. Beth had never skipped school a day in her life and thought her mom should cut her some slack. Her mother refused to discuss it further, and it wasn't until the next morning at breakfast that Beth read the note her mother had written. *Please excuse Beth O'Brien for being absent yesterday. She was out due to illness. Thank you, Mrs. O'Brien.* Beth smiled at her mother who was leaning against the kitchen counter.

"I didn't say you were sick but I'm sure someone was ill somewhere," her mother stated with frustration.

"I'm sure it will be okay. Thanks, Mom!" Beth hugged her.

She arrived at school and entered The Center. It operated at a slow roar as the students shared the story of how the principals headed straight to the beach and to Ron's parents' vacation home. They wrote down every single tag number on the cars parked there. The kids got called one by one to the office to suffer a two-day suspension. No one really cared about being suspended since the seniors didn't have to take final exams and just filled in time anyway.

In homeroom class, the teachers checked signatures on the excuses with the signatures of their parents on the Emergency Information cards. Even Mrs. Hart became frustrated by the intensity the administration gave the whole ordeal.

It had been done for the past ten years and it would continue to be done for years in the future. The more upset the administration got about it, the more the students became determined to see it through. None of Beth's friends had a problem, but each of them sweated the intercom beep as it buzzed classrooms all day. Beep! "Excuse me, Mr. So and So? Could you please send the following students to the attendance office...?"

Finally, the chaotic day for teachers and seniors came to an end. The detention room was moved to the cafeteria for the next five days to accommodate the large number of seniors parked there.

The principals decided not to suspend any of them but forced them to endure five three-hour detentions to be called "extended days."

Beth felt grateful she was not among them, thanks only to her mother who, it turned out, was pretty cool.

The following week was the seniors last full week of school. The pressure was on the esteemed Letterman's Club to perform a lasting prank at the high school, especially since last year's class let the white mice loose in the cafeteria. They wanted to top that. On Monday, a brown paper bag circulated around the Center. Everyone was asked to pitch in a couple dollars for the "Big Event."

Beth and her friends wanted to know more, but the guys wouldn't tell. Most of the seniors pitched in a couple dollars after being assured by the boys that no one would be hurt, and no property would be destroyed. By Wednesday, the rumor mill had the total dollar amount collected at over five hundred dollars. The seniors were instructed to be in the Center Friday morning and to make an open space to create a trail from one side of the Center to the other. Each side had doors that went out to the school's parking lots.

When she arrived on that day, more students packed the Center than Beth had ever seen. The principals milled around the area and watched anxiously, knowing something seemed out of the ordinary. The energy was high, and the kids were excited with anticipation.

"Pop! Pop! Pop!" Firecrackers went off down the far hallway headed towards the gymnasium. Both assistant principals took off in a run. Once they left, the side parking lot doors flew open and two naked figures ran toward the Center. The crowd started hooting loudly, clapping and cheering. The pathway was opened further as the guys streaked through the Center towards the back parking lot doors to a getaway car. Each boy had a burlap bag tied over his head with eyeholes cut out. No one except the other lettermen knew their identities and how much they had gotten paid. The noisy crowd alerted the head principal who emerged from the cafeteria before the boys could run all the way through. That was not part of the plan. Beth and some of the others became quiet.

The principal strode through the crowd and into the pathway of the boys. One of the streakers ran into him, knocking them both to the ground. The other boy jumped by him and escaped to the back parking lot. The Center became completely silent.

The principal stood and grabbed the naked, unknown streaker by the arms. He made the boy stand there naked as the other assistant principals came to help. The three of them marched the hooded, naked boy down the hallway to the principal's office.

Beth and her friends looked at each other and burst into gales of laughter.

"Wow! That even topped last year." Susan laughed, tears streaming down her face.

Good old Lynne frowned and said, "I hope they don't get expelled. What if they can't go to graduation?"

Her comment put a damper on the girls' high spirits, and they all attempted to stop laughing.

Thankfully, the boys did not get expelled. The senior class advisors were given strict orders to watch the two boys at the graduation ceremony to make sure neither of them removed their clothes and ran across the football field. It seemed likely that the administration was happy to see the wild class of 1980 graduate.

CHAPTER 67

Beth drove the girls out to The Boat on Friday night. A full moon hung among sparkling stars in the night sky, and the warm temperature soothed Beth. Jackie told them her father offered them the use of the beach house for the ten days before graduation. They were dumbfounded.

"That's cool, but I doubt our parents will let us go," Beth said.

On Sunday, Beth pressed her parents for permission to go to the beach house. Finally, her father said, "Well, you'll be away at college in a couple of months. I don't see why you can't go."

She threw her arms around her dad and kissed his cheek. Then she hugged her mom and ran to her room to call her friends. To her relief and surprise, all her friends had been given permission. Next, she called her coworkers to find someone to work her scheduled shift. It took some begging and promising to return the favor, but Debbie agreed to cover her shift. Elated, Beth turned on her stereo and danced around her bedroom.

~

Beth and the other students received their yearbooks on Monday. Seniors were given extra time in the morning to get them signed. They spread out on the cafeteria deck outside and in the Center. Beth and her friends opted for the Center. The jukebox continued to play as they signed one another's books. As they wrote heartfelt messages to each other, Beth grew emotional. She was touched by the sentimental comments from her classmates and friends. The girls filled two whole pages writing to each other.

On Tuesday, the high school administration told the seniors to report to the auditorium after lunch for a special farewell concert. Beth and her fellow classmates poured into the auditorium. The principal came out in front of the curtain and welcomed the seniors. Everyone quieted down and listened.

He expressed how proud he felt of (the majority of) the students in the class and with that in mind, he hoped they would always remember how much he appreciated their maturity and common sense. The principal also emphasized how important it was for them to act maturely during the commencement ceremony (no streaking, in other words). He told the students to be on the football field at nine a.m. for rehearsal on the Saturday of graduation. No one was to miss the rehearsal. Nonattendance meant you would not be allowed to walk in the ceremony and your diploma would be mailed. He ended his speech by saying, "Now, with all that in mind. Here is my gift to you. Seniors, enjoy the show with...The Travelers!"

Beth, Jackie, Lynne, Susan, and Melissa squealed their delight. They high fived each other and jumped up and down. Their male classmates grinned and fist-bumped the air. The lights were turned down, and the spotlights began to spin around the auditorium.

The curtain went up, and the hottest local rock band drove out a loud, pulsating rendition of The Rolling Stones, "Satisfaction." The seniors jumped to their feet screaming, clapping, and smiling at each other. Beth couldn't believe how cool their high school principal was. The band worked the crowd, and the lead singer did his best Mick Jagger impersonation.

Beth looked around the auditorium. The senior class teachers and class advisors stood along the walls of the auditorium and appeared to enjoy the show as much as the students. She nudged Jackie and Lynne on either side of her and pointed to Mrs. Hart dancing with Mr. Dillard. Beth grabbed hold of Jackie and Lynne and motioned Melissa and Susan with a chin jerk to follow as she pulled her two friends down the row of seats to the aisle. She let go of Jackie and Lynne and clasped Kenny's hand, and the other girls collected the rest of the guys from their lunch table. They headed toward the open orchestra pit in front of the stage. A crowd followed their lead and joined them on the makeshift dance floor. After an hour of The Travelers, the kids clapped and cheered as the band left the stage. Some students shouted, "More, we want more!"

The auditorium remained dark for several moments. As Beth and her friends began to head back to their seats, a voice boomed over the audio system. *"Stay right where you are, my children!"*

The kids turned back to look at the stage. It went pitch-black, and a guitar began to play. Another joined in, then a horn section blew as psychedelic stage lights spun around. The curtain opened, and The Funks took center stage. "When you wish upon a star, your dreams will take you very far, yeah, when you wish upon a dream. Life ain't always what it seems oh yeah..."

Beth, her friends, and the other seniors screamed loudly and rushed the stage again. The black kids ran to the stage with the white kids and for the first time ever, they all danced together. The Funk Band caused excitement Beth had never seen at school. No one danced with partners, they just danced in a large group. The whole auditorium sang the chorus, "You're a shining star, no matter who you are, shining bright you see, what you can truly be, you're a shining star, no matter who you are, shining bright you see what you can truly be..." The music stopped, and everyone sang a cappella. "Shining star for you to see what your life can truly be, shining star for you to see what your life can truly be, shining star for you to see what your life can truly be." The lights went off, and the students roared their appreciation. The guys sang with synthesized voices, "Groove and boogie down, down come on groove and boogie down, down come on, let's groove tonight, share the spice of life…" The Funks continued for another forty-five minutes.

The band thanked the students and the principal for inviting them to perform, and the band members used towels to wipe sweat from their faces and necks.

Beth wiped moisture from her brow with the back of her hand, grinning at her friends.

The principal retook the stage and asked the students to give one more round of applause to The Travelers and The Funks. Both bands entered with their instruments and took a spot on the stage. Beth and her classmates shouted and clapped as they awaited the encore.

The applause and screams drowned out the principal. He smiled at the faculty members at the side of the auditorium, shook his head, and exited the stage. All the musicians smiled at the adulation they received. The drummer from The Travelers began to play, and both bands jointly performed The Commodores, "Brick House."

The entire auditorium did the whistle and swayed as the seniors sang every word. To end the show, the bands performed "Play That Funky Music" by Wild Cherry.

Beth walked on cloud nine the rest of the day.

Wednesday was the last day of classes for seniors. Beth walked through the hallway like a zombie, unable to believe this was it. She and Kenny cleaned out their locker during homeroom, and she felt like crying through the whole process. Kenny would be going to the University of Delaware, and they promised to keep in touch. He also promised he would come to the beach and visit while the girls were there. She had known him well for eight years, since fifth grade, but he'd never been more important to her than that day. They hugged for a long time in the hallway before they left for their first period classes.

At lunch that day, Jackie suggested they go around the table and tell something funny or memorable about each other. Jackie tried to go first but broke down in tears before she could say anything. Fred looked at the sniffling girls, smiled at them, and suggested they each tell just one memory. Kenny and Ron looked uncomfortable with all this sentimentality and started to pretend cry. "Boohoo, Boohoo," they said.

The girls laughed through their tears and smacked them on their arms.

Fred said, "I'll start. My memory is the football team making it to the conference division championship."

They all nodded in agreement. That was a big moment.

Ron said, "My favorite moment was playing quarterback for C.R. and the Dullard game and winning!" He grinned broadly.

Melissa nodded excitedly. "I loved cheering at the football games this year!"

Lynne smiled at them all. "It was an honor to be your Homecoming Queen." She wiped her eyes.

Susan said, "My favorite high school moment was meeting Tyler in ninth grade."

The others booed her good-naturedly and she laughed.

"I loved competing in the Miss Teen USA competition," Jackie declared, and they all smiled at her.

"My favorite memory was sharing a locker with you, Beth, and all your stupid pictures and notes." Kenny looked at Beth. "I will miss that."

Beth's throat constricted, and she had to fight back tears.

She looked around at them all, making eye contact with each of them. "My favorite memory is lunch with you guys every single day for four years of high school. Oh, and the elbow wrestling." She looked at Kenny and smiled.

By that time, the group had become somewhat melancholy and as they glanced around at each other, Kenny held up his milk carton. "To us!"

They all burst out laughing as they raised their cartons to toast each other.

Throughout the day, the underclassmen Beth had gotten to know stopped her in the hallway to say goodbye. During each class period, she couldn't decide which teacher had been the best and finally decided that every teacher was the best one she'd ever had in her entire school career.

The afternoon flew by, and Beth and her girlfriends headed out to the parking lot at exactly 3:10. There would be no more hanging out at the Center after school. It was done! Beth paused a moment and glanced back at the high school, a wistful ache in her chest. The girls climbed into different cars and headed home to pack their bags for their trip to the beach.

Lynne had bought a car, and they were going to use that and Jackie's mom's car. Earlier, Lynne's mother had asked Beth to drive her car because she worried about her daughter driving that far. Lynne still felt a little jumpy behind the wheel and was happy to let Beth drive. A little after five thirty, the girls packed up and piled into the cars.

CHAPTER 68

The first stop on the way to the beach was the liquor store on the highway. Beth was blown away by the amount of liquor purchased. They bought several pints of Bacardi, Sloe Gin, Vodka, three flavors of Schnapps, three cases of Michelob Light in bottles, and four bottles of wine. They put the alcohol in Lynne's car behind the front seat. She and Beth covered it with their suitcases, beach blankets, and towels.

They followed behind Jackie's station wagon. Halfway to the beach, Beth decided to pass Jackie, and a police officer pulled behind her and put on his flashing lights.

"Ah, crap." She gripped the steering wheel and slowly stopped the car on the side of the road.

Her heart pounded, and her palms started sweating. They could get in trouble for having alcohol in the car. The officer would probably just confiscate it, but he could haul them in.

He approached the car and asked Beth where she and Lynne were going in such a hurry. She explained they were seniors heading to the beach for a trip before graduation. The officer looked in the back seat, and Beth worried that he saw the two cases of beer near the passenger's side. Her heart began to beat faster, and her sweating hands started to shake.

"How long are you girls staying down there?"

Lynne answered for Beth. "Ten days."

He asked how many girls would be at the house and if their parents knew where they were headed.

Satisfied with Beth's answer, he nodded and wrote her a speeding ticket. After warning them to be careful, he handed her the ticket, and the girls drove off more slowly than before. Beth made no attempt to keep up with Jackie. She didn't want another ticket.

Beth and Lynne reached the beach house, and everyone else had already staked out their sleeping spots. They would share the front bedroom. Jackie and Melissa stayed in the master bedroom, and Susan agreed to stay up in the loft.

Mr. Angellini sent homemade lasagna with salad and bread for the girls to eat their first night. They spent the first hour unpacking and setting up the kitchen and bathroom. The girls each brought a stack of albums, and they let Beth pick what to play. Her first choice was Jimmy Buffet. Who could be at the beach and not listen to Jimmy Buffet? It would be sacrilegious.

They sang the words to "Cheeseburger in Paradise" and set the table for dinner. Melissa found some wine glasses, and the girls drank wine with their dinner. Jackie found an ashtray and smoked after dinner, offering one to Beth. It felt very grown up. They lounged around the table for quite a while, drinking the wine. The conversation turned to what they would do that night. They decided to travel south to Ocean City and hit some of the bars. They wouldn't get carded. It was Memorial Day weekend, and everything operated in a loosey-goosey manner in the resort towns.

Around eight o'clock, they began dressing to go out, deciding to leave at nine. It would take about twenty minutes to get there. They went to a club called Starry Night. The beers sold for a nickel a piece. They danced a lot to the cover band, drank, and flirted with boys they didn't know. Beth couldn't remember the last time she'd had this much fun. They closed down the club that night.

The next day, they headed to the beach slightly hungover. It was overcast and chilly. The water looked choppy, and a riptide warning was issued. The surfers wore their wet suits, and the girls stayed out of the water altogether. They lounged in chairs and read romance novels, magazines, or slept. After relaxing for a while, they decided to walk the beach. Beth asked the lifeguard if he could keep an eye on their stuff for them. He smiled at Beth, more than willing to help her out. She grinned at him flirtatiously and said, "Thank you."

Once they were out of his earshot, Jackie said, "That lifeguard is hot, and if you play your cards right, you might just find out how a real man can make you feel."

Beth jumped on top of Jackie's back and messed up her hair. "Is that right? How does a 'real man' make you feel, Jackie? Huh?" Beth laughed as she fell to the sand.

"Dammit." Jackie smoothed down her blonde strands.

The other girls chuckled.

"Beth, she's right." Melissa slanted her head. "You need to 'get with' someone else soon. Another guy would probably do much better than douche bag Danny. Only this time, please use a condom, dipshit!"

All the girls nodded and agreed with Melissa.

Susan told her she needed to go on the pill. Beth silently listened to their suggestions and looked out over the ocean. She didn't need to be on the pill. She would never put herself through that hell again. Beth smiled and nodded as if to heed their well-intended advice.

The weather improved, and the girls spent the next few days at the beach sunning, rafting, swimming, walking the beach, and flirting with the lifeguards. A group of college boys from Washington, D.C. were there for the week to surf. Beth managed to conquer her fear of the water enough to allow one of the guys to give her lessons. Early each morning, she met him and his friends. Jackie came with her the first day and quit. She justified it by saying they went too early in the morning. Beth and the surfers had to walk about a mile and a half south on the beach to where surfing was allowed. Beth developed a slight rash on her stomach from the wax, and her cute surfing instructor gave her his T-shirt to wear in the water. She was having fun and understood the huge appeal when she finally managed to stand up and ride a wave by herself. Beth wanted to buy a surfboard of her own, but they cost too much money. She was bummed that the surfers left for home on Wednesday, ending her access to a surfboard.

Beth and her friends spent Saturday night bar hopping in Ocean City. On Sunday, Kenny, Chris, Ron, Todd, and Fred came down to spend the day. The girls and guys played volleyball on the beach, and Beth got badly sunburned. At the end of the day, Chris Kneeland drove her back to the beach house on a moped he had rented. Beth held on for dear life, wishing she had never agreed to ride with him. The inside area of her ankle set into the exhaust pipe and burned a perfectly round circle on her flesh. By the time they reached the house, Beth was in serious pain. Chris got her a wet, cold washcloth and a cup of ice. The skin swelled up to a huge blister and looked disgusting.

The other boys had gone clamming on the bay side of town. They returned to the house with two buckets full of clams. They planned to steam and eat them.

Beth investigated the buckets. "You can't eat those, they're huge! They will taste awful."

The guys hadn't realized smaller clams were the best for steaming.

Melissa explained that larger clams, ground up, were used for chowder or to slice, batter, and fry. The guys didn't believe her and steamed them anyway.

While the girls changed and got ready to go to Ocean City, the guys cooked the clams.

Beth finished getting ready and entered the kitchen. The guys were sitting at the table chewing on their clams.

"Are they good?" she asked, teasing Fred.

"Yeah, they are," he said with determination as he continued to chew.

She watched each one of them as they chewed and chewed and chewed. Finally, Ron, Todd, and Kenny agreed the clams tasted lousy and threw them in the trash. They ordered pizzas.

The girls decided against going out because the guys wanted to stay in, complaining the night club scene was getting old. They all played a drinking game called "Thumper" and listened to music. A poker game started at the dining room table. Beth felt like a grownup. She glanced around the table at her friends she had known most of her life, and her eyes misted. They were all growing up so fast.

It grew late, and the guys wanted to stay the night, but the girls wouldn't let them, saying their parents would be checking in and they could get in a lot of trouble. Around twelve o'clock, the guys left.

Melissa told the girls Chuck would be coming down to pick her up at twelve thirty. He didn't get off duty until eleven that night. The two of them planned a getaway for the next day and night. Beth looked at Melissa with some slight jealousy. It must be nice not to worry about your parents catching you.

The next day, Tyler came down to see Susan. He brought his friends with him, Rocky included. Beth wasn't quite sure what to do about that. Everyone seemed to pair up for the night as they went out for dinner and to Ocean City to dance. Beth and Rocky paired more out of comfort than real attraction. He was still an excellent dancer and fun to talk to. Rocky could always be trusted to stay somewhat sober and drive everyone where they needed to go.

For the first time since she arrived at the beach, Beth drank way too much sloe gin. At the nightclub, she flirted heavily with the lead singer of the band as she sat on a high stool at the bar. On his breaks, he came over to talk with her and bought her drinks. He asked her time and time again if Rocky was her boyfriend, and she assured him he was not. On the band's final break, he asked her to go back to his bus with him after the show. Beth turned him down, but she was having fun flirting with him. He spoke softly, flirting and complimenting her. Finally, he leaned in to kiss her.

Beth closed her eyes. Nothing happened. She opened her

eyes, and the guy wasn't even near her. He stood several feet away with Rocky. They leaned in close together, speaking in whispers, their bodies turned away from her.

The lead singer turned back to Beth and said, "Too bad, I was looking forward to it."

Beth glared at Rocky. He had made up some sort of outlandish lie to get the guy away from her. Intent on punching Rocky in the arm, she stepped down from the stool, and her feet gave out from under her and she fell to the floor. Beth didn't remember much else except the burn on her ankle hurting her and vomiting into the bay water off the dock beside the beach house.

Rocky stood behind her, holding her waist and her hair back as she got sick in the wavy water again and again. She begged him to help her feel better. Rocky chuckled at her and told her he was really doing all he could now. Finally, the sickness subsided, and he half carried her back to the house.

He took her into the bathroom and set her on the closed toilet seat lid. She caught her reflection in the mirror. Ugh. She looked like Alice Cooper on acid. Her mascara had run down her face from all the crying she'd done over things that no longer mattered. Her sweat-dampened hair was stringy. Thank God, Rocky had held it back for her while she had thrown up. He got a cold washcloth and cleaned up her face. The cool, soapy water felt heavenly to Beth and she repeatedly said, "Thank you, thank you so much."

"Where's your toothbrush, Beth?" he asked.

She opened her eyes wide and pointed to the holder. "It's the yellow one."

As she talked, she covered her mouth with her hand, realizing she must have terrible breath.

Rocky put toothpaste on her toothbrush and brought it over to her along with a cup.

Beth brushed as he handed her a towel and instructed her to spit into the cup. He rinsed it out, added some water, and had her swish and spit. Then, he took a towel and dried her hair around her face and neck.

Throughout the entire process, Rocky kept asking, "You feeling alright?"

She just nodded.

He assisted her to the bedroom. Beth plopped onto the bed and lay down. Her clothes smelled like sloe gin, and she needed to get out of them. Rocky managed to move her ragdoll body around to get her shirt over her head. Her pants scraped against her blistered ankle as he gently removed them, and she whined loudly. He was able to slip her nightgown over her head.

Beth grimaced and looked down at the burn on her ankle.

"Does that hurt?" Rocky asked.

He left, and she heard him opening and closing cabinets in the bathroom and then in the hallway linen closet. After a about a three-minute search, he returned to her with gauze and white tape, cleaned the wound, and wrapped the gauze around her ankle to protect the burn from further infection.

Rocky tucked her into the bed. "I will sleep on the couch, but I will leave your door open in case you need anything, okay?"

She nodded weakly, her eyes growing heavy, only slightly aware of him leaving her room before she passed out.

The next morning, Beth woke up with a headache. She shuffled into the kitchen and poured herself a glass with iced water and then poured one with orange juice for Rocky. There was a lot she couldn't remember about the night before, but she did remember how Rocky had taken care of her.

She exited the opening out to the living area, and Rocky sat up on the couch and rubbed face.

He saw her, and his expression lit up. She was sure she saw desire in his eyes as he swept his gaze over her yellow and gingham nightgown that he'd put on her last night, focusing on her tanned ankles.

She approached him, sat next to him on the couch, and staring ahead, handed him the orange juice.

"Thanks," he said with gratitude.

Beth began to take deep swallows of the water. She looked at him, aware she looked like crap with dark circles under her eyes.

"Are you still feeling bad?" he asked.

She nodded, pressing the palm of her hand against her forehead.

"I don't know why you came down here, Rocky, but I think I'm really lucky you did. What did you say to that guy from the band last night?" she asked.

Rocky chuckled. "You don't want to know..."

She smiled. "I can imagine."

They sat silently for a long time. Rocky finished his orange juice, and she finished her water.

"Hey, can you get me some more water and some Tylenol out of my purse? It's in my room."

He took her empty glass, filled it in the kitchen, grabbed a slice of bread, and handed those to her before he fetched two Tylenol caplets from her purse.

It was still early in the morning, and no one else had moved.

After delivering the Tylenol to Beth, he looked out the front window. "Tyler's car is still here. Everyone else must have gone home last night."

She nodded, slowly eating the bread, hoping it would settle her stomach.

Rocky sat next to her again. He moved his body back onto the couch. When she finished munching on the bread, he pulled her down next to him.

He lay against the back of the couch with her next to him. Rocky wrapped his arm around her, and she placed her head on the inside of his shoulder. She soon fell asleep again. He moved his free arm up closer to feel the softness of her body. Beth felt the sensation of her breasts being fondled as she slept, and it felt nice. She curled her body in a mini stretch. This caused her to press her rear against him. He moaned and began to kiss her on the ear and neck. Beth was sure she must be dreaming. She was warm, comfortable, and it felt wonderful being touched so sweetly. Beth opened her eyes and realized she was with Rocky on the couch. Her headache had subsided, and the bread had settled her stomach.

She turned her body and faced him. He kissed her on the mouth. Beth knew everything about Rocky. She shouldn't be letting him touch her. Still, she considered going forward. The girls had told her to get right back on the horse.

Rocky must have felt her hesitate because he whispered to her, "Don't stop me this time, please."

Beth let him kiss her again. Rocky would have condoms, and she would certainly be comfortable enough with him to ask him to use one.

Then her insecurities began to creep in. *What if he thinks I'm awful like Danny did? What if he hurts me, too? What if the condom breaks? What if I smell bad or I don't move the right way or...?*

"Don't, Beth," Rocky said, interrupting her thoughts. "Don't start pulling away from me now."

He kissed her deeply. His rough whiskers scratched her skin, and she didn't like that. It distracted her. She heard the door to the loft open and footsteps coming down the steps. Beth quickly pulled herself up and away from Rocky as Tyler opened the door from the loft area. He seemed surprised to see Beth pulling her nightgown down to cover her legs and a disheveled Rocky on the couch.

Tyler smiled and said, "Good morning, I've got to get back home. I'm only home a few more days, and I promised my mom I'd help her with some plumbing."

Beth smiled as she pointed to the loft. "I'm sure your mom appreciates your help. Susan misses you, Tyler. I hope you two will be together more often soon."

Tyler smiled and nodded.

Rocky sat up on the couch and looked at his watch as he and Tyler made small talk. Then Tyler used the restroom and went back up to the loft to say goodbye to Susan.

"It's eight fifteen. My class started at eight," Rocky said to Beth.

"What class?"

"I take an accounting class at the tech college."

Beth scrunched her brow, surprised he still took classes.

"Yes, he is," Rocky said snidely and stood up quickly.

"What?" Beth said, confused by his last comment.

"Weren't you wondering if Danny Mitchell was in my class?"

Beth couldn't believe it, but she wasn't wondering that at all.

"No, actually I wasn't."

"Right," Rocky said in an insincere tone. "I need to go."

Beth felt guilty for some reason. "Are you going to come back down?" she asked.

Rocky looked at her with raised brows. "Do you want me to?"

Beth nodded. *What am I doing?*

He smiled. "I'll come back Friday night. Is that alright?"

Beth walked him out to his car. She wanted to ask him if he was still dating that girl, but she didn't. He never wanted her to know anything about that girl. Maybe he would stop seeing her if Beth asked him to.

"See you Friday." Rocky grinned.

Beth leaned in and kissed him on the mouth. "Thank you for helping me last night."

"Hmm, kiss me again. It's a long time until Friday," he said.

Beth smiled and did as she was instructed. It felt good to flirt.

CHAPTER 69

A few days later, Beth was listening to music in the main room of the beach house while Jackie, Lynne, and Susan still slept. Melissa walked in the front door.

Beth looked up at her expectantly. "How was your trip with Chuck?"

"It was great!" Melissa replied, setting down her overnight bag. "He's flying out today for a few days." Her face clouded. "Um, Charlie is coming down tonight."

Beth narrowed her eyes at her. When *was* she going to tell him?

Melissa avoided eye contact with her. "I know I need to tell him. It's just so hard. I do like him a lot, you know."

Beth felt envious and nervous about Charlie visiting Melissa. She hoped Melissa would change her mind about him. Beth smiled tightly, got up and took a shower, and then bandaged her burned ankle. The son of a bitch still hurt a lot. She got her things together for the beach and headed toward the door.

Jackie came out of her room. "Going down to the beach already?"

Beth nodded, and Jackie lit up a cigarette as she went to the kitchen.

Beth laughed at her friend's tangled bed hair. She wondered why Jackie didn't tie it back when she slept.

"My God, Jackie, your hair is everywhere this morning. No wonder it takes you forever to style it."

Jackie flipped her the bird, scowling as she prepared a cup of coffee.

"Hurry up, Phyllis Diller!" Beth headed to the beach to claim their normal spot for the day.

She set up her towel, beach chair, and radio, and then lay down, closing her eyes. The warm sun and soft music playing lulled her to sleep.

"Wake up, Beth!" Jackie nudged her, and the other three girls giggled as they put down their beach towels.

Beth groaned and rolled over on her stomach. "What time is it?"

"Eleven thirty, lobster. You should put on some suntan lotion and rent an umbrella," Melissa said.

Despite the cloudless sky that held no reprieve from the beating sun, Beth ignored her advice and fell asleep again.

"Beth, wake up," Lynne said.

She rolled over and shielded her eyes from the sun.

"You've been sleeping for two hours. You really need to go back to the house." Lynne grimaced. "You've got a nasty sunburn."

"Huh?" Beth felt like shit, perhaps she was still hung over.

She never got badly sunburned and it usually changed quickly to a tan anyway.

Beth gathered her things and admitted her ankle caused her a great deal of pain. Susan offered to go back to the house with her.

As the two walked, Susan asked, "Did you know Rocky is dating someone?"

Beth shrugged.

"What are you doing, Beth? There are a lot of other people in this world besides Danny Mitchell and Rocky Mulinero. Neither one of them is right for you."

Beth stared at her feet as she walked toward the beach house.

"Who is this girl Rocky is dating anyway?" Beth finally asked.

Susan pursed her lips and remained silent.

"Well?" Beth asked again.

Susan reluctantly told Beth that Rocky had been seeing a

certain girl for a couple of years off and on, more on than off. She was from Smythfield High school and had already graduated. Her parents owned a real estate company and were wealthy. The girl had bought Rocky his new T Top car.

Beth gaped at her. She had no idea the relationship had gotten that serious.

"Do you think he cares about me at all?" Beth asked her.

Susan looked sympathetically at her. "Of course, he cares about you! He wouldn't keep coming around if he didn't. According to Tyler and his friends, Rocky likes what her money can provide him, and he's probably not going to be willing to give that up."

Beth didn't like it, but she understood. She would get the truth from Rocky on Friday.

They reached the house, and Beth set her stuff down and went into the kitchen. She had to get herself together. Her body started to return to its proper state after she ate two scrambled eggs, a piece of dry toast, and drank two cups of coffee. Beth went into the bathroom, removed her bathing suit, and gaped at her sunburn. She was as red as a lobster!

After she showered, she gently patted her body dry. The towel felt rough against her skin and caused her pain. She put on a pair of white cotton drawstring shorts and a large pale pink T-shirt she normally wore to bed. No way was she going to wear a bra against her sunburned body.

Beth read a book on the couch until the girls returned from the beach, and they shared submarine sandwiches for dinner. They got ready to go out for the night. Beth tried to change into different clothes, but her sunburn and ankle blister were making her miserable. She told the girls to go without her.

Melissa approached Beth on the couch and asked her if she and Rocky had used a condom.

She told her friend they hadn't had sex, and Melissa seemed relieved.

"There are lots of guys out there, Beth." She patted her

lightly on the head.

"I know." Beth gave her a half smile. Blah, blah. They all seemed to think the same thing.

"Is Charlie still coming down tonight?" Beth asked, hoping he would.

Melissa shrugged. "I haven't called him to confirm anything, so I don't think so."

"How are things going with Chuck?"

Melissa's face lit up and she smiled.

"You need to let Charlie know soon," Beth said in a hard voice.

Her friend nodded and said she would.

"If Charlie does come down, do you think Danny will come?" Beth asked.

Melissa stared at her and blinked.

"You've lost your mind. You have, Beth, you really have. I can't believe you'd even want to see him after the way he treated you," Melissa said harshly.

Beth hung her head in shame. Melissa stood up and walked away from her.

The four girls expressed their concern at leaving Beth alone, but she waved them off and told them to have a good time. After they left, she stacked some albums on the stereo and got a pillow from her bed. She lay on the couch and read a book with music playing low in the background, enjoying the tranquility of the empty house. The collar from her T-shirt dug into her sunburned neck, so she decided to remove it. It felt good to lay there with no shirt on. She spread her arms out and enjoyed the cool air on her skin. Soon, she fell asleep.

She heard the girls enter the porch door and woke up quickly. Beth was freezing and laughed at herself, knowing she lay there exposing herself. She sat up quickly and bent down to grab her shirt from the floor as she stood.

Charlie walked in the door from the front porch with Mike Crowley directly behind him. *Shit, it's not the girls.* Beth was stunned to see the two of them in the doorway. Their eyes widened at Beth's naked breasts. She threw the shirt up over her chest, and the two guys turned their backs, offering her more privacy. They began to apologize immediately. Beth excused herself to the bedroom where she forced herself to put on a bra over her painful sunburn followed by the T-shirt. She came out, and the guys placed beer cans into the refrigerator, grinning. Beth blushed with embarrassment.

"Where's Melissa?" Charlie asked her.

"The girls went out. What time is it?"

Charlie glanced at his watch. "Ten thirty."

They wouldn't be returning anytime soon. Mike and Charlie sat and talked with Beth for about a half hour. Mike went to use the restroom, and Charlie came over to sit next to Beth.

"How have you been?"

Beth's face slackened and she shrugged. The last time he'd seen her was at Danny's cousin's apartment.

"You're okay?" Charlie asked.

Beth didn't know what to say. She wished Danny cared enough about her to ask that. She shook her head with complete honesty.

"It'll be alright, though." Charlie rubbed her back, and she flinched.

"I fell asleep on the beach and got a nasty sunburn," she said.

"Oh, sorry!" He furrowed his brow. "I wish I could do something to help."

Beth smiled. "You can't, but I appreciate you saying that."

He focused on her mouth. Beth wanted to kiss him. Shit! What was wrong with her?

Mike returned from the restroom and suggested they go look for the girls at the bar. They offered to take her with them, but Beth refused. The two guys left, and she felt down in the dumps, unsure why. Was it her sunburn? Was it the burn on her ankle? Was it because Rocky had a girlfriend? Was it because Danny didn't come? Shit!

She trudged into the bedroom, took off all her clothes and climbed into bed. This time she made sure all the doors were locked. She lay in the dark with her arms out to her side, trying to get comfortable despite her sunburn.

Later, she heard Lynne crawl into bed. Her boyfriend, Joey, was with her.

Beth looked at the alarm clock. It was two fifteen. She had to go to the bathroom. Beth pulled her nightgown over her head under the covers so Joey couldn't see her. She got up, grabbed her pillow and blanket, and then headed out the door. It might be polite to give them some privacy.

Beth used the restroom and headed toward the couch, dragging her pillow and coverlet from the bed. Mike was sleeping on it already. Damn! She would try to get comfortable on the love seat.

"Hey," Mike said softly.

Beth smiled and whispered, "Hey, it's a little crowded in the bedroom so I came out to sleep on the couch. Are you drunk?" She set her stuff on the love seat.

"I wish. Maybe then I could get some sleep." He didn't sound drunk.

"What's the matter?" Beth whispered with concern and sat on the coffee table next to where he lay on the couch.

"Seeing your tan lines earlier and knowing you were in that room has been keeping me awake." He wiggled his eyebrows.

Beth's cheeks grew hot as she recalled he'd seen her topless.

He sat up and continued talking in a hushed whisper, "Come here, Beth."

She leaned forward, and he reached for her right hand.

"I know what happened between you and Danny. Charlie told me about it. I'm telling you right now, if it had been me, I would never have done that to you."

Beth wasn't exactly sure what Mike meant but it seemed as if he needed to get it off his chest.

After a long pause, he said, "I'd like very much to date you. Do you think you could ever go out with me and give us a good try?"

She didn't know what to say.

Following a long stretch of silence, she asked, "Are you sure you're not drunk, Mike?"

"No, not at all," he said in a loud whisper.

Beth wished with all her might he had been. This was coming out of the blue.

She sat silently, blinking, not sure what to say. He took her face in his hands and leaned in, kissing her softly on the lips. Both stunned and confused, she pulled away. Where was this coming from? He had to be drunk.

Mike drew back and looked her in the eyes. "Let's go out tomorrow. We can go to dinner and then go dancing at The Rudder. Just the two of us. What do you say?"

Beth stared at him. "I don't know what to say, Mike. I really don't. You're tired, and probably have had a little too much to drink. Maybe we should talk tomorrow in the light of day."

He compressed his lips and nodded tightly. "Okay."

"By the way, where's Charlie?" she asked.

He pointed to the loft. Beth sighed. Apparently, Melissa did not break things off with him tonight. Beth stood, scooped up her pillow and blanket, and walked to the master bedroom where Susan and Jackie slept. She grabbed some more blankets from the closet and laid them on the floor in there to make it softer. After Mike's strange behavior, she couldn't sleep out on the love seat now. Her thoughts whirled, and sleep eluded her.

She lay there, tossing and turning. This was the weirdest week she had ever been through. If she went out with Mike, it would certainly piss Danny off. But that shouldn't be a reason not to date someone. On the other hand, it would be so much fun to really piss Danny off. *If I slept with Mike, that would be the icing on the cake.* Danny could stew about that for years to come. Then again Danny probably could care less and then where would she be? Well, perhaps she could be in a loving relationship with Mike Crowley. Wait, with Shot Man Mike?

It would be a terrible mistake for her to date Mike while she was still so confused about Danny and her life in general. Finally, she fell asleep.

The next day she loaded up on sunscreen and headed to the beach. She and Mike took a long walk. She explained how much she adored him as her friend and why she couldn't date him. Mike seemed disappointed but agreed with her. Melissa broke up with Charlie that same night. Beth thought of the J. Geils Band song. *"You love her, but she loves him. And he loves somebody else, you just can't win. Love Stinks!"*

A disappointed Mike headed back home with a pissed off Charlie. The girls had one more week to spend at the beach and then it would be their high school graduation. Beth smiled at the prospect of finally getting out of high school.

Friday arrived, and Rocky came down to the beach at five o'clock. He and Beth went out to dinner. He took the T Tops out of the Camaro, and they drove down the coast, parked, and strolled the beach. They went up on the boardwalk and entertained themselves in the arcade and bought ice cream. It was a beautiful night, the stars shining brightly. They walked back out on the beach and sat on the sand. Beth needed to find out the truth. She had put it off long enough.

"I know everything about your girlfriend," she said.

Rocky looked at her.

"What do you know?"

"I know her name is Jodi Phillips and her family owns Phillips Real Estate in Milford. I know they are quite wealthy and that you have been going steady with her for a couple of years. Susan told me."

Rocky held his head down.

Beth continued, "I know she bought you the very car you brought to my house to take me for a ride in the day you got it. I'm confused. Obviously, I didn't want to think about you having a girlfriend. I have always taken comfort in knowing you were out there somewhere and that you cared for me. Now I'm trying to deal with reality. I think you love her and want to be with her but I'm not truly clear about why you are here with me. I could understand it if you and I had this great, passionate sex life but that's not true either. I'm a bit lost," she said and waited for a response.

Rocky peered up at the sky. "First, she did buy me the car." He glanced at Beth, watching for a reaction to his honesty.

It felt weird. She nodded and looked away. She hadn't realized he was a person who took advantage of people. Or had she?

"She and I met at a soccer match at Smythfield. She came on strong and we went out. Her parents treated me really nice. Her dad got me the job at the car dealership where I work. He has a buddy that owns the place. The next thing I knew he offered to pay for my college. That's how it got started. At first, I was just in it for the ride, you know. Then it got more complicated because she grew to have strong feelings and I felt a little..."

"Rotten?" Beth smirked at him.

He nodded. "Yeah, rotten, and indebted to her dad. But I do care about her."

Beth took a deep breath and waited for him to finish.

Rocky slanted his head, a touch of sadness in his gaze. "You already know why I'm here with you, and I'm not even going to say it out loud because it doesn't really matter anymore now, does it?"

Beth stared him in the eye. She'd heard enough. It didn't matter. Beth never really loved him and now she never would. She shook her head.

"Come on, let me drive you back to the house." He stood

and held out his hand to help her up.

She accepted his aid and faced him for the last time.

"Thank you for finally telling me the whole truth," she said.

They walked back to the car, and he drove her to the house. She kissed him on the cheek and told him not to get out of the car. Rocky Mulinero had been dismissed.

It was close to nine thirty, and the girls got ready to go out to The Rudder. Beth was upbeat and ready to finally have "some major fun." That night and the rest of the week passed in a blur. The girls spent their time on the beach, shopping, drinking, and dancing. Every night there seemed to be a different crowd hanging out. Staying at the beach was a great way to end their senior year.

Saturday morning came quickly, and the girls rushed to clean up the house and pack their things to head back to town. They had to be at the football field for graduation rehearsal promptly at nine in the morning. If they arrived late, they would not be permitted to walk in the ceremony. It was already eight fifteen, and it took forty-five minutes to drive home with no traffic. They were barely going to make it.

They pulled into the high school parking lot. Everyone already stood in their places on the field, and the teachers directed them with bullhorns. The girls jumped from the cars and took off running toward the field. Beth stopped and ran back to Lynne who carried her shoes.

"Thank you!" Beth yelled as she sprinted to the field and scrambled to get her shoes on.

"Holy shit!" Jackie said and giggled.

They threw open the gate and ran past the bleachers. Mrs. Castle yelled at them as they ran towards her.

"Where have you been? You are all late! Go get in line! Go! Go! Go!"

The girls ran full throttle.

Kenny waved and called to Beth, "Stand here by me!"

She jumped up and hugged him.

"Excuse me, students! Please take your places immediately," one of the teachers with the bullhorn instructed.

Beth could see Jackie and Susan from where she would be sitting. Lynne sat up front, and the two waved to one another. Melissa sat behind her, but she couldn't see her. After rehearsal, the girls had exactly an hour and a half to get home, changed, and be back at the field for the actual ceremony at one o'clock.

CHAPTER 70

Graduation Day

The Inevitable

While I was fearing it, it came,
But came with less of fear,
Because that fearing it so long,
Had almost made it dear.
There is a fitting a dismay,
A fitting a despair,
'Tis harder knowing it is due,
Than knowing it is here.
The trying on the utmost,
The morning it is new,
Is terribler than wearing it,
A whole existence through.
Emily Dickinson

Beth got dressed in a white linen short-sleeved dress with purple and yellow pansies along the bottom hem, and she chose white dress shoes.

Her parents ran around like nuts getting ready, and her sister and brother-in-law were at the house waiting for everyone.

Her grandmother prepared food in the kitchen. She'd already made the coleslaw and potato salad.

Melissa came over to pick up Beth so they could get to the high school early to don their caps and gowns. Her family said they would meet her on the field after the ceremony. Beth smiled broadly and waved to them as they stood in the doorway to see her off.

She and Melissa headed to the high school. Excitement tickled Beth's stomach. They arrived to find Joey and Lynne climbing out of his car. Susan and Jackie pulled up together. They helped each other with their caps, using bobby pins to secure them. The girls wore gold robes, and the boys wore royal blue. Melissa complained about how her auburn hair clashed with the gold fabric.

"It's not majorly attractive on any of us!" Jackie said, losing patience with Melissa's complaints.

The ceremony started precisely at one. This year the boys and girls walked together side by side instead of the usual separation of boys on one side of the field, girls on the other. The program, filled with many speeches and advice, lasted a while. Thankfully, everyone kept their clothes on. At the hat toss, Beth and Lynne teared up, and the boys shouted their excitement. People ran around on the football field and hugged each other. Everyone took pictures. Beth and her girlfriends got together and posed for their parents and then for each other. They separated to speak to individual friends, boyfriends, and family.

The field began to clear as people headed home for their family celebrations. Chris ran up to tell the girls there would be a party at his house tonight. They all agreed to attend. He smiled and ran off. Beth looked up at the bleachers.

"Come on!" she shouted to her friends, and they followed her through the fence up the empty bleachers to the top bleacher seat.

They stood and looked down at the field. The wind blew a strong hot breeze, and their hair and gowns billowed. Beth was overwhelmed by the sight of the crowd on the field and in the parking lot. She turned to the right to look at her high school one last time. The rest of them gazed in the same direction as Beth. She glanced out into the parking lot and watched the crowd of people head toward their cars.

She caught sight of a silver Mustang parked halfway back. Beth stood on her tiptoes to get a better look. It was

Danny's car. The Vietnam MIA bumper sticker on the back gave it away.

"Look." Beth pointed at Danny's car.

The girls smiled at her and gave her hugs, knowing the significance of it. They wrapped their arms together. Wiping the tears from her face, Beth turned to search the crowd for him. She never found him but that was okay. He had come. That was all that mattered.

The girls set up a plan for getting to Chris's party. Tyler had come home for graduation so Susan would ride with him. Melissa would go for a little while but then she had a date with Chuck. She'd drive herself. Lynne and Joey would ride together, and Lynne invited Beth and Jackie to go with them. The girls declined, deciding to ride together. After agreeing to meet at Chris's house at nine, the girls said their goodbyes and headed home for their family celebrations.

Melissa dropped Beth off at her house. Beth's parents had balloons, streamers, and tons of food waiting for her when she arrived. The whole family was there along with close family friends and cousins. Beth was happy. She had missed her parents while she was at the beach. Her parents gave her a three-piece set of luggage for traveling back and forth to college. Her sister and brother-in-law bought her a large book bag with an umbrella tucked in the bottom compartment for walking on campus in the rain. She received gifts of money and a nice pen and pencil set, diaries, and all kinds of school supplies. They ate and laughed.

Ann Marie approached and hugged her.

"I know you're glad this is over, huh?"

Beth nodded as she pulled away from her sister and ate a bite of cake.

"I thought it would never get here! I can't believe it's actually graduation day!" she said, smiling and laughing.

The family gathering began to wind down, and Beth went over to Jackie's house for a short while. Melissa was there and announced she had an emergency and needed the girls to meet at The Boat. Beth got on the phone and made the calls to Lynne and Susan. Before long, the cars pulled into the secluded clearing one after the other. They ran toward one another and sat on the logs, basking beneath the warm sunshine.

Melissa leaned forward. "You guys aren't going to believe this!"

A chorus of groans encouraged her to spit it out and get on with it.

"Chuck asked me to marry him!"

They all looked at one another with wide eyes and open mouths and turned toward her.

"He asked you to *marry* him?" Jackie repeated.

Melissa nodded and told them the details of the conversation, including how Chuck looked, what he wore, and the tone in his voice. He hadn't given her an engagement ring yet because he wanted the two of them to talk to her mother first, just to be polite. Melissa looked so happy, and her legs bounced up and down as she spoke. The girls laughed and hugged her.

"You know what the best part is?" Melissa stood and twirled with her arms open wide.

"What?" they asked in unison.

She stopped spinning. "He's being transferred to Travis Air Force Base. It's in California!"

The girls blinked at one another.

Melissa stopped her personal celebration. "Come on, guys, he leaves in two months. We're getting married before he leaves and I'm going with him!"

Beth didn't know Chuck very well and decided she would have to get to know him quickly. Melissa had always been able to take care of herself. Beth was sure her friend would be fine.

Jackie jumped up. "Oh! Wait!"

They all watched her as she ran quickly back to her car. She returned with two brown paper bags. Each held some type of bottle in it. She pulled out champagne. None of them had ever had champagne, and opening the bottles took a group effort.

"I bought these to celebrate graduation. Now we have something else to celebrate," Jackie said as she hugged Melissa.

Jackie struggled to pull the cork.

Melissa grabbed the bottle and said, "Watch."

She shook it, and the cork popped out as the champagne began to spill over the bottle. The girls drank it quickly, laughing and talking a mile a minute.

So they could hear music, they rolled all the car windows down in both cars and turned both radios on. The music blared in unison. The girls sang and danced as they finished the champagne, and then headed home to get ready for a night on the town. Their first stop would be Chris Kneeland's house party.

Beth arrived home, took a shower and changed. She wore a pair of jeans with a thin white cotton gauze pullover blouse. Her tan looked striking against the white fabric. She was lucky that a sunburn always turned into a tan for her. The blouse had quarter-length sleeves and embroidery across the top in pastel pinks, blues, yellows, and greens. She put on a pair of white linen sandals with ankle laces. The blister on her leg had not healed enough to handle the pain of the tie straps, so she changed into a pair of flesh-colored slide-on leather sandals. She styled her hair straight, and she didn't need much makeup, just some mascara and lip-gloss. Then she left to pick up Jackie.

Jackie's mother hugged her and congratulated her on her graduation. She told the girls to be careful, not to drink too much, and to call her if they needed a ride home.

Jackie got in the car and rolled her eyes. "She has never said anything like that to me before! Oh my God!"

Beth laughed and realized their parents were letting go.

It was dark out when they pulled up to Chris's house.

Cars were parked all along the street, and kids stood everywhere. The music spilled from inside the house out to the street. Mr. Kneeland hugged and welcomed the girls into his home, telling them the food and drinks were in the basement. They headed down the stairs and quickly met up with their friends. Melissa pumped the keg and handed Beth a beer, and Lynne handed one to Jackie. They stood and took in the sights and sounds of the party. Susan came in soon after and joined them. The five girls clustered in the corner of the crowded basement.

"Can you believe we actually graduated today?" Beth squealed as they lifted their plastic cups and toasted one another.

"Nineteen eighty always seemed so far away!" Jackie yelled over the music as the girls laughed and hugged each other. "I'm going to miss you guys so much!"

Beer slopped over the sides of their cups. The noise in the basement had become deafening. Aerosmith screamed out of the speakers. Empty beer cans were stacked in a pyramid against the wall.

Most of the people there were seniors and juniors from C.R. A handful of older guys came in. Beth searched for Brian Knight. She hadn't seen him at the graduation ceremony, which both surprised and disappointed her. Beth wasn't going to let anything get her down tonight. Everyone around her seemed happy, and she focused on that. Chris walked up to Beth and hugged her.

"I'm glad you came. Did you see my dad? He's drunk!" He laughed, and the girls did, too.

It was surprising to be around their parents now that they started to treat them like adults instead of children.

Beth searched the room again and hoped to see Charlie, Danny, or Mike. She was anxious to talk to Charlie. They hadn't spoken since Melissa had broken up with him. Beth felt hurt that he hadn't come to graduation. Maybe he had and she didn't see him. Maybe he had been there with Danny.

Would they come to the party?

The girls laughed and talked for over an hour about the ceremony and what was going on around them at the party.

It was Chris's house, but no one had seen him in the past half hour. He could either be throwing up somewhere or screwing a girl in the back yard. The pool table, which normally stood in the center of the room, had been pushed to the side to accommodate the number of teenagers squeezed into such a small space.

As she celebrated happily with her friends, Beth drank down the rest of her warm beer. Amid gales of laughter and self-indulgent praise, she saw him. Her stomach dropped as Danny Mitchell descended the stairs. She was even more stunned to see Rocky Mulinero right behind him. She moved her plastic cup up to her face as a shield so she could watch Danny walk down the basement stairs. He scanned the room then turned away to look anywhere but at her.

"What the hell?" Beth said, and her friends followed her stunned gaze.

"Don't let them ruin your night. This is your night, Beth, not theirs!" Lynne said, and Joey nodded in agreement behind her.

Even Tyler moaned his displeasure at his friend's appearance.

Rocky approached Beth as Danny headed to the keg. He looked quite pleased with himself.

"Why are you here with him?" she snapped.

Rocky's smile faded as he stared at her with wide eyes.

"I just came to tell you congratulations, that's all."

Beth rolled her eyes in disgust. The two probably talked about her, sharing details, and laughing about her. Hell, they probably had a bet going as to which one of them could get her to leave with him tonight. She hated them both right now.

Rocky headed to the keg. Before long, she had lost track of him in the crowd. Danny still stood by the keg. She never lost sight of him. Beth was angrier with him than she was with Rocky. Pain swelled in the back of her throat. She hadn't seen him since he'd told her it had been a mistake to sleep with her. She hadn't seen him since her pregnancy scare. He smiled and shook hands with people, congratulating them. She clenched her hands into fists. God, she hated him! She wished she had never laid eyes on him.

Jackie leaned into her ear, "Easy, Beth. Keep it together."

Beth swung around toward Jackie and put her back to Danny. She didn't want to see him and his mean, hateful face ever again.

"Rocky better not come over here to talk to me again," Beth said in a low deliberate voice to the girls.

They searched the room and said they didn't see him anywhere. Maybe he had left. Maybe he and Danny hadn't come together after all. She looked down into her plastic cup. It was almost empty. She swirled the cup while trying to steady her nerves.

"Hi Beth," Danny said gently to her, approaching her from the side.

Beth's heart sank, and she said nothing. She was on the verge of tears.

The girls remained silent and glanced from Danny to her. She turned her head in the opposite direction and began to bounce her right leg back and forth in agitation.

Danny came around to face her again. "Beth, can we please go somewhere and talk?"

She scowled at him and shook her head.

"Please? We really need to talk. I know you're mad at me, and I don't blame you. Please, let's get out of here and talk." He continued to hold her cold stare.

She compressed her lips, nodded once, and turned to walk up the stairs, and he followed her.

Beth was so confused. She wanted to see him on one hand, then didn't on another. She wasn't sure why he had to pick her high school graduation night to talk with her.

Where had he been the past six weeks? She was supposed to be having a great time, not suffering through some emotional scene. At the top of the steps, she stopped and motioned for him to lead the way. Danny led her into one of the bedrooms. He walked her over to the bed piled with jackets and purses and they sat side by side on the edge.

"I feel like I haven't talked to you in years," he said. "I'm sorry I took advantage of you."

Beth drank the remnants of her beer, crushed her plastic cup, and tossed it in the small trashcan by the bed. "Danny, I know you're sorry for taking advantage of me. I know you're sorry you ever touched me and that it ever happened, but I'm tired of hearing you say the same things over and over." Her voice dripped with sarcasm.

Danny widened his eyes at her.

Mr. Kneeland opened the bedroom door and looked startled to see the two of them in the room.

"Oh, I'm sorry!" He turned the light off as he shut the door.

Beth and Danny looked at one another and chuckled despite the gloomy atmosphere in the room. It was enough to break the ice.

"He is cool but kind of strange," Beth said, a slight smile tugging at her lips.

Danny stood and took Beth by the hand. "Come with me."

He led her down the stairs, through the party crowd, and outside. They walked down the road. Streetlights illuminated their path in the dark night.

"Beth, I'm sorry about things not working out between us. I wish things could've been different. So much has happened, and so much time has gone by..."

Trying to maintain her dignity, she blurted, "Absolutely, I agree completely."

Danny smiled at her.

They walked down the street to his parked car and

leaned on it.

"I want you to be happy, you know. You'll be going off to college and having lots of fun. It'll be more fun than you could ever imagine," he said.

"Danny." She sighed and steeled herself to tell him what she'd been wanting to say for years. "You know I've always loved you, ever since I met you in ninth grade."

There. She'd said it. No more pretending or misunderstanding. She had spoken directly and honestly.

Danny smiled at her uncomfortably.

"I know," he said and nodded as he looked down at the ground.

Beth watched his awkward reaction, and a crushing ache spread through her chest. "But you don't love me."

He rubbed the back of his neck.

She looked up at the sky and took a deep breath. This was the most awkward moment she'd suffered through in her entire life. She felt sick to her stomach first, then her legs went weak.

"I'm seeing someone, Beth," he said in a whisper.

"Are you in love with her?" she asked.

Danny met her gaze and nodded. "I think so."

Beth wanted the earth to open and swallow her. Nothing in her life had hurt as much as this moment. Nothing.

Then without warning, her anger flared.

"Just why are you here, Danny? What did you really want from me tonight? Why did you have to tell me this on my graduation night?" Her hands started to shake.

Danny held his head down. "I don't want you to hate me. I really do care about you. I kept that ring forever. I just sold it not long ago to a couple who were really in love."

Beth snapped her head up and looked him in the eye. Why was he doing this?

"Did you sell it to Rocky and Miss Polaroid?" she said, laughing. That would top the whole night off, wouldn't it?

"What are you talking about?" he asked.

Beth shook her head and dismissed the comment. She turned to walk back to the party, unable to talk to him anymore. He was hurtful and mean. Her throat felt ready to explode from pain, and her feet and legs felt like lead.

"Beth?" Danny called out.

She turned back and faced him.

"I need to know something," he said.

"What?" she said, sounding worn out, caved in, wrecked.

He hurried toward her. Her shoulders drooped, and she leaned her head back slightly. She couldn't take one more mean and hurtful comment. He took hold of her arms and looked into her eyes. His expression was so serious, his gaze so intense. Beth thought he was going to kiss her or start to cry or something. She stared at him, waiting for him to ask his question.

He pinched the bridge of his nose. "Are you pregnant?"

That's what this was all about! He'd been worrying about her being pregnant. Beth's mind had been put to ease several weeks ago. If he had bothered to call her, he would've known that, too. She was glad he'd suffered. He deserved to worry. She gaped at him. Her silence caused him to shuffle on his feet.

Beth almost screamed. God, the desperate look on his face spoke volumes. She really hated him at that moment, but she began to laugh in disbelief. "You're asking me this now? It's been six weeks! You're just now asking me this?"

Danny's face was white, his brows drawn together with concern. Beth enjoyed the fact that he was uncomfortable. Good! He stared at her, waiting for the answer. Typical Danny.

Beth's temper flared and she said, "You know, Danny, if I am pregnant, it wouldn't be your problem at all."

"Come on, Beth. I know you haven't been with anyone else."

It pissed her off that he knew her that well.

"No, I'm not pregnant."

Danny relaxed his shoulders but surprisingly he didn't smile and jump up and down with joy.

"No happy dance?" she asked with sarcasm.

He looked at her as if to apologize.

"I have to go," Beth said with disgust as she marched away from him, back to the party.

She heard his car door shut and the engine start. He drove away in the opposite direction. Now, at that very moment, she could feel him smiling with relief and joy. She turned back towards the car and held her middle finger up in a final, silent declaration.

This time, she was finally going to move on with her life. She vowed to forget all about Danny "douche bag" Mitchell.

CHAPTER 71

Beth walked up and down the street in front of Chris's house attempting to assuage her anger. Finally, she calmed enough to go back inside. She found Melissa as she was leaving to meet Chuck.

"I need to talk to you," Melissa said.

"I just need a beer first," Beth said.

The two went down the stairwell and ran into Charlie Cahall at the keg.

"Hey Beth," he said sullenly.

Melissa politely said, "Hi Charlie."

Charlie looked her in the eye. "Go to hell!"

Beth's mouth dropped open. She had never seen this nasty side of Charlie.

Flustered and embarrassed, Melissa told Beth she had to leave. She ran up the steps and out the door to the safety of her future husband's arms. Fortunately for Melissa, she had someone who would be able to comfort her.

Beth stood there feeling like stone as she stared at Charlie. She tried to convince herself this night wasn't really happening. It was a bad dream.

Charlie looked down at the floor and shuffled his feet. He blinked his eyes as if ashamed she had seen him at his worst. She decided she didn't need a beer after all and walked silently away to ask Susan and Tyler to give Jackie a ride home. They agreed, and Beth grabbed her purse and headed out to her car.

Charlie now sat on the front steps of the Kneeland's home. The two made eye contact as she exited. Beth shook her head at him.

"Don't look at me like that," Charlie said as she walked

past him.

"Did you know she dated someone else while we were together?" he yelled.

Ignoring him, Beth continued to walk away.

Charlie jumped up and followed her to her car.

"Hey! Hey! I'm talking to you!"

Beth turned around, swinging her fist as hard as she could. She connected with his left upper arm.

"Hey!" Charlie's eyes widened.

Thinking he might hit her back, Beth quickly ducked.

He just stood there and rubbed his arm. "What are you hitting me for?"

"Because you're an ass! How could you embarrass her like that?" Beth screamed.

"How could I embarrass her? I'm the one that looks like the idiot! You have no idea how I feel," Charlie yelled, equally as loud.

Beth searched his eyes. He stared back at her in silence.

"I do know how you feel," she finally said.

"No, you don't."

"Danny came to my graduation party to tell me he sold the ring he bought me, letting me know that now we are really finished. Oh, and to tell me he's in love with someone else, he thinks. Ha! Poor girl. Oh, and one more thing. He asked me if I happened to be pregnant!" Beth's volume increased as she spoke.

Charlie winced as if in acknowledgement of her pain.

"I don't know why you're friends with him, either. He's a complete *ass*!" Her body shook wildly with anger and nerves.

With his arms held out, Charlie approached her. She walked into them, and then she fell apart.

Charlie walked her to her car. The two sat inside, listened to the radio, and confided hurt feelings and anger to one another. Beth was heartbroken in the truest sense of the word. Eventually, they were talked out. They sat quietly for a long time.

"Mike told me that he asked you out at the beach. He would be good to you, Beth," Charlie said calmly.

Beth shook her head. "No, I don't belong with Mike. Where is Shot Man anyway?"

Charlie explained Mike felt too uncomfortable to come around.

More silence followed.

"So, you'll be heading off to college in August, huh?" he said, stating the obvious.

Beth nodded.

Charlie leaned forward in his seat. "I think I'll miss you, Girlie." He smiled at her and pinched her cheek.

She threw her arms around him. "I'll miss you, too."

Beth would miss everybody. Her life as she had known it was coming to an end. It felt devastating and exciting all at once. Everyone around her seemed to be in a rush to finalize or resolve relationships and issues before they moved away. It was as if every decision she and her friends made at that moment would affect the entire rest of their lives. For Beth, it was almost too much to bear.

They hugged for a moment too long. Charlie held her tightly and then drew back to look in her eyes. Beth smiled brightly, embarrassed by the hug. Charlie pressed his lips to hers lightly, and she didn't pull away. She felt a little nervous and unsure of herself. He leaned in again, this time Beth moved in to meet him and turned the simple search for kindness and security into passion. Charlie kissed her deeply.

She remembered him lying next to her on the beach grinning at her and sitting close to her at the freezing football games to keep her warm. Warmth bloomed in her chest as she recalled running into her house with a smile after the mailman had delivered a letter from him.

Charlie continued to kiss her, and she continued to respond.

She pictured him at the keg the first night they'd met and

how he'd made her feel safe and secure at the picnic table when she'd gotten a little buzzed and giggly from the beer.

She leaned in and held tightly to him while recalling his face in the dark of the nurse's office asking her how she really felt about Danny Mitchell. She remembered watching him kiss Melissa at Danny's party and feeling jealous. She remembered him holding Danny protectively back at the party at Brian's. She remembered the embarrassed and disappointed expression he'd had on his face when he'd seen her standing at the door of the apartment after she'd returned with Melissa, and the surprised expression when she'd been topless in the beach house.

Their kiss ended, and he drew back from her.

"Let's get out of this car. My house is right across the street. We should go there."

She nodded, and the two exited her car. They walked arm in arm towards his home.

Beth stopped just before they reached the door. "What time is it?"

After glancing at his watch, he told her it was still early, only nine thirty.

They entered his house, and his parents were watching television on the couch.

Beth smiled and said, "Hello" as Charlie introduced her. He took her hand and pulled her into the kitchen. Charlie reached into the refrigerator and gave her a Coke and took one for himself.

"This way." He directed her down into the basement.

Charlie's bedroom was on one side of the finished basement. She followed him in only after he assured her his parents didn't mind him having girls in his room. He turned on a small television on his dresser.

They kicked off their shoes and climbed up to sit on the bed. The room was small with a large stereo and miniature slot machine on his bureau. Several beer signs and a poster of Farrah Fawcett hung on the wall.

Beth smiled, comfortable and happy to be invited into Charlie's private world. She relaxed her head back against the headboard and stretched her legs out in front of her. He maintained a safe distance by lying on his stomach in the opposite direction facing the television set. Worn out but calm, Beth took a deep breath, sighing as she let it out. They watched the second half hour of Love Boat.

Charlie produced a deck of cards and turned the volume down on the TV. They played War and listened to Bob Seger. The card game turned into a dirty battle. They shared easy laughter often. While Beth used the restroom, he left to get them another soda. He returned to the room with two more Cokes and a box of Ritz crackers.

After setting the food and drinks on the nightstand, he put a Van Morrison album on the stereo. He turned the light switch off. Unsure of his intentions, Beth looked at him. Charlie avoided eye contact with her. He picked up the deck of cards and tucked them away in the nightstand drawer. Charlie placed a pillow against the headboard and sat up against it. He pulled her over to him, and she leaned into him and relaxed against his shoulder. The tension left Beth's shoulders.

"You know, it doesn't always have to be so difficult and complicated between two people," he said.

Beth looked up with a questioning glance.

He smiled at her, and she longed for uncomplicated right then. In fact, she craved it.

"I wish we would've..." Beth began.

Charlie silenced her with his mouth, passion in his kiss.

The stereo played "Moondance" which heightened the element of romance.

"Your parents?" she asked breathlessly, her body tingling from his tender caresses.

"My parents don't come down here and the door's locked."

Before she knew it, Beth lay on the bed with Charlie on

top of her kissing her deeply.

"I'm scared," Beth said, being totally honest with him.

Then she felt his body start to react to her. Concerns raced through her mind. If she had sex with Charlie, their friendship would change forever. But maybe, just maybe, Charlie was the one. What about Melissa? Would her friend hate her?

Charlie stopped kissing her but did not move away.

He gazed in her eyes. "I want to show you that it can be wonderful. I want you to know that. I won't do anything you don't want me to."

"I'm afraid it will hurt again."

"It's not supposed to hurt, Beth. Let me show you how it's supposed to be. I promise I won't hurt you, not at all. Will you let me show you?"

Beth was overcome by his tenderness. He talked to her and listened to her fears.

Charlie slowly rose from the bed and tugged her up with him.

"It's too light in here," she said as she stood on her knees on the bed.

He smiled at her shyness and turned the television off. The light from the stereo cast a slight golden hue over the room. Charlie pulled the covers down on his bed. He held her hands in front of her.

"Talk to me, Beth. Will you trust me?"

She nodded shyly. He pulled her top up and over her head.

He stared into her eyes. "You really are beautiful."

She reached up and helped him remove his shirt. "So are you."

He softly touched her face, her neck, her shoulders, and arms and complimented her repeatedly. His words didn't ring hollow to her, and she found herself telling him how wonderful he was. Beth closed her eyes and savored the wonderful sensations he created.

"Take your pants off and get into the bed," he said softly.

Beth tensed. "I don't know. I'm not on the pill or any-thing."

Charlie smiled at her. "It's okay. We don't have to do that if you don't want to. I just want to touch you."

He pulled the covers even further down on the bed, and he lay down. Beth smiled and moved next to him, feeling assured and relaxed.

He lightly traced her arms and stomach. Beth closed her eyes again.

"Turn over. I'll rub your back," he said.

Once he began to knead the tense muscles in her back and neck, Beth felt more relaxed than she ever had before. She was in heaven. No one had ever given her a back rub before. Her legs and arms turned to rubber as he worked his fingers over her flesh. He spoke to her softly, and after a few minutes, she felt indulgent and guilty.

"Let me do you now," she said, and Charlie turned over on his stomach.

She imitated his hand movements, and he moaned in pleasure at her touch.

"You're very good at this," he said.

Beth felt more confident and wanted to make him feel good. They talked in hushed voices about his time in college, his job at the post office, and her work at the store. Neither of them brought up school, Danny, or Melissa.

After a few moments, Charlie turned over and tugged her onto him. Again, they shared kisses filled with passion.

"Beth, I want to make you feel good. We don't have to go all the way for that to happen."

Her breathing was uneven from the kissing.

"I'll turn away. You get out of those pants and under the covers."

Beth wanted to but she was afraid. "Why do you want to do this, Charlie?"

He looked at her. "I just do."

She did as he suggested but left her bra and panties on and climbed in between the sheets.

Charlie left his pants on. He reached for her under the covers, touched her satin undergarments and chuckled softly.

"You really don't trust me, do you?"

Beth felt embarrassed by the teasing.

"It feels so good to kiss and touch, but it hurts so much to, you know," she said, lowering her eyes. "Everyone says it won't hurt the second time, but I don't believe them."

Charlie softly touched her face. He listened to her and gazed in her eyes.

"We won't do that then. We'll just kiss and touch. Okay? I promise to leave my pants on."

Beth smiled, unable to contain it. He smiled back at her.

"I swear I won't hurt you. I'll only make you feel good. Let me do that." He trailed one hand down to her thigh and inched it toward her sex.

"What if I'm gross or something?" she asked seriously.

Charlie chuckled and halted his hand on her thigh. She didn't laugh, and he lifted both eyebrows "Good Lord, Beth, you're not gross. Is that what you think? You think there is something wrong with you?"

She nodded, and tears instantly fell from the corners of her eyes.

He kissed her. "Hey, I promise there's nothing wrong with you."

"You don't know that."

"I've already seen you topless and I can assure you, there is nothing wrong at all in that department."

Beth smiled at him, feeling somewhat reassured.

"Yeah, but you don't know about the other department."

She was convinced something awful existed about her. She believed Danny had cared about her for years until he experienced her intimately. That night, he'd stopped caring at all. Making love was supposed to bring them together, not tear them apart. There had to be a reason why he didn't want her at all anymore after they had been together.

"I'm telling you, Charlie, I really think there's something wrong with me," she said again, believing it more than ever.

"Okay, Beth. How about this? I'll tell you if there's something wrong, okay?"

Beth stared into his eyes to see if he could be trusted.

"I'll tell you, only you, no one else, okay?"

She saw sincerity in his expression and nodded. Van Morrison crooned, "She give me love, love, love, love, crazy love. She got a fine sense of humor when I'm feelin' low..."

Charlie's gaze softened, and he touched her face and kissed her gently, reassuringly.

Beth touched his cheek and searched his eyes for meaning.

She took his hand, guided it to her bra strap, and allowed him to pull it down. He followed her lead and removed it, then took off her panties. Charlie gently caressed her stomach, relaxing her again. He kissed her passionately and then focused his attention on her chest, assuring her she looked beautiful and there was nothing wrong with her. Reassured, Beth smiled. She even let him remove the covers so he could look at her as he touched her. After kissing her and causing her nipples to harden, he trailed his hand down her stomach. Pleasant tingles coursed through her entire body.

Charlie spoke to her again while he caressed her. "You are beautiful, Beth. Never doubt that. Your body is perfect. I love the way you feel and the way you make me feel."

He made her believe she was beautiful, and she felt more comfortable with him looking at her.

Charlie murmured again, "You are perfect."

Believing him, Beth smiled. He touched her body with a sensual rhythm, and she began to move with it. A strange but blissful sensation she couldn't suppress rose within her. She became warm and flushed, and she closed her eyes.

Beth opened her eyes and admired his handsome face.

Every so often she would shut her eyes as she responded to his gentle touches. As he stroked her sex, her breathing became heavy, and her lips were swollen from kissing him. She responded as a woman to his touch, moving her body in time with his strokes. Beth grasped Charlie's shoulders and looked in his eyes as she leaned up to him and arched her back. She held him closely to her and tilted her head back. Charlie kissed her intensely, and her body shuddered its final response. Relaxed and blissful, she fell back onto the pillow. She was unable to repress a smile. Charlie allowed her to recover silently and then moved to lie next to her and held her close.

He whispered, "That's how it is supposed to feel. That's how you should be made to feel every time."

Beth smiled and stretched. When her breathing returned to normal, she said, "Charlie, it's okay if you want to..."

"No, not tonight. Be quiet and still for a minute. I'll do it again," he whispered.

Before long, Beth let him guide her through the process again. To her surprise, it felt just as intense but didn't take nearly as long.

Van Morrison seemed to know exactly what they were doing. "I want to rock your gypsy soul," he sang.

"Let me touch you. Show me how," Beth whispered to Charlie.

He groaned and drew her close. "There is plenty of time for all that."

"You're not going to let me?" she asked.

Charlie looked at her and shook his head.

"It doesn't seem fair," she whispered, averting her gaze.

"Tonight is for you, Beth. It's more than fair. You looked beautiful tonight, and I'll have this memory forever."

Her cheeks heated, and she glanced at the digital alarm clock. It read ten past twelve.

"I think I'm hungry," she said.

Charlie chuckled. "You should be."

Beth laughed with him. They sat up in the bed, ate Ritz crackers, and drank their Cokes. He burped out loud, and Beth matched his with intensity and volume. The two of them burst into laughter.

She touched her head and widened her gaze. "Oh my God, my hair must look awful."

"It doesn't, but you can use this." He grabbed a comb from the top of his dresser and handed it to her. "Can you stay the night?"

Beth shook her head. "I actually need to get going soon. I told my folks I'd be home by twelve thirty."

Charlie rubbed the back of his neck, disappointment lining his features.

He left the room while she dressed and combed her hair. Charlie returned and escorted her out. Thankfully, his parents were in bed. He walked her out into the cool night air to her car parked across the street. They moved slowly, their arms wrapped around each other.

"I think we should go out on a real date. What do you say?" Charlie asked as they reached her car.

Beth smiled at the idea. "Are you finally asking me out?"

She turned to hug him, and Charlie nodded. Beth smiled and nodded, too.

He hugged her and drew back. "I'll call you tomorrow, and we can make plans."

She bristled, suddenly feeling strange and awkward with him. What if he didn't call her? She opened the car door and slid inside.

"I will call you, I swear," he assured her, holding the door open.

"You better."

He grinned at her and shut the door.

She drove home in a blissful state, hardly believing what had just happened.

Relaxed and gratified, Beth slept better than she had in a long time.

The next day, Beth blushed deeply every time she thought about how she had responded to Charlie in his bed. She wished Danny had been tender like that with her. The difference was unbelievable. Charlie was so concerned for her feelings and fears. He enjoyed her company and talked to her. Charlie knew when to be quiet and when to reassure her. He paid attention. Danny could use some lessons from Charlie.

True to his word, Charlie called her on his lunch break and then again at four to confirm their plans for dinner that evening.

Melissa called Beth around two that afternoon and wanted to talk about how badly Charlie had treated her at the party. Beth listened to her friend rant, and she felt like the scum of the earth. She justified her actions with Charlie by pretending it wouldn't matter to Melissa. Melissa didn't love Charlie and was marrying another man. However, the truth was Beth had broken the girl code and felt like crap about it. She wondered how Danny would feel about them dating. He probably wouldn't care at all, but she hoped it would drive him into an insane asylum.

When Charlie called at four, she asked, "Do you think we are doing this just to piss off Melissa and Danny?"

"I hope not. Do you?"

She paused and said, "I feel like that might be possible."

He told her he would come over to her house after work and they could talk.

Charlie arrived, and her parents were polite. Beth felt sick to her stomach. After her parents retreated to the kitchen, they sat in the living room and talked quietly. She explained that she thought she was betraying Melissa to get revenge against Danny. She felt uncomfortable about getting involved in a relationship and then going away to college.

Charlie nodded and listened. "I think maybe we'd better wait if you feel that way. We don't have to rush into anything."

He'd given her the out she needed.

He smiled at her and took her hands in his. "Beth, I love you to death. We've always had a great friendship but maybe it's not enough to base a relationship on. Let's not mess it up by pretending to be something more because we think it's what we *ought* to do after last night."

Relief oozed from Beth's body. He gave her a genuine smile. Why prolong it into a long relationship that would fail in the end?

He took her in his arms for their last hug.

"Thank you for last night," she said quietly.

He patted her on the back.

"It was really my pleasure."

Pulling away, she began to cry. "Is this the right thing? Are we doing the right thing?"

Charlie nodded.

"I care about you, Charlie. I love you in my own weird sort of way," she whispered.

"I know. Walk me to my car, girlie," he said in his normal tone.

She did and waved goodbye to him as his car left her driveway.

Beth walked upstairs to her room and tried to process the events with Charlie. He had always cared for her, and she had taken a great deal of comfort in that through the years. Beth desperately needed someone to be kind and loving like Charlie had been last night. Did she love him? Deeply. Was she in love with him? No. The parallel of her relationship with Danny crashed over her like a tidal wave. How could she be angry with Danny when she played the same role with Charlie? The difference remained in a small fact. Charlie had known what he was doing and had comprehended the situation. He had entered it with a clear understanding. When Beth had given herself to Danny, she had lacked experience and hadn't understood the real situation. She believed Danny loved her even if it was delusional.

Charlie had taught her so much. She had learned how to be selfless, and she had discovered she couldn't make herself feel something she didn't. Finally, she understood being sexually involved with someone who loved her was so much better than with someone who did not. She never imagined she'd be able to feel the way she had last night, but even though Charlie had made her feel special and not just like a piece of ass, something had been missing. Would she ever find a guy who could give her everything she wanted and needed?

CHAPTER 72

Beth worked on Sunday from twelve to four. Brian Knight came in the store.

Thrilled to see him, she ran over and hugged him. "Hi Brian. I missed you at graduation."

"I missed the ceremony because the baby got sick and needed to see the pediatrician, but I got you a graduation card." He smiled and handed it to her.

"Thanks," Beth said. "Is she better now?"

"Yes. Ann is home with her now."

"Gosh, I miss Ann, too." Beth clutched the envelope holding his card. "I never see her anymore now that she's not working here. Is she coming back?"

"I'm not sure," Brian replied. "It's been difficult financially so she may be coming back. I'm driving myself crazy working and going to college at the same time. It hasn't been easy." He had a pensive glimmer in his eyes. "Once I get my degree, I hope it will be better. I think I want to be an accountant or work in finance."

Brian looked tired and miserable. He was trying to be a responsible husband and dad, but anyone could see this was killing him.

Beth's other coworkers circled around them, ending any further conversation between them. They chattered away, asking about Ann and about the baby. Beth studied him as the others conversed with him. He was still very handsome and pleasant, but something was off.

Finally, the others wandered off, and Beth asked, "Do you have a few minutes? I have a twenty-minute break. Can you wait a minute or two?"

Brian nodded and grinned at her. He waited for her out

in the parking lot. The two walked over to the deli and had a cup of coffee and split a piece of cheesecake with cherry topping. They sat and talked quietly, but she could tell Brian was uncomfortable. Ann would probably be angry with him for visiting her even though they'd been friends for years.

"So, what else is new? I don't hear too much about anybody anymore," he commented as he took another bite of the cheesecake.

Beth told him about the false pregnancy scare.

He frowned at her. "You told me before that wasn't an issue."

"I lied. I'm ashamed of my own stupidity," Beth said. They sat in silence again, and then she muttered, "It doesn't matter now anyway."

"What doesn't matter?" He looked up from the plate.

"Danny," she said firmly.

She told him she went to Charlie's house on graduation night, leaving out major and important details he didn't really need to know. Brian leaned back in his chair and smiled, swallowing hard, a tic pulsing in his jaw.

"You two would make a good couple," he said lightly.

Beth sent him a hard stare. He just didn't seem himself. "Well, Charlie and I decided we are better as friends. I don't think I should date him. I mean, I love him to pieces but not in a dating way. You know?"

Brian chuckled ruefully. "I do know. I think you once said the same thing to me about us."

Beth was quiet a moment or two. She had forgotten that, but it was true. Thankfully, they had remained friends. Beth shared so much with Brian and looked to him for guidance and support. She stared at his unhappy countenance and wondered why she thought he was so wise about love and relationships. Clearly, he had gotten himself into a very difficult position.

"The University of Delaware isn't that far away. You'll be seeing Charlie from time to time. If you two are meant to be together, it'll happen," he said, interrupting her thoughts.

Beth gently asked, "Brian, what's up? You don't seem happy."

He shrugged as if brushing off her comment. "Oh, I'm fine. We're fine. Things will get better." Brian sounded like he was trying to convince himself, not her.

"Okay. Tell me about Emily."

Brian perked up. He showed her pictures of his daughter that he kept in his wallet.

They finished their snack, and Brian walked her back to the store. She thanked him again for the card and moved to hug him. Brian embraced her stiffly.

She smiled, and he touched her chin. "Goodbye, Gorgeous."

Huh, he hadn't said that to her in a long time. A strange, prickling sensation went up her arms as he left the store.

CHAPTER 73

The summer passed quickly. Beth and the girls spent every free moment at the beach or at The Boat playing rock music.

The night before Melissa's wedding, the girls gave her a private bridal shower at The Boat. They decorated it with flowers and candles and bombarded her with gifts. The girls got incredibly drunk and cried as they thought how much they would miss one another.

Jackie lifted their moods and did her Janis Joplin imitation to "Piece of My Heart." Her hair flew all around, and her body jerked in rhythmic convulsions. The girls laughed, blown away by her accuracy. Lynne did a fantastic female imitation of Mick Jagger prancing around singing "It's Only Rock and Roll, But I Like It."

The next day, Beth, Jackie, Susan, and Lynne attended Melissa's wedding at the Justice of the Peace office downtown. Chuck was dressed in his uniform and looked very handsome. Melissa wore a mid-length off white lace dress with ankle-strap off white shoes. Her auburn hair was pulled up in a loose, romantic bun with wisps of hair dangling elegantly down her neck. She wore emerald stone earrings and a matching necklace, a wedding gift from Chuck. Several of Chuck's Air Force buddies were there and appeared happy to finally meet Melissa's friends. Jackie tossed her blonde curls around a few times in front of them. Beth shook her head at her friend and smiled.

Chuck had no family there, and Melissa's mother didn't come to the ceremony. Beth knew Melissa was hurt, but her friend seemed happy about starting a new life with Chuck and leaving town. The nine of them went back to Chuck's house off base and had wedding cake and champagne.

Beth gave Melissa a card from her parents. The outside read "Mr. and Mrs. Charles Weismann." Melissa opened the envelope and smiled. As she opened the card, a check for one hundred dollars fell out. Beth's eyes widened, and Melissa began to cry. The two hugged, and Beth promised to thank them for her. Once again, Beth felt proud they were her folks.

The wedding cake was delicious, a gourmet treat created by Mr. Angellini. Everyone laughed and smiled while the photographer took plenty of pictures. Soon, Beth and the other guests left so the newlyweds could begin their wedded life together. Melissa beamed happily as she and Chuck waved goodbye from the front door.

Beth glanced back at her friend with tears in her eyes.

~

The summer season began to wind down, and Beth and her three remaining girlfriends prepared for college. Melissa was already gone, somewhere in a U-Haul headed to California.

During their last trip to The Boat, Jackie said, "I wish I were going to the University with you guys. I'm excited about college, but I'm not sure an all-girls school is right for me. I'm a little sad about it. I don't know why my parents have insisted on this."

Beth and Susan looked at each other and started to giggle, looking pointedly at Jackie.

Lynne added dryly, "I can't imagine why they want you in an all-girls school, Jackie."

Jackie scowled at them. "Oh shut up!"

All four girls erupted in amused laughter, and then they grew quiet and pensive.

"We need to get together on holidays. Maybe we can rent a place during the summers and all work at the beach," Jackie said, wiping the tears from her eyes.

The girls agreed excitedly and promised to do that.

"You will be okay, Jackie. You'll meet new friends and

feel right at home in no time," Susan said. "And we will come visit you, and you can come visit me and Beth at the University."

Beth nodded her agreement. She was glad to be leaving town soon. Finally, she'd gotten over the hurt from Danny and the confusion of the emotional attachment she had to Charlie. She no longer saw Mike anywhere in town and the rumor was he'd fallen hard for a girl in Dover.

Susan's eyes widened as she looked at Beth. "Oh, I have news! Rocky will be at the University in the fall."

"What? Why?" she asked, surprised. "Did Rocky break up with Miss Polaroid?

"No, apparently they're both going, and her parents are paying for an off-campus apartment for them," Susan responded.

Beth shook her head in disbelief.

Susan went on, "I wish Tyler would be there with me. I'm so worried about him. He is convinced I will break up with him when I go to college. That's not going to happen." She shook her head for emphasis.

They ended the night with hugs, tears, and promises to stay in touch.

Susan and Beth went to Pippy's for dinner the night before they left for college.

Beth said pensively, "It's weird how much has changed already. Melissa is gone and I miss her. Now Jackie is gone, too."

Jackie had left a week earlier for freshman orientation.

"I know," Susan agreed. Thank goodness we will be going together. Lynne will be the only one here. I think she might be lonely."

Beth laughed. "Yes, but Joey is going to the University, too. I think she might be up to visit a lot."

Beth was surprised to see Danny enter the restaurant with two guys she didn't know. She'd seen him around town a few times but never to say hello or to talk to him. He laughed loudly and looked a little drunk. Susan rolled her eyes at Beth. Danny soon noticed her seated at the booth, walked over, and squeezed into the seat next to her.

"Hey Beth." He gave her the intense stare that used to send her reeling with joy and excitement.

"Hi," she said and continued to eat her pizza.

"What are you guys up to tonight? I just moved into my own place. You should come see it," he suggested.

"Wouldn't your girlfriend be upset?" Susan asked with one raised eyebrow.

Danny shook his head, dismissing the notion and told Beth he wasn't dating her anymore. Beth smiled, remembering Danny's declaration of love for this girl.

"Yeah, sorry, we can't come. We're going home after this. We both leave for college in the morning," Beth said with a smirk.

Danny looked taken aback by her rejection. He said goodbye then stood up and left.

"You okay, Beth?" Susan asked.

Beth pursed her lips. "I'm fine. I mean look at him. What is he doing? What kind of person is that?"

Susan followed her friend's gaze. Danny drank from a mug of beer and made large arm gestures and movements as he spoke. Beth wondered what she ever saw in him and briefly remembered what it felt like long ago. He was no longer that young boy, and she was no longer that little girl.

On Sunday afternoon, Beth rode up the highway with her parents to college in her parents' Chevy Blazer. Everything she could possibly need to survive her first year in the dorm was packed tightly in the back. Her parents helped her unpack as she met a girl from New Jersey who would be her roommate. After her father brought the final load in, it was time to say goodbye. Beth walked them out of the dorm and to the car. She hugged them and smiled at her mother, crying just a little.

Walking back to the dorm, Beth looked around the campus. People were coming and going everywhere.

Beth looked up into the face of a boy about her age.

"Excuse me, I need to find the community center and I have no idea where I am going," he said.

She glanced around and searched the buildings for signs but was unable to help him. They decided they would help each other figure it out. Both had to be there for the freshman orientation meeting in a half hour. At the meeting, Beth saw Susan and Joey at different locations within the large, packed room. They each waved to one another and smiled broadly.

"My name is Phil, by the way," her new friend said.

"I'm Beth." She smiled as she held out her hand to shake his.

It felt nice to meet someone new. Phil didn't know about anybody she knew or anything about her. She could start all over here.

Beth continued to smile at her new friend. College would be another long, strange trip. She looked forward to it with bravery and new excitement.

EPILOGUE

2000

Proof
That I did always love,
I bring thee proof:
That till I loved
I did not love enough.

That I shall love always,
I offer thee,
That love is life,
And life hath immortality.

This, dost thou doubt, sweet?
Then have I
Nothing to show
But Calvary.
-Emily Dickinson

"Hurry up, Beth! We're running late," her husband called.

She ran out of the bathroom and shoved her hairbrush in the outside pocket of her duffle bag.

"I'm ready." Beth stepped into her sandals and grabbed her purse.

He picked up the bag, and she followed him down the steps. She looked around the kitchen for anything she might have missed.

Her mother-in-law stood in the kitchen, smiling at them. "We'll be fine. You two have a wonderful time!"

Beth hugged her tightly. "Thank you so much for staying with the kids."

She turned to hug the two boys who stood near their grandmother. The twins, Charlie and Brian, were already as tall as their mother. They had their father's athletic build, even at eleven. Charlie was the football and baseball player. Brian enjoyed hunting, fishing, and lacrosse. The boys groaned through the kisses she gave them.

"Make sure you behave and listen to your grandparents while Dad and I are gone."

They nodded and smiled.

Her husband reentered the kitchen after loading their bags in the car. "That's right. Be gentle to Grammy and Grandpop. Don't be loud and no roughhousing."

He tousled their hair, and the boys hugged him in return. The twins smiled devilishly at their father and agreed to be perfect angels.

He grinned at their teasing. "We'll be gone for a week, and we'll call every night, okay?"

The boys nodded again. Beth looked up at her husband and smiled. Brian smiled back at her as he took a large tote bag from her hand. He kissed his mother and thanked her for coming to stay at their house.

Beth and Brian walked out the door with another quick "goodbye." He carried their final bag to the back seat of the Land Rover. Beth slid in the car with a handful of CDs she'd grabbed on the way out. He situated himself behind the steering wheel.

"I'm so excited!" She bounced in the seat.

Brian laughed at her as he backed the car out of the driveway. "No kidding?" He smiled at her. "I have to say I am, too!"

She admired his handsome face. Why had it taken them so long to realize their love for one another?

Beth recalled, how, after college, she had returned home and married a local man. The marriage lasted only two years, ending in divorce. Beth had been teaching English at Colonel Roberts High School for two years. Brian had remained in Dover for several years and had tried to make his young marriage work. He attended a local college and continued to work at the grocery store. Three years later, he moved to Connecticut after his marriage fell apart. He stayed with his grandparents while he completed his senior year of college and went on to graduate school.

Beth remembered how she and Susan Pallace were having Sunday brunch at The Town Squire Restaurant in 1987 when Brian Knight and his brother walked in. She had locked eyes with Brian, and the rest of the world had disappeared for her. They had spent several, inseparable days reminiscing and catching up. By their third evening together, they were inseparable, and they became lovers. He had told her he loved her soon after that first special night.

Brian still took her breath away. He was tender and strong and enjoyed learning how to please her. Likewise, she learned the secrets of giving pleasure back to the man she'd always loved.

After their wonderful time together, Brian had to return to Connecticut, but long weekend trips and expensive telephone bills had consumed them both.

Exactly one year from the day they'd reunited at the beach, they married in a small chapel in Connecticut. Their wedding plans had started small and soon blossomed into a huge affair. Many of their old friends had attended the beautiful ceremony, and they'd honeymooned in Martha's Vineyard. The bed and breakfast owners had provided a romantic setting. Their wedding night had been full of tenderness and love.

"I can't believe we're actually married," Brian had said as he'd held his new wife in his arms. Beth recalled how she'd smiled contentedly and how he'd coaxed her face up with his hand and made her look at him. He'd spoken of the love he'd always felt for her, and her heart had burst with emotion. They'd made love with an intensity neither had ever known.

Beth smiled to herself. Brian still loved to tell her that

he'd fallen in love with her the moment he'd seen her at Melissa Walter's keg party.

Brian had a job in Connecticut as an investment banker, and Beth had found a job teaching English at a high school in Connecticut. He shared custody of his daughter Emily who stayed with them during her vacations from school. Beth and her stepdaughter got along well, and she enjoyed Emily's visits a great deal.

After a year of marriage, Beth gave birth to twin boys. Brian was supportive and helpful. He knew how to help her even when she wasn't sure how to help herself. They had spent many sleepless nights caring for the two small babies.

Beth smiled at the memories and patted her husband's thigh. As the years passed, they had grown together as a family. Brian spent his spare time coaching his sons' sports teams and he often sponsored them financially. Every few months, Beth and Brian went away for a weekend while his parents or hers babysat the boys. This time they were going somewhere special, and excitement tickled Beth's stomach.

As the car traveled down the bypass, Beth said, "Twenty years is a long time. Do you think we'll recognize everybody?" She checked her face in the rearview mirror.

Brian laughed. "Oh, you'll recognize everyone. There might be some people with a little less hair and a lot more body, but you'll recognize them all!"

"I can't wait to see the girls!" she said.

Brian reached over and held Beth's hand. "I love you, you know that?"

Beth smiled and leaned in to kiss him on the cheek. "I love you, too."

The women had planned a pre-reunion cocktail party at Susan and Tyler Jenkin's home in a new housing development near the high school. Beth and Brian arrived first at six o'clock. The girls hugged tightly as Brian and Tyler shook hands, genuinely glad to see one another. The guys drank beer and made small talk.

A very pregnant Jackie came to the door with her husband. Susan and Beth squealed as she entered the room. She worked as a lawyer in New York, and her husband was an attorney in the same firm. This was their second child. Jackie had kept her hair long and it was still just as curly. Tyler introduced Jackie's husband to Brian, and the women congregated in the kitchen.

Melissa arrived next, and she looked fantastic. Her boys were teenagers, and she worked as a surgical nurse at a hospital in Illinois near Scott Air Force Base. Her husband, Chuck, was a Lieutenant Colonel and still very handsome.

Lynne and Joey Griffin arrived last. Joey worked as an architect in town, and Lynne was a happy, stay-at-home mom with four children between the ages of two and twelve.

They all drank wine and complimented one another on how fantastic they looked. Beth listened to the gossip as they caught up on the lives of old friends and old loves.

Charlie Cahall still worked for the U.S. Postal Service and was a Postmaster in town. He was still married to the girl he met the first year Beth went to college. Beth remembered meeting her once when she was home for Christmas. Charlie had brought her to a party at his brother's house. The girl had watched him with adoring eyes the entire evening, and Beth had thought to herself *This is how it should be for Charlie.* They had two girls and one boy. Beth smiled, recalling her graduation night when he had been so kind to her, and she hoped he was living a happy and comfortable life.

Susan filled them in on all the town gossip. Danny Mitchell still worked in the family restaurant, married the daughter of a judge, and had no children. Mike Crowley was divorced and had sole custody of his two children. He was working at Colonel Roberts High School as the wrestling coach and Driver's Education teacher. Rocky Mulinero and "Miss Polaroid" were long divorced. He'd been married and divorced four times. He worked as a radio disc jockey on the local rock station. He wasn't currently married but was liing with a waitress from Hooters.

Billy Englehart had recently married a much younger woman, and they had a small baby. He worked for years as an engineer and now held a position with the FBI at the World Trade Center in New York City.

Susan also told them Chester Black's Bar had burnt down over a year ago and that Greg Black owned a liquor store where the bar once stood, and he was known to be a heavy drinker. He also married one of Rocky Mulinero's ex-wives, possibly the first one.

Beth laughed as she thought of Greg marrying "Miss Polaroid."

Tyler called out, "Susan, did you show them yet?"

"Not yet. Is everything ready?" she asked.

"It's ready whenever you are!" he replied.

The women looked at Susan with raised eyebrows. Susan grinned and motioned for them to follow her outside. The guys were sitting together on the back deck, and Brian grinned devilishly at Beth when she walked past him. She couldn't help but blush while she smiled back at him. He still looked as handsome today as he did twenty years ago.

"Come this way," Susan said.

She led the women through the backyard and around the shed. Tyler motioned the husbands to follow. There was a beautifully landscaped terrace and several weeping cherry trees beside a beautiful goldfish pond. The women followed Susan around a privacy fence and toward a hot tub.

"This is beautiful," Jackie said in awe.

Beth and the others chimed in their agreement.

As they rounded the corner to get the full view of the hot tub, Melissa called out, "Oh my God!"

Beth and the rest of them crowded around to see what she was gaping at. Sitting in the clearing next to the goldfish pond was The Boat—the actual dilapidated old boat! A circle of logs sat in front of it.

n squealed and screamed with excitement. aced flowers in all the openings and attached to the old boat just as they had always done on spe- ccasions.

"How on earth did you get this?" Beth asked Susan.

She and Tyler grinned. He answered, "Developers bought the old Jackson farm and were moving in. Susan told me about The Boat, so we loaded it up on the trailer and brought it back here. I think it looks great. It needs a coat of paint, but Susan insisted I leave it this way until after the reunion this weekend."

The husbands watched as their wives walked around The Boat and logs, treating it as if it were a shrine. Beth and her friends gingerly ran their hands over it. She was dumb- founded that it looked the same, no more dilapidated than it was twenty years ago.

"Look at this." Lynne touched the spot where they once wrote their boat name choices with lipstick.

The only name that remained visible was "The Miss June."

Lynne and Beth began to cry, and they hugged one an- other tightly.

Susan popped open a bottle of champagne, poured four glasses, and handed them out.

Jackie held up her glass of sparkling cider. "Here's to old friends. They are the best!"

Susan, Beth, Lynne, and Melissa raised their champagne glasses.

"Hear, hear!" They toasted and drank, asking their hus- bands to take pictures of them in and around The Boat.

They finished their cocktails and then piled in their cars to drive to their class reunion. Beth delighted in seeing her old lunch table friends and catching up on everyone's news. Later that night, Brian and Beth settled in at the Sheraton Hotel.

"I'm taking a bath. My feet are killing me," Beth said as

she removed her high heels.

"I'm going to order a bottle of champagne." Bria grinned and picked up the phone receiver.

"Oh. I like that." She grabbed her overnight bag, went into the bathroom, and filled the tub. After undressing, she climbed in and soaked luxuriously in the heated water.

Beth finished her bath, dressed in a new piece of lingerie, and opened the door. At the sight of her, Brian took a deep breath. She strutted over to the bed. From his reclined position against the headboard, he poured their champagne from the nightstand, handed her a glass, held up his hand, and repeated Jackie's toast. "Here's to old friends. They are the best friends."

"Hear, hear," Beth repeated and drank her champagne.

Brian slanted his head, ogled her, and patted the space next to him on the bed. "You better get over here quickly."

Beth smiled and giggled as he put his glass down on the nightstand and pulled her down close to him on the bed. She set her empty glass next to his.

Brian leaned over and kissed her deeply. He rubbed his hands down her back and whispered, "I love you, Gorgeous. I always have."

Beth returned his kiss and wrapped her arms around his neck. Brian groaned softly as she moved her body against him provocatively. He allowed her to move him over on his back, and she rested on top of him.

"Brian, I thank God every day for you. You are my best friend, and I love you so much." She kissed him passionately.

Brian groaned. "I am a lucky man."

With the radio playing in the background, Brian gently eased her face down toward his and kissed her again. Excitement surged through her body in response to his tender caresses. Soon, the two were consumed with one another and the moment that defined that one thing Beth had always been looking for.

She had found true and lasting love.

LAURA MCWILLIAMS HOWARD

******** ~ ********

ACKNOWLEDGEMENTS

The process of publishing this book has been an act of love for my sister, Laura McWilliams Howard. Laura ("Laurie," as we called her) died of lung cancer on December 7, 2017 before she was able to see the reality of her book come to fruition. Writing this book was a labor of love for her and I am so grateful that she was able to complete her story and can now posthumously share it with the world. This book is a work of fiction but is based on real events that took place during my sister's high school years from 1976 to 1980. The characters and many events in the book are figments of my sister's imagination but the intense emotion and angst will be recognized by anyone who has ever been an adolescent. This book is a coming of age story that will touch your heart and make you root for the protagonist and her friends. Everyone currently raising teenagers should read this story. The topics addressed are timeless and include love returned and love unrequited, friendship, loyalty and betrayal, parent-child relationships, the need for independence and acceptance, and even the balance of power between males and females. Laura will make you laugh, she will make you cry, and she will have you thinking about important aspects of growing up, how the world has changed, how it has not changed, and how it should change. I am so grateful to her for writing this book.

Laura is not here to dedicate this book but, in my heart, I know she would want to dedicate it to her beloved sons, Patrick James Spence and Ray Andrew Bryant. She loved her boys and wanted nothing more than for them to continue living well and loving fully in her absence. I hope that this

...hem of the capacity their mother had for lov-
...s world and beyond. She would also want this
...cated to our sister, Julie McWilliams Ellwanger,
...iflessly cared for her during her long illness, and to her
...ther, Betty Erdle McWilliams, whom she loved dearly. Without doubt, she is with our father, James Andrew McWilliams, and they are watching over us all. I can only assume that together they are proud of her accomplishments and their remaining family. Finally, my sister would want to thank her husband, Brian Howard. She feels his love even now and she knows he misses her.

Thank you, Laura. You have given us an amazing gift. Our love for you endures.

Finally, I would like to thank our editor, Kelley Heckart, for the time and energy she spent helping me to perfect this book. I could not have completed this project without her.

Vicki McWilliams Stephens

ABOUT THE AUTHOR

Laura Mcwilliams Howard

Laura McWilliams Howard was born Laura Elizabeth McWilliams and called "Laurie" by her family and friends as a child. She was the third daughter of Jim and Betty McWilliams and lived her entire life in Dover, Delaware. A 1980 graduate of Caeser Rodney High School, Laura went on to get her teaching degree from Wilmington College in Delaware. Not one to venture far from home, Laura taught at Nellie Stokes Elementary School for most of her teaching career. She was blessed with two remarkable sons, Patrick James Spence and Ray Andrew Bryant, whom she loved with all her heart.

Laura lived with her husband, Brian Howard, and her dogs, Archie and Mac Daddy and was adored by them all. She had ve, and she was always available to her sons, er parents, her sisters, her friends, her various nephews, and her students. She loved to write, and care for her parents, husband and sons. She was at mother, wonderful sister and daughter, and beloved friend.

Laura was diagnosed with lung cancer in March, 2017 and died on December 7, 2017 at the age of 55. She has left a legacy of love for us all.

Made in the USA
Middletown, DE
12 January 2021

31494682R00345